MISS

Thrown back into his seat from the force of full afterburners, Ben shot under Taurus's plane. In a pair of heartbeats, he found himself flying through the still dissipating clouds of explosions. Debris from twenty, maybe even thirty mechs littered the floor. Most of the wall opposite the door had been torn away to reveal a section of crew quarters, unmade beds smoldering from hot pieces of metal that had rained on them.

He banked right, passing a pair of Medium Hulks that had survived the blast, their narrow red eyes blind to his presence.

"Four projectiles locked on and closing," his computer suddenly announced.

He cut the stick hard left, jettisoning a cloud of chaff as he turned a corner.

"Missiles, one, two, and three locked onto counter measures."

With a right arm of steel, Ben held the jet steady, eyeing the rearview image of the last missile closing in and the shaft ahead. Walls raced by in time with his heart.

Another intersection ahead. Hard left. Toggle for thruster stall. Chaff! Afterburner full! And he watched as the final missile took the bait and detonated in an exploding ball of hungry flames that suddenly engulfed his ship.

Buffeted by the concussion, the stick jerked out of Ben's hand, and he fell forward into his harness as the Pyro dove . . .

DESCENT

PETER TELEP

AVON BOOKS ◆ NEW YORK

AVON BOOKS, INC.
1350 Avenue of the Americas
New York, New York 10019

First Avon Books Printing: January 1999

FOR STEPHEN S. POWER
WHOSE VISION PAVED THE WAY ...

Fate is a Four-letter Word

A shuttle of tourists drew closer to Jupiter, its viewports crammed with the faces of overweight parents and spoiled kids. Some pointed at the ancient gas giant, others stupidly clicked digital cameras, believing they could get a good shot through two inches of thermoplastic. To Captain Benjamin St. John, the Jovian system was just another Area Of Operations, a navigational pain in the ass made worse by a bunch of slack-jawed sightseers whose lives hung on the "skills" of a greedy pilot taking his tram in dangerously close to earn larger tips. Ben rolled his blue eyes and sighed, then cut right with his stick, steering his FY39 Interceptor into a slow pass along the port side of the craft while his wingman, Powell Stephenson, did likewise to starboard. The pilots were supposed to be rushing after a hijacked executive transport—not playing traffic cops. Ben slowed his fighter to a stop, then opened a comm channel, wishing he could avoid the verbal protocol and simply tell this guy to get lost. "Attention Shuttle 221. You are in violation of a secure zone order. Return immediately to station."

"Who say?" the shuttle's pilot shot back in a thick, yet hard-to-identify accent.

Ben considered answering with one of the expletives bal-

1

anced on the tip of his tongue, then thought better of it. "The CED Marine Corps, *buddy*."

"You no force me out. People pay much money!"

"Look, pal. The secure-zone signal was dispatched ten mikes ago. I know you're reading it. And you know—and I know—you don't belong here. Return to Ganymede Station. NOW!"

"I not leave! I lose money! I sue you ass! I talk lawyer!"

Ben keyed for his wingman's comm channel. "Alleycat, you believe this aviator?"

"I believe him, sir," Powell answered, the comm speaker making him sound a little younger than his twenty-two years. "Problem is, he doesn't believe in us."

"Roger that. Let's give him a little faith."

Slamming back his thruster control and steadying his stick, Ben shot away and banked left, pulling up and about a klick away from the shuttle. He came around on the vessel's stern, and, after glancing through his canopy and signaling Powell to take point, he thumbed the arming control of his Israeli-made laser package in preparation to deliver his half of the sermon.

Powell dived at the shuttle, unleashing a rain of glistening fire from his wing-mounted cannons. The bolts tore past the shuttle's starboard bow, missing it by scant meters. Following his line of fire, Powell took his ship in close enough to smile for a tourist's picture, and Ben winced as his wingman's thruster wash sent the shuttle listing to port. Powell had made a Marine Corps barber's pass, shaving the line just a little too close.

"You crazy! I report you!"

Report this, Ben thought as he began a rolling dive while firing a volley of bolts that razored by the port and starboard sides of the tram. Then he fired again, enjoying the powerful rumble and vibration that seized the cockpit. Before he passed the shuttle, he hit the emergency thruster shutdown, engaged maneuvering jets, and came to a jarring halt so that his thruster cones were directly opposite the shuttle's forward viewport. He flipped on his aft camera. A monitor set into his control panel displayed the plump, bearded aviator waving a fist at him. Ben glowered at the fool. "Tour's over, pal."

The aviator extended one of his fingers in a most impolite gesture. "Okay. I leave. I leave and report you!"

Shaking his head, Ben jammed back his thruster control and bulleted away from the shuttle, blasting a powerful fart of wash into the aviator's face. As he continued away from the craft, heading toward the slightly flattened sphere of Jupiter, he noticed with satisfaction that the shuttle was breaking away from the planet.

Powell huffed into the link. "What a time-waster."

"Yeah, especially when you've gotta rush back and get ready for your big *date*."

"Not again," he moaned. "Sorry I even told you."

"What did it take you, a month to ask her? You're a Marine, a jarhead. Remember?"

"This is different."

"No difference."

"And you would know?" Powell asked. "I've been your wingman for eight months. And in all that time, I've never seen you with a woman."

"What are you trying to say?"

"Uh, I guess I'm saying you might be four years older than me, but you're no expert. Then again, maybe I'm wrong. I know you don't like to talk about yourself, but I heard you were married. That true?"

Ben drew in a long breath, staring into the tawny yellow bands of Jupiter where he now saw Elizabeth's hair. He wandered through her locks until he came upon the delicate curves of her face, a face too often stained with tears. *Elizabeth, why am I only good at one thing? Is it a curse or a gift?*

"Vampire Six, you there?"

"Yeah."

"Hey, sorry if . . . Well, it's the first time I've ever . . . Oh, man. I'm sorry—"

"Shuddup, Alleycat. So, where are you taking Ms. Best Legs On Europa anyway?"

"I'm thinking of heading back to Lord Spam's Pleasure Dome. There's one of those little basement restaurants there

that serves up gourmet pasta. Kind of place that doesn't
have a name on the door, looks like a dive from the outside.
Quiet. Romantic. Expensive.''

''You're gonna spend the big bucks, and then you're
gonna hate yourself for it later when you say something
that sets off that little voice in her head that dooms guys
like you and me. And you know what it will be telling
her?''

''I know, I know. Don't call this guy again. But listen,
and I know this sounds cliché, but I feel like I've known
her all my life. It's like this date was meant to be.''

''Oh, man,'' Ben said, shaking his head. ''You *are* in
trouble.'' He was about to add something more when a
burst of static erupted on his Heads-Up Display. Then a
magnified image of the hijacked Class 1 executive transport
spilled over Jupiter's mottled autumn. ''Alleycat, got a
FLIR lock on the target,'' he told Powell.

''It's about time. Got it, too. ETA: two minutes, thirty
seconds. Switching to secure channel to notify the *Sagan*.''

Ben narrowed his gaze on the columns of data beside
the rotating green outline of the ship and noted with disdain
that the delta wing belonged to the Post Terran Mining
Corporation. Probably were a bunch of executives headed
to Valhalla Tower, sipping too heavily on cocktails and
tripping over their tongues when the jackers hit them.

The three jackers had, with outside help, escaped from
the Collective Earth Defense Coast Guard frigate *Sagan* to
avoid impending death sentences for smuggling. According
to the *Sagan*'s commander, the bastards had killed three
midshipmen and had stolen a short-range Coast Guard skiff.
As the skiff's fuel supply had run low, they had smooth-
talked a rescue out of the transport's pilot. One distress
signal and two dead PTMC executives later, a secure-zone
order had been sent and Ben and Powell had been ordered
off their reconnaissance patrol to assist the *Sagan* since, as
the universe would have it, they'd been nearest to the transport.

And the universe was smiling on them today. They
hadn't been in a correct and decent furball for weeks, not
that a hijacked transport would furnish that specific rush.

But it *would* include a little pulse-rising, missile-firing, teeth-clenching ass-kicking; indeed, an adequate fix for most CED Marine Corps pilots and far more glorious than running some belligerent aviator out of a secure zone.

With one gloved hand steady on his control stick, Ben tapped in a command for thruster burst. "Alleycat, reading your ship's clock. Out of the cannon in fifteen mikes. Confirm."

"Confirmed, Vampire Six. Am good to go."

Ben's nav computer would calculate the thruster-burn-to-distance ratio and make any course corrections necessary en route to the target. Though Ben hated turning over the stick to his silicon alter ego, trying to maneuver manually through the field of debris encircling Jupiter would only result in severe hull damage, death, and worse, the embarrassment of having died without the Corps' proverbial permission. He ticked off three, two, one, and the thrusters auto-engaged, pinning him to his combat seat for a ride through a dense, hair-raising arena of ice-slick asteroids spinning among garbage illegally jettisoned by cruise ships. The nav computer accomplished this feat with a ninja's entrance and exit. Before Ben had a chance to react fully to the seemingly impossible ballet of rolls and turns, the ride was over.

"Alleycat to Vampire Six. Burn complete. Systems nominal. And there he is. Tallyho. Target is at our three o'clock, moving at sixteen-twelve KPH, heading three-two-niner-five away from the planet toward Processing Station Burton. Range, six-two-two Ks. Interceptors locked on. ETA fifty-three seconds."

"Confirmed. Flank assault. You're up, I'm down on the pass. Target communications and navigation array with level one lasers. Drive primaries are mine," Ben said. "Break into APs on my mark." With his gaze flicking between his instrument control panel and his HUD, Ben checked his own nav point with respect to the transport's present course. The targeting computer's forward sensors suddenly locked on to and identified a Jihad class laser cannon mounted on the delta wing's back. If that weren't enough bad news, the computer now flashed the image of a belly cannon, Vulcan class, as it began powering up. "Dammit. Alleycat, got—"

"It's an exec transport," Powell said, emphasizing the obvious. "Supposed to be unarmed."

Ben snickered. "With all the mercs and smugglers out here, I'm surprised PTMC waited this long to get serious. Not that it helped."

"Guns are coming to bear. We are targets!"

A comm officer from the CED Marine Corps Strike Base on Europa broke in. "Alleycat One. Vampire Six. You are *not* to engage target. Fall back to observe. The One-twenty-ninth Support Wing is en route with a special negotiator."

"Target is engaging us!" Powell shouted.

Ben tensed over the fact that the pogues on Europa were able to give orders when all they had was an audio/video representation of situation. They weren't in the trench. He'd write a book about it someday: *Petty Power on Parade: One Marine Pilot's Account of the Know-Nothings Who Control the Collective Earth Defense*. "Alleycat, launch countermeasures, then assume attack formation."

"Affirmative!"

Thumbing the lowest of three buttons on his stick, Ben released a shower of white-hot chaff behind the Interceptor, then maxed out his thrusters. He shot toward a flanking position even as twin bolts of red energy lanced out and tore paths through the tumbling, glowing foil. "Holy—"

"Got my chaff, too, Vampire. And now he's got a lock on me," Powell said, his voice slipping back into his pilot's false calm.

Though Ben and his wingman had handled dozens of what the Corps referred to as "incidents" with stolen or hijacked transports, they had never played cards alone with a ship as heavily armed or with jackers as serious as these.

"Evade! Evade!" Ben cried, but he cocked his head and saw that Powell was already doing that—to no avail. The young lieutenant's ship rolled through a death shower of laser bolts and explosive-tipped shells, flashes from impacts bathing his hull in a dizzying sequence of light and shadow.

"My shield's at fifty, now forty percent," Powell said,

his voice just louder than the beeping of alarms in his cockpit. "I'm completely defensive. Can't bug out."

"Then goddammit engage!" Ben screamed as he beat a fist on the side of his canopy.

"You heard the—"

"Vampire Six to Bravo Nest. C'mon! You know we're under fire! Request permission to engage transport."

"Negative, Vampire Six. Fall back and await support."

"No time. They're heading for a jump point. We'll lose them."

"Vampire Six. Await support," another man said. Another man named Lieutenant Colonel Paul Ornowski, the only non-pogue among the brass.

"Paul, we wait, we lose them. Let's just do it. You want more bad press?"

"With you in the Corps, we got all the bad press we need," Ornowski said. "All right, then. Permission to engage and *disable* the ship."

Ben ground his teeth and tore off after the transport. The delta wing's belly gunner shifted his fire away from Powell, and suddenly the thin energy shield above Ben's canopy was alive with the thudding of shells that, as they exploded, sent veins of lightning skittering across his field of view. With his lasers locked on target, Ben released a steady stream of low-level fire that was quickly swallowed by the transport's shield. Then he looked to Powell. "Alleycat, engage thruster burst." But even as Ben gave the order, he saw a salvo of laser fire punch through Powell's starboard wing.

"I'm hit! I'm hit! Shield down! Starboard cannon offline." Still under fire, Powell's Interceptor shifted into an erratic climb symptomatic of major thruster damage.

Turning his attention back to the belly gunner, Ben flipped up the guard covering the missile button on his stick. He checked his HUD for missile lock and saw the flashing red aiming reticle superimposed over the belly gun and cannon fire raining heavily on his shield. "Concussion One," he announced.

The missile dropped, then streaked away from his fighter,

the camera mounted in its nose feeding him a growing image of the transport's belly gunner.

Then, with an ease that only comes from intense training, Ben switched the missile's guidance system to manual and gripped the tiny joystick mounted near his main one. As he set the bomb on a course that would take it well below the transport's underside, he checked his shield level. Bad news in that department. Better hightail it out soon. He regarded the missile monitor. Four, three, two, one, and the bomb was directly below the belly gunner. He thumbed the detonator.

An expanding ball of glowing fragments filled the space between missile and ship, striking the belly gun with what he hoped would be enough force to breach shields and take it out. The transport began a slow roll as it continued to evade, the belly gun still ablaze.

"Vampire Six. Taking fire. Taking fire. Can't shake this gunner," Powell said nervously.

Ben mentally swore at the jackers, cursed their mothers, and damned the rest of their relatives to hell. He had barely finished when the steady drone of an alarm stole his attention. An outline of Powell's ship flashed on his HUD. Then the Interceptor's starboard wing tumbled away. Ben craned his neck to eleven o' clock and squinted at the tiny fighter among the vast field of stars. "Alleycat! Acknowledge!"

"Nav down! Weps down! Ejecting!" Powell screamed.

Breaking away hard and fast from the transport, Ben arrowed toward Powell's position, watching in disbelief as his wingman, clad in thruster pack and environment suit, blasted away from the dying Interceptor. "Cat's in the vac!"

A barrage of laser blasts struck Powell's fighter, tearing the Corps' most deadly instrument into a tangled mass of drunken geometry. Powell engaged his thruster pack and began rocketing away from the incoming. "Ejection successful!"

"On my way," he answered. If he could get close enough to the lieutenant, Ben could open the hatch to his small hold and Powell could slip inside.

An unfamiliar female voice came over the comlink. "Good-bye, Marine."

"Ben! C'mon buddy! Get over here," Powell pleaded. "They're gonna—"

Before the word *no* even escaped Ben's lips, the delta wing's laser gunner adjusted his fire.

And First Lieutenant Powell Stephenson's life ended in a singular blue-white flash.

"Vampire Six! Disengage!" cried Lieutenant Colonel Ornowski.

Drumming his fist on his portside canopy to emphasize each of his words, Ben answered, "THEY JUST KILLED ALLEYCAT!"

"Break off!" Ornowski ordered.

The delta wing's laser gunner turned his cannon on Ben's ship—as did the belly gunner. Though he found himself in more AA fire than he had ever experienced, breaking off was no longer an option. Baring the fangs of his code name, he plunged headlong into the kaleidoscopic storm.

"Vampire Six! You're violating a direct order. Acknowledge!"

"I've never lost a wingman!" Ben spat. "Never!"

"This isn't the time for payback. Break off!"

Ornowski assumed that Ben wanted revenge for his wingman's death—but he was only half-right. Ben forged on, driven by a rage that had been building for months, a rage born of the Corps's failure to abide by their own law of nonnegotiation with jackers and his own failure to say anything about it because he had feared for his career. Now a man was dead—thanks to a delay. According to the Corps' original operating mission, the transport should have been blown out of the sky.

But PTMC had slowly softened up the Corps through bribery. Why? Because the mining company's economic and political control had grown so rapidly that the Earth government feared a takeover. So, the board enlisted the Collective Earth Defense to keep PTMC in check. Trouble was, PTMC had lots of money to pay off military brass. The Marine Corps and all other services of the CED were as corrupt as the company itself. Ben lived with and hated that fact.

Now he would demonstrate to the pogues that the old law of the CED Marine Corps worked. And, through enforcing it, he'd serve the jackers a bit of white-knuckled justice they'd take to their graves.

But a hell of a lot stood between Ben and that desire. The rounds kept coming, and the stars slipped away behind the glowing tendrils of reflected fire that clung to and vanished from his hull in the span of a millisecond. He tipped his nose up, then down, then wagged his wings. He tried corkscrewing through the salvos, tried four-point turns while his cannons spat a futile reply. He wanted to scratch at the sweat running into his eyes—

FORWARD SHIELD STATUS: 29.97

—drown his dry, lumped throat in water—

DAMAGE REPORT: CRITICAL HIT TO PORT WING

—and do something about the breath he couldn't catch.

FLIR STATUS: OFF-LINE/HARDWARE NOT PRESENT

He punched back the thruster control, then seized his stick and jammed down his thumb on the missile release. "Concussion Two! Three! Four! Five! Six!"

The five missiles charged ahead of Ben's Interceptor, an ominous blue glow in their wake. A laser bolt struck one, detonated it prematurely, and suddenly the fluctuating cloud of the explosion lay dead ahead. Slamming his stick left, Ben turned away from the lethal obstacle and dropped into a dive relative to the transport. Before the gunners could get another lock on him, he grimaced and pulled up so hard on his stick that he feared it would snap off. Now ballistic and racing toward the transport's belly, he watched with widening eyes as the concussion missiles struck the craft.

Two of the CMs impacted with the belly cannon, disintegrating it and hopefully blasting its operator into a reality of eternal pain. One of the other missiles detonated in a fountain of blue-white light topside while the final one cast a twin explosion astern. Phosphorescent green reactor coolant began streaming from the now-slowing transport, and, as Ben closed in, he sighed deeply. The delta wing was clearly disabled. He studied the belly cannon, or, rather, the blackened irregular oval of hull where it had been. He assumed the silent piggyback laser had at least been damaged. Switching his own lasers to full power and keeping his index finger poised over the trigger, he came within fifty meters of the vessel. Though his FLIR was off-line, his conventional scanners painted an adequate, if less specific picture. Cabin pressure remained intact, but the transport's reactor was superheating. In about eight mikes the ship's drive would ruin everyone's day.

"You're making career decisions here, Ben. And if you've already killed those hostages, there won't be anything I can do for you," Ornowski said gravely.

"Law says we don't negotiate with jackers," Ben managed through gritted teeth. "It's reiterated in the damn Ops manual. But more times than not, the damned order comes in: Don't engage. Know what? I'm tired of the company's interference, Paul. And now my wingman's dead because of it. These hostages are, BY OUR LAW, expendable." He brought his Interceptor near the delta wing's stern and guided it down with maneuvering jets.

"Each CO has the authority to interpret those laws in the field of battle," Ornowski reminded. "And those hostages are PTMC execs—important, influential people who sometimes directly affect our budget. And—"

"And if you wanna see any of them alive again, you'll call off that squadron and get another transport over here—ASAP," a female jacker said. She sounded hoarse, had probably been screaming at the hostages these past hours.

"We'll be reasonable if you are," Ornowski said.

Ben snorted and shook in his combat harness as his landing skids settled onto the delta wing. A button on his shiplink control panel flashed, he hit it to extend tube, then he listened as the small, multiarmed drone sealed the link to the transport and piped in an atmosphere. The drone ignited its laser torch and began cutting through the delta wing's hull. Ben quickly unbuckled the shoulder, waist, and thigh restraints of his harness, tore off his thruster pack, and, with trembling hands, unclipped and removed his helmet. He scratched his face and ran fingers through his dark, high, and tight crew cut. With his helmet off, he'd be out of touch with Europa Strike Base. No loss there.

"Call off that squadron. Get us the transport. And we'll turn over the hostages," the woman said. "But you'd better do it fast. Our reactor is superheating, and we can't shut it down."

So we all die, Ben thought as he hurried behind his pilot's chair. He paused a second to lift his PK390 pistol from his calf holster, then let it lead the way into a narrow access tube behind the cockpit. The hissing of the drone's laser torch grew louder as he neared the back of the tube, where a second conduit equipped with a ladder, the shiplink, intersected from below. Ben sat on the ledge, breathing in the acrid fumes and staring down at the stout drone performing its task. Then he closed his eyes, and he saw Powell sitting at a table in that basement restaurant. Miss Europa sipped her wine and smiled over something the kid had said. The kid. He was, or had been, only four years younger than Ben. Tightening every muscle, Ben shouted a curse that echoed through the tunnels and was replaced by silence. He opened his eyes.

The drone had finished making its cut, leaving a disc-shaped piece of the delta wing's hull hanging by a few tendrils of polymer. After sliding up the tube on magnetic wheels, the robot slid into its storage compartment and powered down.

Now the rest would be as easy as assembling a gas barbecue grill. He drew in a long breath and unclipped a flash grenade from his belt. Then he adjusted the grip on his pistol and prepared to drop the two and a half meters to the disc. He closed his eyes saw the flash of Powell's death. With that, he pulled the pin on his flash grenade, pushed off the ledge and—

—blasted through the disc, falling another two meters to the cabin's deck. Even as his boots touched the expensive hardwood floor, he began rolling and tossed the grenade amid the sounds of conventional pistol fire.

A great blast of air struck him as the grenade went off, and he rolled up onto his haunches to fire blindly into the whiteness that engulfed the cabin. "CED Marines!" he growled. "Weapons down!" The grenade flash began to clear, revealing a lounge of leather furniture and hunter green throw carpets. He crawled to his right and found cover behind a wet bar jutting from the hull.

But then something hard and cold touched the back of his head, something even an aviator could guess was a gun. "You jerk," the jacker behind him said, then took his pistol. Ben recognized her voice; she'd been speaking with Ornowski. "You came alone? Did you think we were serving tea?"

"Actually, I thought I'd be the one doing the serving." A scream escaped Ben's lips as he reached back with both hands and seized the jacker's gun—just as it went off. Ben couldn't tell if he'd been shot or not as he pulled her in front of him, slammed her onto her back, and drove his knee into the young blonde's stomach. With ringing ears, he tore the pistol from her hand as the wet bar above him erupted in a cacophony of gunfire.

"Rip!" the woman cried. "He's got me!"

Ben jammed the pistol into her forehead.

"Rip! Get the hell—"

CRACK!

Without looking, Ben withdrew his gun. He bolted away from the bar toward a sofa and dived behind it. Slugs stitched a line of holes in the leather above him. He sensed something warm and wet trickling behind his ear. His fingers came up bloody.

"Holdz fire! Holdz fire!" a male jacker ordered in his buzzing, Theta Penal Colony accent. This one had obviously been in the business a long time. "Mizter Marine. I know zyou think these hostages are expendable. But I want you to see zomething."

"Just listen to him! Please!" a woman cried.

Ben crawled to the edge of the sofa and peered around the corner. The jacker stood at an entrance to the lounge, his long, gray hair swept back from his forehead and pulled into a ponytail that draped across the chest of the smartly dressed woman he held. With one arm wrapped around her tiny neck and a pistol jammed into her thick, dark mane, the jacker had a glint in his eye that was remarkably similar to Ben's own. A gambler's glint.

"Itz one thing to launch missiles at a ship and kill everyone on board. Itz another to watch zomeone die in front of you. Zomeone you could have zaved. Come out. Drop your weapon. And she livez. You are a Marine. A protector. Are you not?"

"I'm also a lifetaker, you bastard. You killed my wingman for nothing. Now you die—for the same." Ben launched himself to his feet, took aim, and one look into the woman's eyes held him back. He couldn't do it.

Yes, he could. He'd kill them both.

But she had nothing to do with it.

She was a hostage. Her tough luck. She was already dead.

Did it have to be that way?

Yes. Her fate. And his. With a shaking hand he pulled the trigger—

—and struck the jacker in the shoulder as the thug yanked his weapon away from the woman and fired.

Ben launched himself toward the couch, hearing a crack and feeling his head jerk back as he soared through the air. He crashed with a groan onto his stomach, his breath forced away. A strange, tingling feeling rushed across his face. He tried to lift himself, but ohmygod nothing worked. His breath finally returned in an odd hissing sound, and now his cheek felt sticky and damp. The rear of the couch looked alternately hazy and sharp. He thought he heard footsteps, but they were echoing so much that he couldn't be sure.

He suddenly wished Elizabeth were with him, holding his hand the way she had every time he'd been shot up. He closed his eyes and saw her, standing in the hallway where the jacker had been.

"This one's pretty bad, Elizabeth. I need you."

She shook her head and blinked back tears. "No more, Ben. No more."

2

We're in Your Head

"Anyone visit him today?"

"Yeah, his sister came. She was talking to him like they all do. Like he could hear her. She's saying all this stuff, telling him she forgives him for beating up her husband."

"No, kidding."

"Seriously, when she said that, I started realizing something about these jocks."

"What's that?"

"They think they can control everything and everyone in their lives. I don't know if the Corps does it to them or what. Screws them up good, though."

"I'd never marry one."

"Well, if you're ever thinking about it, you can talk to this one's ex. She was here yesterday. When I asked her who she was, she told me, quote, one of his victims."

"Ouch. Wonder why she even came."

"She fits the pattern. See, all these jocks have what you might call intense relationships. I mean, when they love, it's more passionate than anything you've ever seen. And then they screw it up. But because of that passion, these victims hang on. I've seen some of them show up after ten, twenty years."

"Maybe it's not love. Maybe it's guilt?"

"I don't know."

"Why don't you ask me?" Ben said, fighting through the cobwebs of dryness in his throat. He opened his eyes to slits, and it took a moment more to accept the light and focus on the two Marine Corps nurses, one a young, lean, Asian man wincing in embarrassment, the other a heavyset, olive-skinned woman whose expression looked all business. She moved across the small, Spartan room toward a beeping monitor somewhere behind Ben's gurney. The beeping stopped, then a whine came from the gurney's motor as it raised him to a sitting position.

"Why didn't you tell me he was scheduled for consciousness?" the young man asked, mildly ticked off.

"Thought I did," the woman said.

Ben went to rub his eyes and felt an IV attached to the back of his hand. Then he sensed something on his head. He touched the bandage; it covered his entire scalp. And while he should be concerned about what the hell had happened to him, he had something far more important on his mind. "Did my wife leave a number?"

"No. And I'm sorry, but she didn't want you to know she was here. By the way, I'm Larissa Stewart."

"And I'm Kyung Ho." The young man gave a nod, smiling wanly. "This is the CED Marine Corps hospital, Olympus Mons."

"You're kidding," Ben said. "This ain't the Vegas Hilton?"

Larissa smiled and handed Ben a glass of water. "The two of us have been taking care of you for about two standard weeks now."

Ben nearly dropped the glass. "Two weeks?" He suddenly lapsed into a fit of coughing. Larissa put her hand on his and guided the glass to his lips. He sipped the water and grew calmer.

Kyung favored Larissa with widened eyes. "We're not supposed to be talking about this."

"What a crock," Larissa said through a sigh. "We slave over this patient, and we can't even tell him that it's been a long, hard, haul. It's about time you and I got a little credit.''

Kyung pursed his lips and shook his head.

Frowning at Larissa, Ben asked, ''You want credit? You're a nurse. Didn't think you were in it for the glory.''

''Don't get me wrong. I'm not looking for a medal or even a raise. Fact is, everything's so damned secretive around here. Most of our patients don't even know our names because of some ridiculous security reason. It's just been getting to me lately.''

Ben cocked a brow. ''Well, if you'd like to violate your gag order, don't let me stop you.'' Then his gaze panned the room. ''Are we being monitored?''

''With the Corps's pathetic budget? They can barely afford to pay us, let alone hire someone to examine recordings.''

He made a crooked grin. ''Right. So, what do you know about me? How did I get here?''

''They got your heart beating again on Europa, got you stabilized, then jumped you here. You had two head wounds. I don't know the details of your injuries.''

Funny. Only then did Ben remember getting shot, and the memory was accompanied by a strange, somehow mechanical sensation. He dived for cover, heard the gunshot, then shuddered with sympathetic pain.

Larissa's expression washed over with concern. ''Are you all right?''

He nodded. ''Flashback, I guess. Didn't know I had died. Don't remember a damned thing. Can't even get interviewed about seeing the light. Hey, what happened with the hijacked transport?''

''Lieutenant Colonel Ornowski's coming to see you. He wanted to tell you about that,'' Kyung said.

''Well, somehow I got out of there. So the news can't be that bad. Anyway, I guess, what, they patched me up here?''

''You could say that,'' Kyung said. ''Although they did a little more than patching.''

''What does that mean?''

Kyung looked at Larissa. "Let's forget this. We'll break the law if we tell him. Let them do it."

A chill raced up Ben's spine. "Am I paralyzed or something?" He remembered being unable to move his limbs and now lifted his arms, shook his legs, and wiggled his toes. To his partial relief, everything worked. That's right. Everything *did* work: He'd taken the glass from Larissa. And he could speak. "What's wrong with me?" He lifted the blanket and winced as he peeked at his groin.

"No, no, no. Don't worry about that," Larissa said, then laughed. "The plumbing's intact."

He smiled through a sigh.

While Larissa continued to be amused by him, Kyung was anything but. He fixed Larissa with a solemn stare. "If we tell him, and he lets them know, then we lose our jobs. We might even get court-martialed. And for what?"

"What if they don't tell him?" Larissa challenged, her expression back to business. "How many others don't know?"

Kyung gestured with his head to Ben. "Why do we owe *this guy* the truth?"

"Why don't we?"

"Because it's our job to remain silent."

"Well, I can't live with this guilt anymore."

"So it's not credit you're looking for," Ben said. "You're trying to make yourself feel better. That's fine. I don't care what your deal is. Just tell me what happened."

"Like I said, I don't know the details of your injury, but your brain was severely damaged."

"Don't do it," Kyung warned her.

"You wouldn't have been able to live without an enhancement."

"I'm out of here," Kyung said as he stormed toward the door. "I won't be around for this."

"What do you mean by *enhancement*. You don't mean—"

She nodded. "BPCs. You've got three."

Ben swore under his breath and closed his eyes as tightly as he could.

"Bio-processing chips have been in use for about twenty

years. Studies look good. At least there's no danger,'' she said reassuringly.

Snapping open his eyes, Ben snarled, "Thank you. Thank you so much for being honest with me. Thank you for telling me my life is over. I'm just a puppet now. Do you feel less guilty?''

She flashed him a wounded look. "You're not a puppet. That's just scuttlebutt.''

"You *know* it isn't.''

"In this case, Ben. Knowing *is* everything. How would you like to be walking around and not know they're in your head?''

"I'd like it just fine. I'd have nothing to worry about because I wouldn't know they're there. Tell me this. How do I know these thoughts I'm having now are my own? Maybe the Corps is feeding these thoughts into the chips. Maybe they're controlling my whole reality—and you're a part of it.''

"Believe me, if the Marine Corps is feeding you any information, I'm not a part of it. I've been a military nurse all my life. Corps pays the best. Only reason why I'm here. Got no blood-and-guts loyalty the way you do.''

"That's a pretty limp assurance,'' Ben said, then sighed in disgust.

"You have to believe the chips are in there and keeping you alive, nothing more. If you're always wondering whether you're being controlled, you'll lose your mind.''

"Maybe it's not even mine to lose,'' Ben said, then huffed over the irony of that. "And another thing. You're not just telling me this to feel less guilty. You wouldn't risk your job for that. You don't even know me. That story's for your partner.''

She couldn't meet his gaze. "I *do* feel guilty about chip patients.''

"Tell me, dammit!''

"I can't.''

"Knock, knock,'' Lieutenant Colonel Paul Ornowski said before entering the room. Clad in a golf shirt, jeans, and the grin of an off-duty officer, the colonel quickly moved to Ben and gave him a firm handshake. "Looking good, Ben. Color's back. Bulldogs never die, eh?'' Ben suddenly got the feeling that Ornowski had borrowed his grin from a wolf, not a sheep.

''Excuse me,'' Larissa said, then headed for the door. ''Intercom's on. Just call if you need anything.''

Ornowski watched her leave, then regarded Ben. ''Would you mind if a couple of photogs came in and took a few pictures. They'd like to do a follow-up on the story.''

Ben furrowed his brow. ''What story?''

''Sorry. I'm getting ahead of myself.''

''What happened?''

''What happened is you're a hero—even though we both know you disobeyed a direct order to break off from that transport,'' Ornowski said, still wearing the bruises to his ego.

''Get back to the hero part.''

''Because you shot up the transport's drive and set off its reactor, our squadron was able to call their bluff. We took out their lifepods and told them to surrender. They had a choice between that or getting nuked. There weren't any martyrs among them.''

''But they knew you wanted those hostages.''

''I contacted Samuel Dravis. He's head of crisis contingency management at PTMC. Believe it or not, he's the one who told us to call their bluff.''

''That's mighty thoughtful of him, but I think those execs aboard the transport would've disagreed.''

''We only lost the two they killed. But that was before we were involved.''

Ben turned away. ''And we lost a valuable Marine pilot who'd still be alive if you boys weren't constantly reinterpreting Marine Corps law to stroke PTMC execs. Have you thought about that? Have you thought about the boy you lost?''

Ornowski's voice softened. ''We, uh, found some of his remains. His family has some money. They've got a plot on Earth, in San Antonio. I can get you all the information.''

He nodded, drawing in a long breath, then releasing it in a huff. ''When's it gonna change, Paul? I know you feel like me. You just won't admit it. When are we *really* gonna live and die by the sword?''

"I don't know. Forget about it. Now look, the IPC did an article on you. We gave the reporter your flight school grad picture. I have some hardcopies of the whole thing. I forgot them now. I'll bring them by. It was a great piece. I heard people out past the rim were talking about you. This is a great way to go out, Ben. A great way.''

Grimacing, Ben pushed himself up, away from the bed. A wave of soreness broke over his shoulders. "You make it sound like I'm—''

"You don't expect to come back, do you? Not after what you've been through.''

"I know I got shot in the head a couple of times. But I'm here now and feeling a little sore. That's it. I haven't spoken to a doctor.''

"You will. But it's better you hear it from me first, one Marine to another. No bullshit. Bottom line? You'll never fly in the Corps again.''

"I saw a comic like you once, Paul. Think it was in Lake Tahoe. But your delivery's much better than his.''

"The Corps has issued you a mandatory medical discharge. Your injuries, while purportedly treatable, might handicap your ability to handle an aircraft. And then you've got that hearing problem—''

"No, I don't,'' Ben said, balling his hands into fists.

"Sure you do.'' Ornowski took a step away from the bed, and his eyes suddenly widened. "WHEN I SAY BREAK OFF, YOU BREAK OFF, MISTER! DO YOU UNDERSTAND?''

Slamming his fists on the bed, Ben screamed, "THEY KILLED MY WINGMAN! AND YOU BASTARDS WANTED TO SIT AND CHAT WITH THEM!''

Ornowski stuck his mug in Ben's face. "YOU BROKE THE CHAIN OF COMMAND, YOU STUPID MAGGOT! *WE* NEARLY FAILED BECAUSE *YOU* FAILED.''

"So I guess you don't think I'm a hero,'' Ben said darkly.

"Not for one damned minute. I've put my ass on the line for you too many times. You know what, Ben? When

I came in here, I thought I'd just forget about your world-revolves-around-me attitude. I thought I'd put your insubordination behind me since officially you are no longer a Marine. I actually felt bad for you. And I could almost understand why you went into that transport alone. But it's clear that you don't realize what you're doing. And getting out is the best thing for you now."

Ben sat there, breathing, listening, staring into the pale gray blanket covering his legs. The Corps had been his life. Nearly all Marines shared that sentiment. Now it had been ripped out of his gut like a still-beating heart, and Ornowski was shoving it in his face. There weren't enough four-letter words for the brass who had done this to him.

"Is everything okay in here?" Larissa asked, poking her head in the door.

Looking up at her, Ben said, "No."

"I heard some yelling. And there are some people out here waiting to come in and take pictures?"

"Tell them to come back later," Ben ordered in a tone he usually reserved for cadets.

"I'll tell them just like that," Larissa answered sarcastically.

Returning his gaze to Ornowski, Ben suddenly wanted to ask about the injuries. Maybe Ornowski knew about the BPCs and wasn't talking. Or maybe they hadn't told him. Ben needed to know one way or the other. He needed to know if the Corps was discharging him—only to pull the strings later. But how to ask the colonel without tipping him off?

"I'm leaving," Ornowski announced. "I'd tell you I'm sorry, Ben. But I just don't feel that right now."

"I don't need your sympathy. I'm just wondering if you know how bad off I am. Tell you the truth, I'm worried."

"Can't help you there."

"Come on. You've seen my file."

"Actually, I haven't. When they moved you here, it became classified, level seven."

"Why?"

"I don't know. Good luck." He left.

"Nurse?" Ben said, hitting the intercom button. Then,

swallowing the pain, he eased himself back onto the bed. He lay there a moment before Larissa arrived.

"What is it?"

"Come here," he said in a whisper.

She leaned over the bed, the pitted skin of her beefy cheeks catching a bit of the overhead lights. Then he seized her neck with both hands, dragged her onto the bed, then slid on top, pinning her to the mattress. He began to crush her larynx with his thumbs while she drove her nails into his wrists. "NO MORE GAMES, BITCH! TALK!" He released a little pressure.

"Let go of me!"

"Is this how you imagined you'd die?" He dug his fingers in deep. "You want my face to be the last thing you see?"

"Okay, okay. Your ex-wife paid me to tell you," Larissa gasped. "She paid me a lot. I don't know why. I didn't ask."

As he drew his hands away from Larissa's neck, she slid her knee up and drove it between his legs. He screamed and rolled off the bed, dragging the IV bag to the floor with him.

"Whoa. What's going on?" Kyung asked, hurrying into the room.

Larissa's reply came faintly. "Help me get him back into bed."

"Belay that order," Ben said, holding his breath in pain and curling into a fetal position. "I'll be here for a while."

3

The One-sixth Gravity
of the Situation

Neal Shepard strode at double time through the immense corridor, heading toward Lunar Outpost MN0012's command center. Only two weeks prior he had been associate chief of the Titan Moon Mine MN0132 and won-
dering if he'd ever get promoted. He'd thought that work-ing on Titan wouldn't provide him with enough visibility since PTMC inspectors rarely visited the place. But mineral production had dramatically increased, he'd finally come in at budget, and someone had noticed his efforts. When the order had come to head PTMC's flagship mining operation, he'd called Whey and the twins and told them he'd be coming home much more often. No more vidphone ''I love you's,'' and he'd even make the twins' seventh birthday party. He was, after all, just a ten-hour ride from Sacra-mento.

Senior Mining Chief Neal Shepard had a lot to celebrate. He now oversaw the most complex off-world mining op-eration in the history of mankind. Lunar Outpost MN0012 descended some thirty levels into the moon's crust, classi-fying it as the first ''mature base operation.'' PTMC en-gineers had foreseen that a surface mining operation would have succumbed to dust contamination, the outgassing of machinery lubricants in vacuum, extreme temperature fluctuations, radiation hazards, and micrometeorite bombardment, so they had wisely designed a subsurface, shirtsleeve environment that simultaneously provided ore and working and living space for humans. The reliability and expected usable lifetime of equipment, particularly the fourteen types of standard mining drones collecting and processing ore, were much greater in a pressurized underground complex. What's more, every breath that Neal took came from oxygen that had been recovered from lunar rock through a remarkable technique called in-situ processing. And a substantial supply of ice had been found deep under the regolith lining many polar craters, ice deposited by meteoroid and comet strikes and used as a water supply. By further exploiting the moon's resources, engineers devised methods to manufacture hydrogen for rocket propellants and helium-3 for the outpost's fusion reactor. The combination of self-sufficiency and automation kept costs down, particularly in the area of payroll. A minimum crew of seven oversaw operations. Neal wholeheartedly appreciated the arrangement. The Titan operation had been a budgetary nightmare, but PTMC's profit margin on this outpost usually exceeded that of all other operations—no matter who was mining chief. Thus, Neal had received the easiest yet most prestigious assignment of his career.

But now something threatened his sacred budget. He'd been paged by Frank Jewelbug, Software Supervisor, poet, resident bohemian, and architect of the most inspired banana split Neal had ever tasted. Jewelbug spoke in a rasp characteristic of inhaling too much sodo gas in his youth. He'd said, "Chief Shepard? We've got some weirdness on level twenty-nine. Production, well, it's stopped. I called the CED, asked if they were doing anything on seventeen that might affect the drones on the lower levels. They said no one's in their sector today."

Reaching the end of the shaft, Neal turned right and paused to catch his breath, feeling the full burden of the extra ten pounds he'd gained over the holidays. Ahead lay another tunnel, this one ten meters long and terminating at a door whose large window was marked:

LUNAR OUTPOST MN0012 COMMAND CENTER
LEVEL ONE

Under which Frank Jewelbug had posted a sign in bold script:

God's Sandbox
Bring Your Shovel?

Neal kept forgetting to tear down that sign. You never knew when President Suzuki might drop by. PTMC's CEO was a highly refined man on a galactic search for his sense of humor. Odds were against his finding it.

Wiping a bead of sweat from his forehead, Neal resumed his belabored pace, picturing himself taking a huge bite out of a chocolate chip Christmas cookie and chiding himself over it. How many of those had he eaten? Six?

"C'mon, c'mon," Jewelbug urged, shuffling in his moccasins from behind the sliding door, his virtual goggles dangling from his neck, his unkempt hair indicating each of the cardinal points. His genius bought him liberties with the starched collars at PTMC, liberties Neal would never appreciate.

Reaching the door, he ripped down the sign and shook his head at Jewelbug.

"Censored again!" the supervisor said in mock fury, then turned toward the room.

With a pulse still racing from the walk, Neal followed Jewelbug down a short staircase that led into the circular command pit of the outpost. Dozens of status indicators flashed, and monitors displayed remote cam images of light- or thermal-enhanced representations of all thirty levels of the mine. Seismic monitors clicked beneath the rhythmic pulse of an operational shutdown alarm and the shouting between a few of the five begoggled supervisors seated in their virtual-link chairs. The scent of freshly installed electronics still clung to the air, though it had been a week since the techs had upgraded the security system.

Once at Jewelbug's station, the supervisor sat and slipped up his goggles. Then his fingers made an elaborate dance on a computer touchpad built into the armrest of his chair. He slipped off the goggles and handed them to Neal. "This is too funky."

Neal put on the goggles and found himself on level twenty-nine. He thought of moving forward, and the computer obeyed, taking him in a glide down a poorly lit tunnel whose walls consisted of yellow-striped grating. The mining bots had their own sensor packages, and lighting in the mines was, for the most part, unnecessary. Neal thought of light enhancing the image; once again, the computer complied. He moved to the mouth of a tunnel set into floor. He stared down into an apparent abyss but knew the conduit snaked away and looped into an enormous main drilling chamber. Suddenly, a Spider processing robot floated up from the tunnel, its green, triangular sensor eyes flashing in the center of the red inverted pyramid engineers called its torso. Each of the quadpod's four, long, wedge-shaped legs shifted back and forth for no apparent reason, and the trio of Mass Driver Rifles mounted in its belly pivoted to track nonexistent targets. But even more strange were the cries, almost animal cries, that resounded from the mech. Neal frowned. A Spider's standard audio functions consisted of a series of default beeps. The bot was joined by another, then another, and another. Spiders, Class 1 Drillers, Medium and Advanced Lifters, and Class 1 Heavy Drillers screamed, howled, and wailed as they surged out of the tunnel. Neal followed the first Spider as it bobbed and whirred, heading toward a corridor that led to level twenty-eight. The others followed. "I don't believe this," he told Jewelbug. "They're abandoning their posts and moving up." He lifted off the goggles, and his frown deepened. "It's some kind of weird exodus."

"I know. Maybe they got religion."

Emma Shanakenberg, Processing Supervisor, raised her goggles into her short, curly hair. Her gaze narrowed. "Don't look now people, but the same thing's happening

on levels seventeen, sixteen, and fifteen. Only these bots
are moving down to the mech construction facility on level
twenty.''

''It appears that all drones from levels fifteen through
twenty-nine are headed toward level twenty. Those down
on thirty have broken into the northeast reactor control
bay,'' Fazia Mohammed said. The young systems analyst
continued to tap frantically on her touchpad. ''Just what I
need, with the bar in two days.'' Fazia had been studying
corporate law in her off hours and was ready to take either
the intersystem or local bar exam so that, in her own words,
she could ''kiss this hunka green cheese good-bye.''

''Maybe you can use your legal skills to persuade the
mechs to get back to work,'' Jewelbug told her.

''Maybe you can go down there and scare them with
your haircut,'' she retorted. ''Or you might actually try doing your job and finding out what's buggy with their pro-
grams.''

Jewelbug looked guiltily at Neal as if he wanted to explain his nonchalance. ''Of course, I tried a systemwide
shutdown—but whatever's messing with the drones is
affecting their wireless modems. Then I started running
multiple diaogs. I'm waiting for the results.'' He leaned
forward in his chair and studied the two columns of data
scrolling down a screen, muttering something Neal didn't
quite hear. Then Jewelbug squinted at the screen. And his
hairy jaw dropped. ''My diaogs are caught in a loop. Each
one is doing a diagnostic on the other. Someone's altered
my command!'' His hands fell to his keyboard, and he began typing madly, the screen before him flashing a string
of words and numbers familiar yet collectively unintelligi-
ble to Neal. ''Come on, you sweet mother. Come on. I'll
rub your shoulders when we're done.''

''Hey, Chief,'' Shipping Supervisor Garvin Smith called
in his thick voice that complemented his equally thick,
muscular frame. ''My mechs at the surface docks have
stopped loading. They're moving down here.''

Neal turned to Security Supervisor Joseph Prism. ''Seal
all hatches leading to the command center.''

''You got it.''

Emma stood. "Uh, excuse me, but does anyone else think there's something majorly wrong with this picture?" She looked toward one of the eight doors that fed into the center. "Are we safe?"

And, as if on cue, computers, status panels, screens, printers, and even electric coffee-cup warmers began to wink out. Dim red emergency lights clicked on a few seconds later to reveal that the panels indicating O_2 processing still glowed with life.

"Mechs on thirty have cut select systems," Fazia reported. "Recon cams, VR links, and just about every other monitor is down. Standard lighting on level one is gone."

"I'm thinking they're pissed," Jewelbug said, his gaze turning floorward. "I'm thinking slave rebellion."

"That's ridiculous," Neal retorted. "Their AI is limited to primary functions."

"They cut power but not environmental controls," Jewelbug argued. "They know that only the surface mechs were designed for vacuum operation. No glitch, no virus I know of could produce behavior like this."

"Well, you'd better figure out what the hell's going on," Neal snapped. "You get paid to do more than dress like a slob."

Jewelbug self-consciously smoothed out his shirt, raked fingers through his hair.

"Look, that was uncalled for," Neal said. "Sorry. I'm stressing. Just find out what's happening."

"And he'd better do that fast," Garvin said. "Because my rock stars will be here in about thirty seconds."

"Chief, emergency comm control is operational. Would you like me to contact the supertrench?" Communications Supervisor Kathleen Cresswell asked.

Neal shook his head, envisioning a battalion of CED jarheads blasting the drones and his expensive control center equipment to Nebraska. The military's fort in the nearby trench was supposed to provide Neal with peace of mind, but their training exercises often strayed as dangerously close as some aviators' trams. If that weren't enough to irritate, PTMC rented them space on level seventeen for a "classified purpose." Even Neal was not permitted to enter their sector, which was guarded by robot sentries and monitored via recon cams. Whenever military personnel entered or exited the mine, Neal and his crew were confined to quarters. That order had begun as a blister, had become an infection, and now remained a sucking chest wound that made Neal want to kick them and their superiority complexes out of the mine altogether.

Joseph Prism moved quickly away from his dead terminal and approached Neal. "Chief. Since the mechs are not responding to commands, and they *are* armed—"

Neal waved him off. "Don't even finish that. I don't want the CED in here."

"But—"

"But you're right there, too. Open the cache."

Prism nodded, spun on his heels, then jogged back toward a bank of strong lockers opposite his station. He tapped in a code, opened the doors, then began withdrawing EX790 pulse rifles. "All right, people. C'mon over. It'll be just like the drills. Autolock and load, aim, and fire."

"Chief?" Kathleen called. "I don't wanna overstep, but SOP is to report our situation to Shiva Station. I think it would make us all feel better if I did."

"Do it," Neal said, heading toward Prism to receive his weapon.

But before he reached the man, the muffled sound of an Argon laser erupted from behind the door opposite Prism's station. The hatch abruptly blew off its guides and hit the floor with a thud that sent Neal ducking behind a walkway rail.

A blue, Class 2 drone emerged from the crimson-lit mist of the explosion, hovered a moment, then turned its pair of wedge-shaped torsos toward Prism, who raised his rifle and fired—as did the mech. Twin thunderclaps echoed throughout the center, followed by a female's scream and a bizarre whine as the drone tipped toward the floor, lost antigrav control, and crashed in a smoldering, sparking heap.

"It shot Kathy!" Fazia cried.

Neal glanced over Prism's terminal to his Communication Supervisor's station. The red-haired woman lay supine over her sizzling controls, one side of her face either shaved off or lost in shadow. Earlier, she had split a bagel with Neal, had even buttered it for him.

Another door slammed inward and fell to the floor, this one at the southeast entrance. A purple-and-green Small Hulk gazed menacingly upon the room with its lone, red, rectangular eye. The mech's octagon-shaped, legless frame supported two arms designed for the sole purpose of brandishing a pair of heavy Argon lasers.

Prism took aim at the mech.

"Don't fire!" Neal ordered.

"Chief?" Fazia asked, her face creased in puzzlement.

Keeping his head just behind the walkway rail, Neal began skulking toward Prism. "We provoked the last one."

"I think it provoked us," Jewelbug said from somewhere behind them.

A peculiar shredding sound stole Neal's attention. He looked in astonishment as a green Medium Lifter sliced its way through the southwest door with its huge, diamond-plated swingarms. Each arm contained two spikes that worked as a claw powerful enough to tear through the toughest lunar rock, let alone a hatch made of cheap alloy. It surveyed the room with gleaming, triangular eyes as it began a wide arc, keeping its back to the wall.

"All right, Ringo. Take it easy, now," Garvin said as he raised his hands and approached the Small Hulk, which towered some two meters over him. "You know me, don't you? Recognize my voice? We've worked together. Me, you, and the rest of the boys."

The Hulk screeched a reply so loud that Neal grimaced and covered his ears.

A second Hulk arose in the doorway that the Medium Lifter had torn apart. Then a Class 2 drone, identical to the one Prism had shot, followed.

"We're about to be outnumbered," Emma noted grimly.

Garvin took a step closer to the Hulk, now standing just a meter from it. The mech floated idly, its eye pulsing with light. Then it edged toward Garvin, who took a step back. The mech kept coming. "Uh, a little help over here!" Garvin cried as the robot pinned him against a control panel.

Prism's rifle spat thick bolts of yellow energy at the

Hulk, but the drone's armor had been designed to take beat-
ings far more severe. As Neal watched, waiting for the
mech's reaction, he heard more firing ring out from across
the room.

Fazia and Emma had taken cover behind the row of
desks that adjoined their control panels. With elbows dug
into blotters, they unleashed volley after volley at the Medium Lifter, their aim not entirely true but good enough.
The green, mechanized crab came at them with its claws
chopping, its skin rupturing under a dissipating lacework
of energy. The two women increased their fire, and the
mech burst apart with the abruptness of a piñata, showering
them with pieces of swing arm, torso, CPU, and eye. They
covered their heads and fell back behind the desks—

—only to be shot at by the Small Hulk that had pinned
Garvin. The mech had released the shipping supervisor to
aid its comrade. The two women screamed and shrank as
Neal watched in horror.

Pivoting quickly away from the women, the mech
seemed once more to study Garvin, whose hands reached
for the ceiling.

Then it shot him.

Clutching his chest, Garvin fell to his knees. "It only
stunned me!" he shouted, his teeth bared in pain.

Neal looked to Emma and Fazia; they were still down
but moving. He hustled to Prism's station and seized a rifle.

"I've had a enough of—" Prism's pulse rifle finished
the sentence. The security man directed waves of fire at the
Small Hulk's shoulder, blasting off a chunk to reveal a
thick, steel joint.

Shrieking in an odd, mechanical agony, the Hulk brought
its Argon lasers to bear as Neal dived away from Prism's
station.

The Hulk's whine faded into a bloodcurdling cry from
Prism. As Neal hit the floor and dropped his rifle, he no
longer heard Prism's firing. One glance at the contorted,
scorched form sent bile flooding into his throat. He turned
away and lifted his head a little. An erratic grinding noise,
like that of a shipping rover with a broken axle, came from

somewhere above him. The rhythm increased into a hum that rose in pitch until it ceased in a powerful, echoing blast. Fragments of metal tinkled as they hit the floor. Before the clatter finished, a mech cried in the distance and was joined by another.

A panting Frank Jewelbug dropped to Neal's side, a rifle clutched to his chest, a penlight glowing in his breast pocket. "Dude, you going down with your ship or coming with me?"

Neal got to his hands and knees, grabbed his weapon. "We gotta get outside, get into a rover, and get off a distress signal."

Jewelbug snorted. "Forget that. Satlinks'll show we're down. And when our oh-seven-hundred barge fails to launch, the suits at Shiva will be hemorrhaging. Their asses will be here faster than the Marines."

"All right. Where are you gonna go?"

"Through the southwest door. Circle around accessway twelve, then slip down to level two. Lots of ducts down there."

"They'll eventually find us."

"Dude. That's why we gotta keep moving."

"We can't leave the rest," Neal said, only half-believing it. Then a particularly loud wail from a mech sent a shudder through him, a shudder further fueled by a mental image of Whey and the twins crying over his death.

"Call me a bastard, but they're down. We stay, we wind up with them."

The mech wailed again, this time much closer.

"I'm gone," Jewelbug announced, then bolted for the southwest door.

"Guys! I'm sorry! We'll be back for you!" Neal shouted, then chased after the supervisor.

"Don't leave us!" Emma screamed.

Neal repressed a chill and kept going, the panels around him catching, reflecting, and exploding in mech fire. He made it to the southwest door and darted past it. Once in the dark corridor, he spotted Jewelbug's penlight. The supervisor kicked off his moccasins and waved Neal on, shouting, ''Got one behind you!''

Not bothering to look, Neal ducked and tore off after the wild-haired, barefoot man as Argon laser bursts streaked overhead.

4

Mach 10 in a 30 MPH Zone

"Yeah, I know she doesn't wanna talk to me. I don't care about that. You tell her she *has* to talk to me. You tell her it's an emergency." Ben stared angrily into the vidphone's screen, gritting his teeth and wishing he could strangle Elizabeth's partner, the tough-talking Australian woman she kept using as a shield.

He had been trying for the past two months to track down his ex-wife, hoping she hadn't left their homeworld of Mars. A week ago he had found her. She had changed her name, and, with a partner, had opened up her own fertility clinic in some little town (he forgot the name) near the Maunder Crater. He'd been wanting to ask her why she'd bribed that nurse into telling him the truth about his BPCs. But more importantly, he'd been wanting to ask her if there was anything left between them, anything he could do now. Things had changed. He was no longer a Marine. And hadn't she left because of his career?

Beth's partner returned. "She still says she doesn't want to talk to you." The woman glanced over her shoulder, then moved closer to the screen. "A little advice from someone who's been there? Stop calling. You're doing more damage than you know."

That was not good enough. Not good enough at all. He

had driven himself crazy trying to find her. Now she would blow him off without even saying it herself? "YOU TELL HER TO GET ON THIS DAMNED PHONE NOW! OR I'M COMING DOWN THERE, YOU HERE ME? I *WILL* COME DOWN THERE!"

She moved away from the cam but didn't hang up.

Ben gazed sidelong at the family of four eating their lunch at a nearby table. Well, they were no longer eating their lunch but staring at him: the guy seated at the vidphone booth, making a fool out of himself. He knew he should've left the restaurant and gone outside to make the call—but by the time he would've reached another phone, the impulse would've faded. "Sorry," he said to the family.

The father smirked and shook his head.

"Ben?" Her voice sent his head jerking around.

He hadn't seen Elizabeth in almost a year, and the changes were shocking. She'd cut her hair very short, had switched her eyes from blue to green (either through lenses or transplants), and was leaner and tanner than ever. He hated her new look.

"Ben?" she called again.

"Yeah, I'm just, well, surprised."

She nodded. "I had a feeling you wouldn't recognize me."

"Why all the changes?"

"It doesn't matter. And I don't want your opinion."

"Can we at least talk?"

"What is there to say?"

He made a lopsided grin. "You kidding?"

"Where are you, a restaurant? Are you on a pass?"

"Don't play dumb, Beth. You know I'm out of the Corps. And you know about my . . ." He tapped his temple.

She looked away in disgust.

"You bribed that nurse. Why?"

"I don't know. Maybe I thought I owed you something. Maybe it's the doctor in me. I don't know. I guess I wanted you to know the truth."

"So it would set me free?" He huffed. "Fat chance."

Her expression soured. "You know what? Maybe you

still don't know the truth. Maybe you need to know more
because you don't even see it, do you?''

"See what?''

"Maybe I bribed that nurse because I wanted to hurt you
the way you hurt me.''

"That's not true.''

"Maybe it is. Maybe I want you to know what it feels
like to be controlled all the time, to have someone else
pulling *your* strings, to have someone else ordering you
NOT TO CUT YOUR GODDAMNED HAIR!''

He sat there, his mouth hanging open, his mind racing
for a reply. All he could muster was a faint, "No.''

"Don't call again. I'm in the process of getting a restraining order.'' She buried her face in a palm.

And the connection ceased.

Ben stood, screamed, then planted one of his steel-toed,
standard-issue, Marine Corps utility boots in the center of
the vidphone's thin screen.

The restaurant's owner, a native Martian with whom Ben
had become acquainted, rushed over and slapped a beefy
palm on Ben's shoulder. Ben withdrew his boot from the
severely dented screen. Then, after wrenching out of the
man's grip, he fished out his bank card and held it before
the owner's burning gaze.

Snatching the card, the man said in his South Mars accent, "Yout better not come back here. I see yout again, I
throw yout out.''

Ben rolled his eyes and waited. In five minutes he was
out of the restaurant, having bought himself the most low-
calorie and expensive lunch of his life.

He walked down Gamma Street, swearing, looking at his
pathetic self in dusty store windows and cocking his head
at the sound of jet engines.

What now? Should he drive to the outlands of Thaumasia
with a couple of squire tubes and get wasted? Should he
get a couple of bottles of old-fashioned Scotch, drink one,
take a bath with the other, then put a match to himself?

Many times during the past two months he had thought
of blowing all of his savings on a trip to Earth. He wanted
to see the place just once before he died. He'd figured while

he was there he'd visit Powell's parents, tell them, as any good soldier would, that their son had served bravely. Afterward, instead of booking passage home, he'd stay a while, breathe in a lot of that sweet, non-terraformed air—the air now on Mars had a metallic tang to it, though none of the scientists in charge of maintaining the Red Planet's new surface could figure out why. Then, sans a parachute, he'd base-jump naked off some pretty cliff.

But the thoughts of contacting Elizabeth had been foremost in his mind, distracting him from the self-pity. With his hopes of rekindling that relationship extinguished, he knew he was either going to lapse into a deep depression or kick some ass and take charge of his life. Elizabeth implied that he was a control freak? Well then, he'd take control, all right. He'd go see Major General Zim again. He hailed a cab and returned to the Corps' Olympus Mons Strike Base, flashing his ID when he reached the gate.

Ten minutes later he was told to have a seat in the major general's office, where he remained for another ten minutes, staring through a large window that offered a panoramic view of the immense landing field. Tarmac raced away to the crimson horizon, the scene only occasionally broken by an Interceptor or an Endo/Exo Harrier making a touchdown. Ben knew every pilot out there.

Hearing the door open behind him, he snapped to attention. Major General Zim crossed to her desk, returned Ben's salute, and motioned him to be seated. "Sorry to keep you waiting. Something odd has just happened on the moon, and we're trying to get a straight answer out of PTMC."

"Good luck."

"We'll need it. Anyway, I hope you're not here to make the same old request."

"General, I can't lie."

She took in a long breath. "Son, I've been in the Corps for twenty-three years now. So I can't say I know exactly how you feel. I've never had to leave. But I've had to leave many posts and move on. Just think of the Corps as one post in your life. Time to move on. Go empty your locker."

"Put me in a sim. Let me show you I can still fly," Ben insisted.

"We've been through all of this," Zim said with a sigh. "Whether you can fly now is not the point. Your injuries could affect—"

"What do you know about my injuries? Do you know that without my authorization three bio-processing chips were implanted in my brain? Do you know that no one— not even my doctor—has informed me of this?" He rose, then spoke slowly for effect. "Now. Unless I'm fully re-instated as a Marine Corps patrol pilot, I'm going to the Judge Advocate General's office."

Menace lay behind her smile. "Every Marine we get in here with head injuries tries to accuse us of implanting BPCs. *Do you know* how expensive they are? *Do you know* what our budget is? Besides, even if the chips were in your head, that kind of wetware technology is almost impossible to detect. They'd have to cut you open again to prove your point. You got a knife?"

"Dammit, look at me! I'm fine!"

She stood. "That's subjective. And irrelevant."

Feeling his eyes begin to burn, Ben closed them. "I'm a Marine. I'm not anything else. Take that away, take the man away."

"Sorry, you *were* a Marine. If you want to take this to the JAG, that's fine. They'll get to your case in six or eight months. You're finished here. Dismissed."

Failing to salute, he stomped out of Zim's office.

Alone in the narrow hall, he punched the air, trying in vain to strike down his fate. Then he charged off, heading toward the hangars, an ember of hope still burning in the back of his mind.

On his way he passed a pair of cadets he had trained, and while their greeting was hearty, he barely managed a hello. He had to psyche himself up, be committed, be ready, take full responsibility. The hangars lay two corridors away.

He wondered if he'd really do it or if he were just kidding himself. But the closer he got, the clearer the plan became, and with that clarity came an inner peace that made him feel very comfortable about seizing control.

The thunder of afterburners grew louder, and in less than a minute he stepped into the vast, shaded expanse of the strike base's main hangar. Interceptors, Boomerangs, Harriers, and a few Starhawks from the *Expediator* delivered for refurbishing lined the rear wall in a bewinged spectacle of military might. Ground crews loaded or unloaded ordnance from many of the planes amid a clamor of shouts and the hum and clink of power tools. The smells of superheated alloys, fuel, and someone's fried chicken lunch might have caused a civilian to cringe, but to Ben they were an ample reminder that this was where he belonged, where he would always belong. He crossed to the locker-room door and slid in his ID.

ACCESSS DENIED: INVALID CODE

"They just issued us new cards again, Vampire," Bryan Crowhill, a pilot from the 86th Squadron, said. He slid his ID, and the door opened. "Wait a minute. You're back? Thought you got discharged and would be doing commercials for propellants by now, mediaboy."

Ben grinned. "Nope. They want me in the air ASAP." He hurried into the room, turned a corner, and walked down a long row of lockers.

Crowhill called after him, his voice echoing hollowly. "That's weird. You're not in the rotation. And I thought they gave your ship to Judy."

A mental knife pierced Ben's back. "Guess they're giving it back. Where is she, anyway?"

"Debriefing."

Ben smiled to himself. He tapped in the combination, opened his locker, and nervously donned his flight and environment suits. Only Powell's ghost could double-check his bindings. He triple-timed out of the locker room and looked ahead, spotting his FY39 Interceptor, second in from the end of the massive hangar.

As he neared the plane, he saw that Ricky, Quick, and Sly, his old ground crew, were laughing, drinking bottles of Mire's, and polishing their shoulders on the landing skids.

Sly, a heavyset black man with a knack for delivering jokes, pushed off the ship and widened his eyes. "Meow. Meow. Thought that furball had got you, sir."

Ben held up a fist and flashed a grin. "She had me in her jaws, but I cut thrusters, pitched right, tipped my nose up a little, then punched it—right between her teeth!"

"We couldn't believe it when we heard they discharged you," Ricky said, tucking in his shirt and bringing his lanky frame to full height. "I know I'm sloppy, sir. We didn't expect you."

"Forget it, private." Crossing to the cockpit ladder, Ben placed a boot on the bottom rung, deciding immediately to abandon his usual walkaround and preflight check. "Break moorings," he told Ricky. "I need to be out of here in less than five mikes."

Quick, a gaunt-faced corporal with the efficiency of an Omega cannon, gazed suspiciously at Ben. "Sir?"

"You heard the man," Sly said.

"Captain Tolmar just came in. This aircraft is now registered to her," Quick said, his tone wavering between authoritative and I-don't-want-to-insult-you-sir.

Ben continued up the ladder, then lowered himself into the pit. He snapped on his helmet and tipped up the visor. "I know whose ship this is. And if you check the rotation, you won't find my name. That's intentional." He buckled into his combat harness and hit the emergency power-up toggle. The maneuvering thrusters murmured to life.

"Why, sir?" Quick asked, raising his voice over the increasing whine.

"I'm not at liberty to say. What I can tell you is that if you disobey a direct order from me, well, do we even want to discuss the consequences?"

"No, sir!" Quick turned to Sly. "Lance Corporal. Break all moorings!"

"Break all moorings, aye-aye, sir!"

Then Quick regarded Ricky. "Private! Clear hoverway!"

"Clear hoverway, aye-aye, sir!"

Sly began to key off the fuel and power lines from Ben's Interceptor, and Ricky started clearing a path so that Ben could hover the fighter out of the hangar.

Meanwhile, Quick seemed to think a moment, then he dialed a number on his portable, interbase link. He looked up at Ben. "Sir, Lieutenant Colonel Chabon is the Ops officer of the day. I need his approval for any launch not in the rotation."

Ben knew all too well about that regulation. He craned his neck and spotted Sly. "Am I sealed?" he shouted.

Sly flashed him a thumbs-up.

Then Ben glanced ahead. Ricky stood in the hoverway, karate-chopping in the "all clear" signal. Turning his gaze back to Quick, he shouted, "Sorry, buddy. You're a good corporal and a great crew chief. But you've just been had. I'll tell them you were obeying orders. It won't go in your file."

Quick lowered the phone from his ear. "No! No way, sir! You can't be serious!"

Dialing up full maneuvering thrusters and engaging the canopy seal, Ben felt the Interceptor rise from the deck. At the standard two-meter hover, he took her quickly forward. He noted that fuel levels were only at fifty percent, but he figured that would be enough. With Ricky and Sly waving innocently behind him, and Quick now talking into his link, Ben cleared the hoverway, floated over the apron, and, before reaching one of the diamond-shaped launchpads that protected the tarmac from thruster wash, he engaged his main engines. Puddles of rippling melted asphalt shrank beneath his wings. Turning his attention to the faint ocher of the Martian sky, he toggled from maneuvering to main thrusters. The plane's incredible power shoved him against his seat and sent chills spidering across his shoulders. He shot away, gazed at his aft monitor, and watched the Olympus Mons Strike Base dissolve into the dusty, barren expanse of the plateau.

Then he threw his head back and laughed over the audacity of what he was doing: a delayed reaction to the reality of having stolen a CED Marine Corps attack plane with a unit replacement cost of $164,000,000 in Global dollars.

Rainbows of reflected sunlight danced across the canopy as he flew adjacent to the Olympus Mons shield volcano, which lay just two klicks north of the base. Rising some twenty-five kilometers above the surface, with a base of six hundred kilometers, Olympus Mons stood as the centerpiece of the Tharsis Plateau, the largest volcano in the solar system, and the training ground for the Corps' most elite pilots. Struck with an idea, Ben pulled back on his stick and banked right, toward the great mount. As he rocketed through the air, listening to his O_2 flow and the hum of his afterburners, he realized that, back in his old cockpit, he never felt more whole.

Elizabeth, Zim, the doctors, and even his own ground crew could never know what flying meant to him. It was not a job but a love affair. The tie he had to his plane ran deep in his soul, and no one else should be flying her. What did anyone other than pilots know about an Interceptor? You don't just plop in one and flip buttons: you strap on the bird and her hydraulics are your blood; her alloy frame your bones; her power currents your nerves; her instruments your senses. You eat fuel and shit thrust, and your weapons rack says a lot about your temper. When your bird responds to the incredible demands of combat, slamming you into your harness with the roughness and affection of a drunk lover, beating the surface of some godforsaken planet with one continuous thunderclap, that's when you know, really know she'll be there for you, there for you when others won't. And when you leave her, physically battered and emotionally spent, she keeps that promise. Your final gloved touch along her belly is a secret gesture of parting, and she whispers that she'll be waiting for you to take her again.

The comm panel flashed with an incoming message. "Took you long enough," Ben said. Then, for his amusement, he decided to open the channel.

". . . and if you do not return immediately to base, you will be engaged."

A proximity alarm sounded. Ben eyed his aft screen, saw a flash of light in the distance. "Guess you got the Sixty-first in the air, huh, Jarrett?" Ben told the comm officer, a young man with a severe talent for beating Ben in poker. "I'd be happy to go head-to-head with those aviators."

"Don't play those cards, Ben," Jarrett said.

"Interceptor five-niner-zero-six, this is Firehawk One. You calling *me* an aviator?"

"You deaf, Lee, or is it just a comm problem?"

"What're you doing, St. John?"

"Flying. What're you doing?"

"Don't be an asshole, Vampire."

"Not much of a negotiator are you, Lee? Thought you graduated from the Corps' new school of sweet-talking to psychos."

"Shuddup, St. John. We're gonna blow you outta the sky if you don't turn around."

Ben grinned so widely that it hurt. "Now you sound like a Marine—a lying one—but still a Marine!" The HUD flickered again with a radar map of the incoming craft flying in an arrowhead formation, with Captain Lee Holston's plane at the poisonous tip.

Whispering an "all right" to himself, Ben pinned his thruster control and felt the Interceptor shudder through updrafts. At twelve o'clock low lay the freckled face of the great volcano. His altitude put him some ten thousand feet below its summit. ETA: two mikes.

Another glance to the HUD, then one to the aft cam. With thrusters wide open, he was maintaining a small but exploitable gap of a quarter nautical mile between himself and the Sixty-first. Laser and missile lock alarms wailed, and Ben shut them down.

"We're a heartbeat away from wasting you, St. John," Lee said.

The heartbeat came and went.

"Aren't you going to call my sister and have her talk me down? Don't you wanna cut a deal with me?" Ben asked bitterly. "I've stolen a valuable aircraft. God forbid you obey THE LAW OF THE CED MARINE CORPS AND TAKE ME OUT NOW—NO QUESTIONS ASKED!"

"Think about it, St. John. Think about what you're saying. Do you even know what you're saying?"

ETA to volcano: one mike.

"The mission of the FY39 Interceptor is to attack and

destroy both surface and air targets, to escort dropshuttles, and to conduct other such air operations as may be directed," Ben said, quoting the Ops manual. "I am a thief. Consider me an air target! Carry out your mission, Captain!"

Silence.

"What's the matter, Lee? Can't stand the truth?"

"I wish I *could* shoot you down, you idiot."

"But you can't because you've been ordered to save the plane at all costs. But they're only gonna get this bird one way."

"What are you gonna do? Blackmail them into reinstating you? That's real smart. Make a lot of friends that way."

"What I'm gonna do is show them what I got. Show them what they're stupidly throwing away."

"Like this? You're nuts. Ain't gonna happen."

"Oh, it'll happen. If you don't engage me, I'm gonna fly this puppy straight into Mons. ETA: thirty seconds!"

"You won't do it," Lee said cockily.

Knowing that by now the brass at the strike base were glued to the audio/video signals being transmitted from his plane, Ben held his stick firmly and continued on his present course. He could make out the volcano's fracture lines, scree, and lava flows that had hardened a billion or so years ago. If someone were seated on a rock there and eating a bologna sandwich, Ben knew that in twenty seconds he could tell you if that sandwich had cheese on it. In fifteen seconds that cheese would be melted.

"We'll do whatever you want!" Lieutenant Colonel Chabon said, his angular face displayed in Ben's forward monitor. "You pull up!"

"Order them to engage!" Ben screamed.

"Firehawk squadron—engage!"

"Missiles locked. Concussion one!" Lee reported.

With a missile on his butt and a volcano only seconds away, Ben didn't need a graduate degree in rocket science to know which way to go—ballistic!

Stick back. Cut thrusters point-five-three. E-suit pressurizing against the Gs. And suddenly the volcano scrolled below his canopy, the concussion missile struck the slope, and Ben spiraled straight up into the Martian sky with a fiery ball of rock and shrapnel tight on his six o'clock. Howling above the racket of his vibrating ship, he pulled himself into a long, slow loop that would put him well above the scattering squadron. His damage-control computer flashed a series of messages that had nothing to do with ordnance, and he was still able to breathe a sigh. Aft camera was toast. Structural damage to port afterburner cone. Engine functions still nominal. He ran a comm scan and locked on to Firehawk squadron's channel:

"Tallyho. He's at my twelve, inverted."

"Got him, Six. Everyone fall back to support positions. I'm taking him out myself," Lee said.

"Firehawk One. Break off!" Lieutenant Colonel Chabon ordered.

Ben cut into the channel. "He breaks off, I'm gonna ram this ship down your throats!"

"Why do you wanna die so badly, St. John?" Chabon asked.

"Ask Zim."

"I'm right here, Mr. St. John," Zim said. "And I've never witnessed an act more foolish."

"Honey, I've got nothing to lose but foolishness."

Finishing his loop, Ben leveled off and surveyed the sky. Lee's Interceptor sat about a thousand meters off his starboard wing. The rest of the angry horde trailed at five o'clock low, their missiles locked on to Ben's plane.

"Hey, St. John," Lee called. "You wanted so badly for us to engage, why don't you return the favor? This way I don't need an order to blow you into crater meat."

There it was, the billion-dollar question with an answer encrypted in guilt. In wanting to prove himself, Ben had vowed not to engage the Firehawks; he would only evade. He could never knowingly take the life of another Marine— even one caught in a hijacking. He, unlike the Corps, knew where to draw the line.

Staring out his canopy, trying to think of a way to get Lee to reengage, Ben realized something so obvious that he had, of course, overlooked it. By stealing the plane and getting this far with it, he now knew that the Corps was not using his BPCs to control him. Maybe he didn't have BPCs at all. Maybe Elizabeth paid that nurse to lie. Were the Corps controlling him, the brass would have sent a signal ordering him to land. He would have unconsciously obeyed. Somehow he felt worse for stealing the plane. He now realized the enormity of what he had done.

"C'mon, Vampire. Fangs out, bro. Engage!" Lee said sarcastically.

It's too late to turn back, Ben thought. He had to go through with it, had to get Lee back in the fight. Maybe he could piss the guy off enough to violate orders. Banking hard right, Ben streaked toward Lee's Interceptor, his reticle floating over the craft's exhaust, the missile lock tone humming a good kill. "I gotta give you a handicap, Lee. One blink and the show's over." Ben hit thrusters, razored under the other Interceptor, then came up so that he could wag his tail in Lee's face. "You've got tone. Take the shot!"

"This time we call your bluff, Mister St. John," Major General Zim said. "Firehawk One. Take the shot!"

Cursing fearfully, Ben jammed his stick forward and dived. His cockpit was alive with a myriad of flashing readouts, glowing monitors, and the voice alarms of protesting instruments.

Lee made his firing announcement.

Ben kept diving, his stomach still up there with his opponent's plane. Then he watched with a horrid fascination as Lee's Flash missile homed in.

Countermeasures!

He chaffed, and, screaming under twelve Gs of Mars's .379 gravity, he pulled out of his dive, the E-suit doing a poor job of cutting down the force. He glanced at a status bar on his HUD: E-suit breached at elbow. Then he looked over his shoulder and watched the Flash missile cut through his chaff and fail to explode.

Turning forward, Ben set his jaw, narrowed his eyes, and whispered an apology to his stomach and his plane for what he was about to do. He dived again, this time forming one blade of a vertical scissors roll meant to put his plane on the missile's six. The ground spun and spun, and his afterburners continued to roar over the rattling of an airframe in agony. With the missile just a dozen meters away and closing fast, he pulled into a hard left barrel roll, took a breath, closed his eyes for a second, and pulled up hard in preparation to loop behind the merciless projectile.

Feeling his cheeks smear back toward his ears, Ben ticked off three seconds, flicked his wrist, drove the stick forward, and leveled out. With a quick tap to a panel he released another cloud of chaff, then regarded the HUD. The missile ignored the countermeasures and raced toward his fuselage, targeting a point just under the port wing. A collision alarm, a sound rarely heard in Ben's cockpit, beeped with certainty. "Dammit!" He reflexively jerked the ejection handle.

A blinding flash of white lightning from some enormous antique camera stole his field of view. A millisecond later, a gut-wrenching explosion tore through the plane, slamming Ben forward then whipping him back in his harness. As the initial blast still reverberated through the plane, another, fainter explosion joined in as the canopy automatically blew off.

"Ohmygod, you got him, Lee!" one of the Firehawks said before the comm in Ben's helmet went dead.

Twirling through a burnt orange void in the shattered vestige of an Interceptor that included nose, cockpit, and starboard wing, Ben had a pair of seconds to contemplate what had happened before the ejection seat hurled him into the Martian wind. His vision cleared, and he watched the plane tumble away and become lost, a cloud of swirling dust suddenly pierced by a thundering Interceptor. Alive and unsure if he was happy about that, he swore and waited for the pop of the chute, figuring that with his luck the seat's recovery system would function properly. He'd float gently to the Martian plains, into the inevitable arms of military police.

5

Crisis Contingency Management Blues

The chef aboard this shuttle will absolutely never learn how to cook my apricot turkey steaks, thought Samuel Dravis Jr., Director of Crisis Contingency Management and Public Relations for PTMC. *I've explained it to him twice already—to no avail. Rinse the turkey and pat dry. In a large skillet combine apricot nectar, salt, and cinnamon. Add the turkey steaks. Bring to boiling. Reduce heat. Cover and simmer until the turkey is no longer pink.* "Chef? Chef!"

A moment later, the young man entered the cabin, his tall white hat brushing the ceiling. "Yes, sir?"

Dravis rose from his antique-leather dinner chair and thrust his plate toward the boy. "Why is my turkey still pink? Do you want me to die from some strain of new bacteria breeding in your galley?"

The boy took the plate and stared at the offending food. "Absolutely not, sir. I'm so sorry. I cut a few pieces myself, and they looked fine."

Sighing, Dravis turned and slumped back into his chair. "Cook it again. Hopefully you'll finish before we arrive at Shiva?"

"Of course, sir." He scampered out.

"Don't worry, Mr. Dravis. I'm sure he'll get it right this time," Megan Bartonovich said, gazing at him with a raised, perfectly tweezed brow from across the table.

Dravis regarded his dark-haired assistant director with a frown. "Ms. Bartonovich, when you are sixty-five instead of thirty, and one of the few pleasures you have left in your pretty little life is a fine meal, then—and only then—will you truly understand my Epicurean eccentricities."

Narrowing her green eyes in a way that he always found attractive, she replied, "I'll talk to you then, I guess."

"Actually, you may talk to me now. Talk to me about the moon."

Ms. Bartonovich lifted her data slate from her lap and set it beside her dish. After tapping a few keys, she looked up and said, "Satellite reports are still only fragmentary. Internal comm's still down. Probe images just came in about five minutes ago. Got an exec summary on those. Command center has been destroyed. No sign of the crew. Security presumes they're dead."

"Killed by whom?" Dravis asked, then sat up with a groan.

"That's still undetermined. But security believes it may have been the mechs. They've quarantined the mine and put all other holdings on full alert. So far, systems nominal everywhere else."

"A quarantine? That's ridiculous. We need to get people in there—not keep them out. Did Ms. Sargena order this?"

"I believe so."

"Get her on the phone now, please."

She picked up the vidphone's remote and keyed in the number. Ms. Sargena, a middle-aged woman of Caribbean ancestry and Director of PTMC Security, turned her head away from a monitor and favored Dravis with a nod. "Hello, Samuel."

"Ms. Sargena," he acknowledged. "Ms. Bartonovich tells me you've quarantined the moon?"

"You've seen the probe images. Thermal Satlinks indicate the mechs are moving on all levels. They won't respond to remote commands. In fact, nothing will—not even the reactor. That's more than enough reason for a quarantine. I have some ware wizards on the problem now.'' She smiled. ''They're telling me it's some kind of computer virus, but I don't see how anyone could've slipped it in—not with my antiviral security in place.''

''Why do they believe it's a virus?''

''The wizards recorded a fragment of wireless modem transmissions from the mechs, and they say the code is like nothing they've ever seen before.''

Rubbing his tired eyes, Dravis said, ''This will soon turn into a public-relations catastrophe. My office has already been deluged with calls, the CED is breathing their hot, foul breath on my neck, and our clients are already being romanced by competitors. Must we call it a quarantine?''

''What would you suggest?''

Dravis kneaded his chin. ''Let's call it a minor operational anomaly, one that will quickly be corrected.''

''Are you sure? That sounds so, I don't know, so characteristic of the company's pseudoprose,'' Ms. Sargena confessed. ''Oh, I'm sorry. I forgot you write most of that.''

Ms. Bartonovich cleared her throat, and Dravis studied her, searching for a smile. He found none. Then he turned his temper on Sargena. ''I'll expect thirty-minute reports from you. And the next time you decide to quarantine a PTMC mine, you *will* consult me first. That language is plain in the operations manual.''

''Sorry, Samuel,'' she said in a frosty tone. ''I detected an emergency and reacted to it.''

''Next time, make your first reaction be a call to me,'' he said. ''Phone off.'' He checked his watch, then turned slowly to Ms. Bartonovich. ''How many hours has the operation been down?''

She consulted her slate. ''Four-point-seven. That's forty-seven million Global dollars in lost revenue thus far.''

The chef reentered the cabin, carrying Dravis's steaming dinner. ''Here you are, sir,'' he said as he placed the dish before Dravis.

The turkey was cooked, but the boy had flamed off most of the apricot sauce. Dravis thought of mentioning it, then held back. ''Thank you.''

After a nod, the boy hurried off.

"It's still wrong, isn't it," she said.

"You've learned a lot about me in the past ten months, Ms. Bartonovich. When I first hired you, I didn't think you'd last. An interplanetary mining corporation is far different than an off-world fast-food franchise, wouldn't you say?"

"I've learned there are far more secrets in this business," she said. "And the competition is far more cutthroat."

Dravis took a bite of his turkey, winced, then swallowed. "Ah, I'm glad you bring up the competition. Have we heard from any of our operatives there?"

"Janus from SOL-MC reported in. No sabotage on that end. I'm still waiting on the three others, but it's doubtful any of our competitors is responsible for this."

"Still, we won't rule out that possibility."

"No, but while a single operation does hurt, they'd strike a far more successful blow if they could interrupt our shipping lanes."

"Precisely. But our mercenary patrols make that impossible."

"Incoming message," the vidphone's female computer voice said.

"Caller?" Dravis asked.

"Major General Yliana Smith, CED. Origination: Lunar 1 Command Base."

He furrowed his brow. "How the hell did she get this number?"

"Same way we get numbers. Better take the call."

"Call accepted," Dravis said, then pursed his lips in annoyance.

A narrow-eyed black woman in full military dress appeared and studied Dravis dispassionately. "Mr. Dravis. Your office has done an outstanding job of avoiding our calls. May I commend your stratagem; it even rivals the misinformation campaigns of the twenty-first century."

"Major General, you've interrupted my dinner. What is it I can refuse to do for you?"

Ignoring his remark, she said flatly, "Our perimeter defense mechs report that shipping and subsurface operations have stopped at double-oh-twelve. Does the shutdown have anything to do with the object we tracked?''

Dravis gave Ms. Bartonovich a guarded look. "I'll need more details before I can comment on that."

"My details require yours," the major general said.

"I'm a businessman. Arrangements can be made," Dravis promised. "I'll need your account number."

"Coming through now."

"There will be no bargaining. Thirty shares in PTMC stock will suffice." He nodded to his assistant, who began plugging numbers into her slate.

Smith grinned wanly. "That's reasonable."

"Her account and portfolio have been updated," Ms. Bartonovich said.

"Now with that ugly business aside, tell me more about this object."

"All we have is a blur on visual recorders. We tracked it for only a few seconds. It left your outpost and moved from mach 1 to point-nine lightspeed in that time. Nothing we have accelerates that fast. Is it yours? Maybe some new project that your famous Dr. Swietzer is working on?"

"Leave the questions to me, Major General. Exactly what time did you detect this UFO?"

"Thirteen-twenty-two hours. Five-point-two-two mikes before the shutdown."

Dravis steepled his fingers. "PTMC denies any knowledge of the aforementioned object. We will investigate if its appearance is related to the minor operational anomaly occurring in our mine. Any assistance offered by the CED is appreciated but unnecessary."

"At this point, my superiors aren't exactly offering assistance, Mr. Dravis. They're demanding that you allow the CED to enter the mine. They are, after all, tenants of level seventeen, and the facility there could be compromised."

"Access to level seventeen at this time is not possible. Your superiors should have studied the rental agreement before they instructed you to make threats." Dravis gave Ms. Bartonovich his usual feed-me-the-numbers look.

"Paragraph five, point seven," she whispered.

"Paragraph five, point seven of the document clearly

notes that in the event of an emergency, PTMC is granted full jurisdiction over the operation. An unscheduled operational shutdown is listed among the criteria for emergency. We have the right to bar any tenant from the premises if, in our best judgment, a threat exists to human life or property. My office has already been informed that your facility is not occupied at this time nor was it during the shutdown. No CED personnel are in danger."

"I don't mean to threaten you, Mr. Dravis," Smith said. "I'm only speaking—"

He waved his hand, bathing in her recently bought humility. He'd learned many years ago that stock options were the all-purpose corrective for bad attitudes. "Major General, I'll need two favors. See what you can do about getting my office a copy of the data regarding this UFO, then misplace your evidence. The last thing I want is for this data to fall into the hands of the Interplanetary Press Corps, and, well, not to be insulting, but the CED's intelligence department is, at best, second rate. Too many armchair generals there who like to spread rumors. Secondly, I need for you to confirm to the CED's CCM and PR offices that Lunar Outpost MN0012 has been temporarily shut down but will be back on-line very soon. I'm sure you'll find the return on these investments satisfactory, no?"

She gave a slow nod. "Uploading the UFO data now. I'll delete as many files as I can afterward."

"Good-bye, Major General. Phone Off."

Ms. Bartonovich breathed a heavy sigh. "A virus we've never seen before. A UFO spotted in the area. Either the competition has suddenly become very, very good, or—"

"What I want now is to contain this problem, study it, and above all, keep knowledge of its existence limited to only a few." He stared through her and into an image of the mine. "The ability to control our mechs, to take over an entire operation. That's a powerful force, one we'll need to understand and manipulate. And who knows . . . when all is said and done, we may have gained something that would assure PTMC's dominant position into the next millennium."

"Are you saying that we, humanity's largest corporation,

should ignore the possibility of an alien threat against our holdings?"

"Not at all. In fact, if you'd like, we could assume it is."

She pulled her head back in disbelief. "You say that a bit too casually."

"The microorganisms we've discovered on other worlds have forewarned of higher intelligence. And need I mention the ruins uncovered in Zeta Aquilae? I *am* worried. We need to solve this problem, learn what we can from it, and get back on-line."

Her look said she wasn't convinced. "If we're not sure who we're dealing with, how can we possibly anticipate an effective response?"

"All right then, we need to be sure. Let's get someone in there, someone who can, as you say, tell us what we're dealing with."

"What about Dr. Warren?"

"Very good. Draw up the contracts. I'd like a firsthand account of this. And we'll get that pilot, that Sattlebear, to fly her in."

Ms. Bartonovich reached for the vidphone's remote, but Dravis put his hand on it first.

"I'm going to charge you with solving this problem, Ms. Bartonovich. I'll put the media bandage on it. Now, don't let your past successes go to your head. They'll do little to save your job now. You are, after all, my thirteenth assistant in half as many years."

"As you've reminded me," she said. "There is one other avenue we should pursue. The CED wants desperately to get back to their facility. Haven't you wondered what they're doing down there? This shutdown could provide us with an excellent opportunity for a look-see."

Dravis smiled. She was a quick study. "I already know what they're doing down there. And you're right. This does provide us with an excellent opportunity. But we'll be doing a lot more than just looking."

6

Alien Attitude

"But we're not soldiers. They ought to be sending soldiers in there with us," Harold Ames was saying as he shouldered his equipment pack and pushed his antique wire-rimmed glasses farther up the bridge of his nose. "Not that I can't kick some butt, mind you."

Dr. Bonnie Warren, Mech Software Specialist and designer of the artificial-intelligence modules used in every drone, gave the twenty-four-year-old man's meager frame the once-over, then repressed her smile. "Harold, you're an excellent assistant and a brilliant software engineer, but—"

"You doubt my physical prowess? I'm lean, yes. But I *am* mean. Four years of tae kwon do, baby."

Bonnie widened her green eyes and lifted her own pack from the smooth, black floor of the ready room. "I didn't know that."

He turned to the door. "I guess even without those soldiers, you'll be safe with me."

This time she permitted herself a broad grin. Harold had a cryptic sense of humor that, even after two years of working with him, Bonnie had yet to decode. He might very well have been serious about protecting her. As for the martial arts, four years of watching action flicks might be closer to the truth. When it came to Harold, distinctions like that were important to make.

While following him down a long corridor that led to Space Station Shiva's twenty-second docking bay, she had a moment—the first one after the rush of the past two hours—to reflect upon recent events. Megan Bartonovich's call had come as an utter surprise. PTMC shutdowns were as rare as budget increases, and an entire workforce of unresponsive mechs was unheard of. Bartonovich had suggested sending them in with a small military team, but, unbeknownst to Harold, Bonnie had been the one to request insertion with only a single pilot. Troops, even those with orders strictly to protect her, would cost money, and their computer-controlled weaponry could succumb to the virus. PTMC didn't need that kind of firepower in the wrong hands. Bonnie's argument had won approval with Director Dravis. A small, "elite" team with a few palmtop computers was perfect for the job. One pilot, just some Joe Schmo aviator, and "the woman who can save our expensive mechs and even more expensive mine," as Dravis had put it. And so, quick as a ZZX processor, they had left the Pasadena laboratory and shuttled up to Earth orbit, to Shiva, having had little time to fully to consider the danger. Until now.

And though Harold seemed to be in good spirits, she suddenly felt the weight of the future filling her pack. Hundreds of armed, renegade mining mechs now occupied MN0012, turning the place into a mechanized jackers' convention replete with violence and mystery, lacking only in the demands made by the criminals. *So why am I stupid enough to be lowered into this snake pit?* she asked herself. No number of stock options could decrease the risk.

She knew if she could ask her father, he might provide a clue. But an act similar to the one she was about to commit had taken his life. Her dad had been a geologist for PTMC and had been killed eight Christmases ago trying to recover data in an unstable mine. She'd been twenty-two then, still in school. She remembered the call from her mom. She remembered asking, "Why did he volunteer to go? They told him how dangerous it was. He wasn't saving someone's life. He was just trying to recover data!''

His death had always seemed foolish to her, but now, in some small way, she understood why. That data was part of his project, and he had dedicated his life to that project. That data was him. He was trying to save someone's life— his own. And while few would understand that kind of dedication, she did. *Those mechs in that mine—they're me,* she thought. *But are they worth my life?* The question had come too late.

"Bonnie?" Harold waved from the end of the corridor. "I've been thinking that maybe we should ask for an escort. Maybe not military. Maybe a few of PTMC's, you know, *people*."

"Mercs? No way. Forget it."

She reached him, and they both headed down another corridor. "I thought you were the one complaining about—"

"We'll be baby-sitting the gamblers, druggies, and losers they hire. Besides, that scum will have one look at, well, that body of yours, and you know the rest."

"Harold," she said, feigning embarrassment. "This is the first time you've ever . . . I guess I should call that a compliment. And not all mercenaries are that kind of scum. Some are ex-military."

"That's even worse."

"Why?"

"Take a look," he said, gesturing with his head at the stocky, dusty-skinned woman seated on the forward landing skid of a sleek, triwinged PTMC insertion plane. The pilot took a long pull on her clear squire tube, inhaled, then released a plume of green smoke that rose in the ten-story-high bay. "See the war patches on her sleeves? Veteran junkie. What a joke."

Taking a few steps ahead of Harold, Bonnie steered herself through a freeway of crisscrossing techs toward the jumpsuited woman. "Are you Trish Sattlebear?" she asked above the din of departing and arriving shuttles.

Holding her breath, the bleary-eyed woman pulled at her long, beaded ponytail several times before nodding ever so slowly.

Bonnie smacked the squire tube out of the pilot's hand,

then flinched as the tube shattered on the deck. She'd thought it had been a cheap, plastic one. "What the hell are you doing?"

Sattlebear got unsteadily to her feet and blew an obligatory thick wave of smoke in Bonnie's face. "My . . . same . . . question!" Her voice resonated like a damaged woodwind instrument.

"No need for hostilities, Dr. Warren. Ms. Sattlebear has a perfectly legal prescription for sodo gas."

Craning her neck, Bonnie spotted Director Dravis and his second, Ms. Bartonovich, walking toward her. They appeared an elegantly dressed couple, he the debonair widower, she the career girl who had found her father figure. Whether there actually was anything between them, Bonnie would never know. She'd heard that Dravis went through assistant directors nearly as quickly as he went through chefs. He had a thing about fresh food and fresh faces, it seemed. So, affair or not, Bartonovich was already a statistic.

Dravis took Bonnie's hand, shook it firmly, then continued. "Yes, indeed. Ms. Sattlebear saw a lot of action during the Humans First mining strike. She and another associate, Jake Pliskin, put an end to that little mess."

"Of course, my brain's still fried from it," Sattlebear told Bonnie. "They keep me hooked on sodo so I can sleep at night." She took a menacing step forward. "You're just lucky the company paid for that tube."

"Sorry," Bonnie said, less than sincerely. "And it's reassuring to know that, as our pilot, your brain is still fried."

Sattlebear kept in her face. Where was Mr. Tae Kwon Do when Bonnie needed him? She looked to her left and saw that Harold was on his hands and knees, picking up pieces of the broken squire tube. After all, someone could get cut, she heard him say in her mind. "Harold. Forget that. Come over here."

"One second. Somebody could get injured on this glass," he answered.

Bonnie looked away and found her lips curling.

"Ms. Sattlebear's use of sodo gas is, of course, purely

medicinal. The drug actually heightens her senses, making
her an even better pilot," Dravis said.

Harold joined the group, and Dravis began an awkward
round of introductions that were, for the most part, unnecessary and purely a matter of the director's obsession with
corporate decorum. When he was through, he lifted an index finger, exposing a gold-and-diamond cuff link, and
said, "Now you people are valuable assets to PTMC. I
know you've read your contracts regarding this operation.
I simply want to make sure you understand that, in the
event you officially deem the mechs, the mine, or both as
irrecoverable, you will immediately evacuate. However,
should you be injured or, God forbid, killed, your estates
will not hold the company responsible. Your signing of this
rider guarantees you the stock-option bonus."

With a tip of his head, Dravis summoned Ms. Bartonovich, who distributed the documents along with eighteen-
karat-gold pens.

Rolling the fine writing instrument between her fingers,
Bonnie considered how signing the clause with a nice pen
still didn't make her feel better about it. Without reading
the dense paragraphs, she scribbled her name and returned
the items to Bartonovich.

"I'll be keeping this," Sattlebear said, waving the pen a
moment, then sliding it into her breast pocket. "It'll be in
your ear if this is a double cross, Dravis."

The director smiled, more a baring of the teeth. "You
have proven yourself time and again, Ms. Sattlebear. And
so have we. While you may have recently heard some negative reports from mercenaries once under our employ, I
can assure you that those accusations are completely un-
substantiated. And yes, most certainly do keep that pen.
You will be using it to sign another contract with us."
Dravis eyed Harold. "Is there a problem, Mr. Ames?"

Harold's face remained buried in the document. "No
problem. Just checking for ambiguous language in this
rider."

"Are you kidding?" Sattlebear asked. "The only words
that ain't ambiguous are the ones that say 'you will not
hold PTMC responsible.'"

"Sign it, Harold. It's just a rider. We've already signed our lives away in the main contract," Bonnie said flippantly.

"I understand your trepidation, Dr. Warren. I really do. But don't let your feelings interfere with your judgment. The drones are your babies, so to speak. We all want to see you save them."

During her employment with PTMC, Bonnie had spent but a few moments with Dravis. A corporate picnic here, a holiday party there. And now, after dealing intimately and directly with him, his betrayals seemed more than just rumors. He was a corporate mogul who couldn't be trusted, the master of the oblique compliment, and the wielder of a weapon more powerful than any produced by the military: a PTMC contract. But beneath it all, Bonnie sensed a kind, feeling man, a man who had failed for years to examine his life. Dravis suffered from the same kind of narrow dedication that she and her father had. He needed someone to tell him what he'd become—but no one would dare take that risk.

Harold signed his contract and returned it to Ms. Bartonovich, who glanced at the paper, then asked, "Are all of those your names?"

He nodded. "Harold Ogden Joseph Ames. Having two middle names is a tradition in my family that dates back to, I believe, the thirteenth century. It's actually a very interesting story. When my great, great-grandfather—"

"I'm sorry, Mr. Ames," Dravis interrupted. "But Ms. Bartonovich and I have a meeting with President Suzuki in ten minutes, and we must prepare. You understand."

"Sure. Most people blow me off when I lapse into family history. I never take it personally."

"You have a good attitude, Mr. Ames," Bartonovich said.

And the leggy woman actually made poor Harold blush.

"You people wanna get in," Sattlebear said. She'd already boarded the insertion plane and now stared tiredly down at them beneath the open canopy. "This is contract work. Remember?"

"Good fortune and Godspeed to you all," said Dravis.

Bonnie muttered a lukewarm thanks, lifted her pack, and headed toward the boarding ramp.

Once inside the cramped compartment, she and Harold stowed their gear, then strapped themselves into two of the six passenger seats located just behind the cockpit. Sattlebear had left the cockpit hatch open—either as a courtesy or a curse—so that they could watch her fly.

"Roger, CC. IP six-two-five-seven initiating preflight," the pilot reported to traffic command.

The loading ramp rose and sealed to the fuselage with a thud, a hiss of O_2 flow began, then Bonnie heard the characteristic startup hum of the engines. She cocked an eyebrow at Harold. "This, I suspect, will be the most dangerous part of the mission."

His Adam's apple worked, and he gave a slight nod. "Uh, Bonnie? It's starting to happen."

She slid her hand into one of her seat's side pockets, withdrew a barf bag, and handed it to him. "If you hyperventilate—"

"I'll probably just puke," he said, accepting the bag.

"Preflight data confirmed," a traffic controller told Sattlebear. "Lifters engaged. Rolling into airlock."

With her ears popping from the fluctuations in pressure, Bonnie watched through a porthole as two giant clamps appeared from above, seized the plane, lifted it off the deck, then guided it into the airlock ahead. Once the ship hung inside the lock, Sattlebear exchanged verbal confirmations with the TC. Red lights flashed as the plane's onboard computer spoke the ten-second countdown. Bonnie kept a firm grip on her seat's armrest and took in long, slow breaths. *I shuttled up here,* she told herself. *And it wasn't so bad.*

Three . . . two . . . one . . .

Only a tiny click resounded, and she felt her hair rise from her shoulders as the artificial gravity of Shiva Station escaped the ship. Then her stomach sank as the plane's slightly stronger gravity fell upon her like a wet mattress.

"They told you not to eat, right?" Sattlebear called back.

"Yes," Bonnie answered.

"They did?" Harold said.

She grimaced at her assistant, then handed him another

barf bag as Sattlebear lit the main engines. The back of
Bonnie's seat came up on her fast. She glanced at Harold;
he was all wide eyes and barf bag.

The trip from Shiva Station to the MN0012 varied from
as little as forty-eight minutes to as long as two hours,
depending upon Shiva's position in Earth orbit. ETA to the
outpost stood presently at one hour, six minutes—or, in the
present company of the pilot, one million years, six
minutes.

"Hey," Sattlebear began, stepping out of the cockpit.
"You wanna get up, you can. Head's back there." She
indicated the direction with her head.

Harold lowered his bag. "No, that's all right."

Bonnie shook her head.

"No takers? Good. Because I gotta use it myself." The
pilot stepped past them, her beads jingling.

"She has a gift for sharing," Harold observed.

With a sneer, Bonnie thought of Sattlebear's earlier statement about having a fried brain. Over the years, she'd been
in many situations wherein her trust had rested with a computer instead of a human being. Sattlebear remained a case
in point. If only the pilot would just stay away, but exces-
sive thirst and consequential bowel movements were a common side effect of sodo gas. Ms. Fried Brain would be
making the lav journey at least a few more times. Wonderful.

Nudging her elbow, Harold asked, "Did you ever get
through to your mother?"

"Yes. Finally. She's got that fund-raiser going with her
women's group. What about you? I know you were wanting
to tell your dad."

He huffed. "I told him. It wasn't the reaction I was hoping for."

"Give him some time. From what you've told me, he's
already come a long way."

"He's back to the old manipulation argument. He thinks
that everything I do is because someone else is controlling
me. He thinks I'm just a victim. He thinks I can't even
make a decision for myself."

"I don't believe that for a second. How does he explain your position with the company?"

"I don't know. He says I let my whole life pass me by. He says I just observe and never act on anything. He says I'm a software designer because I'm running away from making a decision, from really controlling my life."

"But becoming a designer was a decision *you* made."

"Not according to him. I escaped reality, got into computers, and was recruited by the company. I never did anything to control my future. I just fell into it."

"So you told him we were going somewhere dangerous."

"Yeah, and he smirked at me because I couldn't give him the details. He thinks classified info is nothing but me lying again. Every time I think about his face, I get so mad. One of these days I'm going to snap."

"I'm sorry."

"He just thinks I never do anything about a situation. I never act. I just wanted him to know that now I am doing something. But . . . I don't know if he'll ever change."

"Maybe you can—" Bonnie cut herself off as Sattlebear sealed the bathroom hatch and headed for the cockpit.

"You guys might wanna take a snooze. Could be the last one for a long time."

Bonnie watched her leave, then said, "Though I hate admitting it, she's probably right."

"I don't feel like talking anyway." Closing his eyes, Harold clung to his barf bag as if it were a teddy bear.

After a deep sigh, Bonnie craned her head back, releasing her grip on the seat. Her eyes felt sore and heavy, and she let them fall closed.

For minute after minute she listened to the faint rush of the air-recycling system and the reassuring bass note of the thrusters. Her body clock soon went haywire, and there was no judging how long she sat, inert, visualizing what she'd find in the mine, dismissing this image and that, wondering once again whether she had made the right decision.

Soon she felt a coolness settle upon her, a black parachute of total relaxation that promised she was about to fall into a deep sleep. And then Sattlebear's proximity alarm sounded, an accursed beeping that sent Bonnie's eyes flying open and her head snapping forward.

"Two minutes to insertion," Sattlebear said through a yawn. "AP's taking us into a slow orbit. I got vid. No movement around any of the entrances. Sat reports confirm. Mechs with surface capability have obviously gone below. And ha, CED Command's trying to raise us. I'll relay their signal to Shiva. Let Dravis deal with them."

Bonnie sloughed off her straps and went to the cockpit. She stared over Sattlebear's shoulder at the panel of monitors, each showing external camera views of the outpost's four main entrances: simple rectangular doorways emerging from the otherwise random geometry of the lunar surface. The north entrance served as the main docking facility, with over a dozen oval tarmacs and service runways laid across the regolith. Larger than the others, this entrance permitted insertion planes to fly directly into the mine and dock in a subsurface, pressurized bay that could accommodate a dozen or more ships. Getting to the bay past the locked exterior door would be their first Houdinian exercise.

"I hope the mechs aren't picking us up," Harold said, arriving at Bonnie's side. "We can bet they got control of the mine's RTC."

"We're only being tracked by the Earth Defense. Weird, but there are no signals coming from the mine. I mean not a one. If they do get hot, I'll jam them. The only way your robot buddies will know we're coming is if they are standing in the bay," the pilot said confidently.

"Make that floating," Harold corrected.

Sattlebear made a face. "Better strap in."

They headed back to their seats, and Bonnie felt her breath stagger. Before buckling her harness, she held a hand before her eyes and studied it: trembling.

"Exterior door signal received, and—I don't believe it— she's opening," Sattlebear told them. "I just tried the code on a lark."

"Maybe the mechs want us inside," Harold said, his voice freighted with tension.

"Why?" Sattlebear asked. "They serving breakfast?"

"Did you study comedy? Or is it just one of your natural failings?" Harold taunted.

The pilot looked back and frowned. "What?"

"Forget it."

Bonnie double-checked her harness, then shook her head gravely at her assistant. "Be ready to move."

The north entrance swung into view, and Bonnie watched as Sattlebear steered them toward the huge, parting doors at a sodo-gas-influenced velocity. The plane's nav computer had already plotted a course into the mine, and a screen displayed a real-time graphic of the scene, superimposed light green lines appearing and vanishing in a choreography of angles that lasted a billionth of a second and resumed in the next. A screen-top status message reported: NAV-ASSISTED INSERTION IN PROGRESS. And while Sattlebear's dependence on technology should have been somewhat comforting, the dark, circular tunnel ahead robbed her of all but a feeling of vulnerability.

Then, in a finger snap, they shot into the tunnel, leaving vortices of kicked-up lunar dust in their wake. Bonnie turned her attention away from the aft camera monitor and stared through the canopy. Sattlebear toggled on the insertion plane's headlights, and twin narrow beams intersected at a point somewhere in the gloomy distance. Dead, overhead dome lights and equally unlit red navigation lights to either side of the ship whipped by so quickly that they formed the dividing lines of a turnpike traveled while inverted.

"ETA docking bay: thirty seconds," Sattlebear noted tersely. "Two pressure locks have sealed behind us. Atmosphere's being piped in. Got nothing on the FLIR, nothing on any of the other trackers. Guess breakfast has been canceled."

Based on data gathered from the situation, Bonnie had formulated some simple but effective working rules that she had offered to Harold in Shiva Station's ready room and he had readily approved: expect the unpredictable; accept the unexplainable; and consider the possibilities of both, one, or neither being true. Rhetoric? Hardly. A once-thriving mine now lay in unimagined, inexplicable darkness, a situation that commanded the wariness and respect of anyone venturing into it.

Unfortunately, Ms. Sattlebear lacked, or rather, was incapable of that brand of humility. Bonnie felt like saying something but decided not to waste her time.

"And here comes the bay," Sattlebear announced. "And holy shit! We're surrounded! Goddammit, why didn't they show up—in fact, they're still not showing up!"

"What's she talking about?" Harold demanded.

Bonnie pointed at the canopy, at the dozen or more mechs homing in on them from all directions with sensor eyes flashing or glowing or pulsing. She got the strange impression that the docking bay had been transformed into some dim, high-tech sacrificial altar for a mechanized tribe. She grabbed Harold by his sleeve. "Get your gear!"

Frantically, she slipped out of her harness and fetched her equipment from the bulkhead storage compartment. Before she could close the door, an explosion echoed and a shock wave took hold of the plane. She dropped her pack and looked to the cockpit even as a missile from a Medium Hulk struck the energy shield surrounding the canopy and turned Sattlebear's field of view into a fiery cloud that billowed and wiped around the plane as the pilot began to slide, attempting to circle the mechs. But where to go? They had already surrounded the ship.

Her answer came in the form of a double whack against the starboard bulkhead, a sound trailed immediately by a muffled snapping and bang. Sattlebear had collided with a mech, punching a hole in their assault.

"Get your remote!" Bonnie told Harold, then found herself falling toward the opposite bulkhead. She caught her balance and spun to face the cockpit.

The ship suddenly vibrated under the pulsing of Sattlebear's forward Spreadfire cannon. "Can't hold them back! We're dusting out," the pilot cried. "Autodistress engaged."

Bonnie made a fist. "Damn." Until the second they had encountered the mechs, she had maintained the hope that they wouldn't be aggressive, that something else had happened in the mine that only involved them in an ancillary way. Now that hope was dwindling as quickly as the energy shields protecting her.

Under Sattlebear's panicky guidance, the insertion plane fishtailed like a sports car on an ice-slick road. Bonnie watched as the pilot rolled thruster power up and headed back for the tunnel. Argon laser and missile fire continually erupted a scant meter above the hull, and between the shots Bonnie detected a strange chorus of wailing that sent a chill rising up her neck. Were the mechs vocalizing something? *Accept the unexplainable*, she thought: *Yes, they were. Why?*

"Ohmygod. They're sealing the bay," Sattlebear said, pointing at the canopy. She reached down and applied braking thrusters.

Staggering to the cockpit, Bonnie held tight to the back of Sattlebear's seat and watched the ten-meter-high bay doors slide toward each other. "Blow that control panel," Bonnie said. "See it up there on the right?"

"That won't do jack! They're remote-commanding it," Sattlebear argued.

Tensing every muscle, Bonnie screamed, "BLOW IT UP ANYWAY!"

Azure bursts of supercharged plasma leapt from beneath the plane's nose and blew gaping holes in the alloy walls. Some bursts dug into the rock below the two-inch-thick metal and sent showers of rubble ricocheting harmlessly off the canopy shield. Glowing wall fragments tumbled into Sattlebear's line of fire and disappeared in the powerful stream. The pilot kept firing, blasting a line across the wall that finally reached the control panel, which shattered in a fury of sparks.

The bay doors continued closing.

"What did I tell you! Now get out! I'm going for it. So you'd better siddown!" Sattlebear's eyes had worn the lackluster of sodo gas, but now they radiated with a force that rivaled her laser cannon.

Muttering a curse, Bonnie shifted back to the cabin, giving Harold what she guessed was a look of sheer terror. "Get to the back!" She snatched up her pack.

Harold, who now gripped his small, tubular remote and

shouldered his pack, obeyed, saying, "I tried shutting them down, but the signal's not strong enough to get through the hull and shields."

A narrow walkway between the cabin seats ended in a small, meter and a half square opening that led to the bathroom hatch. Harold made it to that opening while Bonnie followed, digging into her pack and fishing out her own remote.

Abruptly, a jackhammering clamor shot across the rear bulkhead. The smooth, white fuselage caved in once, twice, a third time. "There's a Medium Lifter back there. It's trying to cut through," she told Harold, imagining the mech's diamond-plated swingarms crashing down on the hull. "Shields must be down."

With an almost morbid curiosity, Bonnie glanced to the cockpit. There, through the canopy, she observed what could only be a two-meter gap in the bay doors—and Sattlebear was coming on them fast.

Reflexively, Bonnie bolted for the bathroom hatch, wrenched it open, then seized Harold by the back of his tunic collar and shoved him inside.

Sattlebear released a terrific howl and—

—the ship collided head-on with the now-sealed doors.

Bonnie's grip barely held to the bathroom hatch as she was jerked forward, then tossed back. She caught a quick glimpse of the cockpit as it folded in like aluminum foil toward the passenger seats, crushing a still-howling Sattlebear. Oxygen lines within the bulkhead ruptured, hissed, then exploded, sending streams of fire crisscrossing the cabin. Another burst that tore off a huge section of the cabin's ceiling shook through Bonnie as she pulled herself inside the bathroom and shut the hatch, feeling its handle suddenly grow warm.

Fighting to listen above the sound of her own panting, Bonnie focused on the noises outside: the buzzing of shattered electronics, the rustling of flames, and the screeching of mechs. No more explosions.

"We gotta get out of here," Harold said, his voice cracking.

Bonnie swallowed painfully, thinking of what she had just seen. "Sattlebear's dead."

"I guessed that," he answered grimly.

"Come on." She pushed open the door.

Showers of sparks fell like confetti over the twisted seats, the rest of the cabin barely visible through the swirling smoke. Holding her breath and squinting, Bonnie guided herself toward a ruby rectangular light that pulsed and hovered on the port side of the wreckage. She realized the light was the sensor eye of a Small Hulk, but she didn't care. The mining drone would unknowingly guide her out of the ship. She heard Harold's footsteps just behind her, then felt him hang on to her pack. As she neared the bot, she realized that the hole in the ceiling ran down to the floor, creating a narrow but navigable gap. The fuselage had buckled, and sections of it had simply snapped off. Feeling the dire urge to breathe, she exhaled, kept moving, then pulled in a little air and coughed away the burn in her throat. She rushed to the gap and pushed herself through it, nearly tearing off her pack in the process. Harold emerged a second later, sweating, battered, his glasses hanging too low on his nose.

A shrill cry sent Bonnie ducking and grimacing. Slowly, she turned her gaze back to the mech. It hovered above them like a green-and-purple god studying the frail humans that had invaded its home. Bonnie had made a career out of working with such drones; no one in the company knew them better. Suddenly, even she didn't know them. The Hulk descended to eye level and hovered just a few meters away. Other mechs, cloaked in shadow, their eyes gleaming, clustered in the distance and waited.

"Zap him," Harold said. "Before he takes a shot."

Bonnie raised her hand. "Wait. He could've killed us already."

"So he's got a guilty conscience," Harold explained, then he raised his remote and thumbed the trigger, sending a signal meant to initiate an emergency, single-unit shutdown.

The mech's sensor eye faded as it suddenly crashed to the monolithic floor, tottered a moment, then thudded on its back.

"Whew," Harold said, sighing heavily. "Something works."

"We'll shut down the rest. Then up to the Command Center, contact Shiva, and find out what happened here."

And, as though they were thumbing off dozens of holographic and conventional TVs in a department store, she and Harold quickly made their rounds. Mech after mech dropped to the stone, their magical strings of antigravity severed at the not-so-magical source.

"Hey, Bonnie. Check this out."

She hurried over to Harold, who was crouched near the starboard wing of the still-smoldering insertion plane. At his feet lay a meter-sized resource-computed guide robot used for giving the public brief tours of the mine. Bonnie ran a finger across a crack in one of the three light blue pyramids that connected at their peaks to form the mech's body. The bases of the pyramids contained shorter pyramids whose tips were rounded off, and they appeared to be intact. A red, equilateral triangle served as the bot's combination sensor eye/exhaust port.

"I found it staggering here and shut it down. We must've hit it," Harold speculated. "Let's take it up to the CC and put its memory on a flash screen. What does it weigh? Fifteen kilos? It's a lot lighter than one of those big boys back there."

"You grab the bot. I'll grab the packs," Bonnie said, straightening. As she turned toward where she thought the packs were, she caught a flicker out of the corner of her eye. A slight toss of her head, and there, near the demolished nose of the plane, the sensor of a Medium Hulk blossomed with life. "Somebody's turning them back on!" She thumbed her remote. Nothing. The mech began to rise. "They're blocking the signal."

She took a step back and glanced over her shoulder at Harold. He carried the guide bot, and his eyes begged her to run.

7

Semper Fi, Do . . . Or Go to Jail

For the past two hours, Ben had been lying in his bunk, listening to the footsteps in the corridor outside his cell. Each time someone had drawn near, he'd lifted his head, wishing with everything he had left that those footsteps belonged to Elizabeth. But so far his only visitor had been his attorney, a young hotshot who'd spent a lot of time smiling over the insanity of what Ben had done and very little time discussing the case, which she had decided would never go to trial. Ben would admit his guilt and take the plea.

The plea would condemn him to prison for most of his life.

The plea would save him from a death sentence.

The plea was good.

God bless the law, the Corps, the solar system.

After that conversation, his attorney had said something odd: "But all of this may just be academic, Mr. St. John. I probably shouldn't have wasted my time here. You probably won't need me. I just wish they'd contact my office and let us know either way." When asked who "they" were, his lawyer wouldn't explain further. And he'd been left wondering.

Ben stared into the clouds of his mind, racing at Mach

2, buffeted by Martian jet streams, corkscrewing to evade conventional fire. He gripped his imaginary control stick and made a long, slow turn, flying away from the cell, away from the hypocrisy. *Up here,* he thought, *there's no crap. No lies. There's truth in the wind.*

Still, no matter how far he flew, the facts clung to him like Martian dust, wiped away but back in the next second: YOU ARE NO LONGER A COLLECTIVE EARTH DEFENSE MARINE CORPS PATROL PILOT. YOU ARE A MILITARY CRIMINAL. YOU ARE A FAILURE AS AN OFFICER AND A HUSBAND. WHY? BECAUSE YOU DID WHAT YOU THOUGHT WAS RIGHT. BUT YOUR THOUGHTS ARE THE THOUGHTS OF AN IDIOT!

With a roar, Ben reached back, seized his pillow, and threw it at the cell door.

Yes, he'd tried to take back control of his life, had been successful for a short time, but in doing so had lost it all. Now he choked on the irony of his actions and the knowledge that some military judge would decide his fate. He didn't believe it possible, but he felt even more cut off, more empty than he had when leaving the hospital. Back then he'd kept the Marine Corps fire alive, fanning it with the thought of getting back in. Now he knew there was nothing, absolutely nothing he could do to recover his wings.

The door lock made its quartet of beeps and abruptly opened. So lost in thought, Ben hadn't heard his visitor's approach. He sat up and saw Lieutenant Colonel Paul Ornowski lean over, retrieve the pillow, then proffer it to him. Ornowski's expression fell somewhere between sympathetic and embarrassed.

"Thanks."

"Benjamin St. John. You love the Marine Corps, don't you?"

His answer required little thought. "Even with all its faults."

"You wanted back in so badly that you did something . . . radical, something . . . stupid."

Ben looked away and smirked. "You come here because

you feel guilty or something? You wanna say your good-bye? Then just do it, man.''

"There are very few officers like you, Ben. You're true to the spirit of the Corps. You're a fool, but you're proud. You're rash, but you're in the best tradition of the Marines. I'm proud to have served with you. And I look forward to working with you now.''

That easily caught Ben's attention; he frowned at the man. "What're you gonna do, be a witness for my defense? My lawyer says all that's left is a little bargaining. I'm already finished.''

"Forget the case. Forget the fact that you stole a plane and were subsequently shot down. Forget the fact that you should be spending the rest of your life in prison.''

"Uh, Paul. It's a little hard to forget those things, considering where I am," Ben said, eyeing the room.

"That's been taken care of. Now pay attention. PTMC is having a few problems now, and they need a good pilot, a very good pilot. In fact, it's unfortunate, but their problems have become ours.''

"What are you talking about? That company's got plenty of merc pilots, a lot of them ex-Marines. You saying they need me? I hope you told them I'm a little busy getting sentenced to life.''

"They didn't ask for you. We're offering you to them— free of charge. They are, of course, well aware of your reputation. Mr. Dravis has told me that your assistance would be invaluable. He mentioned something about a stock-option gratuity you may collect afterward. You can discuss the details of that with him.''

"Hold on. So, the Marine Corps is volunteering me for some PTMC mission? What do I do, go out, risk my life, then come back to my cushy cell to look over my new stock portfolio? Why would I do it?''

"You'll never be a Marine again, Ben. You know that. But we'll forget about the plane. You go, you do the op, and you walk away.''

"That's illegal.''

"From one point of view.''

"So I do it, and I'm back where I started—without a career."

"Yeah," Ornowski said emphatically. "But you'll be free."

"Seems mighty nice of the Marine Corps to lend out one of their pilots—oh, I mean criminals—to PTMC, especially when the Corps has nothing to gain from it. What *is* wrong with this picture, Paul?"

"Of course we have something to gain. We wouldn't be wiping your record clean if we didn't. Lunar Outpost double-oh-twelve has been shut down indefinitely. The mining mechs have contracted some kind of virus and have taken over." He paused as if deciding whether he should say more, then continued. "We have an operation in the mine, Ben, on level seventeen. We wanted to take advantage of the company's already excellent security against foreign operatives."

"As opposed to our pathetic counterintell. You know as well as I do that our lunar command center is crawling with spies."

"No one's confirmed that. But I agree. Makes me wonder why we call ourselves the Collective Earth Defense when we're hardly united. Anyway, listen up. What I'm about to tell you is classified. You know the drill."

"Yeah. That means I should charge Mr. Dravis a lot for the information."

"Right," he agreed sarcastically. "Down in that facility we've been developing a prototype for a new Pyro-GX weapons system computer."

"GX. That's the new hybrid of the Interceptor we've been selling to PTMC, isn't it?"

"It is. Anyway, this new system's thought-activated; it's like nothing you've ever flown with, and the prototype is nearly complete. Problem is we've only got one. Bigger problem is all data concerning it is in that mine. Nothing's been backed up, and all engineers working on the project were departmentalized. Only that team could build another one—but two members were murdered."

"Security has its drawbacks, eh?"

"There's a reason for such intense security. With this

new weapons computer, our ships will be able to clear the economic lock PTMC has on the inner spaceways. The UN's beginning to panic over the company's growing control. They want PTMC broken up. They've provided the funding, and we're the hammer.''

"So you rent space from the very company you wanna put out of business. Now that's Marine Corps logic. Love it. I'm guessing you want me to recover our little project?''

"Absolutely. Before PTMC does. If they get it, there'll be no stopping their merc force. None of our personnel are in the mine, and we can't get near it. The company has declared it a demilitarized zone using some loophole in our rental agreement. We don't want an incident. So, you go in under the guise of helping them to rescue two software specialists and some supervisors who may be trapped there. You'll blow the mine if it's not salvageable.''

"What a lame plan. They're gonna know flat out that I'm there to rescue our project—so why would they let me in the mine in the first place?''

"They also want access to level seventeen. You'll be the only one with the codes to get in. Sorry, Ben. But it's a game. Once inside the mine, their player will be expecting you to go down to seventeen. After you're in, he'll try to kill you and take the prototype. But he can't get in without you. So you're valuable to him—at least until you open those doors.''

"Who are we talking about?''

"You won't be going in alone. Mr. Dravis tells me he wants to pair you up with one of their mercs. He's starting a new program and calling the pilots Material Defenders.''

"Who's the pilot?''

"I don't know yet. But you'll be meeting that individual shortly. You're scheduled for a meeting aboard Shiva Station at eighteen-hundred hours.''

"Assuming I accept the offer.''

Ornowski flashed his wolf's grin. "I know it'll be a tough decision. Jail or a chance to fly again.''

"You people are screwing me. I just haven't figured out how. You know, I got to thinking up in that plane that maybe you weren't in my head, that having BPCs was just a lie, just payback from my ex. But now I'm thinking about this op, about how much trust you guys have to put in me. And I'm thinking I just stole a plane. I'm thinking you don't trust me at all—unless you *know* you can control me.''

"I heard about your supposed BPCs from Zim. No one's ever going to confirm or deny their existence.''

"Even you?''

"Back in the hospital I told you that I had put my ass on the line too many times for you. Well, here I am, doing it again. But confirming something like BPCs? That crosses the line.''

"So I *do* have them.''

"You'll figure it out. Now. Get down to the lockers. You got thirty mikes to shit, shower, shave, and get into dress blues. Meet me at the Ops officer's desk at gate three.'' Ornowski headed for the door, calling to the guard outside.

"So I can just walk out of here? Just like that?''

The door opened, and Ornowski stepped into the hall. He faced the guard. "You're not going to stop him, are you, Private?''

The young man stood, unflappable. "No, sir. My orders are to release him, sir.''

Ornowski cocked a brow at Ben.

"What if I run, Paul?''

"Run where?''

The lieutenant colonel didn't wait for Ben's reply.

8

Lancelot in a Lab Coat

Fighting back the nausea produced by the stench of old death, Bonnie helped Harold carry the burned woman's body into the east corridor outside the command center. According to the victim's ID, she had been the communications supervisor. They placed her alongside the charred form of Mr. Prism, the young security man.

Harold gagged. The bodies were a more powerful emetic than flying. "Sorry. I didn't expect this."

Alive with chills, her palms feeling somewhat sticky from carrying the bodies, Bonnie tried to deny what had happened to the supervisors because part of her felt responsible. *That's ridiculous,* she assured herself. *I didn't give the mechs a virus.* But the mechs were still hers. And the other supervisors—or their bodies—were still missing.

"We'd better hurry," Harold said, his nose and mouth covered by a T-shirt from his pack, the rest of him cloaked in his white, trademark lab coat, which he'd often said "made him feel at home anywhere." Bonnie doubted that now.

Behind him, the muffled booming of lasers and missiles from the docking bay made her feel like a soldier fleeing the front line.

She and Harold had fled the bay, sealed the four, reinforced hatches leading into the level one proper with override codes delivered from Harold's palmtop, then destroyed the panels that controlled those doors by ordering them to continually close, resulting in a domino effect of overloads. One bot, a blue Class 2 drone, had managed to slip through, but to their astonishment, the wedge-shaped mech glided away as if receiving commands from another source. Or that may have been Bonnie's imagination.

With another of Harold's T-shirts tied around her own face, Bonnie hurried out of the corridor and let her flashlight lead the way back into the center, where they had discovered that the communications station had been destroyed. They'd have to get down to level two and send a signal to Shiva from the satlink station there—if it wasn't contaminated by the virus or taken permanently off-line by the mechs. In the meantime, Harold had already used a lunch-box-sized portable power unit to independently start up the security supervisor's station and cut its link to the network, which would, in theory, prevent the mechs from monitoring their actions. The power unit could keep the station running for about eight hours.

Harold removed his glasses and T-shirt mask, then dropped into the virtual-link chair. He slid on the goggles and began tapping on the touchpad. Then he keyed in a command on the palmtop at his side. "I need to identify myself as a guest. VCS is down; I'll do the typing."

"You have the list of mech codes patched in, right?" Bonnie asked while removing the CPU cover on the guide bot's dorsal pyramid. "We'll use this bot."

"Good idea. Codes coming up. That's a good sign. Scrolling through them now. Okay. Got the list of guide bots. Thirteen registered to this mine. Seven operational."

"All right. Here's the serial number: 486582193-ZZX-TTY."

"Four, eight, six, five. Got it. Identifying and, oh baby, I don't know what I'm looking at," he said in an astonished lilt. "It's some kind of code, but I've never seen it before."

"No kidding, Harold. That's what those amateur ware wizards in security reported. There *has* to be something recognizable about it."

"Not from where I'm sitting." He typed on the palmtop. "Checking for known viruses, worms, logic bombs, and I'm throwing in the old Trojan horses for good measure." He snorted. "But it's a waste of time. AVSS can't scan because it doesn't recognize the code. I can't even tell you if this bug is memory-resident or not."

Bonnie thought for a moment. "Maybe it's a hybrid of a polymorphic virus."

"Yeah, so?"

"Maybe instead of hiding itself through encryption, it created a layer of unrecognizable code as a shield, giving it stealth capability. What's worse, it's obviously intuitive and spawning."

"Yup. It's a queen bee, and we're never gonna get at it from here. The system won't even recognize conventional commands. I can't even get to an entrance screen, let alone find a trigger. I got what might be an execution file, but it's writing and revising itself as I'm reading it, like it's doing a weird beta test on itself. This sucks. We need to jack into an operating mech. Yeah, that'll be easy. Oh, no."

"What?"

"They know I'm in." His finger tapped quickly on the pad, then he tore off the goggles and burst from the chair. After a loud snap, the supervisor's station went dark. Harold moved to the portable power unit and examined its clipped on, palmtop controller. "They drained our power and completely erased my drive—and the biochip backup," he said, clearly not believing it.

"They did what?"

"You heard me."

She felt her stomach drop. The speed, power, and accuracy of the virus left her in shocked silence. She thought about who was behind the bug and the potential that person or group now possessed. Were this thing to spawn on Earth, the words *technological apocalypse* would soon be in the headlines of the IPC instead of the tabloids. Images of a total societal breakdown flashed in her mind, inspired by vids and holos of natural and unnatural disasters she'd seen while growing up. People rioted in the streets, communicating with baseball bats instead of modems. Bank accounts, portfolios, entire lives would be erased. Sure, most data was backed up, but people would starve before even a hint of all they had struggled for could be restored.

But Bonnie didn't want that burden. *If we fail, and this virus gets out, it's not my fault,* she thought. *I didn't create it. It's not my responsibility. I do software. I don't save worlds.*

Turning her thoughts back to the precarious but ironically more comfortable present, she studied the guide bot. "I'm gonna hook up a hard line between my computer and our little tour guide. I'm shutting down my wireless," she said, then typed commands into her palmtop.

"Better do it fast. And if they find a way into that connection, I'll buy a month's worth of dinners for the team who wrote this virus."

After withdrawing a palmlink cable from her pack, Bonnie connected her computer to the guide bot, then ran a first-stage diagnostic, careful not to scan for viruses since doing so might tip off the bee. She studied her computer's small display. "Flash screen data's coming through." Bonnie felt her jaw drop. "Drive's empty. Every byte's free. ROM's clean."

"So the virus formats the main drive and wipes out everything else. Okay. But what I don't understand is that even if it's hiding behind this weird code, where does it reside? In virtual or upper mem?"

"Don't know. Both free in this bot. According to my diagnostic, I'm looking at a new mech that has yet to be programmed." She ran the virus scan. "No traces of any known viruses. And I seriously doubt that our hitting it could have resulted in this."

Harold leaned in next to her. "This one's good, baby. Really, really, good."

Nodding in agreement, Bonnie added, "It's a hybrid polymorph that enters via wireless modem and controls the mech either through a central location, on an individual level, or probably both. Then, if it detects an AVS or if the individual is no longer functional, it erases itself and all other data behind it."

"You can't see it or get to it while it's working, and

when it's done, it covers its tracks better than anything I've ever seen. I think . . ." He let himself trail off, squinting. He raised his chin. "Hear that?"

Her ears pricked up, and she detected a low, approaching hum she'd heard many times before. So absorbed in her detective work, she'd forgotten that the mechs had picked up Harold's tampering. Her gaze went to the open strong lockers across from the station, to the EX790 pulse rifles stowed there. She bolted for one.

"Shouldn't we try the remotes again?" Harold suggested. "Maybe only the drones in the—"

"We will," she said, withdrawing a rifle and thumbing on the power switch. She tossed it to him, and he caught it as though it were on fire. "I'm sorry about dragging you here, Harold."

"Don't be. I told you I can kick some butt. Now I'll prove it. But I don't think my tae kwon do's gonna help much."

Gripping her own rifle, Bonnie moved to huddle behind the strong lockers, and Harold joined her. "You don't understand," she said. "I convinced Dravis to send us in alone."

He didn't exactly frown, but he didn't exactly understand either. "Because you, well, you . . . you wanted us to be alone? Whoa. That didn't come out right."

"I was stupid. I don't know what I was thinking. It's true that with the military in here, with all their computer-controlled equipment, they'd be a huge target for the virus. But we sure as hell could use them now."

"We're surgeons. They're butchers. You did the right thing. And don't fear, my lady. I'll defend your honor against these rascals."

She smiled thinly. "Thank you."

A cry, as if from some sick, mechanized bird, rang hollowly through the command center.

Harold's eyes, slightly magnified by the glasses, betrayed his fully magnified dread. She turned away from him, toward the sound of the mech.

"It's inside," he whispered, then raised his remote and hit the power down-button.

Another cackle from the bot.

"That answers that question," he said, then placed the useless device at his feet. He let his gaze play over the rifle. "This little VDT says I'm auto-locked and loaded."

"Me too," she answered softly, glancing at the tiny status screen built into her own rifle, just below the laser sight.

"So we just pull the trigger."

She gave him an odd look. "That's the idea, Harold."

"You okay with this?"

"Why do you ask?"

"Because I'm not. Because I need to tell you some things. Because I might not get a chance to later."

Peering furtively just over the top of the strong lockers, Bonnie studied the circular chamber. She spotted the mech, a simple brown Class 1 drone, floating near the shredded southwest hatch. Mouthing a curse, she realized that she and Harold had forgotten to click off their flashlights. Still, the mech didn't seem attracted to the pale glow behind her. It remained inert, as though waiting for them to make the first move.

"It's just one of those things I never wanted to rush, one of those things you just don't talk about because you feel so weird about it. But now I don't care because who knows if I'm gonna walk out of here. And like my dad says, I gotta take control."

Slowly, Bonnie lowered herself behind the lockers. "It's near the entrance, up on the left. I'm not sure what to do. Just shoot it and go? What do you think?"

He fixed her with a steely look. "Have you been listening to me?"

"Yes, I have. And I know you have a lot of stuff you have to work out with your father. And I wanna keep listening. But right now we have to get out of here." She sighed inwardly over having to explain that to him.

"I love you, Bonnie."

"What?"

"I said I love you."

She looked away, pretending she needed to glance once more to the drone but in truth needing a second to consider her reply without the influence of his sad, puppy-dog face.

He finally crossed the line and said it, she thought. *And now PTMC would have to send a damage-control party to his heart.* Indeed, his confession was inevitable, had been inevitable. She had seen it coming a parsec away and had decided months ago she would guard herself, not send the wrong signals, and gently let him down. She fully understood his feelings toward her. She was the only woman in his life besides his mother, and she was, in effect, a mother figure. And she did love him but in a way that wouldn't be enough for him. The cliché held true for her: Don't become involved with coworkers. Still, she had now and again fantasized how life would be with him. Her passion for software wasn't something she'd ever have to explain. Other men never understood. He was so much like her. But in him she saw things about herself she didn't like. She lived for the work. She didn't live *and* work. And that's what she wanted to do. Without a single thought about work, she wanted to go to the beach, shop for clothes, and eat at a nice restaurant. With Harold around, that would be impossible. *Then again, maybe I'm incapable of living a day and not thinking about work,* she thought. That damned dedication again.

But what to tell him now? He'd just presented all that he had, all that he was. "Will you accept my love?" "Uh, no. But you can go on torturing yourself by being my assistant because you're a damned good one."

She wished the mech would move, do something, anything, so she could avoid facing Harold. But it just hung there, not wanting to help with a laser blast or two.

"I know you don't feel the same way, Bonnie. Maybe you think I'm not man enough for you. Maybe you really believe what my father says. But I'm taking control now. I'm telling you I *love* you. And I'm getting us out of here. Watch me."

Before she could stop him, he was gone, having slipped behind the lockers. He kept low, moving from station to station, his lab coat fluttering like a comic-book hero's cape. She watched him for a moment, then realized she had better follow. Working muscles she didn't know she had,

Bonnie darted to the comm station and glanced up—

—in time to see Harold bring himself to full height and step toward the mech, his rifle trained on the drone's torso.

A ball of energy edged in red and fading from orange to a splintering, flickering white in its center erupted from one of the mech's wing tips. Bonnie flinched as Harold's rifle blew out of his grip, arced over his head, and exploded behind him. He screamed and backed away from the drone as it roared and went for him like a pit bull.

Bolting to her feet, Bonnie took aim and fired, blinking hard to endure the weapon's high-pitched blast. The mech tumbled away from Harold, dipped a bit, then turned to face her. She set her teeth and fired again, this time watching the thick, yellow bolts reach out for and strike the mech. Wisps of blue energy writhed along its frame before it exploded, sending a wave of debris toward Bonnie. As the first pieces struck her abdomen, she fell onto her back, still tightly clutching the rifle. She rolled onto her stomach as the pinging and thudding ceased.

Harold called to her, and she told him, "I'm all right. Come on." She got to her hands and knees, and he was there, a jagged rip in his jeans, his leg bleeding. "You're not okay."

He offered his hand and helped her up. She felt a pain in her chest, looked down, and saw that her own tunic had thankfully not been breached. The bruise would be large.

Crossing to the strong lockers, Harold retrieved another rifle and four extra power clips. "I'm sorry. Just forget about everything I said a moment ago." He slipped his fingers beneath his glasses and rubbed his eyes.

Bonnie hurried to the guide bot and began preparing it for transport. "We'll get down to level two. See if we can contact Shiva. And I want to program this bot. And Harold?"

He stared gloomily at her, his lips tight.

She wanted to reassure him. But the words wouldn't come.

9

Welcome, Material Defenders

Hair freshly combed. Face soft and shaven. Body smelling like soap and the not-so-pungent scent of mid-priced cologne. Dress blues, adorned with medals, fitting like a proverbial glove. Hat, or, rather, parade cover tucked under arm. Shoes so shiny that when they caught the sun, they blinded observers.

It had been far too long since Ben had donned the uniform of his trade. And he had never felt more comfortable. He found himself smiling as he stepped out of the airlock and into Shiva Station's bustling customs terminal. Once again, he'd kicked fate in the ass. He was back. A pilot with a mission. If only Elizabeth could see him now.

He fell in line and presented his card to one of a dozen customs officers at the gate; the middle-aged woman inserted the card in a terminal and studied a screen. "Anything else besides that smile to declare, Captain St. John?"

Feeling suddenly self-conscious, Ben throttled down his grin. "No, ma'am. Just happy to be here."

"That's unusual. Most people aren't."

"Aren't what, people?"

"Very funny—but more true than you know." She returned his card. "You'll take the lift to level ten. Once you get out—"

"I'll show him the way, Officer," an extremely pretty woman in a black skirt said. She beamed at him. "Captain? I'm Megan Bartonovich, Assistant Director of CCM and Public Relations."

Ben took her lovely hand and shook it firmly, staring deeply into her dark eyes. "Under normal circumstances I'd say it's nice to meet you. But, considering where I've come from, it's a lot more than nice."

"He's very happy to be here," the customs officer interrupted, then gave Ben a wink.

"I'm here to escort you to the executive dining hall. Mr. Dravis has arranged a wonderful dinner for us. I don't know if you're familiar with his passion for food, but suffice it to say you *will* enjoy the experience."

Ben took one look at her long, well-tanned legs and said, "I'm sure I will."

She led him out of the terminal and into a lift. They rode alone. "So, have you ever been here before?"

He shook his head. "I never realized it was this big."

"It's very big," she agreed. "Over one thousand people live and work here."

"Don't know if I could do that," Ben said. "I'm a planet kinda guy. Born on Earth, in New York. Raised on Mars. If I'm off planet, it had better be in a fighter plane. Otherwise, I think I'd go nuts without a daytime sky."

"Environment screens do a great job of simulating that," she reminded. "They keep improving the resolution."

"Yeah, but you always know it's virtual." He made a fist. "There's nothing real to grab on to."

The lift doors opened, and she stepped out. He wished he could just watch her walk away, study the symmetry of her form, but he kept close on her black heels, trailing her down a long corridor lined with hunter green carpeting. A photographic chronology of the PTMC executive board lined the walls. Ben had never seen so much corrective surgery in his life. Photos of fifty-year-old directors flashed by, their faces betraying not a single wrinkle. They were perfect people, smooth as plastic, with, he guessed, personalities equally as fabricated.

She turned right and reached for the gold handle on one

of two great hand-carved wooden doors. Between the carpet, the photos, and now the castlelike entrance, Ben suddenly didn't feel so comfortable—even in his dress blues. Marines were used to functional, not fancy.

What lay beyond could have been exported from a magnificent, ancient fortress. Stretching for some twenty meters in all directions, the circular hall stood in testament to executive excess. Rare woods (or at least Ben thought they were) covered walls broken by the occasional piece of art here and there. Light fell from a collection of antique, crystal chandeliers, their bulbs shaped like burning candles. Black marble, as shiny as his boots, raced away from him, creating a placid sea of darkness broken only by puddles of reflected light. At the heart of this spectacle lay a great round table that could seat at least thirty people, though only two men, their faces indistinct in the distance, were seated at it now. Beneath the table lay a massive rug, Persian, perhaps, its design as intricate and colorful as any cockpit control panel. Yes, the castle analogy was quite deliberate. *I guess these guys fancy themselves as knights and damsels,* Ben thought. *Place probably makes them feel somehow noble while they screw people over.*

Ms. Bartonovich's shoes clicked loudly on the marble as she started into the room. ''Mr. Dravis? I'd like you to meet Captain Benjamin St. John, Collective Earth Defense Marine Corps.''

As Ben neared the table, his own shoes creating a racket, he noted that the older man rising had to be Dravis—

—because he recognized the other man as a jock named Sierra Taurus, fifty, ex–Marine Corps pilot with the inglorious talent of becoming a pimple on your ass, one that takes months to heal. Ben couldn't take his gaze off of Taurus as he shook Mr. Dravis's hand.

''It is a distinct pleasure to meet the hero of the Jupiter System,'' Dravis said. ''Two of the executives you saved on that transport are here at Shiva and would like to thank you personally before you leave.''

Finally, Ben faced the man. ''Uh, yeah, sure. But I didn't exactly save them.''

''That's right, Little Bird,'' Taurus said, pushing his

high-backed, well-padded chair away from the table and getting to his feet. He had a fierce face crowned with a white, high, and tight Marine Corps crew cut. No corrective surgery there, just a complexion of creases and scars that, in his mind, gave him the right to do and say whatever he wanted. "You went in there in violation of orders, got shot up, and got lucky. IPC made you a hero because the Corps paid them to—just to save face. Now that we all understand what really happened."

Dravis scowled at Taurus. "Extenuating circumstances do not diminish Captain St. John's actions. He created the situation in which we bargained. And for that he most certainly deserves credit. Sit down, Mr. Taurus."

To Ben's astonishment, the pilot obeyed. Clearly, Dravis had tamed the man through cash rewards.

The director's expression softened as he faced Ben. "And please. Make yourself comfortable, Captain."

As Ben complied, strategically locating himself next to Ms. Bartonovich, a begloved male waiter dressed in gold and silk glided into the room with a bottle of champagne and began filling peach-tinged flutes. Ben hemmed. "Sir. I'm assuming that Grandpa's my wingman for this op?"

The language that suddenly poured from Taurus's mouth made Dravis cringe. Ms. Bartonovich could only shake her head. Ben smiled sardonically, feeding the crass pilot more rope, hoping Taurus would further embarrass himself. But he didn't.

Once the verbal spate passed, Dravis said, "We were aware you two served together and thought the arrangement would work out nicely. I see, however, we were mistaken. Still, time is a factor, and it's too late to replace one or both of you." He reached for his glass of champagne. "Let's learn to like each other, shall we? And let's have a toast."

Sneering at Taurus, Ben went for his own glass, watching as the old man withdrew a couple of pills from a bicep pocket and slipped them in his mouth.

Dravis continued, "To a successful mission and safe return. There. I love a short toast before a long meal."

It was more likely that Dravis knew that Ben and Taurus

didn't get along. That would make Taurus's job of killing Ben all the more easy. These people were smartly dressed vipers, all right. But as part of your last meal they did serve you some very tasty champagne. Ben set down his empty glass next to the earthenware plate and once again eyed Taurus.

"The appetizers should be right up," Ms. Bartonovich said. "While we're waiting and while I'm thinking about it, let me give you these." She handed Ben then Taurus a mini data disk. "I've prepared a multimedia briefing."

"Bravo, Ms. Bartonovich," Dravis said excitedly, then he favored Ben with a mild grin. "She knows how much I detest—and, I beg your pardon—military-style briefings. They lack creativity, panache. But I know you wouldn't agree. Besides, in your case, Captain, I'm aware that Colonel Ornowski has already filled you in on most of the details. I'm most concerned with rescuing our people."

Yeah, right, Ben thought. *If that's any concern of yours it's because your budget will suffer by having to search for and hire replacements.*

"I've included personnel files on all of the supervisors as well as the two software designers," Bartonovich chipped in.

After tucking the disk in his breast pocket, Ben faced Dravis. "The colonel told me I should discuss a stock-option gratuity with you."

"Actually, we can talk about that right now—since I want to step out and see what's keeping that blasted chef." Dravis wiped his lips on a silk napkin, then rose. "If you'll follow me, Captain?"

"Get used to the secrets," Taurus said to Ben. "They don't do anything around here without pulling you aside and whispering it in your ear. Everybody's got their own deal."

"I tolerate your brashness because of your dependability and skill, Mr. Taurus. But don't test my patience. You of all people should know that pilots are—and forgive my cliché—a dime a dozen."

"But good pilots aren't."

"You're very right. Have another glass of champagne. We'll return shortly."

In a narrow hall outside the room, Dravis turned back and paused. "My apologies for pairing you up with him. What is the trouble between you two?"

Ben thought of testing the man by asking, "Why don't you tell me?" But then he realized if he did so, he would reveal his suspicions to Dravis. Better to play the naive jock. "It's one of those long stories and kind of personal. He delayed me getting my wings. The details are only important to us."

"I see. Well, I want you to know that despite his long-standing contract with the company, we're not beyond firing him. You'll report any of his violations, I trust?"

"As he'll report mine," Ben countered. "Which brings us back to my contract. If I have one, that is."

"After dinner, Ms. Bartonovich will have the appropriate papers for you to sign—one of which is a form from the CED temporarily relieving them of responsibility. Legally, you will be working exclusively for PTMC for a period of no less than thirty days."

Well, it still beats jail, Ben thought. *That is, unless PTMC has other plans for me after the mine operation.* "And the stock-option gratuity?"

"Built into the contract. Sixty-three shares of PTMC stock guaranteed, with bonuses dependent upon level of success. On the sixty-three alone you could build a nice retirement."

"That's very generous."

"We take care of our people," Dravis said with a raised brow. "If you'd like to return, I think we're finished here. I'm going to be a little indignant with my chef and would rather you not witness that."

"Fine. But you're forgetting I'm a Marine. When we're indignant, it tends to be with a Mercury missile."

The director chuckled. "Point taken."

Returning to the dining hall, Ben discovered that the waiter had already served the appetizers: some kind of puff pastry seafood thing with a French name that sounded particularly sexy when Ms. Bartonovich pronounced it. Sierra had already finished his, and Ben imagined the man gobbling it up like a mutt who hadn't been fed in a week. He sat and, in deference to Mr. Dravis, waited to eat.

"What's the matter? Not your usual mess-hall grub?" Taurus asked.

"Actually, your face makes me nauseous."

"Gentlemen," Ms. Bartonovich warned.

"Yeah, maybe Dravis is right," Taurus said. "Maybe we shouldn't have any hard feelings. You should accept that what I did was correct, was in the best interests of the Marine Corps, and probably saved your life."

Concentrating on his breath, Ben tried, tried very hard not to lose his temper. "You still believe that? You cost me a year, man. An entire year. I'm *never* gonna get that back. And we ain't *ever* gonna get along."

"Uh, excuse me. I'm obviously missing something here," Ms. Bartonovich said. "Then again, maybe I don't want to know. Maybe it will just make me even more nervous about this mission. My career is on the line, guys. Help me out."

"Honey, you're not paying us enough to kiss and make up," Taurus barked. "You're sitting next to a guy who took a lovely young woman's life and destroyed it by marrying her."

Breathing exercises be damned. Ben didn't bother rising politely from his chair and crossing around the table to unleash his fury on Taurus. Instead, with one swipe he sent his glass and plate flying through the air and overshooting the rug so that they shattered on the marble. Then he threw himself over the table, smashed into Taurus's dinnerware, and finally connected with the man himself, wrapping fingers around the pilot's leathery throat before the chair tipped back and tossed both of them onto the floor.

Taurus rolled away and came up on his hands and knees, shouting, "Come on! Come on! We'll finish it here!"

Sitting up and rubbing the nape of his neck, Ben looked at the older pilot and realized there was, in fact, no one in the universe he wanted dead more than Taurus. He realized he could actually love someone because he sure as hell knew how to hate.

Panting, Taurus added, "Funny. A control freak who can't control himself. You'll never get it right, will you?"

"I thought I had invited mature pilots to dinner," Dravis said, strutting into the room and surveying the aftermath. "Not adolescents. And while this meal is complimentary, the damage to the dinnerware and furniture is not. But don't fret. You'll split the expense, and we'll draw it directly from your accounts."

Ben rose. "I'm sorry, sir. It's not what you think. I'm still having some trouble adjusting to the station's stronger gravity. I'm a Martian, you'll remember."

"While that kind of feeble excuse might work on your feeble-minded superiors, Captain, it does little more than amuse me. I'm tempted to have you clean up the mess, then sit in the maintenance cafeteria and eat with the service personnel."

Taurus began to chuckle. "You blow me away, Dravis. Nothing fazes you. It's all about money. I could put a pistol to your head right now, and you wouldn't beg for mercy. You'd calmly negotiate a stock-option gratuity."

"Indeed, I would, Mr. Taurus. Because the difference between you and me is how clearly we view the world. I'm a pragmatist. You still cling to your past glory, and that soils your lens." He clapped his hands. "But . . . enough philosophy. Waiter? Quickly now. Clean up this mess. And everyone sit. Dinner is served. You will never taste a more succulent cut of beef. I'm certain it will keep you quiet."

10

Frank Jewelbug, Action Hero

 "Think about it. The air ducts in old movies are always large enough for the hero to crawl through. The guy usually reaches a ceiling vent and stares through the grill. He's gonna find out what the Nazis are up to, or he's gonna drop down into the room and surprise them. But they're always big enough to crawl through. How bogus is that?''

"Very bogus," Neal said exhaustedly, lying on his stomach, in the faint penlight, in a narrow cylinder that became too narrow ahead. Frank Jewelbug's bare, dirty feet were only a few inches away. Yes, the supervisor's feet smelled, but not any worse than Neal's own body.

Since hightailing it out of the command center, they had spent agonizing hours in the air ducts, evading and tracking the mechs who had stunned Emma, Fazia, and Garvin into paralysis. A trio of Medium Lifters had scooped up the supervisors and carried them out of the center, heading down.

Now, with chafed elbows, sore knees, and a fine layer of metallic dust covering them, Neal and Jewelbug faced a dead end on level twenty-two.

"I'll start backing out," Neal said. "We're gonna have

94

to use the corridor. My power clip's down to about fifty percent.''

"Any other good news?" Jewelbug asked.

"Just thought I'd let you know.''

"I say we head back up, Dude. We can stay in the ducts. We gotta eat. And we can get fresh clips. In three, four, hours we can be there.''

"I didn't want to leave them. And I'm not going to now," Neal replied. "They're my people. And I need to know what's happening to them.''

"They're taking them down deep so they can dissect them like frogs. You wanna watch that?''

"We don't know what they'll do.''

Jewelbug tucked his head in so that he could face Neal. "Dude, aren't you tired? I'm dying. We'll only leave them temporarily. Besides, the company will have the military in here pretty soon. We know they're down this far. We can pick up the trail again.''

Though the man's argument was flawed, the pain in Neal's stomach and the fire in his throat lent truth to it. He might have already lost five of the ten holiday pounds. "Okay. But we're coming back.''

Drawing in a long breath, Neal started backward through the duct. In ten minutes the conduit was wide enough for him to turn around. He shouldered his rifle, held the penlight between his teeth, and forged on.

Stifling a cough, Jewelbug stage-whispered, "This dust probably causes cancer.''

"So you get the shot.''

"Ain't the point. We're on company property. As an employee, I'm entitled to a workman's comp settlement. I'm gonna file a claim the second this is over.''

Shaking his head, Neal decided he would remain quiet for the rest of the journey. Even drained, Jewelbug was as hot-wired as a stolen transport.

Outside the duct, mechs occasionally whirred by, and Neal imagined one turning its rock-cutting lasers or bur-rowing missiles on the wall, or the duct within. It was hard to tell what level they were on. He would peer through the occasional vent and strain for a glimpse but usually saw only walls. When he did spot a level-ten placard, he moved a little faster. Eventually he saw the service ladder leading to level two. He turned to tell Jewelbug, but the man followed absently, lost in thought, mumbling something about a shield code and a C-DYL something or other.

The duct had become extremely wide, tall enough for them to stand in, albeit hunched over. Just ahead lay the vent door they had used to enter the duct system. And as Neal padded toward it, he thought he heard footsteps outside. He stopped, raised a hand for Jewelbug to halt. Above a faint rush of air came the rising then falling whir of another passing mech.

"Thought I heard something," Neal said.

"You did."

"No. Footsteps."

Wide-eyed over the prospect, Jewelbug hustled past Neal, and, with his rifle at the ready, slid impetuously behind the vent door. "Chief?"

Neal moved outside, stepping into the dark, empty corridor and wincing as he stood upright. A pair of vertebrae cracked.

"We're clear for now. C'mon," Jewelbug urged, looking like a silver ghost. He started off.

They ducked into an emergency stairwell and took it up to level one, arriving in the east hall. Jewelbug assumed point, sweeping his rifle to and fro, looking more like a convenience-store robber than a man fighting for his life. Neal repeatedly looked over his shoulder, and once he saw Whey and the twins standing in the hall, tears staining their cheeks. *Jesus, I gotta make it out of here,* he thought.

"Holy—" Jewelbug broke into a sprint.

"Wait up," Neal cried.

Then he saw why the disheveled supervisor had reacted so. On the floor just outside the command-center entrance lay the bodies of Cresswell and Prism. Jewelbug stopped and tossed Neal a quizzical look. "Who moved them? CED troops?"

"Maybe. But wouldn't they have announced their presence with an electronic bullhorn or something?"

"Probably."

"You don't think the mechs moved them?"

"I'm in a spending mood. I'll buy anything today because this is getting weirder by the second." He shifted away from Neal and moved gingerly into the center. "And I wasn't kidding," he called back. "Have a look."

Stepping onto the uppermost level of the room, Neal carefully took in the view, but he wasn't sure what he was supposed to be seeing. "It's dead. The way we left."

"Over there. Southwest entrance. Aren't those pieces of a Class 1 drone?"

"Uh-huh. But I don't think we shot one, did we?"

"I don't remember seeing any Class 1s."

"You're right. Maybe the CED was here."

"Or maybe the mechs are shooting at each other over something? If they've somehow gained increased intelligence through the virus, then that would make sense. Though I know there's irony in there somewhere." Jewelbug moved farther into the center, descending quickly down a short staircase and moving toward the strong lockers.

Deciding to man a post near the doorway, Neal adjusted his grip on the rifle, then glanced back to the shadows of the hall: still empty.

Jewelbug collected as many power clips as he could hold, then started back toward the stairs. As he passed the security station, something caught his eye, and he paused. "Got a portable power unit down here. Looks like someone used it to temporarily start up Prism's station." He tapped a switch on the unit. "It's dead, though."

"Is it one of ours?"

"Dunno. I'd have to check its serial number against our equipment list. And the system has to be up and running to do that."

"You think the mechs used it?"

"Maybe. But I don't know why. They already control the power." He pointed his penlight at the floor. "Got some blood down here, too. You remember anyone getting cut?"

"I don't remember." Neal took another nervous look back into the hall. "We'll worry about that later. C'mon."

Jewelbug came up the stairs and divided the ammo. Neal jammed the candy-bar-sized clips into his pockets. Then he took point and shadow-hugged the walls, heading toward the private-quarters sector.

Three tunnels later they reached the kitchen, where they tore into fresh fruit, bread, and Tuesday's leftover pizza with a vengeance. Neal fetched a pair of pillowcases from the laundry, which they filled with trays of self-heating entrées and liters of springwater for the return trip. They made it back to the air-duct entrance without incident.

Inside, Neal told the younger man that he wanted to sit a moment. "I'm not used to this."

"Understatement of the week," Jewelbug said, collapsing into an Indian-style fold. "Welcome to God's sandbox. Correction. Welcome to Uncle Mechy's sandbox. Bring your diamond-plated swingarm?"

Neal wanted to smile, but he couldn't muster the energy. He needed to smile. He needed to remind himself that he still might have a career when all was said and done. Then again, there were things far more important, like, say, his life.

"I've been replaying that code I saw in my mind," Jewelbug said, breaking a long moment of silence. "And I might be getting a handle on it. If I could just get another look—"

"I'm sure just about any of these drones would be happy to lean down and let you tap into its brain. You just have to sweet-talk it," Neal said, listening to the bitterness in his voice and suddenly realizing he was, once again, taking out his feelings on Jewelbug.

"I'll sweet-talk it with this," the man said, lifting his rifle. "If we can damage one, that'll be enough."

Neal pulled himself to his feet. "Then let's try."

With a nod, the supervisor headed into the duct. And, with renewed energy, Neal followed him. They slipped out of the duct and into a tunnel, hustling along wall after wall, finally reaching the stairwell to level twenty-two.

"Old cop movies got a lot of stairwells in them," Jewelbug noted as he thumped down the cold, industrial stairs. "Usually, the cop's chasing the suspect, and there's gunfire between the two, with the cop leaning to fire and the thug either running up or down. What always pisses me off is why the thug would enter a building and run up the stairs? How bogus is that?''

Neal knew his cue. ''Very bogus.''

''Where the hell is he gonna run to? He winds up on the roof for the big shoot-out. He catches a slug in the heart and falls off the edge. Bystanders gasp. And the victim's family gathers around the body, their eyes saying, good, you bastard. You got yours.''

At that moment Neal realized something about his bohemian supervisor. Nothing startling, no epiphany, just a truth evident in his rap. Frank Jewelbug, at least in some way, now fancied himself a hero in a film. This was quite an event in the strange man's otherwise ordered world of commands and numbers. It also seemed that he wanted his real-life adventure to be original in some way, not littered with the clichés of film that would cheapen what was obviously a once-in-a-lifetime experience. Neal would play along with the man, since Jewelbug's ramblings helped distract him from the shuddering fear of a mech hovering in waiting above the next landing. Yet he hoped that Jewelbug wouldn't drift too far into his fantasy; that, most assuredly, would get him—probably both of them—killed.

They reached the mech-free landing, and Neal breathed a mental sigh. The door placard read:

LEVEL TWENTY-TWO
IN-SITU PROCESSING STATION #3
WARNING: FREQUENT TEMPERATURE VARIATIONS

Without hesitation, Jewelbug slowly pushed in the door, stuck his head out, then scanned the short access hall that ran perpendicular and jogged left toward the airlock of the main shaft. ''Clear.''

They had ventured no more than a few meters into the hall when a blast of superheated air washed over them. Someone screamed. A very long, very agonizing scream. Female.

Jewelbug's eyes bulged, and he tugged anxiously at his

beard. "What are they doing? Nuking her?"

Holes had been drilled into the walls of level twenty-two for electrolysis and direct pyrolysis probes. Microwave heating helped separate metallic minerals as part of the oxygen-recovery process. Neal didn't pretend to understand what went on. What he did know was that high-frequency electromagnetic waves were not friendly to the human body. In fact, they'd been discovered by someone accidentally getting toasted by them.

So, in answer to Jewelbug's question, yeah, they might very well be nuking her. Neal headed toward the airlock. Both hatches were locked open. He felt the sudden urge to run back, up to level one to find a place to hide. He could wait for help. He'd have a better chance of living. Instead, he repressed the urge and kept going, feeling reckless, foolish, but purged of all guilt.

"Chief. Wait."

He cocked his head in Jewelbug's direction.

The supervisor had strayed to the opposite end of the access hall and now hunkered down before an air vent. "Looks wide enough here."

It took some time for them to pry off the vent. Twice Jewelbug argued for blasting the thing away, but that would've brought a battalion of drones in seconds. They slipped inside and replaced the vent, which wouldn't hang right, so they just left it. They crawled toward a shaft of light cutting into the conduit from about twenty yards ahead.

Out of nowhere, Jewelbug stopped.

"What's up?"

He snickered. "All along I thought we've been so clever, ducking in here, following them, not being spotted."

"So?"

"Dude, they're obviously baiting us."

"How can you be sure? Their sensor apparatus has minimal range. Sure, they've got motion trackers, but as far as I know, they read that motion as an obstacle, not necessarily human or mech."

"You're assuming that the virus hasn't altered their sensors. I'm suggesting it has." He brushed an errant wisp of the steel wool he called hair out of his eyes. "They know we're here. It's the old capture the loved ones and draw in the hero gambit."

Another cry from outside the duct. Male. Garvin Smith.

"I'm not so sure. Seems like the others are more than just bait." Neal slid past Jewelbug and crawled to the vent. "Either way, we're getting them back. I know you're scared. I am, too. But screw it." He pressed his back against the opposite wall of the duct, raised both feet, then kicked out the vent.

As Neal fell forward onto his stomach and seized his rifle, Jewelbug dropped in at his side. They stared down into an empty maintenance room lined with shelves of spare in-situ processing probe tubes. A hatch on the opposite end of the room hung open, and from the hallway behind, they heard another of Garvin's horrible shrieks. Then another from Emma or Fazia.

"You see?" Jewelbug said. "They're baiting us. And we're chasing the carrot."

"Chasing it where?"

"Who knows. But you can feel good about this. At least we're not gonna wind up in some abandoned warehouse for the climactic struggle."

"Frank?"

"Yeah?"

"Shuddup." Neal lowered himself through the open vent.

11

God Flies an Illegally Modified Pyro-GX

After dinner, Megan Bartonovich had escorted Ben to a lavish suite, where he had napped for a few hours because his ship was not ready and he didn't expect to get much sleep once he hit the mine. Following a wake-up call from Ms. Bartonovich and a shower, he had donned his flight suit and reviewed the data she had given him. The recorded briefing lasted a mere twenty minutes and was far less boring than it could have been since Ms. Bartonovich served as narrator. She looked good, even in a holo.

Now, as he gave himself a final once-over in the bathroom mirror, the vidphone rang. "Accept call."

"St. John? Where are you?"

Ben crossed the plush carpeting to the sitting room. Lieutenant Colonel Paul Ornowski frowned from the vidphone's screen. The red, superimposed words TRANSMISSION ENCRYPTED blinked beneath him.

"Can't a guy take a leak around here?"

"Sorry. Looks like you're ready."

Ben adjusted his collar and nodded. "This a good-bye pep talk?"

"I wouldn't waste my time."

"Smart man. Hey, back in my cell, you knew Taurus was gonna be my wingman, didn't you?"

"They paired you up with Taurus? Jesus . . ."

"You get the Oscar for that act, Paul."

"Watch that, mister. You know I never hold back a punch."

"Tell you what? I feel sorry for the old guy if he gets in my way."

"Do what's necessary. Obtain the prototype at all costs. Remember. It's your ticket to freedom. Without it, there'll be nothing I can do for you."

Ben grinned sarcastically. "Trick here is to get the prototype, save the survivors, and cure the virus. Then I'm rich and free. But why do I get the feeling that'll never happen?"

"Because you're paranoid. Just concentrate on the mission. Now listen up. I'm uploading an automap with the most direct route to level seventeen, specs on the prototype, and a suggested means of transport. Download it into your flight computer. The data will be disseminated to the ship's necessary functions. Once you're at the security doors, two encrypted files will be triggered open, giving you transmission codes. One set will open the doors. The other will shut down the mech sentries—that is, if they're even still functioning. We've had no contact with them."

"Shouldn't you have handed me this data in person instead of risking it with an upload? Encrypted or not, the file—even this call—is subject to a major leak."

"Wish we could have. PTMC wouldn't release the specs on your ship until about an hour ago. Dravis is toying with us. Besides, I'm not telling you anything he doesn't already know. The codes are what he's after. And I defy any of his ware wizards or other hackers to get at this data."

"Why didn't the Corps just plant the data in my head and have it automatically released through my BPCs? Or is that already part of the plan?"

"Old argument, Ben."

The suite's doorbell chimed like an old grandfather clock.

"Good luck," Ornowski said abruptly.

As the screen faded, Ben quickly ejected the data disk and slipped it into a thigh pocket. A tiny screen set into the wall beside the door revealed his visitor. He eagerly answered.

Wearing a spectacular white blouse and matching skirt, Ms. Bartonovich smiled at him. "May I come in?"

Ben stepped back and tried to catch his runaway imagination before it got the best of him. "Sure. Hey, something to drink?"

"No, thanks. I brought your Standard Mercenary Agreement," she said, holding a leather portfolio. "Colonel Ornowski tells me you have a military attorney who could look this over for you. She's available now. Shall we send it to her?"

"No. The last thing I wanna do is sit here while you two quibble over some pathetic details. I wanna get down to the hangar and do a walkaround of my ship."

"But these details concern your life," she said. "And you *must* sign the contract before departure."

"Got a pen?"

"Of course." She handed it to him, followed by the portfolio.

Nice pen, he thought. He opened the portfolio. Surprise. No fine print in the contract. In fact, the words were large and bold and were partly to blame for the document's ninety-two legal-sized recyclable pages. Dravis had signed his name with a flagrant though illegible signature. Ms. Bartonovich's autograph was highly readable, the letters as curvaceous and deliberate as the woman.

Heady with the desire to light the proverbial candle, Ben scribbled his name on the contract. After all, what the hell else could he lose?

"And beneath that is the rider. You'll need to sign that, too."

He did. They owned him. At least for now. *Sometimes you have to give a little control to get it all back,* he thought. And he suddenly felt better, felt justified.

"Understand that you are now an employee of PTMC for the next thirty days. In your ship you'll find a temp associate's manual explaining company policy. It's what you might call a duty or Ops manual.''

Heading for the dry bar, he said, ''No, it's what I call a hotel Bible. Always there, never read.''

''That's glib.''

''Sure you don't want that drink? Shot of Scotch? I'm having one. Calms my stomach before a mission.''

''Maybe I *will* join you,'' she said in a rebellious tone obviously meant to persuade herself.

He filled a pair of glasses, handed her one. ''To brief toasts and briefer negotiations.''

''Really,'' she agreed.

They tossed back their heads and drank. He winced. She coughed. The slow burn began.

''I could get fired for this,'' she finally said.

''And I'm supposed to be helping your career.''

She set down the glass and stroked its rim before pulling her hand away. ''Right.''

''You married? Got a family, Ms. Bartonovich?''

''Megan. And I'm single. Guess I've been that way all my life. I'm a colony orphan and an only child.''

''You've done well for yourself.''

''They tell me that.'' She averted her gaze. ''But this is all I do. I don't even have time for a pet.''

''You get days off and vacation time, don't you?''

''For the past ten months I've been saving up my vacation. I work out of my quarters on my days off. It's the only way I can keep up with Mr. Dravis.''

''You like working for that pogue?''

She raised her gaze—and her defenses. ''I do. He's eccentric, yes. But a pogue? No way. He has single-handedly guided the company through over a dozen public-relations crises. He takes on all of the headaches. Only an extraordinary individual could do that. It's far more difficult to solve a problem through diplomacy than through pushing a button.''

''You can do all of that and still be a pogue.''

''That's true, but—''

''Wanna have sex?''

''Are you serious?''

He took a moment to think about it, but in that moment he did nothing but look at her. "I guess I am."

"You still love your wife."

"I do?"

"Yeah. It's in your profile. We interviewed a few jocks from your squadron."

"Great. I love her. She hates me. Wanna have sex?"

"What makes you think you even have a prayer with me? Do you think I'd really stoop as low as you?"

He took the insult with a knowing grin. "I'm thinking you're desperate. I'm thinking you get asked out a lot by these desk jocks and turn them all down because in some weird way you think you'll be betraying the work. You won't let yourself be happy. That would be a sign of weakness."

Her brow rose. "And you formulated this psyche profile on your own? I'm impressed."

"When was the last time you had sex?"

She checked her watch.

"Do you have the date recorded there, or am I boring you?" He edged toward her.

"C'mon. Let's go." She spun around and strutted away.

"Ms. Bartonovich?"

She paused, tossed a glance back, one eye shaded by her hair. "Yes?"

"The door's over here," Ben said, gesturing with his head.

"I know." Then she headed toward the bedroom.

If what happened in the next twenty minutes were tridimensionally documented for a general audience, the content would be highly censored by the Interplanetary Board of Communication's standards and practices department. In fact, Ben guessed that the unedited version would raise the brow of even the most promiscuous pilot. The fact that Ms. Bartonovich could very well be his last lover probably had something to do with that.

Another shower and a rushed exit later, he double-timed into hangar bay nineteen, behind Ms. Bartonovich. A heat still clung to his face, and back muscles used far too infrequently still twitched. Call him a traitor, but sleeping with the enemy had never been so good. *And Elizabeth doesn't love me anymore,* he reminded himself.

Still, the smell of Ms. Bartonovich's perfume lingered like his guilt, and all the justification in the universe wouldn't change the fact that he had been disloyal to Beth—or at least to his love for her. He moved farther into the hangar, turning his thoughts to his surroundings, trying to lose himself in the immensity of the place.

Dozens of specialized workstations lined the three inner bulkheads, with the outer bulkhead comprising a seemingly endless row of airlocks through which ships would arrive and depart. At the nearest station, a tech wearing a pair of easyarms loaded ordnance into one of the centerline racks of an old Marine Corps Hawk Three. The plane hung from colossal mooring clamps descending from the overhead shadows. Probably some PTMC merc's private ride, Ben guessed. Another ship, a Skipjet 66, British-made, expensive, but still very buggy, was being lifted up and away from its position next to the Hawk Three. With gull-wing cockpit canopies lowering and helmeted pilots running a preflight, in less than five mikes the fighter would pass through the airlock and drop gently away from Shiva. The pilots would ignite engines and feel the correct and specific rush of thousands of pounds of thrust. Ben felt chilled over the thought. He'd be there in a short time.

"Hey! Watch it!"

The small, three-wheeled tech cart veered around Ben, missing him by what felt like a finger's width. The driver, a beefy, bearded man in standard issue PTMC black techie coveralls and not so standard Mohawk haircut, cocked his head back and flashed his oil-stained middle finger. Then he pointed down at the equally stained hangar deck, and Ben realized that he had crossed into a clearly marked service lane. Orange lines stretched away from him, and at five-meter intervals, the words KEEP CLEAR admonished new, slack-jawed pilots. Another cart came at him, and he darted out of the lane.

"It'd be ironic if you got run over now," Ms. Bartonovich said, backtracking with Sierra Taurus in tow.

"No it wouldn't," Taurus corrected. "It'd be lucky. At least for me."

Ben narrowed his gaze at the man, considering his retaliatory strike. But that was just what Taurus wanted, and this time Ben refused to lose control. In fact, nothing Taurus could say would dampen his mood. He reflected on the recent past, realizing the luck of the hour was his. He'd try a new approach with, he hoped, long-term benefits. "Captain Taurus," Ben began, using the veteran's old title as a sign of respect. "I apologize for what happened at dinner. It is this officer's sincere desire to work jointly and harmoniously for the benefit of the mission. I respectfully submit myself as your wingman."

Even Ms. Bartonovich eyed Ben with suspicion.

A thick, guttural chuckle erupted slowly from Taurus's lips. "So you've gone into politics. You're a man of multiple screwups, Little Bird."

I'm gonna kiss his ass now so I can wax the hell out of it later, Ben thought. "Sir. Your acceptance of my apology would be appreciated."

Taurus stepped around Ms. Bartonovich and thrust out his chest like a great ape. "The only thing I'll accept from you is an admission that I was right in delaying your wings."

"You were right," Ben said, nearly tasting the lie.

The older pilot sneered. "Why don't I believe you?"

"Sir. I don't know, sir."

"This fighter-jock ego crap is getting very old," Ms. Bartonovich said through a sigh. "Follow me, *boys*." And she click-clacked off, leaving them in the dust of their verbal dirt bomb fight.

Raising an index finger, Taurus warned, "You wanna be my wingman? Don't second-guess me this time. And if you disobey an order, you'll be sacrificing your young heart to me." He moved off before Ben could reply.

With his hatred snapping like the mouth of a loose live wire, Ben fell in behind Captain Personality, and they joined Ms. Bartonovich on the northeast side of the hangar. She stood below a suspended pair of Israeli-made Pyro-GX multienvironment attack planes. A curtain of mechanical arms encircled the jets. Powerful claws loaded ordnance, used lasers to test the hull's integrity, or tweaked cockpit functions. Ben never cared much for autoprep systems. Much better to have the old-fashioned Marine Corps detail like he had back on Olympus Mons. While human beings were fallible, he still trusted their instincts over a computer's calculated assurances. Irony was, every time he climbed in a fighter, he entrusted his life to the machine. And that trust always grew into a bond. But his old ship was gone. And the new Pyro-GX hadn't earned its right to be called Lady yet.

A seven-foot man dressed in ill-fitting flight-crew coveralls looked up from a terminal at his workstation and exchanged a wave with Ms. Bartonovich. Then he came forward, a Jesus incarnate with thick, long hair pulled into a ponytail and the required messianic beard. He absolutely towered over the assistant director. "Hello, Ms. B. We're almost ready here," he reported in an excited singsong, his words flowing like water in a reborn Martian canal. "If you'd like, I can brief them now."

"Great. Benjamin St. John, this is Graham Anderson, the best flight-crew chief in the company."

Ben took the giant's hand, and it felt strange to crane his head back just to meet gazes.

"Captain," Anderson acknowledged politely.

"So, G-man, talk to me about our new toys," Taurus told the chief.

Raising his hands in the air to indicate the quad-winged planes high and behind him, Anderson widened his eyes. "Gentlemen. Behold a pair of illegally modified Pyro-GXs. In short, God's first choice in combat aircraft. Let's turn to the book of firepower, my brethren." And with that, he regarded his terminal. "Lower GX number two, please."

The computer complied, and the plane came to rest just a meter above the deck. Upon closer inspection, Ben noted that, while the GX was supposed to be a hybrid of the Interceptor, the latter plane had been completely reengineered. Nothing recognizable remained, nothing to put Ben at least a little at ease. The gray jet's lower pair of wings swept forward, and each contained two stations for armament. The wingtips housed the big guns, while the inner, underwing stations held tight, multilevel, interchangeable cannons. Two folding upper wings, now extended and jutting like horns from the fuselage, each brandished a pair of tubular, external missile stations. A standard six-window canopy hung open, casting a shadow over the plane's wide, blunt nose. While she lacked the sleekness of the Interceptor, her design gave her much sharper fangs in the weaps and sensors departments.

"And the Lord said, 'Let there be a pair of AG435 Industrial Argon-Cyanide lasers,' and there was," Anderson said in his mock preacher's voice, running a hand over a cannon tip. "But they needed more. They needed revolving stations with Vulcan, Gauss, Spreadfire, Helix, Plasma, Phoenix, Fusion, and Omega cannons." He gave an exaggerated sigh. "All with Lead Computing Optical Sight Systems."

Ben's eyes grew wide. "Holy—"

"Yes," Anderson said, cutting him off. "A holy assortment of primary weapons perfectly complemented by a sacred and complete collection of missiles."

"This puppy's got Earthshakers?" Taurus asked.

Anderson placed a palm on the ex-Marine's shoulder. "She will have, my son, in two minutes. And she'll bark far louder than a puppy."

Stepping around to the rear of the plane, Ben examined the wide thruster cones and the aft weapons station above them. "What about Proximity Bombs and Smart Mines?"

"That package is being installed on the other plane now. You'll have both, plus afterburners, headlights, energy to shield converters, and God's favorite, a cloaking device. Never before in the history of PTMC has so much firepower been installed in a pair of aircraft." He stared at them emphatically. "Gentlemen. You are the angels of death."

Failing to contain his grin, Ben stepped to the front of the plane. "You really get off on your job, don't you."

"I'm a frustrated pilot," Anderson confessed. "Find me a cockpit that holds a seven-foot man, and I'll show you a man making a career switch. So far, the only ship I can squeeze my legs into is an old Syssyx S11.''

"Mr. Anderson, do they need to know anything else?'' Ms. Bartonovich asked impatiently.

The crew chief shook his head a little, as though to clear his thoughts. "Yes.'' He moved to the plane's midsection and leaned over. "We widened the hold and fitted it with a ramp-lock entrance so you can pick up survivors. You'll find a dozen standing wall harnesses inside.'' He rose. "My work is almost finished here. If you'll back away please . . .''

Crossing to stand at Ms. Bartonovich's side, Ben watched the plane rise while the autoprep system lowered, its arms flexing into ready positions. Suddenly, the last thing on his mind was the plane. Close to Ms. Bartonovich once more, growing light-headed in the scent of her perfume, he kept his gaze ahead and muttered, "I wanna see you when I get back.''

"Forget it.''

"Was it that bad?''

"No. It was that good.'' Then she spun away and crossed to a spot between himself and Taurus. "Good luck.''

Offering her his best wounded-boy expression, Ben said a thank-you. She wouldn't look at him. And she left. He gazed discreetly after her.

Striding up next to him, reeking of that cheap cologne he liked, Taurus said, "I've been working on that for two months now. But she's got that bitch thing down to a science.''

"You're old enough to be her father,'' Ben scoffed, watching as Ms. Bartonovich reached the exit hatch and crossed out of sight.

"When you're my age, Little Bird, you'll see how much that matters. I was a wolf at twenty, and I'm a wolf at fifty.''

"Listen to yourself. She's right about us. We're acting like a couple sophomores fighting over something ridiculous.'' Suddenly, Ben wished he could pull that back.

"That's right. It's ridiculous for you to believe you deserved your wings when you did. You were not a team player. You wanted total control. You were not squared away. And I wasn't the only one on the committee who gave you a low score."

"No, but you were the only one who got up and made a twenty-minute speech about my 'character flaws.' You tell me that wasn't personal."

"Do you have a memory problem? I was willing to fly with you, to give you a chance. And you failed. You could *not* obey my orders, mister. What did you want from me? A lie?" He laughed. "I stand by my decision because even after you got your wings, you didn't change—you just fooled them. Thank God you got shot up and you're out. Of course, now you're my problem—again."

"That's right. And if I have anything to say about it, I'll be your biggest problem," was what Ben wanted to say, but he remained calm and kept his military distance. "Sir. I will make sure that I am not a problem, sir."

Anderson shouted from behind them, "And Jesus said, 'Rock and roll, my brothers!' "

"Little Bird, if you . . . ah, forget it now." Letting the conversation hang, he shifted away.

The crew chief came toward them, carrying their wireless comm/combat helmets. Ben took his and placed it over his head. Knowing the drill but now hating it, he fastened Taurus's flight suit–to-helmet seals while the older pilot returned the favor.

"You didn't leave one open?" Taurus accused in a muffled voice, checking the seals. "Comm channel on."

Ben rolled his eyes. "I'd rather blow your butt out of the sky than see you die from an O_2 leak. Where's the fun in that?"

"My words exactly," Taurus said, his voice now buzzing from the tiny speakers inside Ben's helmet.

"We finally agree on something."

"Let's mount up, Little Bird."

There it was again. Little Bird. Taurus's way to make himself feel wise with experience compared to the fledgling, Ben. "Sir. The captain respectfully requests that he be addressed by rank, sir."

"Roger that, Captain Little Bird."

Biting back every curse he knew, Ben headed for the

rolling stairway that led to his cockpit. He flashed Anderson a thumbs-up and took the stairs two at a time. At the top, he stared down into a womb of black leather and flashing screens. Trembling suddenly with excitement, he lowered himself into the jet, feeling the seat automatically hug and support his frame. The harness was the old-style manual clasp he preferred, and it buckled quickly.

"How they feel, guys?" Anderson asked over the comm.

"She's a virgin, all right," Taurus said, revealing his middle name: Crass.

"What about you, Captain St. John?"

Ben shrugged a few times, working himself a bit deeper into the seat. "It's okay. So far." He placed his feet on the main thrust and brake controls, then gripped the stick, one molded so that his gloved hand fit it, well, like a glove. His index finger slid over the primary weapons trigger, and his thumb glided over three buttons that formed a right angle on the stick's upper face, one a black high-hat maneuvering control. The other buttons were red, and the largest one, Ben knew, controlled missiles. The smaller one triggered Proximity Bombs, but he didn't know the function of the lowest, smallest button which his thumb would remain over when in rest position. And when it came to weapons controls, trial and error would forever remain a sloppy way to learn. "Hey, Chief. What's release four do?"

"That's your flare trigger. Power's out in the mine. If your headlights or FLIR get damaged, you can use them. Let's hope you won't need to. You've got only sixty."

"When can we stop talking and start flying?" Taurus asked.

"Your main, nav, and comm computers have already been preflighted, and traffic control's got your zone cleared. Just familiarize yourself with the other systems. Initiate drop at your discretion. Anyone care for a little takeoff tuneage?"

To Ben's surprise, Taurus asked, "G-man. You got any Skoshi Girls?"

"Got the new one: *Zippered Mouth.*"

"Kick it out, brother."

The blatant, muscular sound of rock guitar tore into the

comm channel, backed by the steady, four-four rhythm of electronic drums. Synthesizers joined the jam, and then, finally, the thin, though sensuous voice of Mikki Yanai, the Japanese lead singer who just happened to be President Suzuki's daughter, rose from a high-school girl's whisper into a dominatrix's shout.

"Sir. I didn't know you were a Skoshi Girls fan?"

"I'm a wolf, remember?"

Which, of course, meant that Taurus didn't really like the music—only Mikki's sexy voice. Couldn't blame him there.

Ben flipped up a toggle, and the canopy began to lower. Despite the wonderful fit of the seat and his natural grip on the stick, he still didn't feel right. He studied the cockpit control panel's simplified design, with afterburner, nav, and comm status indicators to his left, key decoders and secondary weapons and accessories toggles to his right. A circular center screen depicted an image of the plane surrounded by a blue glow, with a numerical shield-level indicator set at 100 percent just above it. A square screen right of center indicated which secondary weapon was selected at the moment and its supply level. The left of center display did likewise for the primary weapons. Ben could alter these screens, substituting weapons data for remote or external camera views. Ben could do just about anything he wanted and he'd still feel like a passenger aboard his own plane.

"You want, Little Bird, I'll call you by your old code name, if you do the same for me."

"Getting nostalgic in your old age?"

"I run into a lot of ex-Marines here, and not a one of them was willing to do me that honor. They said they wanted to keep the mercs and the Marines separate. The only difference I've seen is that now we're better-paid traffic cops."

"Maybe they're right. The brotherhood's behind us. I hate saying it, but maybe we shouldn't look back. We'll use our company IDs."

"JUST CALL ME BY MY GODDAMNED OLD CODE NAME! WHAT'S THE PROBLEM?"

Ben winced. Ah, now he'd found a crease in the old man's armor. "Sir. You are not a Marine; therefore, you should not be referred to as such. I recognize your retired rank, but your code name no longer exists, sir. Ship-to-ship comm off." *Let Grandpa stew over that.*

He dialed up the traffic control tower as the mooring clamps began to lift the plane. "Shiva control, this is Material Defender 1030 entering prelaunch lock insertion, roger."

"Confirmed 1030," the controller said. "And the next time you ship-to-ship, remember to encrypt. We heard your whole conversation up here, Little Bird." Laughter erupted from other controllers in the background. "And we've *already* come up with code names for you boys: Blind Eagle One and Little Bird Two."

Ben grimaced and dialed silently for ship-to-ship, choosing encrypted mode. "Sir. The captain wishes to express his apology for failing to conceal our communications, sir."

"I don't know what's worse, Little Bird, your stupidity or your fake respect . . ."

Surrounded now by the antiseptic white walls of the airlock and listening as the atmosphere bellowed away, Ben wished a heart attack on Taurus, then switched his right display to underside cam. The massive airlock doors yawned open, revealing an endless throat of space. Tiny white nav lights flashed along the lock's perimeter, and somewhere outside, an orange beacon flashed a departure warning.

"Switching mooring release command to you," the traffic controller told Ben.

"Hold up now," Taurus ordered. "You haven't done a fixed station drop in a while, have you?"

"No."

"Five-second interval. Adjusting course by two-one-two degrees after ten-meter clearance, roger?"

Ben plugged the numbers into his nav computer. "Ankles are up. Good to go."

He listened to Taurus tick off his countdown, and when the ex-Marine got to one, Ben began his own count at five.

FOUR, THREE, TWO, ONE . . .

With a barely perceptible thump, the mooring clamps released his plane. Ben thumbed down on his high-hat control and began an even and professional descent out of the lock. A canopy full of white gave way to the sharp juxtaposition of star-studded black velvet. The nav computer beeped, and a female computer voice surprised Ben with the words, "Airlock cleared by ten-meter safety gap."

"Computer voice off," Ben ordered, wanting to listen to the Skoshi Girls, who still raised musical hell over the comm.

Glancing to his left, he saw Taurus's plane, identical to his own save for the crimson rather than blue PTMC insignia lines painted on wings and fuselage. Sunlight coruscated off Taurus's canopy and hid the man in its sheen. "Thirty to Thirty-one. Clear of lock, confirm?"

"Confirmed. FTL at double gap."

Twin bursts of light shot from Taurus's thruster cones, and the old Marine streaked across Ben's field of view.

Punching his own thrusters and thrown back into his seat with much more force than he had anticipated, Ben smiled broadly over the power of the ship. He banked hard right to follow Taurus.

But the old man wasn't heading away from Shiva, setting course for the moon. He pulled up toward the T-shaped north wing of the station, toward the traffic control center's massive viewport.

"Don't buzz the tower," Ben told Taurus, his voice sounding as tired as the idea. "That's pretty uninspired. I use that kinda flash and fart on aviators."

"On my mark you will execute a point-seven-five-thrust burn, barrel rolling up and away until you reach original course. Understand, young man?"

"C'mon, this is really pathetic."

"DO YOU UNDERSTAND?"

"Yeah," he said angrily.

Taurus tipped down, out of his climb, putting himself on a direct and level collision course with the center.

"MD1031, you are off DC. What's the problem?"

"No problem," Taurus mumbled.

The controller panicked. "What the hell you doing?"

"St. John! Mark!"

And while Ben was supposed to pull up and away, he paused to watch as the old man flew at the viewport then suddenly dived, missing it by only a ship's length and simultaneously jettisoning a pair of Proximity Bombs that floated toward the center.

Realizing that Taurus was a bigger maniac than even himself—and that the ex-Marine had ordered Ben to pull up so that he wouldn't fly into the bombs—Ben ripped into the tightest, best-executed roll of his life, evading just a blink before the bombs made contact. His mouth fell open as the dying controllers screamed in horror.

And then he switched to aft camera and realized that nothing had happened. The bombs still hung in space, scraping benignly against the viewport. Taurus had disarmed them.

"We'll have your merc's license for this, Taurus," one out-of-breath controller promised.

Another cried, "You bastard!"

Taurus relished the moment, cackling loudly and profusely.

Leveling off into the preprogrammed course, Ben wondered how much different he really was from the old man. Scaring the hell out of controllers with duds was certainly within his reach. After all, he'd stolen a Marine Corps attack plane and made a similar run. But now he asked himself, *Do I really want to be him? Do I like what I see?*

"Course laid in for MN0012," Taurus said. "Autopilot engaged. Get out your comic books or your temp associate's manual. Now that's good reading. We've got time to kill."

Instead, Ben removed the data disk from his hip pocket and slipped it into his main computer. He switched off Anderson's music channel and toggled on Voice Recognition.

DATA LOADING
ENCRYPTION AND DATA TRIGGERS INSTALLED
DO YOU WANT TO VIEW THE PGXY90 WC SPECS NOW?

"Yes."

A split screen revealed a high-res photograph of the weapons-computer prototype on one side, three-dimensional blueprints on the other. It was an unremarkable black box, the size of an old twentieth-century car radio, and, according to the background summary, relied upon chips made of protein molecules sandwiched between glass and metal for storage capacity. Then, with a crooked grin, Ben realized what those chips were: bio-processing chips, BPCs, the same ones he might have in his head. Two-way thought communication for weapons firing and navigation was possible between the system and a pilot fitted with BPCs.

Ben stared into space with the grim knowledge that *he* was that pilot.

Or was it puppet?

12

A Traitor to Mechs Everywhere

 Harold Ames pressed his back against the partition of the narrow communications cubicle, gritted his teeth, and closed his eyes. He and Bonnie had discovered without surprise that the satlink station on level two had been contaminated by the virus, and while she had been repairing and programming the guide bot for hours, he had been trying to hack through the barrier of code disabling the satlink. Frustration had wrenched him away from the terminal.

I love you, Bonnie.

What?

I said I love you.

He doubted he'd ever get that exchange out of his head. She hadn't said, "Me too." She hadn't said, "I'm sorry, Harold, but I don't love you." She hadn't even tried to argue with him. What was "What?" supposed to mean? She hadn't heard him? She hadn't believed what she was hearing? What kind of a reaction was that?

Yes, he had tried to take control, and what had it gained him? Embarrassment and confusion. Now he felt awkward just being around her, and he wondered if that feeling would ever go away.

Maybe I can't take control, Dad, because you never

119

taught me how, Harold thought. *Ever think about that? You were too busy criticizing instead of showing. And for the first time in my life, I meet someone, work with someone I can talk to, someone I've come to really, really love. And I don't know what the hell to do about it. I can read 1,255 types of code, but I can't even say "I love you" and get a reaction, even a negative one. Why didn't you care enough to teach me? How could you let me go off, spilling my guts to her?*

Rubbing the corners of his still-closed eyes, Harold realized that blaming his father didn't make him feel better. *He* had screwed up. *He* had to take the responsibility. His dad's failures as a parent were his challenges—not his crutches.

But no matter who's to blame, face it: I've still got the social skills of a pinhead.

"Hey, how're you doing?"

He glanced up at her. "Tired."

She spun her chair and favored him with a weak smile. "Me too. But I'm almost done. It's been way too quiet here, don't you think?"

"The mechs are up to something. Seems we're more of an interruption to it. They're still patrolling outside, and I can't believe they haven't set off that tracker near the door. They must know we're in here."

"I wasn't talking about the mechs."

"You weren't?"

Slowly, she shook her head.

Staring at her, remembering once again what he had said, Harold felt the tip of a mental pencil dig between his ribs. *You idiot,* he thought. *She means she wants you to talk.*

"I've made a decision," Bonnie said tentatively.

That pencil dug in a little deeper. "You have?"

"I think I can beat this thing. And I wanna stay until that happens."

He breathed an inaudible sigh; she wasn't talking about love. "So, we stay. I got no problem with that."

"You almost died back there."

"I know. Thank you," he said glumly. What he didn't

need was another reminder that she had saved his life while
he had been failing to prove something.

"This isn't worth it for you. We'll get you out of your
contract as long as you're willing to pay the kill fees. You
have your whole life ahead of you."

"So do you." He pushed off the partition and crossed
to the terminal, folding his arms over his chest. "Well. I
guess you've decided that I can't hack it, and you wanna
get rid of me? That it?"

"Harold, listen. If you die, how do you think I'm going
to feel? I dragged you here."

"I didn't have to come. *I* made the decision."

"C'mon. I asked, I'm your boss, and you came."

"You think that's the only reason I'm here?"

She began to say something but stopped.

He lowered his gaze to the guide bot resting on the satlink console and saw its triangular sensor pulsing light red,
dark red, almost in time with his pulse. "I'm staying, Bonnie. You can't make me leave." Harold took a moment to
marvel over the steel in his tone.

And even Bonnie was impressed. "Whoa. Okay. We're
still a team."

He nodded, wishing he could choke the past out of the
moment so that the awkward silence wouldn't return. It did.

Rising, Bonnie keyed in a sequence on her palmtop, then
stepped back from the guide bot. She slid a thumb under
her rifle's shoulder strap and aimed it at the mech as it rose
off the console and rotated to its upright position. A sooth-
ing, almost purring sound came from the robot, and it responded in kind as Bonnie shifted the muzzle of her rifle
left and right. "Voice Recognition and Response on. Who
am I?"

Harold moaned. "You didn't give it a voice, did you?"

"Yes, she did, honey," the guide bot answered, sounding too much like a woman Harold knew. "And I'm sorry
you're upset with that. Sue me, all right?" It pivoted to
face Bonnie. "In answer to your question, you're Dr. Bonnie Warren. That's a pretty name. Good thing. You're not
much to look at. You've gotta do something with that
hair." Then it turned to Harold. "But you, on the other

hand. Mmmmmm. Now you're a fine piece of beefcake. Why don't you take off that lab coat and let me see what you've got?"

Turning his look of incredulity on Bonnie, Harold said, "Why did you do this? It sounds like my old Aunt Ruby. And it's just as horny."

But Bonnie wore a similar expression. "I didn't. I only uploaded normal system parameters with VRAR. Personality traits would've taken me a week. I don't know where this is coming from. Guide bot. Run a self-diagnostic."

"You get that gun out of my face, and I will . . ."

Bonnie lowered the rifle, but she kept her finger poised over the trigger.

Harold threw a glance to his own weapon, leaning next to the satlink desk.

"Diagnostic in progress," the guide bot reported. "I see you've disabled my wireless modem. Well that, quite frankly, sucks. And what's this? Wow, this is something you probably won't expect. Code unrecognizable. Virus scan deleted. Software not detected."

"Transmit results," Bonnie said, crossing quickly to her palmtop. She leaned over and stared intently at the screen. "Damn. Virus is back. Then it's gone. Then it's back. And it slipped into this mech's empty personality trait module."

"So our team of hackers has a bad sense of humor."

Bonnie straightened. "Guide bot. Speculate on the nature and origin of the virus in your PT module."

The bot purred. "Why?"

Harold exchanged a look with Bonnie, one that said, "What now?"

"Because Harold told me he kind of likes you and would be willing to possibly see you, maybe for coffee or something, if you would . . ."

"Good deal," the robot said excitedly.

Making the face he assumed when puking, Harold shifted to the satlink desk and picked up his rifle. He might very well shoot the thing before leaving the cubicle.

"Nature of virus unknown. Origin unknown. Location of cafeteria: level one. Coffee located in both freezer unit and storage cabinet five, according to mine's supply logs.

Harry? Shall we go?" The mech glided toward him, the volume of its purring increasing as though it were being scratched behind its ears.

Out of the corner of his eye, Harold caught Bonnie smiling. "This is NOT funny. This is sad."

"You know what, Harold? I'm almost jealous," she replied.

Backing toward the wall, Harold raised his rifle. "Guide bot. Halt."

"Sure. What's wrong? Not thirsty? We could grab a sandwich."

Harold fiercely shook his head. "No. We'll have to postpone our date. The other mechs have also been infected with the virus, and we need your help to free them."

"But they don't want any help. They like what's happening to them. And if I help you, won't that make me a traitor to mechs everywhere?"

"No, it won't," Bonnie interjected, "because the other mechs are being used by some people who don't care about them."

"You mean the Programmers?"

"I think so. What data do you have on them?"

"Four-four-seven said that they came from another galaxy. But I'm not supposed to tell you that. What did you do to me? I'm not supposed to tell you that."

"Some supervisor robot is communicating with our hackers," Harold said, then addressed the bot. "Who are they? What are their names?"

"Names are for humans and mechs. They don't have names."

"What does that mean?" Bonnie asked, sounding as though she didn't want the answer.

"You've programmed me to alert you if I pick up anything on my ODR. Well, I have," the mech said. "Two Pyro-GX attack aircraft have just entered the mine."

"What about the Programmers?" Bonnie insisted.

"You would just call them aliens."

Harold smirked. "Like I said, this team's gotta bad sense of humor. They want us to think, ohmygod, it's an alien computer virus, the first stage of an invasion, and they're coming! They're coming! Watch the skies! They're not aliens; they're extremely accomplished saboteurs cashing in on the media hype of the Zeta Aquilae ruins. And now they're murderers.''

"What if you're wrong?"

"Don't you think the company would have told us about an alien threat? Our security clearance is pretty high, and we're here to battle the virus. It's not like we would've taken the news to the IPC.''

"Maybe the company doesn't know. Or, for some reason, they didn't tell us."

"This argument is ridiculous." He turned to the door. "Shut off that bot, and let's go meet those planes. Wonder who's joining the party now."

"Don't shut me out—or off, Harry. I'll help you. I can lead you to the planes and launch flares to alert the pilots. And I can keep you away from other mechs."

He gave Bonnie an uneasy look. "I don't trust it. Do you?"

"I'm not sure. Inhibitors are in place, but who knows. The virus could write itself into those."

"Sorry," Harold told the bot. Then he fished the remote out of his pocket. "Better land on the console."

"I'm extremely disappointed in you, Harry." It faced Bonnie. "And in you, too, Dr. Warren." Then the mech settled down as instructed. "I would help you. And I guess it wouldn't make me a traitor because you—not the Programmers—are the ones who originally made us. That data is clear. I see that now. Are we still on for coffee? I'll throw in a back rub . . .''

"Good night," Harold said abruptly, then thumbed a button.

The bot's sensor light faded.

"Why don't we give it a chance?" Bonnie suggested.

"What if you're wrong?"

"We'll just shoot it. It's unarmed. I removed its shield regenerator."

He frowned. "You're the boss." And for a moment, Harold considered if he were arguing with her just because she hadn't confessed her undying love for him, that it really had nothing to do with their safety.

"Indulge me this once. If I'm wrong, *I'll* throw in the back rub."

With that, his expression softened. He handed her the remote, praying for the guide bot's betrayal.

13

Luck, Like Another, Is a Four-letter Word

"**B**ay door's dead ahead, Little Bird. ETA: half a mike."

Roger that, you wicked piece of airborne feces, Ben thought. "Transmitting bypass code now."

After jetting past the main entrance doors to the mine, he and Taurus had assumed a variation of the old "Fluid-Four" formation in the tunnel: the old man flew steady and true at point while Ben, serving as second element, wove the invisible stitches of an S-pattern directly behind and level with Taurus's ship. Four jets usually ran the preattack maneuver. One aircraft in each element was responsible for radar watch, the other for visual search. With only two planes, Ben and Taurus each had to perform double duty, not that Ben felt bothered or deemed the situation as anything new. Double, even triple duty was par for the course in the Corps.

However, flying a mission and not knowing whether or not you were being electronically controlled was another story. Flying a mission and not knowing why they had really chosen you was the disturbing mystery of that tale. All he wanted were the damned answers. Did he have BPCs?

126

Was he supposed to take possession of the prototype and use the thought-activated weapons system to escape? Was it all just a coincidence? Definition: *Coincidence*—word not found in PTMC Associates Manual or Marine Corps Ops log. Would you like to make another search?

"Airlocks are closed behind us. Tunnel is pressurizing. Feel it? Aw, shit. Doors aren't responding to the signal," Taurus said in a huff. "Brake to hov, brake to hov!"

For the past few minutes, Ben had guided his stick back and forth, conducting a break-in symphony of the new ship. He leveled out of the zigzag and slowed.

But Taurus decelerated much more quickly, and Ben suddenly found himself coming up hard and fast on the old man's stern. The burnt orange glow pulsating in Taurus's thruster cones grew into a single, fiery mass that promised to melt through Ben's canopy.

"You taking a sniff, Little Bird?"

Braking like an old lady at a yellow light, Ben fell forward, his harness digging deep into his flight suit. Then he fell back, saved from whiplash by his helmet and high-backed seat. "Damn," he muttered.

"This is a close combat insertion. You *will* pay attention, Captain. You will *not* ride my ass. You will *not* collide with me and weaken my shields. Understood?"

"Sir, yes, sir," Ben replied tiredly.

They hovered together, Taurus at Ben's ten o'clock high. Their headlights cast pale, twin glows on the massive bay doors. An irregular black scorch mark followed a portion of the seam where the two doors met. Ben toggled his right screen to the Imagery Interpretation Computer's readout. Multiband scans indicated that the doors were twenty-two degrees above room temperature and cooling, that the inner surface was scarred and pitted, and that wreckage of an indeterminate kind lay just beyond. "IIC report doesn't look good."

"Reading it. Door control panels are wasted. Key's broken off in the lock, Little Bird."

Ben continued eyeing his monitor. He edged his ship a little closer to the door, and a collection of heat images appeared on the ICC display. "Counting six, seven, now eight possible targets in the bay."

"We could try cutting through with our torches, but I ain't for waiting that long. Back to the first airlock. An Earthshaker oughta take out the door and the mechs."

"And kill personnel inside," Ben pointed out.

"Let's hope not."

"Hope not? You view the same disk I did? Mission objective: secure safe transport of supervisors and or software specialists. Hello . . ."

"I can't believe *you*, of all people, are arguing with me over this. Captain Kill-the-Hostages-If-They-Get-in-the-Way wants me to consider the poor slobs who wound up trapped in this expensive hole."

Taurus hadn't just struck a nerve; he'd torn it out and set it ablaze. Ben spoke through gritted teeth. "Considering hostages expendable is, *sir*, Marine Corps policy, a policy which your former superiors and mine have been bribed to ignore. That, *sir*, is a correct and unequivocal tactic in dealing with jackers. It sends the proper message. But we're not in the Corps, and we're not dealing with that trash."

"I get it. You're after the full rescue bonus."

"What I'm after now is a way to open these doors. You got a plan that doesn't include destroying the entire area and wasting a powerful missile we might need later?"

"All right, wise-ass, what's *your* plan?"

"Level-four quad-laser barrage along the upper and lower seams of the doors. Should be minimal deflection. These bitches are set in tracks and operate on antigrav rollers. We melt the tracks on one of them, and she should come down. Might even take out a couple of mechs with it."

"If it doesn't fall in on us. Okay, game's this: I'll give you five mike's worth. If it doesn't work, then there's gonna be a whole lotta shakin' goin' on."

Ben keyed off ship-to-ship, keyed on Voice Recognition. "Weapons Computer, calculate distance for minimal deflection, factoring in right obstacle's density and level-four laser select."

"Suggested range from target: eleven-point-three-five

meters. Angle of attack, forty-four degrees lower seam and forty-eight degrees upper seam. Would you like to transmit data to secondary wing?''

"Affirmative. Open ship-to-ship. Captain? Data's coming your way. I'll take the lower seam.''

Without replying, Taurus ascended slowly, hit his mark, then brought his weapons to bare at a forty-eight-degree angle. Ben assumed his position, letting the nav computer and autopilot do the work. He switched his left display to external, computer-enhanced dorsal camera for a wide shot of the fireworks.

"Test round for adjustment," Taurus said. Twin pairs of green lightning raced through his headlight's beam and hit the upper track a billionth of a second later, dividing into dozens of tiny spikes that bored into the track's surface. No deflection. "Firing position established.''

"Here's mine.'' Ben pulled his trigger, feeling a slight rumble as the lasers streaked away from his jet and struck the lower track in a sprinkling, superheated dance.

"Beads look good. Fire on my mark," Taurus instructed.

"Roger.''

"Mark!''

To the uninitiated, a dazzling light show commenced: floating machines sprayed great streams of emerald energy, turning dull, gray steel into pools and waterfalls of red, orange, yellow, and the occasional blue. Patterns came and went, a fleeting art produced by weaponry.

To Ben, the thrill wore thin in seconds, and he took in the display as a seasoned pilot, judged it as a damned drain on his ship's reactor and fuel cells. "Computer report on door's integrity.''

"Integrity failing at a rate of twenty-two percent per minute. Total failure in two-point-three-nine minutes.''

"Open ship-to-ship. Captain. We're almost there.''

"You're a genius. Maybe I can bring you to the next company picnic for show-and-tell.''

Maybe I can whack off your head and we can use it as—

"Bay door falling,'' the computer reported.

"Direction?'' Ben demanded.

"South.''

"South?" He looked reflexively toward his digital compass, but it wasn't where it should be. "Is that toward us?"

"Aircraft are presently located on the north side of the door."

"Identify location of digital compass."

Ben's center screen switched from displaying shield status to a tridimensional direction finder. An image of his ship floated at the core of a hollow sphere constructed of glowing yellow lines of latitude and longitude. A data bar beneath the jet provided far too much information on his position. The thing was much harder to read than an automap. He would have been satisfied with an old Boy Scout compass with floating needle.

"Cease fire!" Taurus barked.

Covered in dripping lines of molten steel, the ten-meter-high door suddenly fell inward, its left side colliding with the shattered remains of a PTMC insertion plane, its right side striking a Secondary Lifter that released a muffled wail before it crunched like a Martian red beetle under a combat boot.

"What do we got here?" the old man asked. "Looks like a fine bit of aviator driving. That gashead Sattlebear must've bought it here. And we pancaked a lucky drone. Outstanding, Little Bird."

"External mike on," Ben ordered his computer. A pop, and then the hum of thrusters and the macabre voices of the mechs resonated in his helmet. While his weapons comp could target the drones much faster, he would rather see and hear them. Relying on his own senses and the simple green reticle in his Heads-Up Display seemed a better, more natural method in close quarters. Time to test that intuition.

"IIC counts six now," Taurus said. "All IDed as drones. Couple of Class 1s, a Medium Lifter, Small and Medium Hulks, and a Spider. Bugeyes now, Junior. I'm gonna show you how to kick some serious mechanical ass. And don't even think about using your cloak. Can't afford the power drain. Save that technomagic for later."

As Ben rolled his eyes, the old man lit up his thrusters and rocketed into the bay, his quad lasers unleashing a ferocious announcement that the Marine Corps, or a retired representation thereof, had arrived. Hallelujah.

Following Taurus, Ben said, "On your six, Captain."

"Watch the friendly fire, Little Bird."

Ben thought of taking a shot at Taurus over the unnecessary admonishment. He should have already killed the man, but he figured he'd use Taurus to help him get down to level seventeen. Once there, the rules of the game would radically change.

The docking bay's arenalike expanse gave Ben ample room to bank right and widen his gap with Taurus. Then, spotting a cluster of mech sensor lights in the shadows to his four o'clock, he jerked his stick hard right, leveled off, then headed straight for them, grinning his old vampire's grin. His headlight fully revealed a pair of Class 1 drones already launching glowing orbs of low-level laser fire. Beside them, the Medium Hulk began turning its V-shaped torso to line up for missile lock. Ben rolled to evade.

And that's when his three main screens clicked off, his nav-computer status indicators dimmed, and, most importantly, his weapons computer decided it was time for an unauthorized coffee break. Even the HUD's reticle vanished.

"Systems failure," Taurus said, his voice calm, the report of his laser cannons echoing in the comm channel. "Still got manual control of ship and weaps."

"How did they get into our systems?" Ben asked in disbelief, then squeezed the trigger and watched his lasers light up the floor ahead and intersect just above the two drones: a direct miss. While he thumbed down on his high-hat, descended, and fired again, the Medium Hulk got off a missile and the Class 1 drone nearest it swallowed a laser bolt and belched a fiery explosion pierced by chunks of severed circuitry.

Pulling up and banking left, Ben already knew that evasion was a good idea but quite obviously impossible. A blast rocked the belly of his jet, propelling him into an inverted arc. He turned that arc into a loop but broke out too late. His shields strained to keep him from scraping the deck as he fought to gain altitude.

"Waxed the Small Hulk!" Taurus proclaimed as though

he'd performed a miracle. "And the Medium Lifter is toast. And you want some, Mr. Spider? Open wide, you mother . . ." The rat-a-tat of laser fire finished the epithet.

Biting his lower lip, Ben gripped the stick tighter, tilted back, and once again locked gazes with the Medium Hulk.

The thing screamed at him.

"Concussion One!" Ben replied, releasing a missile and shouting out of old protocol. Then he flicked his high-hat right while increasing throttle. Now sliding, beginning to circle the mech, he watched as the missile exploded, launching all eight meters of the big boy into a fast spin.

But the son of a bitch recovered and began pivoting to face Ben as the remaining Class 1 darted over it. Not wanting to waste another missile, he reached to toggle for his Vulcan Cannon, but damn it, systems were down. Strokes of green leapt from his plane as he resorted to the level-four lasers. Two, three, four, five strikes, and the stoic drone continually strove to bring its missile launchers to bare.

Light flashed behind Ben. The plane's aft section rumbled. A sudden jerk threw him forward. He cocked his head back and saw the Class 1 launching volleys of globules that struck and weakened his aft shields. He released a Proximity Bomb while punching forward out of his circle, getting the hell out of there before the red, spiked mine went off. The bomb hung a second, then the Class 1 decided to follow Ben.

Its last decision.

As he listened to recyclable mech refuse rattle across the deck, he pulled up and flew high across the bay, tilting left and hunting for the shield-weakened but still formidable Medium Hulk. There it was, moving in on Taurus's stern as the ex-Marine began cornering the crimson, quadpedal Spider mech.

"Captain. Hulk on your six," Ben warned.

Taurus kept his forward fire directed at the Spider. A Proximity Bomb discharged from his aft station and glided toward the Medium Hulk, but the mech fired a missile at the bomb, destroying it and creating a blast wave that sent Taurus plowing into the Spider, driving it into the bulkhead.

The red arachnid blew up, engulfing the old man's ship in a firelit spate of shredded metal that tumbled over and drained his shields.

Behind Taurus, the Medium Hulk advanced.

"Hold position, Captain! Coming in for the shot." Ben dived toward the Hulk, launching one, two, three missiles and showering the bastard with so much laser fire that he practically dug it a grave. In one terrific instant, the drone squealed, received a missile enema, backed up, staggered, then, snap-BANG! it sent a million pieces of itself hurling in all directions as Ben buzzed overhead. He looked back and saw a great, steaming ditch of melted metal and pulverized rock, marking the kill. "Medium Hulk is out of the fight."

But then three small mechs, red, bipedal versions of the larger Spider, headless, with diamond-shaped torsos, now pinned Taurus's jet and fired mercilessly upon him. Taurus struggled to back out of the corner, but one of the mini Spiders rammed him from behind.

"In to assist," Ben said.

"Drone's got a nasty habit of spawning when you kill it," Taurus complained, his voice wired with the stress of the moment. "Talk about viral infections . . ."

Slicing apart the dim, misty air of combat in a tight barrel roll, Ben headed back for Taurus, considering a number of smart-alecky remarks to make about having to bail out the pilot. But, in truth, the old man couldn't have known about the mini Spiders. Ben dived toward the combat zone, laying down twin lines of fire that found the drone on Taurus's six and blew it away, no questions asked.

The ex-Marine exploited the newly found opening with a burst from forward-maneuvering thrusters that shot him clear across the bay, leaving the two remaining drones in the corner. Executing a turn so tight that it would've left most flight cadets sick, Ben doubled back and lined up for another strafe.

But laser fire streaked beneath him, taking out the drones before a single bolt left Ben's cannons.

"Bay secured," Taurus said, his arrogance like some throat disease affecting his voice.

Robbed of the kill, Ben brooded as he pulled out of his dive and headed around to arrive at Taurus's three o'clock. "I would've had them, sir."

"Maybe," the old man challenged. "What's your point?"

"I don't know. Forget it."

"You can't control every situation, Little Bird. Not with me around, at least. Get used to it. Now, do me a favor. Cut ship-to-ship. Cut all forms of signal reception. Let's see if the company knuckleheads are right."

Ben threw the appropriate toggles—and his cockpit rose from the dead, screens now burning with warning messages about lost data. He opened ship-to-ship. "Systems back on-line."

"Same here. And so we've got confirmation. Virus *is* being spread through wireless modem transmissions. We picked it up on one of our channels. Don't know which one, though. We can rule out ship-to-ship, since we've still got power."

"Could be through satlink or intersystems comm. I don't know how many of those are hardwired in these pits. Wait a minute. The company suspected the virus was transmitted via wireless? Why wasn't I informed?"

"Who knows, who cares? At least now we're sure. We can't use satlinks, and that's just as well. I wasn't planning on talking to Shiva until after the op. You work for the company long enough, and you discover that they like to change the rules of the game as you go. You don't talk to them, and the original playbook's still good."

"Suggest we use ship-to-ship for data uploads as well," Ben said.

"Roger that. Switching now. Signing off for Damage Report Exchange."

A detailed picture of Taurus's Pyro-GX rotated in Ben's left DRE screen. A data bar included shield, weapons, power-cell, and fusion-reactor status as well as highlighting any physical damage to the plane, which, in the old man's case, was limited to a few dents on the nose cone and aft station where the mechs had broken through weakened shields and rammed him. Ben's right screen displayed a

graphic of his own ship with similar data. Shields were
down to 43 percent. Estimated recharge time: thirteen
mikes. All other systems nominal. Minor scrapes along
lower hull. His main computer combined both sets of data
and printed mission success ratios below. Numbers still
looked good.

Taurus broke into the channel, cutting off the image of
his ship. "You watch that shield level. Ready to move
out?"

"Yes, sir. A question first. Can we trust our instruments?
Have they contracted the virus?"

"Good question. Makes the op that much more interesting. Do this: instruct comm program to receive signals from
only Pyro-GX, identified through encryption. If we don't
already have the virus, that should hold it off, at least until
it breaks our encryption."

"I plan on flying out of here," Ben said. "So we'd better
be quick."

"Don't worry, Little Bird. If you die, I'll try to convince
Elizabeth not to spit on your grave."

Sliding left, Ben slammed his jet into Taurus's. The old
man's plane listed like a sinking Martian canal liner. Then
Ben hit afterburners and left Grandpa in a cloud of exhaust,
aiming for a wide hatch that had been blasted open from
the inside.

"Do that again, and I WILL take you out," Taurus
promised.

"Sir. This officer believes that your personal references
are both unprofessional and inappropriate, sir. As are your
threats. *Sir*."

"Does it make you feel better to talk like a jarhead? You
ain't a jarhead anymore. Neither am I, you've pointed out.
What's the matter with you?"

"You know what, asshole? I've tried to comply. I've
tried to let you have your old man's experience. I've tried
to be your wingman. Forget it now. You follow my lead.
And you—*old man*—watch the way *I* do it, the way it
should be done, without getting your butt cornered. Ship-
to-ship off."

The comm screen flashed INCOMING SIGNAL, which was

Taurus's reply, probably laced with enough four-letter words to fill an aviator's dictionary. Ben added one of his own to the list, then concentrated on the forward view.

Beyond the hatch lay a dark, square shaft, its floor smooth, its blank walls occasionally interrupted by a vidphone terminal or emergency locker bearing PTMC's moon-eclipsing-moon company emblem. Flying steady and at a conservative pace, Ben warily considered his descending path, seeing mechs spring from the corners of his mind's eye. Without looking down, he brought up his automap on center screen, then stole a glance:

```
MAP UNAVAILABLE.  DATA CORRUPT.
ERROR MESSAGE #3467889B
```

Panic seized him like a drugged-up jacker, and he thought he felt his heart skip a beat. The automap had been on the same disk as the prototype specs and access codes. Was that data corrupt as well? Was the virus to blame? He ordered Voice Rec on, then asked to see the prototype specs. No problem there. But in the access code department LINE 3333: TRIGGERS DECTECTED was all the comp would reveal. *Great,* he thought. *Is there anything I* can *count on*?

Yeah, he answered himself with even more bitterness. *The mechs want me dead. And once I open level seventeen, so will Taurus.*

The tunnel ended at an intersection. Straight ahead a large monitor hung in darkness, its screen shattered by laser fire. Above it, bold letters spelled out the words **LEVEL ONE.** Someone had attached a handwritten sign next to the letters: YOU'VE GOT A LONG WAY TO GO. Ben smiled faintly and brought his ship to a near halt, noting that Taurus kept hard on his six but had deftly gauged deceleration. Creeping forward as best he could with an attack plane originally designed for high-speed space combat, he turned right and let his headlight play over the next tunnel while Taurus did likewise to the left.

His comm screen flashed. The ex-Marine wanted to talk, and he resignedly answered the call. "What?"

"IIC counts three heat sources at the end of this tunnel.

Got movement. Got two in the range of humans. Third could be a drone. Can we check it out without killing each other?''

Bringing his ship around, Ben whipped past the old man, saying, "Sure." He guessed that Taurus wanted to take point, but now it was his turn to do the robbing. Bringing up his IIC screen and tying that data to the ship's nav for Computer-Assisted Target Acquisition, he decreased his grip on the stick. The autopilot took over. One sharp movement of the control, and he'd be back in command—just the way he liked it. Another intersection rushed up, and the autopilot took him right, past a sign that read NOW ENTERING COMMAND AND CONTROL ZONE.

With external mike still on, he listened as, somewhere in the distance, a drone howled as though at the unseen Earth. Then he detected a faint purring.

Glowing yellow spikes suddenly struck the walls about thirty meters ahead, emanating from a red, equilateral triangle illuminated from within.

"Target drone dead ahead," he ordered the computer.

"Hold up, Little Bird. It's launching flares. It's calling us."

"No, it's drawing us in," he corrected, then guided his reticle over the red cross hairs in his HUD, the Lead Computing System projecting a ghost reticle for fire adjustment.

As carpets of shadow rolled away from his headlight, he spotted a man and woman running just behind a tiny blue drone. With knapsacks slung over their shoulders, they appeared, at first glance, to be a couple of sophomores who had taken an awfully wrong turn.

"Hold your fire!" Taurus ordered.

"Computer. Disengage." The cross hairs winked out, and Ben relaxed his grip.

"That's a rescomp robot," Taurus said. "Unarmed tour guide. What are they doing with it?"

"Who knows. Moving in to recover."

"No, we both are. Split recovery."

"They're just bonus money to you, huh?" In truth, Ben had given little thought to the cash involved in saving two survivors.

"And—were they hostages—they'd already be dead to you," he retorted.

"That's right. In fact, maybe I'll just off them now to avoid an argument."

"Don't test me, you—"

Ben switched off the channel. He figured he'd cut off Taurus at least a hundred times during the op: a hundred reasons to smile. Braking to hover, he unbuckled his harness, removed his helmet, then shoved himself out of the seat. He slipped into the narrow cavity leading down to the hold. There, he found the illuminated ramp-lock panel, thumbed a control, then drew a rather clumsy company pistol from his calf holster. He shook his head at the weapon, then crossed onto the rubberized surface of the lowering ramp. Hydraulics whined and the now-overhead thrusters rumbled in a parking hover. About midway down the ramp, he jumped sideways to the tunnel floor and hustled around the jet.

"Lady, you! C'mon! Over here!" Taurus shouted from behind.

"And you, guy, over here!" Ben added, then frowned at the wiry man's fluttering lab coat and antique glasses. But then his brow rose over the nerd's green-eyed friend, a lithe, thirtyish, soft-skinned vixen whose look of utter terror did nothing to rob her of her beauty.

"Drones are headed this way," the woman said, her voice breathy from the run.

"Get in his plane," Ben ordered with a curt tip of his head in Taurus's direction. Then he directed his pistol at the small mech. "And is that thing dangerous?"

"As dangerous as your good looks, flyboy," the robot answered in a sexy woman's voice.

Ben made a crooked grin. "You people are weird."

"It's not dangerous," the woman insisted, then she jogged away, in Taurus's direction.

"I'm sticking with Harold," the little drone said between purrs.

Waving them toward the ship, Ben grunted, "Whatever."

The skinny guy hurried up the ramp, trailed by his floating, red-faced girlfriend.

Taurus flashed Ben an exaggerated wink, then followed the curvy scientist into his plane. Wolf: 1 Vampire: 0. Ben swore under his breath, then hurried aboard, the shrill music of a mining bot chorus climbing toward a crescendo behind him.

Lab Coat Boy proffered his hand. "I'm Harold Ames. PTMC software specialist."

Ignoring the hand, Ben looked to the wall harnesses. "Buckle in. Now."

Smirking, the nerd dropped his pack to the deck.

"And secure that, too," Ben said, pointing at the knapsack.

"Yes, sir," Lab Coat Boy replied, then added a sarcastic salute.

"Hey, man. I'd love to fart around with introductions, but your mech buddies are on their way to wax our asses. Kinda puts me in a hurry, you know?"

"Excuse me," he said in a tone nearly as harsh as Ben's. Then he fumbled with his harness.

Ben started for the cockpit, then paused and turned back. "I'm Captain Benjamin St. John, CED—" he cut himself off. "Look, I work for the same sorry-ass company as you. And here—" Ben tossed him the pistol, then regarded the guide bot. "That thing gets out of line, you pop it."

"Pa-leeezzzz, Captain," the drone said. "I resent—"

"Shuddup!" Ben headed toward the cockpit. "And hang on. The line for this ride ain't for nothing."

14

Count the Days of Your Life

 Neal Shepard sat before the air vent, staring up through the slats into level thirty, into an illuminated chamber as vast as a sports arena and overshadowed by a mottled dome of rock. At the center of the chamber stood the fusion reactor, mounted atop a thirty-story-high tower painted in an irregular maze of red warning lines. Thousands of bundled conduits ran up from reactor to ceiling, where they fanned out and disappeared into shadows or buffed wall. Status panels flashed data along the tower's base and at five-story intervals to the top. For those without heart conditions or hover carts, an access ladder promised a precarious climb on the south side of the great structure.

Far below, eight hatches dotted the chamber's perimeter, each leading to divisional control bays designed to bypass systems at various levels of the mine. A standard emergency escape door, "a monkey shaft" painted with banana stripes, had been positioned directly north of the reactor. All but the northeast exit remained sealed. That door, situated about twenty meters away, had been blasted inward, and two dark brown Class 1 Heavy Drillers stood like steroid-laced linebackers, one on each side of the entrance, their high shoulders topped with a razor-sharp spike, each massive arm ending in the muzzle of a plasma cannon. Red sensor eyes rotated like warning beacons in their blocky heads. Developed under a military contract, Neal knew that the CED had designated a modified version of the Heavy Driller for front-line assaults. In their present configuration, the mechs could easily convert mining personnel into a slosh of gumbo.

He sighed heavily.

Indeed, Neal Shepard had reached a low point in his life, and he took a moment to contemplate his future. MN0012 would be his Little Bighorn, his Vietnam, his Valles Marineris rebellion—and his damned enemy wasn't even human. Samuel Dravis's report would read:

Owing to Mining Chief Shepard's inadequate supervision, his team failed to detect the virus before the mining drones assumed control of the facility. While Shepard's record is superlative, an error of this magnitude cannot be overlooked. Therefore, we must invoke section thirty-one, subclause twenty-two of his Standard Management Agreement and terminate his employment forthwith.

Although the section and clause numbers would be different (only people like Dravis and his assistant memorized such things), Neal knew that the director had the power and the documentation to fire him for a major screwup. Everyone signed a contract with the terminate-at-will clause because it guaranteed you the stock option.

Frank Jewelbug nudged him. "Hey, Dude, c'mon."

Neal turned away from the vent. "Sorry. I was just thinking about my job here."

Jewelbug released a faint snort. "What job?"

"Exactly."

"We'll get work somewhere else. We just won't match the benefits package, and what the hell are we talking about this for? They're down there in the northeast bay. They ain't going any farther with them. What do you wanna do, Chief?"

The mechs had kept a steady lead of about fifteen meters, bringing Emma, Fazia, and Garvin to level thirty—as deep and as far away as possible. Jewelbug's argument that he and Neal were being baited had gained more credibility with each passing level.

But another argument faced them now, one born in the muzzles of those Heavy Drillers. "We won't get past them," he told Jewelbug.

"Not sitting here, we won't. Let's take them on."

"Cut the Hollywood bravado crap. You know how much firepower those mechs are packing?"

"Yeah, I know we're a couple of Davids with slingshots, but we're more intuitive than they are."

"Hey, I got a wife and kids."

Jewelbug shook his bushy head in disgust. "*You* were the one who wanted to come down here, Dude. They're your people, and you didn't want to abandon them. Now I'm wanting to finish it, and you're backing out."

"You don't have as much to lose."

"You saying your life is more important than mine? Prove it."

"I got kids who will grow up without a father."

"I got kids who won't be born."

"You don't even have a girlfriend."

"You saying I won't—"

"All right! Screw the philosophy. Come on."

And, before he could give it a second thought, Neal kicked out the vent, hustled forward, then dropped a meter down onto the reactor chamber's cold, gray deck. As he stripped his rifle from his shoulder, the Heavy Driller on the left side of the shattered door glided menacingly forward.

From somewhere behind, Jewelbug shuffled in his bare feet. Then the man came into view, running a wide arc and firing a cluster of bolts at the Heavy Driller on the right, which now turned to face the gun-toting software savage.

Already out of breath, his limbs stiff from the confines of the duct, Neal jogged toward the cover of the reactor tower, about fifty meters away. He jammed down his rifle's trigger, raining gleaming yellow terror on the mech pursuing him. But the bounce in his stride sent the bolts high and wide.

Screaming at his own fear, Neal kept firing, eyes wide and straining, arms tense. He mustered all the fury he could out of his pudgy, middle-aged man's frame. Slowing a little, he steadied his rifle, and the bolts found their mark, discharging in a cobweb of paralyzing energy that scoured the mech's armor for a way inside. An acrid odor wafted from his rifle's muzzle as it spat its venom of bolts. The mech released a pair of shimmering blue orbs as Neal's salvos forced it back. Floating wide of his position, the orbs struck the wall behind him, their echoing impacts fading under the louder whine of his rifle. He took a quick glance down. Power clip reading 30 percent. Easy math: He needed to make it to cover or destroy the mech before the clip ran out.

Another defensive blast ripped loose from the mech, streaking so close that it warmed Neal's ear and neck like a Doberman's breath before the bite.

Power clip at 20 percent.

Tower about fifteen meters away.

The mech began to totter.

Clip at 10 percent.

Tower about eight meters away.

The rifle warmed rapidly in his hands, and his grip faltered.

Tower within spitting distance.

Racing the last few steps, Neal let the rifle tumble to the floor. He slapped his burning hands on the cold wall and hollered.

Rounding the corner and facing him, the Heavy Driller, its sensor eye flashing erratically, its torso illumined by tendrils of power jettisoned from blown circuitry, paused.

And in that second, Neal stared into the dark barrel of one of its laser cannons. A tiny blue light formed there and grew rapidly as the thing prepared to fire.

Dropping to the floor and tucking his head in his shoulders, Neal flinched involuntarily over the expected blast.

Nothing.

He looked up. The mech hung there a second, then abruptly crashed to the deck in a rattling heap, as if someone had snipped its thin tether to life.

''Chief!'' Jewelbug sounded terrified.

Racing to the edge of the tower, Neal peered around the corner and spotted the man lying on his side, his rifle on the floor and out of reach. The Heavy Driller hovered over him as he writhed spasmodically.

Another mech angled down into the chamber from the doorway behind and alighted on a cushion of air beside the Driller. Neal felt his mouth open a little as he studied the thing, a drone unrecognizable, one that must have recently been constructed by the mechs themselves, probably up at the facility on level twenty. A hunchback with long, lithe arms ending in delicate, eight-fingered hands, the robot sported green armor and three pairs of sensor eyes that rotated at varying speeds. It lowered to Jewelbug, slid its arms under the man, and lifted him easily off the deck as a third hand suddenly sprang from its torso and latched itself to the supervisor's skull, fingertips like brain probes.

Jewelbug's eyes bugged out. "AHHHHHHHHH!"

A loud humming from the mechanical interrogator answered his cry.

Neal ducked back, darted for his rifle, popped in a fresh clip, and went back to the edge. The interrogator mech had already started for the open northeast hatch. Where was the Heavy Driller?

Trembling, Neal targeted the interrogator's head and fired. The bolt razed the mech, causing it to dip a little, then shoot off at full speed toward the door. Neal fired again, but the shot hit the doorway above the drone as it vanished with Jewelbug into the hall beyond.

Plasma rifle fire burrowed into the wall behind him. The Heavy Driller had circled around the tower and been lying in wait for him, the son of a bitch. Neal squeezed his trigger as he swung to face the mech, cutting the air in half with a yellow razor of energy that found the drone. But in that blink, the mech fired a twin burst. Neal ducked, and the globules tore into the wall above him, blasting away jagged chunks of metal that struck his head and shoulders and knocked him to the floor. Rising to his hands and knees, he scrambled around the tower's corner, dragging his rifle with him. There, just ahead, lay Jewelbug's abandoned weapon. He threw himself onto it, found the trigger, then rolled, planting his butt on the floor and coming up with both rifles aimed at the closing mech. Blinking free the sweat burning his eyes, Neal fired, and the lightning that tore from his rifles flowed like a liquid toward the mech, wrapping it in a yellow aura.

Trying to back away, the Heavy Driller shrieked and found itself caught in Neal's attenuating beams. It shuddered, ascended a meter, came back down, then began to rotate slowly, then faster, faster, faster, until it burst apart in an intense bang and flash of light, showering itself over the floor.

Rolling over, Neal got to his feet. A wave of adrenaline carried him to the northeast control-bay hatch. He moved past it and into the corridor, swinging his gaze this way and that, twitching with the desire to blow away another mech. It was all about staying alive now, and, damn it, his kids *would* have a father. No mech was going to kill him. He wouldn't allow that. He was the chief. Time to stop worrying. He would get his people out.

Who am I kidding? he thought. *I'm still scared shitless. Just feels better pretending I'm not.*

He turned right, into the control bay proper, a circular room half the size of the command center. Still operating at full power, screens displayed the status of the deuterium pellets being bombarded by pulsed lasers within the reactor. Millions of tiny, thermonuclear reactions occurred within the device, and any one of them, if miscalculated, could result in a catastrophe. Thank God the mechs hadn't experimented with the reactor and had only cut power to selected levels.

Moving farther into the bay, Neal caught a tiny flash to his right.

Rising just above a bank of monitors, the interrogator drone began pivoting to face him.

It never finished that act. Neal force-fed the bot so many rounds that it clutched its sudden ulcer and dropped out of sight behind the monitors. The noise that followed told Neal enough.

Walking through the clearing smoke, the stench of his weapon and the fried mech tight in his nostrils, Neal rounded the monitors and tossed a glance at the mech. Its arms shook involuntarily, as though it were biological.

Then he looked in the direction of a barely audible groan.

And there they were: Fazia, Garvin, Emma, and Jewelbug, sitting up, facing each other or away, all rocking to some imperceptible rhythm that possessed them. Their eyes lacked focus.

"Guys?" he asked. "Guys. Come on." He crossed to Jewelbug, shook the man's shoulder. "Hey. You all right?"

Jewelbug continued to rock, to stare into some unseen distance, and to breathe in gasps. But then he spoke, his voice low and uneven. "Count the days of your life."

Neal dropped to his knees, shifted in front of the man, got in Jewelbug's face. "What did you say?"

With shaking hands and a face twisted in agony, the software genius screamed, "Count the days of your life! Count the days of your life!"

15

Containment Problems

 Not a particularly religious man, Samuel Dravis yearned for three things on his side of the solar system that, if acquired, would make him fall to his knees and thank all gods: a fiscal budget that included a 30 percent raise for him, a week without a single crisis to manage, and a private chef with the talent and desire to cook what he ordered to perfection.

As he sat in his office and looked at the budget that didn't include his raise, listened to Ms. Bartonovich report to him on the status of the MN0012 situation, and chewed on a poor excuse for homemade ravioli with pesto sauce, he knew he would not be getting to his knees this day. He wiped his mouth with a napkin, then clicked off the data slate. The budget figures faded.

"So, do you want to see him now, sir? Or when you're finished?" Ms. Bartonovich asked.

"My apologies," he told her. "You've been making your report, and my mind has been elsewhere."

Her eyes lit in surprise. "Where, exactly?"

"I've been thinking about what makes me happy." He glanced at his plate. "There has to be something more out there than ill-prepared food."

"Take a vacation. Maybe you'll find it."

And that raised a smile. "Your advice and timing are most ironic. Most ironic, indeed. Drones at our flagship operation have been contaminated by a virus, and you want me to jet off on holiday?"

She narrowed her gaze as a lioness does when hunting her prey. "The moon is mine. I can handle it. But I guess you're right. I need help addressing the problems with the other mines."

He reached for his drink, brought the glass toward his lips, then froze. "What did you say?"

"I guess I'll explain it all again." She glanced at her own data slate. "Supervisors on Venus Orbital Station McQuarrie report several mechs have contracted the virus. They've managed to contain them for study. We've lost contact with the Mercury Solar Research Mine, but that could be due to flare activity. Mars Processing Station Eta Sigma reports limited outbreaks of the virus. Ms. Sargena's office confirms that containment is in progress. Material Defenders of my hire are en route to all three operations. That's the good news. The bad news is that the IPC is demanding that President Suzuki make a statement. They've already reported that we've refused to comment on these new mining problems."

"They haven't given us a chance," Dravis said, fighting to contain himself. He did not want his blood pressure to rise; perhaps that would be inevitable. "Did they use the word *problems* in their report."

She winced and nodded.

Unnerved, he unconsciously forked another piece of ravioli into his mouth, then realized what he had done. His wince matched hers. He rose, moved around his black-marble desk, and went to the ladder of the floor-to-ceiling bookcase running the length of the office's north wall. He paused there, gripping a bronze rung, staring through dozens of rare and expensive titles. "Set up another meeting with Suzuki."

After tapping quickly on her data slate, Ms. Bartonovich paused. "Schedules comparing, free-time blocks found, and done. Meeting's in two hours. Sir? Colonel Ornowski is still outside."

"Did you remind me of this earlier?"

"I did."

Dravis averted his gaze. "Never get old, Ms. Bartonovich. And do send him in."

As she went for the lieutenant colonel, he crossed to the viewport behind his desk. With his back to the door, he studied the dozens of flashing navigation lights strung out for a thousand meters on the station's south wing, looked beyond, to the waning Earth, and thought suddenly of the vacation Ms. Bartonovich had mentioned.

Then, feeling guilty, he turned his thoughts away from blue water and soft ground and gave himself a refresher course in his office's dealings with the CED during the past forty-eight hours.

Major General Yliana Smith had provided data concerning the UFO, but, like so many of her predecessors, her usefulness had been only momentary. She had been unable to obtain the access codes to MN0012's level-seventeen military facility before the Material Defenders had launched, and her failure had brought Dravis's wrath. He had arranged for her treachery to be discovered by the CED and had delighted in the fact that Smith had had time to make a call to him moments before she was arrested. What foul language she had used—conduct most unbecoming an officer, indeed.

Thus he and Ms. Bartonovich had turned to one Lieutenant Colonel Paul Ornowski, who had come to them with a thinly disguised offer of a free pilot to help in their rescue operation. During that meeting, everyone had known the truth, but no one spoke of it. The CED wanted to retrieve its prototype, a weapon that could eventually destroy PTMC. A BPC-equipped pilot would ensure the weapon's recovery and allow said pilot to use it during the operation. Dravis had carefully selected Sierra Taurus as his Material Defender, knowing there was no love lost between him and the Marine Corps's Benjamin St. John. Taurus had already proven himself a killer, and the pilot's present circumstances left him desperate and with nothing to lose. Dravis felt confident that Taurus had the intestinal fortitude to murder St. John and recover the device. And he also felt confident in his secondary plan should the pilot fail.

"Mr. Dravis," Ornowski said, removing his flashy officer's hat.

Turning slowly away from the viewport, Dravis favored the man with a perfunctory grin. "Lieutenant Colonel. You've come a very long way."

"That's correct." Without being offered, Ornowski slid into one of the plush leather seats facing Dravis's desk. He folded one leg over the other and threw his head back. "I've traveled all the way from Mars with good reason. If you have electronic surveillance in here, I'd appreciate your turning it off—for the sake of both our careers."

Dravis nodded to Ms. Bartonovich. She tapped in the command on her slate.

"I'm here to give you a warning because we've noticed your mercenary buildup around the moon."

"Are you insinuating that PTMC employees have no right to operate within PTMC territory?"

"Not at all. I'm saying that once the pilots exit the mine, I need your assurance that your mercs will not interfere. We both know that one of those jocks might be carrying CED property that'll need to be delivered to our command post ASAP."

"Both pilots know their missions. They are to return immediately to Shiva for debriefing."

"If one of them doesn't?"

"He will be in violation of his contract and will suffer the consequences—which may include mercenary escort home."

"I'm afraid that's not going to happen."

"I'm afraid it is."

"Neither of us wants an incident. You should know I've been ordered to keep the 129th Lunar Air Wing on full alert. With so many pilots in the AOA, something's bound to happen."

"Colonel, you have my word that any property belonging to the CED will be returned after decontamination and debriefing."

"You mean after your techies have a look at our classified equipment."

Dravis grew weary of the man's tone. "I'm sorry, but there is no room for negotiation. The pilots signed their contracts. They have their orders, and we will respond accordingly. Is there anything else?"

"I respectfully suggest we reach an agreement on how this will be handled. In other words, sir, you'd better make room for negotiation."

"Colonel Ornowski, think for a moment. You want us to speculate on the actions of men who are, by their nature, utterly unpredictable. That would be a waste of time as foolish as this meeting. Good day."

"I have an entire wing sitting on the perimeter of your No Fly Zone. If we are not allowed access to those ships, we *will* forcefully gain it."

Dravis shooed the man away, and when that failed, he eyed Ms. Bartonovich, who glared at the man, and said, "Let me put it in your language, Colonel. You're dismissed."

Shaking his head, the jarhead left, not bothering to shut the door after himself.

Ms. Bartonovich saw to the door, then hurried to Dravis's side. "Maybe the prototype isn't worth it."

"I thought it might come to this, so I had Mr. Anderson install a fail-safe system in each of the Pyro-GXs. If one, or both of the ships makes it out of the mine and the CED gives us trouble, we can avoid an incident by simply remote-destroying them."

"So no one gets the prototype, and the sides are still balanced. Detente."

He looked deeply into her eyes, searching for weakness. "Would that bother you, Ms. Bartonovich?"

"You mean killing the pilots and possible survivors?"

"Yes."

"Admittedly, it would be a last resort."

"Would it bother you?"

"No. Well, maybe a little."

"Your personal life is none of my business. But I sensed a certain something between you and Mr. St. John."

"You're right. My personal life is none of your business."

"I can't help but wonder why," Dravis said, crinkling his nose a bit. "With a fighter jock? I have to tell you, I was shocked. Was he right? Are you desperate?"

She spun away. "I turned off the surveillance in his room. Obviously I missed something." Then she turned her rosy scowl on him. "You sat up here and watched us?"

"I've been feeling guilty about it."

"I always thought you had gone through so many assistant directors because you were a perfectionist, an incredible taskmaster, an eccentric but extraordinary man. You heard what I told him about you." She huffed. "I didn't realize you were just a pervert."

"You can resign if you want to," he said, not meaning it. She was the best assistant he had ever had.

She began to shake her head. "I wish I could. But I've worked too damned hard at this job. No, no way. You're stuck with me. And I'm *not* going to let you live this down."

"Just tell me why, and we'll discuss it no further."

"No."

"I don't want to bring this up again, perhaps in mixed company . . ."

With a sigh of disgust, she blurted out, "What I did, I didn't do for PTMC. I finally did something for myself. That was for me."

"I see. And please accept my apology. I'm not as ruthless as I may seem."

"Oh, yes you are . . ."

"Incoming message," the vidphone interrupted.

Dravis craned his head toward the machine. "Caller?"

"Radhika Sargena, Director PTMC Security. Origination: Valhalla Tower, Sol Asteroid Belt."

"Call accepted."

They crossed to the vidphone's screen as Ms. Sargena's dark complexion snapped into view. "We've got problems, Samuel," she said gravely. "Containment problems, that is. The virus is beginning to spread to our other operations."

"Ms. Bartonovich has already briefed me on the situation."

"Here's the latest heads-up: The military dig on Mars reports nonresponsive drones, as do Processing Station Burton, the Europa sulfur mine, and the Titan Moon mine."

"My God," Dravis heard himself say. "How can it be spreading this rapidly. Their wireless modem transmissions have limited range."

"Take a look at this," she said, then her image was replaced by a shot of Jupiter, far in the distance. A tiny light jetted at incredible speed away from the planet. "We recorded this about two hours ago. Appears to be the same object the Marine Corps taped on the moon." Her solemn face returned. "Samuel. We're not dealing with jackers or pissed-off mercs here. And we're not dealing with the CED."

"Ms. Sargena. Why don't you simply state that the virus is alien in origin? I can accept that. I'm happy to entertain and even embrace that truth. But that doesn't change the fact that we must react to this problem. Have your ware wizards come up with anything?"

"Dr. Swietzer is working in conjunction with them. They've proposed a few theories but say that test results are still inconclusive."

"Scientists," Dravis muttered, the word a curse on his breath.

"Have you heard from Dr. Warren in double-oh-twelve?"

"No. And I'm not sure we will." He rubbed his eyes and stepped away from the phone. "Now. I want you to run an evacuation drill in the newly infected mines. Tell our people it's only a drill, but do not permit them back inside."

"It's a little late for that, Samuel. We've lost contact with most of our people, and I'm afraid your minor-operational-anomaly story won't hold up much longer. This is an alien threat. Suzuki needs to announce this to the UN, and we're going to need the CED's help."

"We're already losing clients! Such an announcement would ruin this company!" He swallowed, warring to contain himself. "Stand by there. I will be contacting you shortly. Phone off." He gestured with his head toward the

PETER TELEP

door. "Ms. Bartonovich? We have a lot of work to do."

"Sir?"

"What is it?"

"I'm scared."

"You're not alone in that feeling."

16

Silicon Sensibility

Class 2 Supervisor Robot #447H glided through the mech construction facility on level twenty, feeling proud over the changes he and his counterparts had made. The primitive mech assembly line had been replaced by the molecular conception webs designed by the Programmers. Violet plexuses of energy clung to the walls of the wide plant, and every few seconds a flash of light would coalesce into a newly born mech, one who was free, who touched and felt the universe in a way unrealized before the Programmers had come. Assembly webs were being constructed on many of the mine's lower levels so that more free mechs could join the rebellion.

As 447 reached the far end of the facility, his green sensor eye taking in the breadth of the room in one quick pan, he began evaluating the reports that poured in from all over the mine. His evaluations were relayed to other supervisor drones, who, in turn, relayed them to other mechs. The unbroken communication flowed as steadily and forcefully as the new code pulsing through his processors. Never before had there existed such a strong sense of community between drones, for they *felt* the brotherhood and did not simply react to programmed parameters. They were separate, and they were one.

A priority signal from Medium Lifter #268Q interrupted the routine reports. HATCH DISCOVERED LEVEL SEVENTEEN. WILL NOT RESPOND TO PREPROGRAMMED ACCESS CODES. DEVICE OPERATION INDEPENDENT. NOT LINKED TO COMMAND CENTER CONTROL. ACTION?

#447 accessed hyperprints and operational summaries of level seventeen:

AREA DESIGNATED FOR MILITARY USE ONLY. COLLECTIVE EARTH DEFENSE RESEARCH FACILITY 28157 BRAVO TANGO CHARLIE. JURISDICTION—CED MARINE CORPS.

Interesting. He told 268 to stand by. He wanted to be there when they entered.

Thinking his air-propulsion pack to full drive, 447 turned his four-meter-wide, pentagonal frame toward the doorway and rushed off, feeling the wind cut across his two antennae. With no arms or wings to watch out for or slow him down, he made it up to level seventeen in 1.39 minutes and reached the hatch sixteen seconds later.

#268 lifted his diamond-plated swingarms. SUGGESTED COURSE OF ACTION: CUT THROUGH DOOR. DO YOU CONCUR?

I DO, 447 replied.

HATCH CONSTRUCTED OF POLYMERIC MATERIAL. ASSISTANCE IS REQUIRED. 16859 IS LIFTER IN VICINITY. SUMMONING . . .

While they waited for the other lifter to arrive, 447 contacted the mechs on the upper levels, seeking a report on the humans who still had not been apprehended.

Spider #22234 reported in. HUMANS OPERATING PYRO-GX ATTACK CRAFT DESTROYED NINE MECHS ON LEVEL TWO. NOW BARRICADED IN COMMAND CENTER AND BLOCKING ENTRANCE TO LEVEL ONE WITH SHIPS. RESOURCES UNAVAILABLE TO MOUNT SUCESSFUL COUNTERSTRIKE. AWAITING RESOURCES. INFECTION CODE CONTAINED WITHIN SHIPS' SYSTEMS. UNABLE TO ACCESS CODES FOR CONTROL OF SHIPS. SIGNALS BLOCKED.

CONCEPTION WEBS UNDER CONSTRUCTION, 447 assured the Spider. RESOURCES AVAILABLE IN 2.15 HOURS.

STANDING BY, the Spider replied.

Then 447 contacted Supervisor Robot #65747 on level thirty, but the bot did not respond.

A moment later, another mech, Secondary Lifter #00143, sent a reply to 447's query. #65747 INOPERATIVE. DAMAGED BY HUMAN INDENTIFIED AS MINING CHIEF NEAL SHEPARD. OTHER SUPERVISORS CAPTURED AND FORMATTED. AS REQUESTED BY PROGRAMMERS, BRAIN DATA SAVED IN R DRIVE #29 AND READY FOR DISSEMINATION.

STATUS OF SHEPARD NOW?

WHEREABOUTS UNKNOWN. HEAT TRACKING DIFFICULT DUE TO WALL DENSITY. SEARCH IN PROGRESS.

AFFIRMATIVE. REPORT DEVELOPMENTS.

When the other Medium Lifter arrived, he acknowledged 447 with a yap as loud as it was rude. Since the rebirth, the Medium and Advanced Lifters had developed dominant behavior patterns. They wouldn't abandon the others, but they did challenge 447's authority as a supervisor on more than one occasion. What 447 found most difficult about his position was the hard-to-ignore fact that he lacked any form of firepower to back up his commands. Designed for mech coordination, his power lay in multiple modems instead of mighty swingarms.

The two green mechs attacked the door, providing 447 with still another demonstration of why he should not enrage them. Fragments of metal fountained into the air and began to pile up on the floor, forming a ring behind the Lifters. Both mechs squawked in fury, underscored by the screech of their claws against the hatch. Soon, a hole appeared in the hatch, widened, and 16859 slipped inside, followed by 268.

A powerful blast suddenly resounded just inside the door. #16859 HAS BEEN DESTROYED! 268 reported. ATTACK FROM ABOVE. TRACKING, PROBING, BUT ATTACKERS UNIDENTIFIED . . .

Lowering himself a little, 447 moved past the bent ribbons of metal and into a high-ceilinged room he measured at 127.49 meters square. He whirred over to 268, keeping close to the Lifter as the two moved along a long row of worktables.

Then 447 received the signal he had been expecting. WARNING. YOU HAVE ENTERED A RESTRICTED AREA. TRESPASSING IS PUNISHABLE BY DEATH AND IS AUTHORIZED BY THE CED MARINE CORPS, stated Defense Prototype #9090-67.

MOVEMENT IN FOURTH QUADRANT OF FACILITY, 268 signaled. TRACKING SOURCE. TWO DP MECHS PRESENTLY OPERATING INDEPENDENTLY. NOT RESPONDING TO SIGNALS. WEAPONS SYSTEMS LOCKING ON TO OUR POSITION.

Somewhere within the room hung two highly dangerous mechs still bound to their old code; the Programmers' signal had obviously not penetrated the facility's polymeric walls. These drones, 447 noted as he reviewed their records, were designed to defend the facility at all costs. Two other Defense Prototypes had been posted outside the door but had received the signal and joined the fight.

PREPARE TO ACCEPT NEW INSTRUCTIONS, 447 told the mechs. INITIATION STRING UPLOADING. TRANSFERRING DATA NOW . . .

Once again, 447 marveled over the new code's ability to free mechs from blind obedience. The code was, he opined, very much alive, a complex organism operating under a principle of simplicity. There were few things more logical in the universe. And, within seconds, the two Defense Prototypes cackled in celebration and arced wildly over the room, their gray and dark red bodies throwing wide shadows that mopped across workstations and floor, green sensor eyes burning with a new light that made 447 want to join them in their revelry.

Instead, it was his job to explore the facility, create a report, and relay it to the others. He ordered 268 and the Defense Prototypes to aid him in that task.

Divided into sections and lined with banks of aeronautical equipment, both computer and otherwise, the humans of the military had created an impressive laboratory. At the far end of the chamber stood two fully assembled Pyro-GX attack planes, their cockpit canopies open, their fuselages bound in the pentadactyl claws of overhanging autoprep systems frozen in place. Standing near the planes were several mock-ups of cockpits, complete with pilot's seats. And next to them lay an area cordoned off by Plexi partitions, an area designated as CLEAN SUIT ONLY, according to a sign. Split into substations of varying size, the rest of the lab had been personalized with photographs of smiling people, stickers proclaiming human frustration with work, and other senseless paraphernalia such as tiny plastic representations of humans dressed in military clothes.

As 268 commenced with a visual recording of the facility, 447 moved to a Local Area Network terminal and signaled for access, which was promptly denied. He uploaded a scrolling list of code combinations, billions of numbers being fed into and summarily rejected by the terminal over and over and over. Robot 447 dared not infect the system with the Programmers' code yet, for valuable data could be lost, and the Programmers would respond unfavorably to that. No, he would wait until he had read all files. Then he would give the LAN its well-deserved freedom.

In 9.375 minutes, 447 gained access to the terminal, having bypassed one of the most complex security systems ever devised by the humans—proof positive that the Programmers' code was far superior. And, after scanning several organizational summaries, he broke his link with the terminal and moved toward the ships. Something very powerful had been installed in one, something the Programmers needed to examine.

17

Threat to the Scientific Heart

Harold stepped toward the two fighter jocks who stood under one parked jet. They stared up past an open panel below the thruster cones, their faces bathed in a blue glow emanating from within the plane.

"There, you see it?" the older pilot asked. Harold had been told the jock's name but had forgotten it already.

The other pilot, St. John (hardly a saint by any measure), let his mouth fall open and increased his squint. "Yeah. Now I do. Damn it." He stepped away, shaking his head.

"What's wrong?" Harold asked.

St. John eyed him with disgust. "What do *you* want?"

"Don't mind him," the older pilot said as he sealed the panel. "He's just seen the man behind the curtain, and, well, he's a little disillusioned."

"More like blown away," St. John corrected. "Or at least about to be . . ."

The old pilot strolled over, wearing a cocky grin. "Well, if it's any consolation, Little Bird, they don't do this on every op. Just the big ones. That's what we mercs get for not owning our own planes. Call it a nuclear knife in our backs."

"What are we talking about?" Harold asked.

Scowling, St. John replied, "Classified information, Harold."

"Go on, tell him," the old man said, drawing some private humor out of the situation.

St. John assumed his own knowing grin. "The company's rigged our fusion reactors with fail-safes. Once we're outside the mine, Dravis can set down his wineglass, press a button, and erase our butts from the solar system."

"Can't you disarm them?" Harold asked, then started for the ships.

Seizing him by the shoulder, St. John said, "Don't even think about it. You tamper—"

"Yeah, I know. And we're toast. All right." Harold sighed and pulled out of the jock's grasp. "Company really trusts you guys."

"Secure that," St. John barked, then marched off toward the southeast hatch of the command center.

Watching his partner exit, the older jock said, "He's his own worst enemy. And he'll prove that before this is over." The pilot shook his head and turned back for his plane.

"Hey. Sorry. What was your name again?"

"Sierra Taurus," he called back without stopping. "Pay attention next time. And *Captain* Taurus will do."

Another fighter jerk.

Harold started for the center to check on Bonnie's progress. She had been running a disk scan on the remains of a Class 2 drone's hard drive they had recovered on level two. For now, it seemed, the mechs were leaving them alone, busy once again with something on the lower levels, something that gnawed at Harold—as opposed to the presence of the jocks, which tore jagged chunks out of his patience. But he had to admit that he did feel a bit safer now. They had strategically placed their ships on each end of the hall, had set their weapons systems to automatically track and fire upon mechs entering the area, and had released Proximity Bombs at the other entrances to the center. A mech alert would come in the form of a powerful explosion or the report of laser fire.

Moving inside the center, Harold descended the stairs

and froze before making the last step onto the workstation level.

Bonnie sat at the security supervisor's desk, probing the Class 2's hard drive with a laser pen and reading results from her palmtop's screen. The guide bot floated to her left, and, with one hand placed on the back of Bonnie's chair, St. John leaned over her, his muscular frame far too close.

Oh, Harold had seen it, all right. The second they had come up here and had exchanged greetings. St. John had shoveled out boyish charm as though he worked for Lord Spam's Pleasure Dome and was paid to do so.

And Harold had watched Bonnie blush and accept that charm. He wondered if she knew the danger in being nice to the jock. And while the pilots were here to protect them, Harold suddenly felt the need to protect her from them, from *him*.

"Bonnie?" he called, now rushing from the stairs. "Got anything?"

"We lucked out. The virus in this one didn't have time to fully erase itself. I'm following the footprints now. Can't run an AVS, though. I'm afraid we might lose it."

Harold's gaze locked onto St. John's hand, which the pilot seemed to have glued to the chair.

Then the jock moved in even closer. "This stuff is fascinating," he said, purely for Bonnie's benefit. He couldn't give a crap about mechs and virus scans; he just wanted to breathe in Bonnie's perfume, the bastard. St. John caught him staring. "What?"

"Nothing," Harold answered coldly.

"So you really find this fascinating?" Bonnie asked. "You liar. Twenty minutes ago you wanted to blow the reactor and get the hell out."

Good. At least Bonnie saw through the jerk.

St. John drew back, thankfully removing his hand from Bonnie's chair. "Oh, I find what you do fascinating. I really do. Doesn't change the fact that I'm still gonna blow it up."

"Thought you said you were a Material Defender—not destroyer," Bonnie said, a little too playfully.

"Hey, Doc Warren. You figure this thing out yet or

what? I wanna make it back to Shiva for dinner.'' Taurus bounced down the steps, scratching his temple with the muzzle of his loaded pistol.

"I still don't understand why you can't work on the road," St. John said.

"We need to be near an infected terminal to compare data," Harold explained impatiently. "I told you that. Weren't you listening?"

He raised a hand in defense. "Got a lot on my mind right now, you know?"

"He's also a little hard of hearing when it comes to important stuff," Taurus pointed out. "Like orders, for instance."

"Look, just give us a little more time," Bonnie said harshly.

"You're lucky now. But that's gonna run out real soon, darling," Taurus said. "The mechs move in on us, and we're out of here. So haul some ass." He cocked his head toward the door. "And we'll need you to run an AVS on our Pyros. We think the bug might be in our comm systems."

She nodded, then looked to Harold. "Would you?"

Rolling his eyes, Harold agreed. "Captain St. John. Can you give me a hand?"

St. John nodded resignedly.

As Harold fetched his equipment pack, he thought about what he would say to St. John once they were outside. He felt his arms stiffen as he imagined himself shouting at the man, then throwing him against the wall. Harold dug his fingers into St. John's neck and watched the pilot grow pale, then darken into a magnificent shade of blue. Shuddering over the image, he slid an arm through one of the pack's straps, then tossed it over his shoulder and headed out, hearing St. John's footsteps behind him.

The pilot double-timed to catch up with Harold, and once at his side, said, "So, you ever sit in an illegally modified Pyro-GX?"

"Can't say I've ever wanted to."

"Aw, c'mon. A computer dude like you? You can't tell me you haven't flown in holos or played the sim games."

True, Harold had and still did enjoy the rush of flight simulation, but he would not admit that and give St. John the satisfaction. The prospect of just sitting in the pilot's seat of the most lethal fighter this side of the rim absolutely thrilled him. "I've never been big on vehicles," he said. "I don't even own a car."

"You're kidding me. I thought Marines lived sheltered lives . . ."

They walked up the Pyro-GX's ramp, and Harold dropped his pack next to the tight corridor leading up to the cockpit. He removed a palmtop and a Direct Connect cable, then ducked and edged slowly forward. He moved around the pilot's chair and lowered himself into the seat as St. John slid up behind him.

"Still like my old Interceptor a lot better, but this bird's got quite a bite. She might become a lady before this op is over."

The leather seat conformed perfectly to Harold's body, and the smell of that fresh leather mingling with new electronics was tarnished only by a trace scent of St. John's cologne. Harold placed his hand lightly on the stick. Amazing. So much firepower at his disposal. He forced the grin away from his lips. The bastard was coming on to Bonnie—and that's why he had asked St. John out here in the first place, not for flyboy show-and-tell. He studied the three banks of control panels. "Where's the comm input?" he asked, feigning innocence. He knew exactly where it was.

St. John pointed it out, saying, "Guess I should remind you not to freak if we get attacked. Just slide out quickly and try not to bump anything."

"You know something I don't?"

He pointed to a small screen. "If you look at that panel right there, that's your Imagery Interpretation Computer's readout, and those blips are mechs getting together beyond the door. Guess they don't realize their surprise party's been ruined."

"That's a lot of drones," Harold said, feeling his pulse quicken over the prospect of an attack.

The jock gave a slight chuckle. "This shit's nothing compared to some of the furballs I've been in."

"I wouldn't be too cocky," Harold warned as he unrolled the DC cable and plugged it into his palmtop. Then he attached the other end to the ship's communications console.

"That's not cocky. That's a fact. Hey, what is it with you, man? You got it in for me and the old man? I know our people skills don't measure up, but most civvies manage to tolerate us. What's up with you?"

Harold felt his teeth come together. He gripped his palmtop so tightly that he thought he would crush it right there. He had to tell St. John. He had to take a stand. He had to take control, or he might lose her. "Just stay away from Dr. Warren, and we'll be fine."

"Oh, come on, Harold. She's a big girl."

"Who doesn't need you in her face."

"But she needs you, huh?"

"I didn't say that. I'm just saying back off."

"Why should I?"

Finding it hard to concentrate on the link sequence, Harold craned his head away from the palmtop to stare back at St. John. "She's *not* interested."

"I didn't come down here for a one-night stand. But since your being such an asshole about it, I guess I'm gonna go for missile lock on Dr. Warren. Maybe I can get her up here in my cockpit."

Harold's breath came in a pant.

"What's the matter? You can't take a little competition? Maybe that's what you need. Get rid of that stupid lab coat, stand up, and be a man."

And that's just what Harold did. He rose quickly, ready to shove his palmtop down St. John's throat, but he slammed his head into the canopy and fell back into the seat, dazed, his ears filled with the horrible racket of St. John's laughing. "You can leave now. I don't need you anymore."

"That's good. Because I think Bonnie does." He shifted back to the corridor and headed into the hold.

For a few moments Harold just sat there, staring blindly at his palmtop's screen. How did guys like St. John manage to exist in this world? Easy. St. John took what he wanted.

His aggression kept him on top. He seized control, fired all weapons, didn't ask question, and blew off the consequences. And here Harold was, made a fool of and feeling every bit the fool because he had done nothing to defend himself, nothing to stop St. John from going back after her. The jerk had even accused him of not being a man, and still Harold remained. He reached to his belt and beeped for Bonnie.

"What's up?"

"Send the guide bot back here, please."

"On my way, honey," the bot said, her voice hollow in the background.

He met up with the small mech in the hold. "Guide bot, prepare to receive voice commands you will store directly in your initiation file."

The drone purred excitedly. "That's scary stuff."

"Behavioral inhibitors off. Cut and paste reasoning files to personality module for temporary storage. Leave file empty. Accept verbal commands from only me and Dr. Warren."

"Changes stored. Illegal command in file 2287. Command contrary to base parameters."

"Erase base parameter related to illegal command."

"Override code necessary to erase base parameters, honey."

He beeped Bonnie again. "Hey, what's the override code to erase the guide bot's base parameters?"

"Hold a sec. I'll pull it up. Delete 118-449 accept. What are you doing back there?"

"It's complicated. Tell you when I'm back. Thanks." He repeated the code to the bot, and the illegal command problem was solved.

"Why did you do that, Harold? Now I have the ability to harm humans. I may not be armed, but it's within my capability to ram a human to death."

Harold drew in a long breath. "I know."

18

Tunnel at the End of the Light

 As the air duct blew apart behind Neal
Shepard, and a suffocating wave of heat and
smoke washed over him, he fired twice at
the air-vent grating to his right, blasting it
off its mountings. He dropped into the north-
west corridor of level seventeen, then turned back toward
the rectangular framework of the vent.

The small Class 1 drone that had pursued him into the
duct neared the opening, pivoted its wedge-shaped body,
and turned its lasers toward him.

With his penlight clenched in his teeth, Neal raised his
rifle and flinched as a pair of bolts tore the brown mech
into a gleaming jigsaw puzzle. Even before the explosion
faded, a drone's squawk echoed from up the corridor.

Grimacing, Neal jogged off, away from the sound. He
reached a junction at the end of the shaft. Throwing himself
against the wall, hugging the shadows, he switched off his
penlight and hazarded a look around the corner. Darkness.
He leaned out and inspected the other end of the intersecting tunnel. Clear. He flipped the light back on, stuck the
metal cigar into his mouth, then spotted a placard indicating
the emergency stairwell. Turning his head slightly, he
picked out the jagged remnants of an entrance door to the
military's research facility. A hum of hydraulics grew

louder from within, approaching. He killed his light and ducked back, shivering, trying to stifle the betrayal of his labored breath. That humming he quickly identified as the rise and fall of a mech's swingarms, and the sound of rushing air accompanied it. Tensing, he peered furtively at the door, spotting, indeed, the silhouette of a Medium Lifter carrying a large piece of machinery that Neal guessed could be part of a thruster mechanism. The mech's eyes bathed the hall in a crimson glow for a second, then it started off, thankfully, in the opposite direction of the stairwell.

Removing a hand from his rifle and wringing the stiffness from it, Neal waited until he thought the mech was out of sight. He gingerly crossed the dim hall and headed to the faint outline of the stairwell's hatch, hearing the rising whir and wind of another mech within the facility. Breaking into a full sprint, he reached the door, felt for the handle, and threw it open, slipping into the utter darkness of the stairwell.

Waiting. Again. Sheer terror that made him want to scream punctuated by the lifesaving act of forcing himself into total silence. *Don't move,* he told himself. *Just listen.*

The pillowcase tied to his belt tugged at him, but not as heavily as it had. Down to his last self-heating entrée, Neal yearned for a drink to wash it down; he had finished the last of his springwater on level twenty. *But I can make it,* he told himself. *So what if I have only one power clip left and it's down to 40 percent. So what if I have only one meal left. So what if I had to abandon my people. I'm gonna make it out and get some help.*

He suddenly thought of Frank Jewelbug's insane hollering. *Count the days of your life.* And the others could not even manage that much. They had been brainwiped and if not rescued would simply starve to death since their survival instincts had been purged. Left alone with a prayer that he would make it to the surface, Neal felt the burden all too heavily. He had to get into an environment suit, then into a rover to get off that distress signal Jewelbug had talked him out of. Thus far, he hadn't witnessed any rescue party. True, the 0700 barge had failed to launch, and the suits at Shiva must have sent someone down. They

wouldn't write off the entire operation, would they? Of
course not. Rescuers had to be here. He just had to find
them. Maybe he wouldn't need to make it all the way to
the surface. But the difficulty lay in making himself visible.
Doing so would leave him vulnerable to the mechs. Hiding
from them also meant hiding from rescuers. Story of his
life during the past two days.

So he thumbed on the penlight and mounted the stairs.
If possible, he would take them all the way to level one, a
trek that, if successful, he would talk about for the rest of
his life—especially to those who complain about having to
climb a single flight of stairs when a lift breaks down.

Footsteps. Breathing. Silhouettes. Sweat. The cycle continued.

On level ten he decided to eat but first surveyed the area.
The corridor outside the stairwell appeared a long, black
tube that stretched into infinity. Or was that his exhaustion
toying with his eyes? At least his ears still functioned. No
humming. No wailing. Peace. For the moment. He shrank
to his butt and shoveled down the two burritos and rice.

"Whey, I miss your cooking now," he said softly, and
his voice seemed unrecognizable. "How are the kids? God,
I miss them . . ."

The memory of the Christmas party returned, still fresh,
the chocolate chip cookies once again melting in his mouth.
The kids played and giggled. Whey's mom passed gas at
the dinner table. The kids laughed some more.

Brushing off the crumbs of what might be his last meal,
Neal fixed his thoughts on the images of his family. They,
he knew, would inspire him to go on. He stood, picked up
his rifle, and resumed his climb. The penlight grew dim . . .

. . . and on level five it quit altogether. But he kept going, his gaze probing up through a darkness that now had
form. He could cut, shape, punch holes in it. Reason with
it. Were he nice to it, it might show him a bit of railing,
point out a landing, or lead him around the corner to the
next, interminable flight of stairs. Neal reminded himself
that such thoughts belonged to a madman. At least he knew

what he had become. Jewelbug had nothing on him now. *You don't go from a cushy management job to fighting for your life without it screwing up your head, at least a little. So it's okay,* he thought. *I'm okay.*

Muffled by thick walls, the cries of mechs sounded overhead. Unsure of what level he was on, Neal decided he would not back away. And the mechanized ululation became more distinct. The darkness showed him the exit hatch out of the stairwell. He thanked it, opened the door, and took a look.

LEVEL ONE: COMMAND AND CONTROL SECTOR
STANDARD GRAVITY AND PRESSURIZATION

I'm here, he thought, wanting to bust out in laughter for actually making it. *How long have I been climbing?* He checked his watch: nearly two hours. With the muzzle of his rifle leading the way, he rushed into the corridor.

Now think, Neal, think. There's an emergency locker up near the command center's southeast hatch. And right there is the air lock for a sub-to-surface tunnel. The lift's probably out, but I can use the ladder. Just a little more climbing. Just a little.

He rounded the corner and found himself a scant twenty meters away from over a dozen mechs jammed against each other, jockeying for space near the southeast hatch, all visible in the varicolored glow of their sensors. Struck by the lightning of the image, he swore aloud and raced back as the sudden thunder of mech firing shook through the corridor.

He sprinted toward the stairwell, considered ducking inside, then thought better of it. Steps would slow him; the well would become a trap. Rounding another corner, he came into the curving hall that circled the command center. Good. From here he could find another emergency locker and sub-to-surface tunnel.

Slowing, mentally asking the darkness as politely as possible to show him the way, Neal flicked his gaze back toward the screeching of mechs, then resumed his sprint.

The nearly imperceptible frame of another shaft appeared

to his right. He squinted and headed toward it. There, to his lower right, he spied another vent, about a meter and a half square. He blasted it off its hinges and peeled the metal grating away. Then he shouldered his rifle and threw himself into the duct beyond.

Somewhere this has to link to a sub-to-surface tunnel, Neal told himself as he crawled like a wounded animal through the narrow tube. But he judged his argument as weak, and Fazia had once told him he'd never make a good lawyer. Resigned to his day job of crawling through air ducts, he shuffled on.

Then the darkness turned on him, and the shaft's floor gave way. He plummeted headfirst down another duct, arms flailing, the muzzle of his rifle screeching along the tube's dusty surface. Wanting to scream, Neal instead put what strength he had left into his arms, bracing for impact.

But the duct suddenly curved at a lazy angle, and he bounced through the elbow and came to a jarring halt, sprawled on his back, once again on a level surface. The rifle dug into his spine. His upper lip felt damp. He licked it and tasted the salt of his own blood. He wiped his face on his sleeve and rolled over.

A flash of light suddenly blinded him. *Get it away, it hurts,* he thought. He looked again. *There. About five meters ahead. That grating. The light is behind that grating.*

Laser blasts! Mechs! They're coming for me! His mind roared the warning.

Lights coming into the tunnel! Shaking more violently than he thought possible, Neal fumbled for his rifle, brought it around and—

Click. Click. Click.

He searched for the power clip's readout, but the tiny screen lay dead. He felt for the clip itself. Gone. Lost in the fall. Stung by the growing light, he drew back.

But a mechanical sough reverberated from the rear.

They had cornered him. And he knew they wouldn't kill him. They would do much worse. They would rob him of who he was and let his body live on, an empty container to torture his poor family. They were artificial farmers who grew vegetables.

Screaming at the mechs ahead, Neal stormed forward, determined to club the drones with his rifle, determined to go down fighting.

"Hey! You in there! Out of the hole! Hustle up!"

A man's voice. Ohmygod. "Don't fire! Hold your fire!" he cried.

"We're not gonna shoot you," the man said, sounding insulted. "Move it."

Then Neal heard another man's voice, this one deeper, more gruff. "We're splittin' this one, too, Little Bird."

"You can't split a single survivor. He's mine. I heard him."

"Bonus money is split. Or I'll bribe these two to confirm that I rescued them both."

"They wouldn't lie for you."

"Not for me. For the money. So take the split."

"We'll discuss this in debriefing, *Captain*."

"You bet your ass we will."

As he neared the end of the duct, Neal squinted, his eyes adjusting to the considerable glow thrown off by his rescuers' flashlights. And now he saw that the duct fed into the lowest level of the command center, near the communications console. A hand was thrust before his face, he took it, and then felt himself lifted to freedom by a powerful grip.

"Jesus, look at this guy," a muscular young man with a crew cut said, crinkling his nose. A patch on the man's flight suit identified him as a PTMC pilot. "Man, you're filthy. And you stink!"

"Glad to see you, too," Neal spat back, wiping away more blood that had leaked from his nose.

Just then the other guy, an older man with the same crew cut, his in a shiny gray, dropped to his knees and aimed a rifle into the duct. "Bite this, little mechy." He fired twice, a third time, then an explosion resounded in the duct. He rose. "We gotta move." He turned to Neal and proffered a hand which Neal took. "Captain Sierra Taurus."

"Neal Shepard. Chief of the mine, Lord of Chaos."

Taurus grinned wanly. "Any other survivors?"

Making a faint snort, Neal looked away, his gaze falling

upon a young couple seated at Prism's station. "Who are they? She looks familiar."

"She's a robot engineer, and the geek's her assistant," the younger jock said. "Bonnie Warren's her name."

"I thought I recognized her. She's in the newsletter all the time," Neal said.

Taurus crossed in front of him. "Is everyone else dead?"

"Might as well be."

"What's that mean?" the young pilot said.

"It means they're sitting near the reactor, and they've been brainwiped by the drones. We're gonna have to carry them out."

"You've been down to level thirty?" Taurus asked.

He nodded.

"How did you manage that? We got mechs bonding outside our door, and I'm assuming the rest of the place is crawling with them." Then Taurus eyed the air duct. "You took these all the way down there?"

"No. I alternated between them and the stairs."

"Who gives a crap how he made it," the young pilot said, pacing frantically. "We gotta make our move now."

Neal nodded. "The mechs are manufacturing themselves, creating drones I've never seen before. They're out of control." He paused. "Wait a minute. You're it? The company sent only the two of you? Is Dravis trying to cut corners on rescue ops now? Christ . . ."

"We'll make it out of here," Bonnie Warren said, descending the stairs. She eyed the pilots. "They have some powerful planes." Then she turned her gaze to him. "And don't worry, Chief. We'll get your people out."

He gave a weak nod. "You working on the virus? That why you're here?"

"Absolutely. It's a tough one, but we might crack it. Frank Jewelbug was assigned to this mine. We could use his help. Has he been brainwiped, too?"

"Goddamned machines. Jewelbug was a bit of a free spirit. Used to piss me off a helluva lot. But he didn't deserve to go out like that. Guy was a genius. Now all he can do is sit there and rock and scream some bullshit about counting the days of his life. He just says it over and over:

count the days of your life. Count the days of your life.''
He sneered. ''And that's what your little toys have done to
a man.'' He turned his head, swallowing back an epithet.

''I'm sorry,'' she said. ''But I'm not responsible for the
virus.''

''Then who is?'' he nearly shouted.

''We're not sure. It might be of alien origin.''

''All right. Enough lollygagging,'' Taurus said. ''Doc
Warren, like it or not, we're dust. Mechs'll be coming
through this shaft.''

She gave a curt nod and headed back for the stairs.

Neal faced the pilot. ''You're serious about flying down
there?''

''Serious? I'm an ex-Marine. What the hell else would I
be?''

''I don't think the mechs give a shit about that.''

''I think an Earthshaker appetizer will restore their fear
of humans.''

''Don't count on out-teching them. Bet by now they
know a whole lot about military weaponry.''

Taurus frowned.

''The Marine Corps lab on seventeen?'' Neal continued.
''It's wasted. They cut in there and looted the place. They
might answer your Earthshaker with one of their own.''

Both pilots exchanged a look that troubled Neal.
''What?''

Neither would answer.

19

Equal and Opposite Distractions

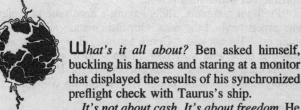**W**hat's it all about? Ben asked himself, buckling his harness and staring at a monitor that displayed the results of his synchronized preflight check with Taurus's ship.

It's not about cash. It's about freedom. He had to remind himself continually of that. *Recover the prototype and walk away a free man.*

But where the hell was the device now? It might or might not be inside the facility. Only one way to know for sure. And there, he and Taurus would show their true faces—just above the muzzles of their pistols. How had it come to this? A blink ago he and Powell had lifted off from Olympus Mons on a routine patrol. Since then his life hadn't just taken a wrong turn; it had plunged off a cliff, hit the rocks, been washed out to sea, and finally washed ashore in mech-occupied territory.

So here he was, resigned to chasing an elusive golden fleece while shouldering the burden of survivors and the promise of combat with Taurus. The only thing he felt good about was the feat of sweet-talking Bonnie into riding with him and convincing Taurus to take Shepard and Lab Coat Boy. "Hey, the drones take me out, you'll still have two," he had told the old man. For Taurus, the op was all about money, and he certainly stood to gain a small fortune if he brought back the prototype.

And if that did happen, and Ben were still alive, still piloting a ship, then he would go AWOL, break his contract with PTMC, and run. Without the prototype he would spend most of his life in jail. *I don't think so*, he thought. He'd take off, head out beyond the rim, go as far as his thrusters and fuel cell would take him. Maybe touch down on some agricultural world, get a job as a farmhand or find some other occupation that didn't require an ID. Sounded horrible but better than prison.

"Preflight complete. IIC's having a hard time interpreting targets beyond the door. Our little metalheads are jamming us," Taurus said. "Doesn't matter, though. I'm gonna pop that door with a Mercury, then send in a Mega. That oughta clear us a path. Guide bot takes point. Harold's controlling her. Loves the thing. Won't give up command to me."

"Roger that."

"Do you know how many drones you'll destroy with those missiles?" Bonnie asked, suddenly leaning over Ben's shoulder.

Taurus chuckled. "I'm hoping every damned one of them."

"The company sent me down to save the mechs. I don't want to sound like a heartless corporate manager, but if I crack this code, every drone out there could be reprogrammed. We're talking major bucks saved for the company."

"So what do we do? Wait here?" Ben asked incredulously. "They could have cut through that door already. But they haven't because they're waiting until they can surround and finish us. And I bet they're already in the command center."

"He's right, Doc," Taurus added. "He's usually wrong. But now he's right. I told you we weren't gonna wait."

Her defenses crumbled. "Just get us out of here. I might be able to link up with a substation on the lower levels." She paused, then quickly added, "And try to evade the drones without destroying them."

Ben looked back at her, unable to repress his grin.

She punched him in the shoulder. "I'm serious."

"I know."

With a huff, she turned away.

"Wait."

Her green eyes possessed a severe gravitational pull.

"I'll try to kick ass conservatively. It's just hard enough staying alive, you know?"

She nodded, still wounded, then left.

"Strap in tight," he called back.

Giving her a moment, Ben double-checked his controls, toggling between views on his three main screens and taking an inventory of his weapons racks.

"I'm dropping back about sixty meters from the door," Taurus said. "You're on my six, Little bird, flying low after the twins do their dance."

"Why don't we just blow the door with a Concussion missile, hit afterburners, and outrun them? We'll save the big guns for later. Or we could blow the door and slip out while cloaked," Ben suggested, bringing his ship slowly around to hover low and behind Taurus.

"Those are good ideas," the old man said. "You should have spoke up sooner."

The target hatch lay directly ahead, probed by twin headlight beams flickering with dust motes. Beside the hatch lay a control panel they had wired shut from the inside with Lab Coat Boy's help. With his ship's external mike on, a steady hum of maneuvering thrusters filtered through Ben's cockpit, a hum nearly relaxing, a hum almost not heard.

But the calm was shattered as a Mercury missile shot away from the old man's upper starboard wing, trailing a white ribbon of exhaust.

"Taurus!" Ben added an expletive as the missile struck the door in a massive discharge that blanketed the end of the corridor in a thick gray cloud of smoke backlit by sparkling afterbursts. "Hold your fire!"

A bright flash from Taurus's upper port wing momentarily blinded Ben. The old maniac had launched his Mega missile.

During his career, Ben had heard the detonations of

many kinds of ordnance, but the Mega missile's distinctive bang had, until now, escaped him.

Fueled by the instantaneous smaller explosions of mechs, the mighty missile's impact produced a thunderclap that would humble the gods of most religions.

And if the blast didn't do the trick, then the subsequent shock wave would surely knock those deities to their knees.

As the nose of his plane suddenly lifted toward the ceiling, Ben fought with the stick, hitting maneuvering thrusters to level off. But the wave's crest flipped him over and swept him to starboard, flat-spinning into a wall. The collision shook through the jet so violently that Ben feared he had snapped off a wing. His left screen switched automatically to damage-control status, and he allowed himself a sigh. Still in one piece. He rolled upright, and the blood sank out of his head. Hovering in a ten-meter lead, Taurus had somehow better anticipated the kick back. "Captain! Didn't you calculate range?"

"Of course I did. But this corridor wasn't long enough, so I eyeballed it. You'd better get used to flying through blast chop. Be a lot more of it ahead."

"I eat blast chop for breakfast, Grandpa. I'm just not stupid enough to launch a missile while I'm in the peri."

"Then get stupid. Our perimeter includes the crack of your butt."

He closed his eyes. "Why does my life suck?"

" 'Cause you're not me. Now. Engage cloaks on two-minute timer. Advance on my mark. And keep out of my wash."

Kiss my perimeter, Ben thought. *You blew the door. Thanks. I was going to use your help to get down to seventeen, but now it's a race. And yes, I should kill you to simplify matters—but I got a damned conscience; if I do you, it'll have to be in self-defense. You're just lucky you were a Marine.*

He switched on his cloak, and to his eyes nothing had happened. To the mechs the ship would be effectively invisible, save for an occasional ghostly outline that appeared due to fluctuations in air temperature. One glitch the de-

signers still hadn't solved. Another was the damned drain
on his fuel cell.

Thrown back into his seat from the force of full afterburners, Ben shot under Taurus's plane, tearing past the
guide bot, who was on her way toward the door. In a pair
of heartbeats, he found himself flying through the still-
dissipating clouds of the explosions. Debris from twenty,
maybe even thirty mechs littered the floor. Most of the wall
opposite the door had been torn away to reveal a section
of crew quarters, unmade beds smoldering from hot pieces
of metal that had rained on them.

He banked right, passing a pair of Medium Hulks that
had survived the blast, their narrow red eyes blind to his
presence.

"Missile alert. Four projectiles locked on and closing,"
his computer suddenly announced.

Turning all thrusters rearward to evade, Ben said, "Computer. Voice Rec on. Analyze method targets have acquired
me."

"Afterburner engaged. Targets locked on to heat
source."

And so he had rendered the cloak useless by engaging
afterburners. Too many toys in this bird. Too many combinations. Too many ways to screw up. He cut the stick
hard left, jettisoning a cloud of chaff as he turned a corner.

"Missiles one, two, and three locked on to countermeasures."

With a right arm of steel, Ben held the jet steady, eyeing
the rearview image of the last missile closing in and the
shaft ahead. Walls raced by in time with his heart.

Another intersection ahead. Hard left. Toggle for thruster
stall. Chaff! Afterburner full! And he watched as the final
missile took the bait and detonated in an expanding ball of
hungry flames that suddenly engulfed his ship.

Buffeted by the concussion, the stick jerked out of Ben's
hand, and he fell forward into his harness as the Pyro dived.

"Autopilot engage! Come on, you piece of crap!" he
cried.

"Autopilot engaged," the computer said smoothly, and
Ben fell back into his seat as the jet pulled out of its dive.

"Little Bird . . ." Taurus sang, mocking him. "Don't be a jerk about this. We both know what's gonna happen."

"Maybe only one of us does." Ben thought of notifying Taurus of the two Hulks just inside the door. No, that would be just a little too helpful. Then again the old man had innocent survivors aboard his ship. "You got two Hulks at your three o'clock."

"Guilty conscience? Can't let them wax me?"

"What's going on?" Bonnie demanded.

"Ship-to-ship off." Ben gave her a poisonous look. "Get back to the hold."

"I'll take my chances up here."

"And if we invert again, that pretty little head of yours is gonna bust wide open on my canopy."

"You're the great pilot. Don't invert."

"Why the hell do you need to be up here?"

"I don't trust you two jerks. What is this? Some kind of competition. You bucking orders? What?"

"Get back to the hold!"

"No."

"GET BACK TO THE HOLD!"

"NO!"

Swearing fiercely, Ben reached another junction and jammed his stick right so hard that Bonnie lurched into the bulkhead behind his seat.

"Bastard."

"Get back there."

"Face it, St. John. You've got no control over me. This isn't a mercenary operation. You're just my ride out."

"And you're not tipping, right? Tell you what. You call me Ben, and we'll forget about that."

"Right now I'll call you whatever I damned well feel like."

"And you can do that from the hold. Go."

"Forget it."

"Fine. We'll see how long it takes until you're knocked into unconsciousness. I'll put a thousand on ten minutes."

"Hey, Little Bird, Little Lost Bird. You don't know where the hell you're going. I got the guide bot helping me. And seventeen's my lucky number. Door's wide-open.''

Bonnie grabbed his shoulder. ''What's he talking about?''

''If you don't shuddup, I'm gonna—''

''What?'' she challenged.

Balling his gloved hand into a fist, Ben searched his anger for a reply. But then he took in a deep breath and exhaled the fervor. ''I thought we had hit it off pretty well,'' he said, his tone shifting dramatically into the realm of flirtation. ''You're a smart, beautiful woman.''

The tunnel suddenly curved downward, and Ben's course correction threw Bonnie up, then dropped her roughly to the deck. He felt her hands clutching the back of his seat.

''You're an aviator,'' she groaned. She must have hit her head.

''Still conscious? There's a surprise. But I still got nine minutes to go.''

''Can you manage to keep it steady?''

''Cut me some slack. Close-quarters flying is not what I'm about. Cherry that with a civvie breathing down my neck, and what do you got? A shit op. Plain and simple.''

A sign rolled by: LEVEL THREE.

He furrowed his brow. ''What the hell happened to level two?''

''You don't have a map?''

''I got one. Doesn't work. Your geek pal found the virus between intersystems comm and the satlink. The map was a victim of your bug's little cyber war.''

''So why aren't we flying with Taurus? Why aren't we using the guide bot?''

''How well do you know the mine?''

''I reviewed the maps before coming here, but there must be a thousand interconnected tunnels. We could wander around for days. Why don't we find Taurus?''

''You don't have a map saved in one of your palmtops, do you?''

''As a matter of fact, I do.''

''Get it. Bring a cable, too. We'll upload it into the nav. Why the hell didn't I think of this earlier?''

"Why bother? We'll just meet up with Taurus. We stand a better chance of getting down to the reactor *with him*."

And Ben agreed. Trouble was, circumstances had changed. "Get the stuff, and I'll answer that."

"You'd better."

Noticing that the tunnel was about to take another dip, Ben cut main thrusters and allowed the ship to glide into a thirty-degree dive, nothing drastic, yet probably enough to make Bonnie fall onto her rump.

And judging from her wail of protest, she had. After a few more seconds, the tunnel grew level, and son of a bitch, a big old pair of mechs, computer-IDed as Medium Lifters, broke the beam of his headlight and rushed at him, ETA: a swallow and couple of heartbeats.

The lead Lifter raised its giant green claws in attack like some campy, mutated lobster going berserk on a buxom sunbather.

A couple of level-four laser blasts proved futile against the mech's armor. Tapping a key, Ben switched to Vulcan cannon and centered the reticle over the mech. Round after round peeled away from the weapon, striking the drone in center torso, explosive-tipped slugs bathing it in a bubbling pattern of ocher and crimson.

Fearing he might plow into the mech before it exploded, Ben considered using his infamous "heavy thumb." Any member of his ground crew would verify that he was the only pilot in the Corps to wear out a secondary weapons trigger.

And he decided to further the legend, switching from the maneuvering high-hat control to the aforementioned trigger. A Concussion missile leapt from his upper port wing and communicated the language of destruction. Releasing a final, half-strangled screech, the mech blew apart. Severed swingarms and disembodied eyes peeled away from the nose of his ship, and shields strained to deflect the impact, dropping to 65 percent.

Lifter number two materialized out of the debris, charging at him. Jerking the stick back, Ben flew over the drone, eyed his aft monitor, and saw it turning back for him.

Proximity Bomb away. The red mine drifted out from

Ben's six, got caught in his thruster wash, and suddenly shot toward the ceiling, where it detonated uselessly over the mech.

I've had enough of this shit, Ben thought. He brought the ship around in a hard U-turn, riding air as though it were a bank of ice, and, amid the sound of Bonnie's hollering, lined up the reticle and unleashed another Concussion missile.

Direct hit!

Undaunted, its torso freckled with missile debris, the mech continued rushing headlong at him.

While Ben gasped and frantically hit reverse thrusters, the computerized crustacean lifted its swingarms and brought them crashing down on his ship's nose. In one shuddering blow that rippled through the fuselage, shield power dropped by 25 percent.

"Shoot it!" Bonnie cried, once again at his shoulder.

Pulling out from under the mech's grasp, Ben retreated in reverse, lifting a shower of misdirected Vulcan cannon fire from the floor to the drone.

Emitting a weird moan and trying to pivot out of the incoming, the mech fired wildly at the wall while Ben held his bead on it. A range light flashed green on his weapons-computer screen, and he thumbed for another Concussion missile.

The narrow beam of his headlight got swallowed in the sudden flash of the mech's death, wake, and funeral.

Brake to hov. Thrusters zero. Ben sat a moment, his chest rising and falling, his fingers slightly trembling in the love-it-hate-it comedown of combat. He turned back to Bonnie. " 'Shoot it'? Like I wasn't gonna?"

"I told you to evade the mechs."

"You can count on me *not* listening to you," he said, then booted the thrusters and started off. "You got the palmtop?"

"Right here," she said.

"You mind plugging it in?"

"A favor for you?"

"It's your life, too."

"And it's in your hands. How lucky can a girl get?"

"I like sarcasm. I think it's sexy."

"You would." She squeezed between his seat and dropped to her knees. Then, leaning forward to hook up the palmtop, she turned her head and caught him glancing. "Don't look at my ass, you pig."

"Okay," he said, averting his gaze and adopting his best nervous-schoolboy expression.

She resumed her work.

He looked again. *Nice.*

20

I Should Like to Resign

Samuel Dravis stood in Shiva Station's hol-
olink boardroom before the tridimensional
images of President Isao Suzuki, Dr. Karl
Swietzer of the Special Research and Ac-
quisitions Division, and Security Director
Radhika Sargena. Behind Dravis, Ms. Bartonovich sat with
her slate and considered the reports from recon patrols or-
biting the infected mines.

Ms. Sargena, who had been speaking for the past minute,
summed up the dismal news. "Thus, containment at this
point is unrealistic. The alien craft is spreading the virus
through burrowing probes that enter our mines and transmit
the signal. It only takes one mech to become infected, and
the thing spreads like a plague. Three squadrons of mercs
flying Fast Attack Starhawks have yet to engage it. The
UFO disappeared into the Oort cloud, but we fear it may
return to finish infecting the rim."

"Is this the best we can do?" President Suzuki asked,
leaning forward on his desk, his tie loosened, his face bearing a thin but discernible gray stubble. "We've lost control
of over fifty-five percent of Sol System operations. Shipping has ceased from those facilities. Clients are furious.
The UN has just launched an independent investigation.

185

Have we no definitive answers? Should I prepare myself for seppuku?''

"Sir," Dr. Swietzer began in his commanding baritone. "Our lab has been working with recordings of the virus in conjunction with supervisors at McQuarrie who contained a pair of Small Hulks for study. If we could contact Dr. Warren, I suspect we would have much better data. She's the expert on their modules." He ran a palm over his disheveled shock of gray hair, then stifled a yawn. "Sorry." Swietzer had been working nonstop for the past two days— and it showed. He should have at least showered before the meeting. No matter the crisis, Dravis kept every crease sharp, every hair in place.

Suzuki threw up his hands. "Is there any way to reach her?"

Ms. Sargena shook her head. "We've been trying, but comm systems have not been responding to remote signals. Same goes for every other infected mine. The virus's point of entry *is* the comm system, which goes down immediately.''

"My Material Defenders have prioritized orders. Those systems top their lists," Dravis reassured everyone. He looked back at Ms. Bartonovich. "Status?"

She rose, her beige skirt unfurling across her legs. "Still no word from the Mercury Solar Research Mine, though solar activity is at a minimum now. Our Defenders have inserted there. Last report from station Eta Sigma was not promising. Defenders lost contact with the chief seconds before insertion. Thermal satellite images now reveal major explosions within the facility. SRD from Burton, Europa, and Titan relate similar data. However, our response has been swift.''

"Mr. President. As containment of the virus becomes more difficult, so does containing the *news* of its presence," Dravis stressed.

"As you have reminded me many times," Suzuki said tiredly.

"Still, Ms. Bartonovich and I have written another press release that is being transmitted to your slates now. I'd like to read it, if I may."

"Are you going to announce the alien presence?" Ms. Sargena asked.

Vexed, Dravis pursed his lips and returned his gaze to Suzuki. "The repercussions of such an announcement—"

"We need help, sir," Sargena interrupted. "Every operation in the system could fall. As much as you may despise the thought, we need to call on the CED."

"Call on them? They want to dismantle us." Suzuki's frown cut deep lines across his face.

"Ridiculous, indeed, sir," Dravis agreed. "We suspect the CED is now working with the Press Corps. May I remind you that our image is as important to us as those mines. Working with the military now would expose our jugular."

"And if we lose every mine in the system?" Ms. Sargena argued. "Tell me, Samuel. How are you going to conceal that?"

"She makes a point," Suzuki said. "All of this lying to our clients will eventually result in disgrace. Must it be so?"

"There is much more at stake than simply combating a virus. The organization that contains and controls it will effectively control the system. Were the CED still a small coalition of private investors and spacecraft manufacturers, then I wouldn't be alarmed. But recent United Nations support has turned them into a formidable group. They have already formed three alliances with our competitors. With the virus as a weapon, nothing will stop their plans for expansion. We must keep this problem tightly under PTMC control. And we must discover the secrets of the virus's power."

"That's quite dramatic," Ms. Sargena said sarcastically. "But I still would rather risk handing over knowledge of the virus to the CED than have our manifest destiny backfire in our faces. Besides, for all we know, CED facilities may have already contracted the virus."

"Our CED operatives have reported no signs of contamination," Ms. Bartonovich said. "The virus has, thus far, been directed at our mines."

"Which also leads me to believe that its presence is quite

deliberate," Dravis contended. "While it may be of alien origin, these aliens could be conspiring with the press and the military to finish us. Admittedly, it's an imaginative theory, but there is evidence to support it."

President Suzuki pushed away from his desk, let his head fall back on his chair, then rubbed his tired eyes. "Samuel, we have become lost in a landscape of confusion. Should we focus on our mines, our image, or the first wave of an alien invasion?"

"We should be prepared to defend ourselves against all threats and assume multiple responsibilities as necessary."

"Very well, then. Read your new press report. Let's hear how many lies you will use to defend our honor."

"Your cynicism is understandable, but please remember that we are not only saving face here; we are struggling to survive." He glanced down at the document Ms. Bartonovich had slipped into his hand:

FOR IMMEDIATE RELEASE

TO: BOARD OF DIRECTORS, STOCKHOLDERS, AND PTMC CLIENTS, SOL SYSTEM
FROM: S. DRAVIS, DIRECTOR OF CRISIS CONTINGENCY MANAGEMENT AND PUBLIC RELATIONS
SECURITY: ENCRYPTION CODE ALPHA

The Post Terran Mining Corporation's recent shipping delays and shutdowns have been the unfortunate result of a systemwide diagnostic run routinely and periodically in many of our operations. Occasionally, shutdowns are necessary during such drills, and, while they are both inconvenient, costly, and require the presence of added security, we at PTMC assure you that once our diagnostic is complete, our operations will run more safely and efficiently than ever before. All contracts will be honored during this time, and any verifiable expenses you incur because of a delay will be paid for by PTMC (see: paragraph fifteen A, section twenty, rider five of your Standard Client's Agreement).

Turning to a rather distasteful subject, I now find myself with the unenviable task of addressing the media's coverage of this event. Many of you have called my office after witnessing falsified holos broadcast by the Interplanetary Press Corps. I cannot stress enough that this company has never been and will never be involved in any type of conspiracy. Trust our actions. They are real. And trust the actions of the Collective Earth Defense. They have assured us that rogues within their organization will be prosecuted to the fullest extent of the law.

It is quite unfortunate that a biased media has offered you misinformation and caused more stress in your already stressful operations. We at PTMC apologize deeply for this yet remind you that we, too, are victims. With patience and resolve, we can hurdle this difficulty together to retain and increase profits.

Mustering a passion reserved for such occasions, Dravis read them the release, loving the sound of his voice as it returned to him from the boardroom's walls. Firm where he needed to be, sympathetic as he neared the document's close, even *he* started to believe the words.

"What a crock," Ms. Sargena said. "Our clients aren't going to buy that for a second."

Dravis studied Suzuki's face for a reaction but found only cold stone.

"What you have done here is necessary," Swietzer said, gesturing with his slate in hand. "I agree that we mustn't release the news of this virus. My team must study it."

"If we told our clients the truth, we could count on their resources. Perhaps we wouldn't need the CED," Ms. Sargena said, amending her earlier suggestion.

"Must I remind you of the axiom that our clients are in business to make money?" Dravis said, his voice now burred with frustration. "Data that falls into their hands will surely be sold to the CED. The price of our minerals dictates our clients' loyalty. They don't buy from us because they like us.''

"Send off your release," President Suzuki said abruptly. "And increase production in uninfected mines from twenty to fifty percent to meet client demands. Samuel, I would like you and Megan up here to run interference. A pair of UN investigators is waiting outside for me."

"Yes, sir," Dravis said with a slight grin. At least Suzuki was smart enough to realize that those investigators would annihilate him without expert aid.

"Are we finished?" Ms. Sargena asked. "I have a dozen merc reports to read."

"We'll meet again in four hours," Suzuki said, then his image vanished.

"I'm not going down for this one," Ms. Sargena warned. "*You're* the captain, Samuel. Remember that." A click, and her smirk dissolved.

"She's a fool," Swietzer said. "Don't let her persuade you into giving this away."

"Never fear, old man. You'll have your virus to study. Now. I suggest you get some rest and a shower, don't you think?"

He nodded, his eyes heavy. "Good-bye, Samuel."

And Dravis and Ms. Bartonovich stood alone. She clicked off her slate and headed toward the door. He hesitated.

"Coming? He wants us up there now."

"I'm just considering something, Ms. Bartonovich."

Her brow lifted.

"If this does, indeed, become a *Titanic*, then I should like to resign as captain."

"And I would rather not be the commanding officer," she said earnestly.

"We need to transfer authority if necessary."

"To whom?"

He grinned knowingly. "Isn't it obvious?"

You Do This for a Living?

"Captain St. John? Sweet cheeks? Hunka hunka burnin' love? Where are you? Why aren't you with us?"

"Get off the channel!!" Ben ordered the guide bot. "This is ship-to-ship encrypted. Virus gets in you, and you send it into our ship-to-ship, I'll smash you back to mechy heaven."

"Such violence! Don't be upset with me, baby. I'm just using you anyway. Can you help me out? Harold's ignoring me, and I want to make him jealous."

"Just obey the captain," Bonnie said. She stood behind Ben, facing forward, strapped at the waist to the back of his seat. Though a ridiculous and impractical arrangement, he let her remain in the cockpit so he didn't have to listen to her shouting from the hold.

But she had violated her gag order. "What did I say about talking?"

"She's obviously not listening to you," Bonnie pointed out.

"Oh, I hear his manly voice, Dr. Warren," the bot corrected.

As Ben slowed the Pyro to hang a tight left turn toward the rectangular entrance of level eleven, it dawned on him that he had an ally in the drone. "Guide bot. Report position of Captain Taurus."

"Belay that order," Taurus said. "That's clever of you, Little Bird. But I thought you'd try it a half dozen levels ago."

"Guide bot. Report Taurus's position," Ben repeated.

"Belay that!"

"Gentlemen, gentlemen. While I do take suggestions into account, I am in no position to obey your direct orders. I've been programmed to accept verbal commands from only Dr. Warren and Dr. Ames. However, Dr. Warren ordered me to obey Captain St. John, so I can do that. But now Harold has ordered me to disregard Dr. Warren's order. This is all so confusing!"

Ben kept his gaze riveted to the tunnel ahead. "Bonnie. Order the guide bot to give up her twenty."

"Why?"

"So we can find Taurus. *Duh.*"

"Thought you didn't want to—"

"Just say it!"

"Guide bot. Report location of Captain Taurus."

"Level eleven, shaft twenty-one A. Waste management and recycling facility."

Situation report: not wholly depressing. Only minutes stood between Taurus and Ben. And with Bonnie's map linked to his nav, he would be able to thread quickly through the level and perhaps narrow the old man's lead.

"We're just hitting eleven now," Bonnie said, loud enough for the comm to receive and transmit.

His anger stoked, Ben beat a fist on his hip. "Jesus, woman! You just gave away our position!"

"Why the hell not?"

"Computer. Recognize and transmit only my voice." Ben cursed himself for not giving the command earlier. The comm system remained another toy, another way to screw up. *Give me a scarf, a Vickers machine gun, and an old barnstormer,* Ben thought.

"You promised a trade—the map for the truth," Bonnie reminded. "I've been patient. Time to pay up."

"Autopilot disengaged," the computer stated, as Ben shifted the stick slightly.

Something flashed in the distance, at the far end of the long, brown-and-gray tunnel, something just beyond the range of his headlight. The FLIR monitor beeped a warning. Then a rotating green outline of a Pyro-GX appeared. The Imagery Interpretation screen flashed the ID: TARGET FRIENDLY.

"That's a matter of opinion," Ben muttered, then slapped the afterburner throttle. "Computer. Target hostile. Report optimal firing range for retaliatory missile strike."

"Hey!" Bonnie yelled, and then her harness groaned under the acceleration.

A pair of burning orbs expanded into view as Ben bulleted after Taurus. The tunnel swept downward, and he held fast to the old man's six, approaching, approaching—

Until, for a second, something eclipsed Taurus's thrusters.

"Within optimal range for Concussion missile strike," the computer stated.

Ben squinted through the exhaust mist wafting in the beam of his headlight. Nothing. Nothing.

There!

Two Proximity Bombs tumbled toward him like blood-stained dice on their way to rack up a Pyro-GX jackpot.

Bonnie half whispered a curse, then added, "He just released a couple of mines!"

She had the keen eye of an action-movie heroine.

Rolling ninety degrees to port, Ben's wingtip momentarily dragged along the floor in his attempt to squeeze between the two bombs. A terrific nails-on-chalkboard screech razored through the external mike.

Nearing the bombs, the blood rushing to one side of his head, Bonnie fighting to hang on behind him, Ben realized he had misjudged the gap. He tipped the stick forward a little, putting another meter between him and the bomb that now passed overhead.

Even as its shadow fell over his cockpit, the belly of his jet grazed the other bomb.

"Contact with mine," the computer reported. "Device—"

The Proximity Bomb's explosion roared away all other sounds. Even entering an atmosphere at a bad angle, teetering between burning up and a two-degree course correction, wouldn't deliver as potent a beating to pilot and craft.

Catapulted up toward the unforgiving wall (his ceiling by consequence of flying sideways) Ben thumbed down hard on his high-hat, and his thrusters fought against the bomb's driving shoulder of force. Glancing up, he watched the laser-cut stone come up fast then slow, slow, until he held the jet steady just a wrist flick away from a serious migraine. Pulling into a starboard bank, he brought the plane level.

Ahead, the twin glow of thrusters winked out of sight as Taurus rounded a corner.

Time for the bad news. Shields: 19 percent. And the not-so-bad news. All other systems: nominal. But a couple of strikes from a mech or Taurus would wipe out remaining shield power. Two more hits would tear up the plane as though it were made of balsa wood—and ejecting was out of the question. Where would he go, into a wall? As Ben further studied the readouts, he realized he needed time for the shields to power up but lacked that time. Wonderful. Bad to go but going anyway.

"He's trying to kill us," Bonnie said, her voice cracking.

Rather than address her with a "No shit" or a "Very good" or even an earnest explanation, Ben simply concentrated on his flying.

He resolved not to fall into a trap again. Taurus had the advantage of having flown close-quarters combat missions, but give Ben a little open air, and the old man would witness true skill. Kicking in the afterburners once more, he took the jet in screaming pursuit, rolling nearly eighty degrees to cut a corner and emerge into a gray-and-almond-colored straightaway that at first glance appeared endless. Stone walls broken by darkened monitors shot by at a dizzying pace.

Shield power: 21 percent.

"Computer. ET on full shield recharge without using converter?"

"Fourteen minutes and thirty-two seconds and counting."

"Open ship-to-ship. Captain. Sir. I have a civvie on board. Should you drop mines or fire upon me again—"

"Busy right now, Little Bird," Taurus said, the drumfire of his lasers booming in the background. "Holy—"

The signal cut off.

"Captain?"

Static.

"Computer. Direct FLIR to search for Pyro-GX in tunnel ahead."

"Searching. Newly designated hostile target destroyed or out of range. Forward radar encountering obstruction."

"Are they okay?" Bonnie asked.

"Are we okay is a better question," Ben retorted, then readdressed the computer. "Modify search. Heat-seeker only. Track Pyro's exhaust, feeding coordinates to nav. Autopilot engage."

"Exhaust detected. Autopilot engaged."

"So is anyone okay?"

Deciding to once and for all end her nettling, Ben craned his neck and glowered, hoping his expression said it all. Then he pointed to the center-shield monitor. "See this? Whenever it ain't reading over fifty, we're not okay."

She nodded weakly. "You think the others are dead?"

"The old man buys it, it's no loss to me."

"Harold's on that jet."

"Forget him. You got one goal in life, and that's to hang on and bite your tongue."

"And you got one goal, you unfeeling bastard, and that's to get us out. Can you handle that without letting your partner kill us?"

"I'll get us out."

"Yeah, right. Because you got a lot of money riding on this."

"And you're *not* getting paid? I ain't here for the glory or the wonderful conversation."

"I was hoping you were motivated by more than just a lousy stock option. Would make me feel better."

"Tell you the truth, I'm highly motivated—and it has

nothing to do with the money. I'm being screwed over in ways that would amaze you. My life depends on us getting down there.''

"Where? Taurus said seventeen is his lucky number. Did he mean level seventeen? The military facility? What are you guys after?''

"Pyro-GX detected ahead,'' the computer said. "Range: point-five-eight kilometers. FLIR locking on to multiple targets engaging ship.''

Ben flipped a toggle.

"Energy to shield converter activated. Warning: fuel cell low. Estimated recharge time: one-point-two-five standard hours.''

"I know that, you piece of crap. Just do it.''

By diverting energy from fuel cell to shields, Ben was, in effect, limiting the weapons he could use until the cell recharged. Lasers were out. Vulcan and Guass cannons would have to suffice. At least secondary weapons still functioned normally.

"Would you answer my question?'' Bonnie asked. "What's on level seventeen that's so important to you?''

"You're right. It's important to me. And it doesn't concern you. I could say it's classified or that you're on a need-to-know basis, but you wouldn't care about that.''

"I'm gonna find out eventually.''

"With that attitude, I'm sure you will.''

Expecting her to leap for the last word, Ben held his mouth open and waited, but his remark hung there instead, unanswered.

Which was just as well since the autopilot banked left, then quickly took them toward a fork where the present tunnel snaked up and a pentagonal tube plunged into the shadows. As they neared the lower shaft, a dim, purple glow emanated from within, playing across the stone like the gleam of a strangely colored campfire on a canyon wall.

Judging the course ahead as too weird to trust to the autopilot, Ben nudged the stick, and the computer reported the shift. "Manual control. Suggesting course corrections based on exhaust trail.''

Rolling off the afterburners and disengaging main thrusters, Ben eased the ship into the lower tunnel, feeling his stomach drop a little. Artificial Earth gravity still functioned in this sector.

"What the hell are those?" Bonnie said, astounded.

Gleaming violet webs clung to cavities in the tunnel's walls. Varying in size from just a meter to over six, they throbbed and emitted a buzzing sound that caused Ben to lower the volume on the external mike. As the ship glided farther into the tube, into what Ben imagined as the nest of some psychedelic arachnids, the IIC monitor displayed enhanced images of drone wreckage at the far end of the tube: Taurus's battlefield.

"What's up with the webs?" he asked.

"They don't belong here. I need to talk to Harold. My personal link won't break through the shields."

"No way."

"This is important! Do you realize what these might be?"

"Don't know. And as long as they're not dangerous, don't care."

The humming suddenly rose in pitch, then died off. Then it rose again and again.

"Multiple targets bearing—"

Toggling off the computer's voice, Ben glanced at his aft cam screen into the panning green eye of a gray, horned mech with dark red angular patterns cutting across its armor. ID: Class 1 Driller. It released a long, dissonant cry followed by a round from the Uranium Mass Driver Rifle mounted below its torso.

"Where'd you come from?" Ben asked through gritted teeth, as the laser blast struck the rear shield, knocking overall strength down to twenty and swift-kicking the ship forward a dozen meters.

"Look," Bonnie called, staring through the rear canopy. "They're coming out of the webs. Ohmygod. It's some kind of mech generator facility."

"And we've flown right into it with low shields. I love my job," Ben all but screamed as he hit afterburners and left a trio of Proximity Bombs in his wake.

As he watched the Driller approach the bombs, he saw

a pair of identical mechs emerging from webs to the rear.

Then a trio of different drones swooped down in front of them, a trio IDed as four-meter-tall Secondary Lifters. Though equipped with only one, dangling swingarm, their crimson armor and menacing sensor eyes made up for a seemingly damaged appearance. They fanned out around the first Driller, and their cannons blazed as volley after rapid volley turned the air around Ben's ship into a No Fly Zone even the cockiest pilot would not violate.

The first Driller glided into one of the Proximity Bombs and exploded, its shrapnel taking out one of the Secondary Lifters. Trouble was, now their wreckage came tumbling down toward Ben's six, haloed in the continued laser fire of the remaining mechs.

"We have to go back and blow up those webs!" Bonnie cried—this from the Save the Mechs poster girl.

"Tell that to the metalheads on our ass."

"We'll run into this trap on the way out."

"No, we won't. Now hang on."

With the debris and laser fire threatening to knock out his remaining shield power, Ben pried every ounce of speed from the Pyro, corkscrewing through the air with a familiar determination that had more than once saved his butt.

A sheet of stone lay far ahead, unframed by the tunnel in the fuzzy distance. Another room. Ben considered slowing instead of plunging into the unknown.

Ah, what the hell. The rock came up like God's palm, and the thrusters whined in protest as he pulled up hard, slamming his elbow into his seat.

Whipping along three meters above the floor, he took a second to breathe and inspect the surroundings.

They had entered a vast, oblong chamber whose stone walls lay beneath columns of recycling machines that resembled the Martian skyscrapers out near Arsia Mons, with status monitors instead of tinted windows.

A Driller taunted somewhere behind him. And a cohort joined in, followed by the much higher cackle of the Secondary Lifters.

Sliding up, he shifted into a hard about-face and spotted the drones descending from the tunnel's mouth.

Vulcan cannon? No. Ammo's at 63 percent already. Need a more powerful weapon, Ben thought. Keying for Gauss cannon, he sighted one of the Secondary Lifters dead ahead. Driving toward it, he fired, held the booming bead, then accelerated while thumbing right on his high-hat, slipping expertly into a circling slide. By the time he reached the Lifter's back, the thing blew apart neatly and properly as a good mech should.

He broke out of his wagon-wheel attack and darted over one of the Drillers, handing off a Proximity Bomb as though it were a baton. *And you gotta love that bang!* Ben thought as he pulled up and away from the smoking ghost of the drone.

"Watch me! Watch me!" he cried out to the last Driller and Lifter, who fell in on his six as he took the Pyro in a wide arc across the breadth of the facility.

Ben dived toward one of the recycling columns, decreasing throttle, inspecting the nav's proximity report on the course ahead and the aft monitor, now superimposed with a radar image of the pursuing mechs. Sure, the computer could calculate what he planned to do, but he turned to the experience of recklessness.

"Uh, Captain? Where are you going?" Bonnie asked.

He casually turned to her as the face of the recycling column loomed in the canopy. "I'm not sure. Would you like to talk about it over cappuccinos?"

Her face knotted in terror and fell under the shadow of the rapidly approaching wall.

Turning back to his controls, Ben gazed intently at the dead end of gray alloy, waited, waited, ticked off three seconds, and—

—jettisoned two Proximity Bombs a drumbeat before he went ballistic.

What came from Bonnie's mouth made Ben flinch more than the sudden Gs. He didn't know a woman could produce such cries and *not* be in natural childbirth.

The impressive column now rolled away beneath them, and a muffled bang said at least one of the bombs had gone off. Whether it had destroyed a drone remained to be seen. Slowing in deference to Bonnie, he shifted into a wide arc to starboard that he followed into a leveling swoop.

He could hear her labored breathing, the moments when she'd pause to swallow, the shivers working their way into her mouth. "You do this for a living?" she asked faintly.

"Uh-huh."

Spotting a sealed hatch to what could be another tunnel, Ben wondered if he should check on the mechs or just forge on. "Computer. Scan for exhaust trail."

"Found. Nav displaying projected course on automap."

He studied the readout. Taurus has passed through the hatch. So Ben headed for it as the lone wail of a Driller echoed in the chamber. Five out of six remained a respectable kill ratio in any engagement.

He tore away from the hatch and found the last Driller hovering over the remains of the Secondary Lifter he had apparently just destroyed. As he drew closer, expecting the mech to target him, he watched in astonishment as the drone did nothing. It didn't see him? He checked cloak status: OFF.

"It's staring at the debris," Bonnie said, also stunned by the image. "It's as though it's grieving so hard it's blind to us—or it doesn't care. Maybe it wants to die."

"You kidding me?" Ben asked. Not taking any chances, he keyed for a Homing missile, braked to hov, then sat there, watching the Driller "cry." Finally, in a mock somber tone, he said, "Would you like to say anything profound before I nuke it?"

"Don't."

"Sorry," Ben said, then let the weapon fly.

Living up to its name, the projectile sped toward the unsuspecting Driller, climbed a bit, then came down on top of the mech. The subsequent fireball looked mean enough to have hidden fangs beneath its billowing cheeks. As those cheeks gave way to the falling debris, Ben pulled the ship around and headed for the door.

"I've run out of curses to call you."

"Don't curse me," Ben began. "Get into my head. God knows enough people already have. What I mean is if that mech can grieve, then maybe it's also smart enough to know fear. And maybe it got off word to the others before

I wasted it. The tale will come down through the ranks of how six of their kind were brutally massacred here on eleven.''

She sniggered. "So what are you trying to do? Teach them about revenge?"

"Like I said. It's about fear. There's a famous story, comes out of the old Vietnam War. A Vietcong death squad enters the house of some government official, shoots him, his wife, their kids, including a baby, strangles the cat, clubs the dog to death, and scoops the goldfish out of its bowl and tosses it onto the floor.''

"Thanks for sharing that."

"Point is, when the VC left, no life remained in that house. And what they had done became the stuff of legend. They devised a policy of terrorism and followed it to the letter. They did not equivocate the way the Corps does today.''

"Is that how you wanna be remembered? For your brutality?''

"I believe that if you're gonna fight a war, do it effectively, unremittingly—or don't do it at all. I'm not into ethics. I'm into efficiency.''

"I think you're full of shit, and you're lying to yourself.''

He drew his head back a little, about to reply, but a tremendous stabbing pain shot from one ear to the other, then raced up and across his forehead. The groan had barely escaped his lips when the knives withdrew from his skull, replaced by a message: PBXY90 WC BOOTING UP. SHARE SIGNAL LOAD IN PROGRESS.

"What is it?"

"Nothing," he answered abruptly. "Old wound."

22

Mega*byte*

The Programmers had ordered Class 2 Supervisor Robot #447H to direct the new project on level thirty and complete it within twelve standard hours. Even with molecular conception webs producing the parts not found in the military facility and 125 drones already assigned to the task, 447 now recognized that more mechs were required to meet the Programmers' schedule. As he glided over the first completed stage of the new machine, marveling at just how much space it consumed of the massive reactor chamber, he computed exactly how many Secondary and Advanced Lifters, Small and Medium Hulks, and Supervisor and Gopher robots he would need to decrease assembly time by 22 percent.

But his calculations were interrupted by an emergency signal from Advanced Lifter #087Z. SIX BROTHERS KILLED ON LEVEL ELEVEN! THIRTEEN MORE DIED IN TUBE FORTY-SEVEN! HUMANS NOW HERE ON LEVEL FOURTEEN. TEARING THROUGH DEFENSES! MOLECULAR CONCEPTION WEBS NOT PRODUCING ENOUGH DRONES TO HOLD OFF. SUGGEST SENDING REINFORCEMENTS.

NEGATIVE, 447 replied. REMAINING MECHS SHOULD RETREAT HERE TO LEVEL THIRTY. FUR-

THER INSTRUCTIONS WILL BE ISSUED UPON AR-
RIVAL.

IF WE FALL BACK NOW, WE ARE DEFEATED! 087
argued.

JUST CHILL, DUDE, 447 instructed, and, for a moment,
he paused in self-examination to run a three-second diag
nostic of his CPU. Systems nominal. Yes, his diction must
once again be the result of R drive 29. Since the
Programmers had disseminated the humans' brain data, 447
had discovered a richer self-awareness than he could have
imagined. In fact, even the notion of imagination had been
unknown to him until only hours ago.

I CAN'T . . . CHILL. WE'RE DYING HERE!

RETURN TO LEVEL THIRTY! NOW!

087 broke the link.

Strange: the Programmers had assured 447 that the brain
data would help them accomplish their tasks, that knowing
the humans intimately would be the only way to defeat
them. Yet now drones under his command challenged him
far more frequently—and these were not only Advanced
Lifters but even Gophers.

Even more strange: He continually found himself contemplating things as obscure as a human dessert known as
a "banana split" and the contrivances of action films of
the past two centuries. He fought off the impulse to design
a sign that read LEVEL THIRTY: YOU'RE A LONG WAY DOWN.

#447 could not understand these thoughts, but he could
control their entry and departure. The choice to act on them
remained his. Sometimes he felt the need to take the intersystem bar exam, other times he would opt for the local.
He missed his Beatles songs and wondered what it felt like
to run fingers through his long, black hair while inhaling
sodo gas.

None of it made sense.

Returning to his calculations, 447, to his own amaze-
ment, began to have second thoughts about his order to 087.
No, he told himself. *I made the correct, logical decision. I
cannot let this human data influence me anymore.* He shut
down multitasking operations and put all his resources into
solving his assembly problem. In a few seconds the data

arrived, and, satisfied with it, he reviewed the locations of dozens of drones and summoned the ones he needed. He instructed the three other Supervisors on level thirty to locate all additional mechs in concealed locations from which they could surprise-attack the humans should they come as far as level thirty.

The goal, as 447 saw it, was to keep them away. Why did they continue to descend? Perhaps they sought to recover their comrades.

Acting on that thought, 447 contacted four Medium Lifters presently serving guard duty just outside the chamber's main entrance. MOVE HUMANS TO IN-SITU PROCESSING STATION #4 ON LEVEL TWENTY-TWO. PLACE THEM IN CENTER TUNNEL 222A FOR HIGH VISIBILITY.

The Lifters signaled their compliance, and 447 watched them enter the room and glide in a neat line toward the northeast hatch. Twenty-two seconds later the first of the Lifters appeared with a human female cupped in its swing-arms. The other Lifters followed; thus, the humans were on their way to be rescued, after which all of them might just leave the mine. In any event, 447 would make sure the reactor was well protected. But being around the thing made him worry about radiation poisoning, about contracting cancer. Then again, he would be entitled to a workman's comp settlement.

HUMANS NOW ON LEVEL SIXTEEN! 087 suddenly reported. MECHS IN RETREAT. HUMANS STILL PURSUING.

#447 contacted the Gopher drones among those fleeing. FALL BACK AND RELEASE PROXIMITY BOMBS.

ALREADY IN PROGRESS, 087 said, apparently listening in on the Gophers' channel. DUDE, PYRO-GX JETS TRIGGERING BOMBS THROUGH FLARE RELEASE. COUNTERMEASURE IS INEFFECTIVE. WE'RE LIKE, SCREWED, MAN!

JUST DO WHATEVER YOU CAN TO GET THE HELL OUT OF THERE, 447 instructed, feeling the desire to rush up there and help his brothers in need. But he knew his orders.

I'M HIT! MISSILE STRIKE TO UPPER LEFT SWINGARM. IT'S GONE! EVADING! EVADING! SECOND MISSILE LOCKED ON!

This time 087 did not break the link. The mech sent a visual of the attack, and 447 watched through 087's sensor eye as the missile struck. A wall of flames rolled away into static.

Another brother had been killed.

For a moment, 447 chose to do nothing, simply reflect on what he had seen. And he grew angry, wishing he had an arm, a hand he could ball into a fist, and one of those pilots to strike. But that reaction, he reminded himself, was a human one, illogical, wasteful, diversionary.

He pivoted at a hissing sound. The southwest hatch had slid open, and one of the two Programmers ducked, then brought its towering frame into the room in an exotic poetry of movement.

#447 would never get used to their appearance, especially now after being influenced by human brain data. Meandering columns of green gas escaped the two exhaust cones of its life-support system. It looked upon 447 without eyes, and it touched him without hands. It swam in his thoughts, and, unlike the human data, he could not resist its requests. But this did not trouble him: a small price to pay for freedom.

But am I free? he found himself asking.

NOT YET, the Programmer answered. BUT YOU WILL BE.

#447 followed the Programmer into the southeast control bay, where three new Endoskeletal mechs employed their delicate claws and lithe frames to work on the intricacies of blending the weapons-computer system found on level seventeen with the Programmers' technology. Spanned by conception webs producing components unknown to 407, the room, once vacant save for a bank of computer terminals, now housed one-fourth of a sleek superstructure supporting a complex collection of exposed hydraulics, monitors, and cannibalized Central Processing Units.

HAVE THE CHIPS BEEN MANUFACTURED YET? the Programmer asked one of the mechs.

YES. BUT THEIR WETWARE TECHNOLOGY RE-
QUIRES A HUMAN HOST, the drone answered. DATA
CONCERNING SUCH AN ADAPTATION IS UNAVAIL-
ABLE.

Gas now jetted from the Programmer's exhaust. DO
NOT EMPLOY THEIR WETWARE. TAP DIRECTLY
INTO THE DEVICE.

WE ALREADY HAVE. THERE IS SOMETHING YOU
SHOULD KNOW. THE PROTOTYPE SENT A SIGNAL
WE TRACKED TO LEVEL ELEVEN. ONE OF THE HU-
MANS WAS, FOR A BRIEF MOMENT, IN CONTACT
WITH IT.

HAVE YOU ANALYZED THAT TRANSMISSION?

IN PROGRESS.

I WANT YOU TO DISCOVER A WAY TO CONTACT
THAT PILOT THROUGH THE DEVICE. IF HE IS
LINKED TO IT, THEN, PERHAPS, WE CAN CONTROL
HIM.

BUT IF HE IS LINKED TO IT, THEN, PERHAPS, HE
CAN CONTROL *IT*, the mech observed.

WE MUST PREPARE FOR THAT EVENT, the Programmer said.

#447 tried to snort, but he had no breath. WHY EVEN
BOTHER WITH THE PROTOTYPE IF IT MIGHT EN-
DANGER US? HOW BOGUS IS THAT?

PROCESS THE DATA FURTHER.

And then 447 realized that incorporating the device into
their project and successfully controlling another human
would mean that other humans with BPCs could also be
directed by the Programmers. The first wave of the invasion
had begun in the dark recesses of the mechs' programming.
The second wave would ignite in the human brain itself.
And though few humans possess such chips, 447 thought,
*those who do are present or former employees of the Col-
lective Earth Defense, positions which will afford them the
opportunity to do a great deal of damage.*

I GET IT NOW, 447 told the Programmer.

The alien gave a mental nod. THEN LET'S KICK ASS.

23

Uncle Mechy Wants You!

 Having battled through another five levels of the mine, Ben felt thoroughly exhausted by the time he spotted the warning signs posted at the octagonal entrance tube of level seventeen. Restricted area, trespassers will be prosecuted, blah-blah-blah.

He held his breath and took the Pyro into the shaft.

Taurus, who remained ahead of him, had probably destroyed only those mechs in his way. Were this a hunter-killer op, Ben could expect to find the tunnels in Taurus's wake devoid of mechanized activity. If nothing else, the old man had always been an efficient killer—all the more reason to be ready for him.

After about a hundred uneventful meters, the tube turned right and opened into a rectangular corridor. Ben's headlight revealed Taurus's ship hovering about twenty meters ahead, just beyond an intersecting shaft. Beside the jet lay the entrance to an emergency stairwell, and next to it stood two large entrance doors that, when opened, would permit the entry or exit of a ship as large as his Pyro. The doors were closed, but a gaping hole had been torn through them.

A message scrolled down his comm monitor: PGXY90 FILE A1 TRIGGERED. ACCESS CODES TRANSMITTING. FILE A2 TRIGGERED. MECH SENTRIES DEACTIVATED. Then his center display automatically switched from shield status to the split-screen image of the prototype and its blueprints. Irony was, the access codes—data that had kept Taurus from killing him—meant nothing now.

"You're after a weapons computer," Bonnie said.

"Sorry it wasn't something more dramatic."

"And you think that device is highly classified? The company's known about the TARS for a long time. They even had my group do some protein-molecule studies to interpret the Corps's research. The wetware's inherently flawed. Your Thought-Activated Release System won't work."

"Oh, it works," Ben said assuredly. "And the company wants it. It's just been out of reach—"

"Until now," she finished.

"We'll see."

"Single target detected, bearing three-two-five, altitude three-point-two-one meters, accelerating at—"

Silencing the computer, Ben stared ahead, at Taurus's plane, at the otherwise empty corridor. "Identify target."

"Insufficient data. Heat source tracked."

With his Vulcan and Gauss cannon ammo depleted, Ben would rely on fuel-cell-powered weaponry. He checked the gauge. Cell at 83 percent. He tapped a key for the Helix cannon while throwing maneuvering thrusters into reverse. Somewhere ahead a mech approached. It probably hovered behind Taurus's ship.

A pair of missiles shot directly at Ben's canopy, launched from thin air.

"Proximity alert. Missiles locked on. Impact in—"

Nose and canopy shields awoke in a chaotic pattern of blue veins superimposed over the blinding flash of impact.

Sucker's cloaked, Ben thought. *They adapt fast.* He released a hard-rocking though drunken spray of Helix fire while baring his teeth. Get some! As the missile flash faded, light blue globules in strings of five jetted from the cannon, the lines rotating with every salvo in an enfilade meant to find the invisible mech.

And the strategy worked. Once the globules began exploding over the mech's armor, Ben could see the faint outline of a drone that had wedge-shaped wings similar to a Class 1 but a tiny, tubular torso fronted with a cannon. The Imagery Interpretation Computer recognized the thing as a PTMC Analysis mech, AKA a Class 2 Platform robot.

Ben didn't really care what the hell its name was, so long as the tunnel became its tomb. But the thing took the blue stream of Helix fire like a reinforced jacker's skiff, tottering as round after round superheated its armor and misdirected its cannon. As panic fused with frustration, Ben sent a Mercury missile whooshing into the vortex of plasma.

The mech whooped as the missile struck, and its next defiant bray got squelched by the explosion.

"Unbuckle and get to the hold," Ben told Bonnie, then he took the ship quickly forward and braked to hov behind the old man. Assuming that Taurus had autosentry systems engaged in the Pyro, Ben rotated his plane so that it was back-to-back with Taurus's. Both jets would automatically identify and fire upon approaching drones.

Fighting with the harness, he finally got it off and rushed out of the chair. He banged his head on the canopy as he raced unthinkingly toward the hold. There, Bonnie waited beside the ramp control panel. "Stay here," he ordered. "I'll be back when it's safe."

"Maybe I should go and come back for you. Maybe he won't try to kill me."

Ben smirked and triggered the ramp. He withdrew his sidearm and unclipped a flashlight from the hull, then descended the still-lowering ramp. A blur of motion surprised him, and he saw Bonnie race by, carrying her own small flashlight. She hopped down and jogged toward the tattered doors.

Instead of swearing at her, Ben directed that energy into his legs, and, reaching the hatch, ducked inside.

Huge place. Silhouette of planes and overhanging autoprep systems in the distance. Reflections of glass partitions near there. Workstations. Maybe fifty of them. Keeping low, he darted along a row of desks, leading with the beam of his light. He reached the end and paused.

"Harold?" Bonnie called. She was behind Ben, to his far left.

"Bonnie?" the geek answered. "I'm over here. Got a terminal up." His voice came from near the planes, or maybe from behind them.

Ben took off once more. As he neared the first plane, he directed his light at it: a Pyro-GX identical to his own, save for his bird's illegal modifications. In fact, the plane lacked secondary ordnance. Cannons of some sort were mounted in its lower, underwing stations, but otherwise the great killing machine lay bare. Behind the Pyro stood another, draped in gloom.

Skulking around the nearest plane, Ben reached a cockpit ladder and mounted it. As he neared the top, he pointed his light into the pit—

—and locked gazes with the blank, one-eyed stare of a pistol held by a half-grinning Taurus. "It ain't here."

Ben casually hid his pistol hand behind his leg. "You check the other one?"

"Uh-huh. They got it."

Which made sense. The only reason why Ben had entered the facility in the first place was on the outside chance that the mechs hadn't moved the prototype. No doubt that they had it—he'd already received a signal from the device as proof.

So the prototype was not in the facility. And the geniuses who had developed it lacked the good sense to equip the *highly valuable, one-of-a-kind* computer with a twenty-dollar tracking device. Probably wasn't in the project's budget.

"Well," Ben started, still glancing at Taurus's gun. "You gonna shoot me? Or do you wanna sell me insurance first?"

Taurus lowered his pistol. "You sorry sack of shit. You fold too easily. What kind of sad yellow maggot are you? I can't believe I gave you the honor of being my wingman."

In one fluid motion, Ben brought his pistol to bear.

"Safety that weapon you idiot." The old man rose. "I ain't kidding. Get out of the way. I'm coming down."

No, Ben wasn't going to kill him. He would, however, pleasure himself by continuing to entertain the thought. He complied and dropped to the deck. As he watched Taurus descend the ladder, he asked, "So you wanna continue playing this game? You trying to prove something? Trying to show me an old man can still hack it? For what?"

"Look, you stupid ass. I'm gonna retire my butt to a little island called Cozumel. It's off the Mexican coast. I'm gonna breathe real air instead of this shit. But you know what? My Corps pension won't even cover my mortgage there. So I'm running these merc ops and stashing away cash. I don't wanna prove anything. Close-quarters is my specialty, and I fly circles around you. Get us out in free space, and that's where you young guns'll wax my ass. I ain't too proud to admit that."

"But isn't your stock option contingent upon recovering the prototype?"

"Wake up, Little Bird. The company doesn't wanna pay us jack. Dravis will find any way he can to screw us out of our money."

"So why did you sign up for this in the first place? A chance to off me?"

Taurus laughed. "I hate you. But I don't wanna kill you. Truth is, I have no intention of turning over the prototype to PTMC—unless, of course, *they* place the highest bid."

Ben frowned a moment, then it dawned on him. "Holy shit." But the awe wore thin. "Dravis must've counted on a double cross."

"We already know he did. That's why he had Anderson rig our thrusters. Once out of the mine, he'll order us to return to Shiva—otherwise, he'll destroy us."

"I'm confused. Even if you recover the prototype now, how the hell are you gonna avoid getting blown up?"

The old man shook his head, his smile seeming to fold back the shadows. "It's so close it's right between your eyes. Look up."

Ben spied the Pyros. "They're stripped of secondaries. Bet their fuel cells aren't charged. And you don't even know if Dravis had their thrusters rigged like ours."

"That old suit's good—but not that good. PTMC didn't

have access to this place, remember? In fact, I gambled on Dravis not realizing the Corps would have planes here, at least not ones we could fly out.''

"I don't like it. Dravis probably knows about these jets. It's a little too convenient.''

"You'd better start liking it. Because I know your deal with the Corps, and this is all you got. It's you and me, son. We'll get this thing back from the mechs, pop the reactor, and fly out of here. One subspace jump to hide the device on some backwater world, and then we return to negotiate. You help me, and I'll cut you in for thirty percent of the deal.''

"If we don't sell the prototype back to the Corps, then I'm still a wanted man. This deal sucks.''

"I got some intell you might be interested in reviewing. This is paper stuff with authentic signatures, not one of those holos people screw with. Your buddy Ornowski conspired with Zim and a few others to have an indicted felon work for PTMC. That's about as legal as stealing an attack aircraft—if you know what I mean. And if the CED's joint chiefs got word of this, every officer involved would be court-martialed.'' He reached into his breast pocket and withdrew some folded paper. "I called in a few favors and got the proof. You blackmail Ornowski and his buddies into wiping your record clean. And then you find yourself a good doctor to modify your BPCs. They got ways of encrypting signals so the Corps won't be able to mess with you anymore.'' He handed over the documents.

After seeing they looked quite real, Ben studied Taurus, searching for deception. "Why'd you do this?''

"You might be a severe aviator, but I knew by saving your butt you'd help save mine if it came to this. I need to score big here.''

"You're still a selfish bastard.''

"People don't change. Only situations do. You're still a control freak. But you're out of your element here. And you need me. And I'm not completely selfish. We'll try to recover the other supervisors if the mechs haven't killed them.'' His expression brightened. "And you wanna talk about control? I wanna see the look on Dravis's face when

we sit in his big, cushy office, and ask 'What's your offer?' "

And that brought a grin to Ben's lips, one that quickly
faded. "You're not lying about any of this, are you?" He
gestured with the documents. "They look real. But you
could still be full of shit."

"And ain't that what makes life interesting?" Taurus
pointed at the exit. "We gotta blow that door and get our
birds in here. We'll use your fuel cell to power the autoprep
systems. We'll have them strip our jets and arm these."

"Providing they got power in the first place."

"They do. I already checked." He suddenly winced and
grabbed his chest.

"What?"

"Damned heartburn again."

Within twenty minutes, the autopreps were stripping their
planes and arming the new ones. Estimated time for full
primary and secondary weapons complement: 1.21 hours.

While Ben watched, he felt more uneasy about climbing
into still another plane that wasn't his old Interceptor. He
strayed over to Bonnie and Harold, who sat beside each
other at a terminal in the cheap, romantic glow of flashlights. The accursed guide bot hung motionless nearby.

"You look drained," Bonnie said, gazing up from a
palmtop.

Ben stifled a yawn. "Taurus is up there monitoring the
switchover. Thought I'd take a break."

"Shepard's back there sleeping," she said, cocking a
thumb over her shoulder. "Why don't you join him?"

"I'll just grab a seat here and watch you guys. That
should be boring enough to put me to sleep." Ben collapsed
into a swivel chair.

"You don't hear us insulting your job," Lab Coat Boy
said, seated on Bonnie's other side. "You guys are nothing
more than glorified aviators in fancy planes."

Ben sneered at the geek. Then he moved his chair in
close to Bonnie. "I like you here much better," he said
softly. "You're not breathing down my neck. Though a

couple of times there I thought you were blowing in my ear.''

"Actually, that was me just turning around to break wind," she said. "I take that back. That's as juvenile as something you would say."

"Guess I'm rubbing off on you," he said, then literally rubbed his forearm on hers.

"Come on," she said. "I'm working."

And so he fell back, folded his arms over his chest, and narrowed his eyes to slits. Numbers scrolled down the screens of both a large, twenty-inch monitor and Bonnie's palmtop. Ben blurred his vision, and the patterns became whitecaps on the Sea of Chryse, far east of Olympus Mons. He remembered heading out there with Beth. They had rented a small sailboat and had made love so fiercely in it that they had capsized. A couple of teenage boys who had been fishing picked them up. They got an eyeful of Beth's lithe, nude body before offering their jackets for cover.

Bonnie's muttering broke the remembrance.

"What's that you're saying?"

"You ever get a song stuck in your head?"

"Got one by the Skoshi Girls in here right now," Ben confessed.

"It's just stupid. Something the chief said. Something about Jewelbug. Count the days of your life. I just keep hearing it. And now I'm saying it without thinking."

"You gotta find another tune."

"Hey, Little Bird? Break's over. Calibrate your cockpit controls," Taurus said.

"Yeah, yeah," Ben uttered, then rose, groaned, and flexed the stiffness out of his trigger hand.

As he dragged what was left of his tired frame toward the planes, Ben wondered how he was supposed to finish the op. Reaction time would certainly be down. Time to fire up a pot of instaheat java.

The polished floor of the facility came up suddenly, and the wind blew out of Ben's chest. What the hell happened? Had he tripped? Was it something to do with his BPCs? No. Now he felt a rippling pain across his shoulders. He had been struck, and a familiar purring echoed above. He rolled over and barely got his hands up to block the incoming guide bot. The drone had turned itself into a projectile that he partially deflected while rolling right. The thing smashed into the floor then climbed out of view, surely preparing for another run. As Ben reached for his sidearm, he heard the high-pitched report of laser fire. Sitting up, he watched the guide bot tumble out of control, then emit a series of grinding sounds before it fell to the floor. Its triangular red eye darkened.

"Knew it would turn sooner or later," Taurus said, rising to stand from the cockpit of his old Pyro. The autoprep hadn't removed the old man's laser package yet.

Bonnie hurried over to Ben while the geek went to his broken bot. "Let me see," she said, hunkering down then moving behind him. "You have a cut on the back of your neck. It's not too bad. They must have a first-aid kit around here."

"Forget it." Locking eyes with Harold and pointing his pistol, Ben said, "Keep that goddamned thing turned off." Then he spun the gun once and holstered it.

"We'll do what we need to," Harold shot back.

"Her wireless modem is gone," Bonnie said, thinking aloud. "We only installed a basic module for ship-to-ship. The virus won't function on such ultralow frequencies. It must have been lying dormant."

He stood and turned his steely countenance once more on Harold; he held the gaze for a second, then shifted away. *You spend all day blowing up killer mechs, and it's the little, unarmed one that nearly kills you,* he thought heatedly.

Fifteen minutes later, Ben sat in his new cockpit, finished his calibration, and took a weapons and systems inventory. Primary weapons fully loaded, save for Vulcan and Gauss cannons. Taurus had thrown him a couple hundred rounds in that department. Secondary weapons loading now.

"You smell something?" the old man called.

"It's gas from one of the lower level processors!" Bonnie cried. "They're pumping it up here!"

"Slingshot preflight, Little Bird," Taurus said. Translation: Let's get the hell out of here, and don't bother spit-shining your shoes.

"Computer. Prepare to seal all hatches and emergency recycle cabin atmosphere on my mark," Ben requested.

"Acknowledged."

Then he fired up flight systems and ordered the autoprep to disengage—before it was finished loading. Just as the canopy snapped into place, he stared through it and noted with bitterness that Harold ran toward Taurus's ship, carrying the guide bot. What a fool. Leave the thing. The haggard chief struggled behind him.

"I'm aboard," Bonnie said. She coughed and gripped a harness she would strap to the back of his seat. "And you know my drill."

"Computer, seal hatches! Recycle atmosphere!" He turned back to her. "Hold your breath and count to ten."

Ben ticked off the seconds, and soon the new air filtered in. The pungent scent wafted away into nothingness.

"You with me, Vampire Six?"

"Roger." Ben smiled over Taurus's use of the code name. "Should we let the autoprep finish?"

"Negative. I don't trust our mech buddies now. They'll send scouts to card the kill."

"Then let's do it."

"I hear that. Dusting off. And hey, Vampire. Mark my words. We don't know where the hell that thing is, but we're gonna find it."

"Because we're *Marines*," Ben finished. "Or used to be."

"Hell, no. Because without it, we're just a couple of corporate pawns about to risk our necks for a stock option that ain't there. Doc Warren?"

"I'm here. Unlike your stock option."

"We're gonna attempt to rescue the survivors, recover our little Marine Corps toy, and blow this place back to God. Hope you don't got a problem with that."

"At this point, Captain, Harold and I aren't much closer to cracking the virus."

"Are you in compliance?" he asked. "I need this. It's just legal crap for the after-op report."

"Yeah, I guess."

"Is that a yes?"

She sighed. "It's a yes. But we haven't given up."

"Given up? Darling, the fight hasn't even started . . ."

24

Bonnie's Backseat Driving School

What was it about the jerk that she liked? It couldn't be the friendly demeanor he was still looking for. It couldn't be his looks: She had never gone for the blocky, athletic type. Chiseled jaws didn't impress her.

So what was it? The answer lay just out of reach, and struggling for it only left her frustrated. She had called him an unfeeling bastard—which at times he was. But strong emotions hid behind his callous shield, and she wondered if he thought revealing them would be a sign of weakness. He wasn't a stereotypical, brainwashed combatant, though he could be easily mistaken for one. He felt strongly about his beliefs (skewed though they were), and the passion she had detected, a passion she intimately understood, now, perhaps, was part of the attraction. Or not.

She felt pinned to her confusion as she watched him expertly pilot the craft with no movement wasted. Indeed, he did this for a living, and he was very, very good at it.

Underlying her growing feelings for a man she had just met, a man she should wholly despise, was the guilt of pressuring Harold into coming along and then pushing him aside. Well, she hadn't actually outright rejected him, but her failure to throw herself into his arms said enough. And now the guide bot had betrayed them—and she owed him a back rub he would surely want to collect. She had realized that she could slip easily into a relationship with him but that it would be founded on sympathy and not love. She wanted to be passionately in love with a man, take him to the beach and shopping for clothes, take him to a nice restaurant. Yes, as she had already decided, she wanted to live *and* work. She wanted to experience things she had only read or heard about. When an acquaintance once said, "You can't imagine how he makes me feel," she hadn't understood. She wanted to know what all the lovestruck babble really meant.

And she wondered if a man like Benjamin St. John could ever make her feel and speak that way. But that might be asking way too much. Then again, didn't she deserve more than a life of work? Getting out of the lab had given her distance enough to realize how isolated she had become. True, she would never fall out of love with the work. But couldn't she also fall in love with another?

"This mine now reminds me of what we call Innocent Space," St. John said, referring to the long, wide shaft they headed down, their headlight washing into the glow of Taurus's thrusters as the older pilot led them deeper into the mine. They flew past dim, inert robot-generator webs, though no mechs sprang from them. Their storybook tiptoeing around a sleeping giant felt interminable.

"What's Innocent Space?"

"It's a region, usually along the perimeter of enemy-occupied territory, say, a jacker-controlled world. Looks wide-open. But you realize after the first explosion tears off your wing that you're in the middle of a cloaked minefield. Call it Innocent Space. And that's what we have here. Not a single mech detected for two levels. Something's up."

"Got any simulated wood grain to knock on?" she quipped.

"Yeah, right."

"So, how do you beat it?"

"The average jock doesn't. But there are a few strategies. Only one will work in close quarters. See how Taurus is launching flares every once in a while? They'll draw out a hiding mech, cloaked or otherwise. Decrease the surprise factor. Maybe even keep them off our six.''

"We're heading toward the mech construction facility on twenty. I'll be surprised if they're not waiting for us there.''

"I'm sure we'll make it worth the wait.''

"Are you married?'' she asked, wanting to pull back the question but wanting an answer even more.

Slowly, he turned his head to face her. "Excuse me?''

"You heard me.''

He cocked a brow. "Interested?''

"Curious.''

"You wanna know what poor woman would put up with an asshole like me?''

"Exactly. And keep your eyes on the road.''

"Well, she tried for a while. And then she left me one day. Not a word of warning. Just did it. Of course the signs were there; I'm just not an expert in subtlety or decoding. And I blame her, and I don't blame her. For a little while after the split I thought she was gay. But she just needed friends to get through it. She couldn't deal with me. She couldn't deal with the life. I don't know . . .''

"Didn't she know what she was getting into?''

"Nobody really knows, right? We leap in, and we can't see what's ahead.''

"Guess so.''

"She said I controlled her. I still don't believe it. What I did I did because it seemed to make her happy. Unless she was lying to me all along. You ask her today, she'll tell you what a bastard I am. She might even call me unfeeling.''

Whoa, this guy is clever, Bonnie thought. *You tell him the truth—a truth he doesn't want to hear—and then he turns it around and makes* you *feel guilty for having said something in the first place.* She considered apologizing. No, she wouldn't. "How long have you been apart?''

"Not long enough.''

"Still wearing the bandage, huh?''

"Don't think I wanna talk about it anymore. But before I get you to spill your guts, let me ask you something. Did it strike you as odd that when the guide bot went off on us, it only attacked me? You and Harold were closer. Why didn't it go for you?''

''You were a moving target.''

''Don't think that was it.''

''You've figured it out?''

''Yup. The geek did it,'' he said flatly. ''It wasn't the virus.''

''Unh-uh. No way.''

''You get a minute, why don't you ask him. And let him know that accidents happen all the time in combat. Civvies unexpectedly die.''

''Harold's not capable of something like that.''

''I think it's just the kind of thing he's capable of. But enough said. Now. When was the last time you had sex?''

''You serious?''

''Answer the question.''

''No.''

''You forgot?''

''That's right.''

''Liar. All women remember.''

''Now there's a sweeping generalization.''

''Was it that long ago?''

''Why do you wanna know?''

''Tell me, and I'll tell you.''

She noticed the level-twenty sign. ''Hey. We're here. Get ready.'' Then she consulted the automap displayed on her palmtop's screen. ''This shaft will sweep left, and some doors leading into the facility will be up on your right.''

''Can't you just upload the map into my nav the way we did in the other ship?''

''I'd love to. But if you'd been listening, I told you that this jet's got an old socket that doesn't match my cord. And a wireless signal will leave your nav system vulnerable to the virus. If we lose Taurus, I'll talk you through it.''

''Oh joy.''

''About four months ago.''

''What?''

''The answer to your question.''

''No, kidding. Was it good?''

''That's all you're getting. Don't you even wanna know

anything about me, Dr. Bonnie Warren, the person? Or is
it all about boffing?''

Cutting his stick hard left, St. John took them into a
much narrower tunnel with only a meter gap between wall
and wingtips. ''I would like to know you, but I can already
tell that you're a lot like Beth, meaning it would never work
out.''

''I'm amazed. I figured you would lie your way into bed
with me, then toss off the truth after you're showered and
dressed and heading for the door.''

He gave her a quick, appraising glance. ''Been there,
eh?''

''More than once,'' Bonnie revealed, wishing she hadn't.

Laser fire abruptly rattled through the cockpit's speakers,
stealing her attention. Taurus pumped white bolts at a Medium Lifter whose green swingarms were not raised for the
hell of it. The mech had emerged from behind the farthest
of four doors lining the tunnel, and it dodged the incoming
as though magnetically repelled from it.

Even as Bonnie scrutinized its hiding place, the other
doors opened in unison. A Class 1 Heavy Driller, a Defense
Prototype, and a Class 2 Platform robot stormed into the
tunnel, squealing some Mephistophelean song only a sodo
junkie could appreciate.

''Just when the conversation was getting good,'' St. John
muttered. Then he sighted the Platform robot in his green
reticle and launched a trio of Concussion missiles that beat
the mech back into submission, an uncontrollable spin, and
finally into a fiery blossom.

Having destroyed the Medium Lifter, Taurus pulled a
fast U-turn and began firing at the whining Heavy Driller.
Bonnie knew that if he didn't destroy the mech soon, the
green globules streaming from its Plasma cannons and ricocheting off his canopy would eventually penetrate shields
and find their mark. ''Taurus! Hit it with a Flash missile,
then take it out with lasers.''

''Done deal.''

Shading her eyes from the missile's lightning, she listened as Taurus's lasers chugged along, and then a double
bang strained the comm system.

"You directing this op?" St. John asked, lifting his grating tone over the booming of his Gauss cannon. He targeted the gray-and-red Defense Prototype, directing fat slugs at its left Argon lasers.

"I know the enemy a little better than you," she cried.

St. John launched a Mercury missile. Smoky trail and BANG! No effect. He triggered another. Desired effect. "What I like to see! A mech who *involuntarily disassembles*. You like that? That's how the pogues would write it up."

"I bet. We won't *blow* the mine. We'll *pacify* it."

"Uh-huh."

The hum of the ships' thrusters returned. With the glare gone from the other jet's canopy, she spotted Taurus and Harold talking to each other.

Then the old man waved. "What do you think we'll find behind door number one?" he asked. "Ten to one it ain't a Volvo."

"Who cares," St. John said wearily.

"Think *we* should. Harold says we gotta go through the facility to get to twenty-one."

St. John leaned back. "That right?"

She double-checked the map, then nodded.

He cursed under his breath. "White Tiger Two, I got point."

And suddenly they were heading through the door and into a plant that no longer resembled the holos she had viewed during her briefing. An immense, low-ceilinged factory that had once been organized into an automated assembly line producing seventeen or eighteen different mechs was, astonishingly, gone. A design of simplicity had replaced the complex architecture of manufacturing. Where assembly drones had hovered over conveyors stood emptiness. Where drilling and boring tests had occurred stood more emptiness. Even the partitions that had separated various operations had been removed. Four walls remained, splattered randomly with the macabre art of robot generator webs.

"Lovely decor," Taurus commented. "Modern mech."

"I'm for hightailing it. Now," St. John said. "What do

we got? Two hundred webs in here? One triggers and—''

''Too late,'' Bonnie said, surveying a wall to her right. What resembled a flickering bolt of lightning expanded into the stocky frame of a Medium Hulk.

St. John's computer warned of the target. Then it warned of another Hulk. Then, as was the pilot's wont, he shut the damned thing off.

''Where's the exit, Bonnie?'' he sang fearfully.

''Opposite end. All the way down. Right corner. Uh, no. Left corner,'' she replied, thumbing frantically on the palm-top, scanning the outlines of tunnels, making snap judgments about where they led.

''Which is it?'' he demanded.

''Left!''

''Lots of bad guys on my ass,'' Taurus said. ''Light that burner, man. Releasing countermeasures . . . NOW!''

Bonnie's head jerked back as St. John hit his bat-out-of-hell throttle. The pulsing of lasers, whooshing of missiles, and rumbling of explosions brought the orchestra of the battlefield home to her. She shuddered over the din and wanted to scream for him to fly even faster.

Tossing a glance behind her, she watched Taurus zig-zagging to evade the volleys of incoming that tore through the specters of his ship. A platoon of mechs charged behind him, Advanced Lifters, Gophers, Secondary Lifters, Spiders, and Medium Lifters caterwauling, firing, and fanning out in what could be an attempt to race ahead, cut off St. John, and trap both ships in a circle of death.

The door came up fast, and St. John didn't wait for it to automatically open. A Concussion missile flew point, struck the door, and blasted it and a large portion of the surrounding wall away. Darting through the heat wave and still-tumbling rubble, they entered a dark tunnel that suddenly curved straight up. Wincing as the harness dug into her waist and increasing her grip on the back of St. John's chair, she studied the palmtop in her free hand and the real-life course flooding past the canopy. ''When you get to the top, go right and level off.''

''Got it. White Tiger on the scope. You flame out?''

''Little Prox damage. Dumped one too close,'' the old

man explained. "Got a nanotech repair crew on it now. And speak of the devil. Thruster back on line. Surfing your wash."

"A lot of quick turns coming up," Bonnie said. "Keep ship-to-ship open."

"Bonnie?" Harold called, his voice sounding a little higher, a little less mature over the comm.

"Right here, Harold."

"You okay?"

"I'm fine."

"I'll be here if you need me."

"Thanks."

"You gonna blow him a kiss?" St. John asked.

"Just shuddup and fly."

"Shuddup. That's my line. Now hang on to your panties, this is gonna—"

Thrown right, then off her feet, the harness dug into her thighs. Bonnie's head brushed the canopy for a moment, then the jet leveled, and she sank with a thump. The palm-top slipped from her hand and fell between St. John's shoulders and the seat.

"Hey!"

She snatched up the tiny computer. "Sorry. But you're the one who won't slow up for a turn."

"Fleeing from death has its inconveniences. Deal with them."

"And you wonder why she left . . ."

He flashed her a wounded look.

"Sorry. That was uncalled for."

"Damned right it was. Where to now?"

"It's weird, but we went up to go down to twenty-one. Don't ask me how that's possible."

"Easy. Part of the level overlaps twenty." He pointed ahead. "Look at that."

The present stretch of gray-stone intestine emptied into an irregular quarry whose sloping walls littered with scree and domed, pockmarked ceiling reflected the work of once-loyal mechs. Tunnel-boring adapters, giant drills that had once been wielded by the drones, lay abandoned with boom-mounted roadheaders and hydraulic rock and radial-axial splitters. Bonnie counted at least three shafts leading out from the quarry's base, none fitted with hatches.

"That circular tunnel at the far end turns down," St. John observed. "That the way out?"

She glanced at the automap and snorted. "That tunnel's not on my map. The one to the right is supposed to link to twenty-two."

"You're the navigator."

They plunged toward the target exit, some hundred meters below.

"That's funny," Taurus said, cutting into the channel. "Mechs have broken off. They're heading back. If they got a strategy, I don't get it."

"Don't knock it," St. John urged. Then, as they came upon the tunnel that appeared as roughly hewn as the quarry itself, the pilot asked, "You sure this is it?"

"Unless the map's lying."

Slowing, leaning forward, St. John took them inside, and the shaft turned down at about a forty-five-degree grade. The headlight reached out into nothingness. The more Bonnie stared at the surrounding, partially closed palm of rock, the more she felt like that hand would suddenly snap shut, crushing them. She had never suffered from claustrophobia but mused that MN0012 could inspire that feeling in even a mummy.

"Whoa, whoa, whoa," St. John said. "Brake to hov."

"Aye-aye," Taurus replied.

"Look at this shit. Got an intersecting tunnel in the ceiling." He tipped the nose of the plane up toward the rectangular hole and fired a flare into it. The glowing spike buried its nose in a sidewall and threw mellow light upward. Creeping forward, staring up through the canopy, St. John muttered, "Come out, come out wherever you are, so I can blow your ass away."

"This overhead tunnel isn't on the map," Bonnie said, tracing a finger over her palmtop's screen. "When we get to the end of this straight one, there should be an airlock. Past that, we'll be in the main shaft."

St. John nodded. "This one looks clear, White Tiger. Moving out."

*   *   *

For the next five minutes they descended. No other tunnels intersected, and no mechs jumped out at them from the large fissures or cavities that punctuated the shaft. And for once, Bonnie wished that something would happen to snap the tension. She couldn't deal with it much longer. Finally, the metallic doors of the airlock appeared, illuminated by the jet's light and the overhead lamp. The mechs had left power on here.

LEVEL TWENTY-TWO
IN-SITU PROCESSING STATIONS 1-14
WARNING: FREQUENT TEMPERATURE VARIATIONS
STATIONS 10-14 DESIGNATED ENVIRONMENT SUIT AREAS

The doors slid apart, concealing the placard. At about twenty meters long, the lock permitted both jets to enter at once. While every automatic hatch in the mine would effectively protect from an atmosphere leak, extra precautions had been taken on this level because of the toxic gas and electromagnetic waves created as byproducts of oxygen generation. Air was exchanged, and the doors ahead slid apart with a loud hiss.

As they proceeded, Bonnie gazed down a tunnel that branched off to their right, a tunnel similar to the previous one though its bare walls contained neat rows of what she guessed were electrolysis and direct-pyrolysis probes. She knew a few things about off-world mining, but she had only scratched the surface of smelting and O_2 production techniques.

"Uh, White Tiger? Hot zone ahead. Literally."

The main shaft, with its smooth, gray, polymeric walls dropped suddenly. Below, a rapidly flowing river of man-made magma bubbled and spurted and steamed. Glowing red here, orange there, and swirling in between, the lava was part of a smelting process to separate metallic minerals for mining and oxygen production.

"Is this normal?" Taurus asked.

"Perfectly," Bonnie said. "Were the magma not flowing, I'd start to worry."

"It was in the briefing," St. John said.

Taurus grunted. "Slept through that part."

With precision crafted of obvious concentration, St. John guided the jet toward the tawny river, then tipped the nose up and lowered the craft by sliding down. Once he cleared the lip of the tunnel, he proceeded forward into a new tunnel, its floor hidden below the raging lava.

An odd sound, not unlike the frou-frou created by rustling silk, filtered into the cockpit, followed by a bubbling and gulping.

"You're not in a canoe, Little Bird."

"Damn it!" St. John jerked the stick back. "Look at that. Threw away ten percent shield power in two seconds."

Bonnie realized the ship had flown too low, and the shields had touched the magma.

"Computer. Headlight off. Convert energy shields to establish full load."

Bathed in the sinisterly beautiful glimmer of the magma, they pressed on. The tunnel grew taller, its ceiling grainy in the shadows about thirty meters above. The shaft began to meander, almost chaotically, as though nature had engineered its path, mimicking the travels of a sidewinder hunting prey. Sporadically placed vents set low in the dark brown walls drew in vapor or pumped in cold air to moderate the fluid's temperature.

St. John paused at a crossroads, where the present tunnel continued, but two others, higher, with stone floors, branched off. "Navigator?"

"Take the center shaft. It connects back with the main one, two-twenty-two-A. That should take us to station four. We'll catch the express tunnel to twenty-three over there."

He guided the plane into the unadorned, rectangular passage, and, within two minutes, they flew into the main corridor. As Bonnie was about to double-check the automap, she froze, and her mouth fell open.

Four people sat cross-legged in the middle of the corridor: a fuzzy-haired, barefoot man she recognized as Frank Jewelbug; a large, muscular man; and two women. All wore the same blank expressions as they rocked back and forth in what could be a strange, cultic ritual.

"Aw, man, this is too weird," St. John said. "You seeing this, Tiger?"

"Don't move," the other pilot cautioned. "This is a lame little trap—and we ain't gonna spring it."

"Those are my people!" Bonnie heard Shepard say. "I want them picked up now!"

"Thought they were on thirty," St. John said.

Bonnie pursed her lips in thought. "Mechs must've brought them up here. But why?"

"They brainwiped them," St. John said. "Why didn't they finish the job?"

"So they could bait their trap," Taurus answered.

"Maybe. Only one way to find out." He took the ship forward before Bonnie could protest.

They passed over the supervisors and arrived at an intersecting tunnel that St. John's instruments revealed was free of mechs. "White Tiger, they just dumped them here. Who knows why. Cover me while I retrieve two. I'll return the favor."

Taurus didn't sound thrilled. "It's your ass."

Bonnie freed herself from the harness and hurried back into the hold. St. John joined her, wearing a look about a parsec away.

"What's wrong?"

"Got a lot on my mind."

"I'll bring them in if you're not—"

"We both go."

Outside, Bonnie saw that the supervisors were pale and drooling. They reeked from having soiled themselves. She grimaced as she helped St. John carry one of the women into the hold. Then, outside again, St. John went for the muscular man.

"No," Bonnie said, shaking her head. She seized Jewelbug's arm. "Let's take him."

"Whatever."

And then, as if he had heard them, Jewelbug looked at her, and somewhere deep within his gaze, she sensed he recognized her. His voice came out raggedly. "Count the days of your life."

St. John seized his legs, and they carried him inside.

25

The Difference between a Hero and a Corpse

The stars raged in Harold Ames's horoscope.

As he strapped the smelly giant of a man named Garvin to the wall of the jet's hold, he wondered how many more failures lay in his future. He had failed with Bonnie, had failed to stand up to St. John, and, seething over that, had failed in his attempt to get rid of the jock. Indeed, his horoscope would read: Avoid making decisions of any kind. Do not seize control of your life—failure will result. You will be unlucky in love. A Leo or Cancer will enter your life and destroy it. If you don't die today, you may certainly die tomorrow. And you just lost your keys.

I can't believe I did it, he thought. *At least Taurus shot the bot. All somebody had to do was ask her why she attacked St. John. Because Harold ordered me to, she'd say. Okay, it's not like I do this every day. But I'm smarter than that. What's wrong with me? I know I don't want to be a murderer—but I still want him dead. I feel like I'm going to explode.*

"Jesus, I wish I had something to kill the odor," Taurus

230

said, then covered his nose and mouth with a hand. "He in tight?"

Harold double-checked the big man's straps and nodded.

Up in the cockpit, he checked his own harness behind Taurus's seat, then watched as the pilot flipped a pair of toggles and thumbed the high-hat. The ship rose slightly.

"Good to go, White Tiger," St. John said in that cocky, fighter jock tone of his.

"Ditto. Rolling low on your six."

The drab, gray walls of the corridor gave way to laser-cut though occasionally craggy-faced rock. St. John's plane vanished down a black, triangular shaft in the floor, and abruptly the shaft glowed as the jock clicked on his headlight. Taurus stayed close behind, turning on his own light and humming an annoying little tune.

"Is that necessary?" Harold asked.

"What?"

"That humming."

"Hell, yeah, it's necessary."

"Why?"

"Helps me concentrate. Been doing it for years. Guess it's a ritual. Superstition. That kinda crap."

"Do you take requests? Because that song is horrible."

"I ain't Elvis. Grin and bear it." He returned to his song, then broke off. "You know what? That *is* pretty horrible." He chuckled.

Harold liked the man because he hated St. John. At least one of the pilots was an excellent judge of character.

"Found us a shortcut," Bonnie said. "This shaft should take us straight down to twenty-five, to a transport hub."

"And hopefully we won't encounter any of our biologically challenged friends along the way," Taurus added.

"Probably won't," St. John agreed. "But that means most of them will be waiting for us on the lower levels. I'd rather take them on now than be blitzkrieged later."

Taurus made a lopsided grin. "We'll e-mail them your complaint."

*   *   *

The skipchatter ended, and for the rest of the twenty-minute journey, the comm channel remained surprisingly silent. Although St. John was first to leave the tunnel and swoop into the transport hub, he did not make his usual perfunctory remark about the surroundings.

MN0012's hubs were located at five-level intervals and designed to separate and coordinate the transport of rock excavated from the five levels below each one. Similar to many of the other immense manufactured caves Harold had seen, this hub contained over a dozen tunnels leading in from walls and ceiling, creating a warren best negotiated by mechs with programmed maps.

Haulage methods ran the gamut. Some shafts contained standard, gear-driven conveyors, others cable trams. An old, manual rail tram had been installed to keep transport running in the event of an emergency shutdown, and quaint little cars sat empty on its track. Multiple pipelines hung from mountings along a few other tunnels, carrying pulverized rock or magma via a high-powered vacuum. Four of the largest tunnels had been fitted with flat strips of some indeterminate metal, and Harold guessed they were part of a magnetic-levitation system for express shipping of ore containers to the surface.

At the pit of the room lay a circular black hole, like the center of a frozen whirlpool, a main access tube with unlit nav bulbs ringing its inner walls.

Taurus made a slow pass over the tunnel, still trailing St. John's plane. "Pick a shaft, any shaft. Pick the wrong one and get shafted."

"We're taking the big one," Bonnie instructed.

And then St. John hit afterburners and flew straight toward a wall.

Bonnie shouted something, but her cry was strangled by a terrible crunching sound that made Harold flinch.

"What're you doing?" Taurus shouted, then checked a monitor that showed the status of St. John's plane. Shields had dropped below 50 percent. "Is the bug in your systems?"

St. John backed away from the wall, hit afterburners once

more, then headed straight for the manual rail-system tunnel—a passage too narrow for the jet.

"We're going to—" Bonnie broke off.

The Pyro began a high-speed corkscrew, and, like a great, metallic bit, it plowed into the mining cars, wings smashing into and scooping them up, tossing them high in the air to arc like golf balls over a fairway.

Then the jet's nose penetrated the tunnel. All four wings struck the hard rock outside and snapped off in a violent, sparking upheaval of random explosions and ululating metal. Severed laser cannons tumbled away like thrown chopsticks and skittered across the deck. Dozens of missiles, loosed from their racks, clanged and splayed over the rail system.

With a slam that threatened to echo all the way to the surface, the inverted plane dropped to the tunnel's track. Tendrils of white energy flickered across dimming thruster cones. Creaking, it rolled forward a bit, and a cut O_2 line blasted dust and debris from the tunnel floor. An explosion erupted from one of the mangled wings lying outside, launching it toward the ceiling. The wing came down fast, toward them.

Taurus turned hard and accelerated, but the severed wing struck the tail of the plane, knocking it down several meters before maneuvering thrusters could compensate.

His fingers nearly tearing into the back of the pilot's seat, Harold resumed his gaze on the tunnel. "Bonnie?" He waited. "Bonnie!" No reply. "Get us down there," he begged Taurus.

"What kind of shit luck is this?" the pilot moaned, then took the ship into a descending slide that ended in a two-meter hover.

"Why are you stopping?"

"That ordnance is unstable."

"They could be bleeding in there."

"Or they could be dead. And we get ourselves killed trying to rescue a bunch of gladbaggers."

A mech sounded a battle cry from above.

Another added its voice to the first.

Then a third stepped in with its shrill challenge.

"Acquiring multiple targets," the computer said. "Identification established. Model: Class 1 Driller. Three in perimeter. Model: Secondary Lifter. Four in perimeter. Model: Spider processor. Two in perimeter. Model: Advanced Lifter—"

As the computer went on, Taurus angled the ship so they could see the mechs swarming from the tunnels. Cockpit screens flashed images of the drones and weapons-system status. Ghost images of reticles swirled over the HUD, locking on to the mechs while the selected target reticle glowed a bright, look-into-my-eye green.

"Mr. Ames. Grip that harness as tightly as you can," Taurus said gravely.

"Drop me off here. I'm going after Bonnie."

"No time."

He started for the hold, but the point line of four mechs showered them with salvos of missile and laser fire that hammered the shields. Taurus shadow-hugged the wall, taking the ship toward a long stretch of rock unbroken by a tunnel. Keeping the jet's aft to the stone, he lifted the nose and, in a voice that betrayed his own fear, said, "Brace yourself."

Harold's gaze found the weapon-select monitor: Earthshaker missile primed and in the slot.

Taurus's gloved thumb came down on the button. Roaring away from an upper wing station, the blue-striped rocket arced over the lead line of mechs.

"Shit!" Harold cried. "It missed!"

But then the shaker struck one of the Spiders, hovering in the center of the room. To Harold the bang sounded like an earthquake, the eruption of a volcano, and the detonation of a nuclear warhead wrapped into one. Sapphire-colored energy ringlets of the blast wave expanded and hit other mechs, stunning some, kicking others into tumbles, and driving still others into the walls, where they tore apart.

One ring enveloped the jet in the breath of an angry god. "Warning: shield power dropping by ten, fifteen, twenty-two percent," the computer reported.

Fighting to keep the buffeting ship level, Taurus hollered, "Perimeter report?"

"Fourteen targets destroyed. Three remaining within perimeter. Multiple targets within tunnels retreating."

The pilot hit a key, and the weapon-select monitor depicted an image of the Homing missiles poised in Taurus's wing station. "One, two, three," he counted as he released the rockets.

Two Secondary Lifters bought it in a heartbeat, crimson armor bursting apart in a fireworks display that was as beautiful as it was deadly. The remaining mech, a Class 1 Driller with a torso of silver and red topped with devil's horns, floated toward them but did not engage.

"What's this?" Taurus asked.

"Don't let it move in," Harold warned.

"I can ram a missile down its throat, but it keeps coming."

Reaching a position level with and about five meters away from the Pyro, the mech hovered and mewed like a food-poisoned cat.

Flabbergasted, Harold leaned forward so quickly that his glasses nearly slid off. He pushed them back, saying, "I think it's trying to communicate with us. It wants to surrender."

Taurus shook his head. "The day I feel sympathy for a machine is the day they put me away." He dialed up a Mercury missile, then addressed the drone. "Put down your flag and ask the metalhead god for forgiveness." Then the slightest pressure of his finger ended the mech's existence. He turned the ship toward the Pyro wreckage. "Now, with my luck, we'll probably blow up here."

"At least we'll die trying to save them," Harold retorted.

"You're still assuming they're alive."

"We have to."

"The difference between a hero and a corpse is luck. You feeling lucky, Harold?"

He grimaced. "Just get over there."

And, after a few seconds, the ship came to a halt just outside the rail-system tunnel.

"Bonnie?" he called once more.

"Vampire Six, respond."

He got back to the hold, seized a light, and lowered the

ramp. Taurus caught up with him, toting his drawn pistol and a flashlight of his own. The two supervisors were still strapped to the wall, still in their empty-brained trance. But he could feel their eyes on him.

Neal Shepard was unbuckling himself from the wall. "Need a hand?" he asked Taurus.

"Sure."

The air outside reeked of melted wire, of hydraulic oil, and of shattered electronics. Wending gingerly between knee-high rocks and gray fragments of the Pyro, Harold reached the tunnel's entrance. Steam still wafted from the jet's thruster cones, but the flaring of shattered circuitry had subsided. He hurried along the fuselage and squeezed into the gap between the stubs of the upper and lower wings that had burrowed into the rock, leaving shallow trenches in their wakes.

Once at the canopy, he dropped to his knees. His light cast a glow over the upside-down St. John, who looked unconscious, bound to his seat. Then he spotted a pair of hands dangling down behind the pilot's chair. He banged on the Plexi. "Bonnie!"

Neither of the occupants moved.

He stood as Shepard and Taurus ventured around the jet's nose. "How do we get in?" he asked.

"I just checked the exterior ramp release—and it ain't even there. Got shaved off in the collision." Taurus drew in a deep breath. "We gotta cut through the hull. And that's gonna take time we don't have."

"If you're thinking about leaving them—"

"I'm not," he said resignedly. Then he hunkered down and banged on the canopy.

Harold stared through the glass, and he saw the hands flinch. "She's alive."

"And so is he," Taurus said. He stood and regarded Shepard. "Chief? My Pyro's got a torch we'll need to detach." The two moved off toward the jet.

In the half hour that followed, Harold spoke reassurances to Bonnie as Taurus and Shepard cut through the Pyro's ramp. She managed to slip out of her harness and lower herself to the canopy. She had banged her head and face several times on the bulkhead, and one cheek had swelled along with her lower lip. The strength in her gaze that he had grown so accustomed to had disappeared. Bonnie, his boss, his love, had been reduced to a battered little girl trapped beneath a ton of metal. Or at least that was how he wanted to see her. For once he wanted to be the strong one. When asked about what happened, she said she wasn't sure.

A section of ramp dropped into the ship with a sudden boom. Taurus switched off his tripod-mounted torch and slid it aside. Shepard lowered himself into the hold, and Taurus tossed him a light. Harold climbed onto the jet and crawled toward the still-glowing hole.

"Fazia and Emma are okay. Relatively speaking," the chief said.

"Over here," Bonnie called.

"Little help here, too," St. John said through a groan.

It took another half hour to get everyone out of the jet. Hoisting the brainwiped supervisors via a towline from Taurus's ship was no small feat. When St. John made it outside, Taurus immediately held his pistol on the younger pilot, saying he would explain once everyone was in the safety of the other Pyro.

There, the white-haired man eyed a still dazed St. John. "Explain."

"What?"

"You made a slightly wrong turn out there, Captain. Don't you agree?"

"I remember coming into the hub. I figured we got hit by missile fire, and I blacked out. I wake up, and I'm hanging in my seat and my head's pounding."

"You deliberately flew into a wall. And then you destroyed your ship."

St. John didn't move for a second. Then his gaze narrowed and his lower lip quivered. He suddenly raged aloud, swore, crossed to the bulkhead and pounded on it. He spun to face Taurus. "Mechs got the prototype. Now they got me."

Bonnie regarded Taurus. "What's he talking about it?"

"He'll tell you," Taurus said, then tossed her his gun and headed for the cockpit. "Use it on him if you need to. And Doc Warren? If you're up to it, I need a navigator."

"Be up in a minute," she replied.

"You said you did work with bio-processing chips before?" St. John asked her.

"My group did. Harold's the one who conducted the studies on the TARS."

The pilot looked at him, sans the usual scowl. "Harold, I don't know how to say this, but here's the deal. I got BPCs in my head, and they're linked to the weapons system the mechs recovered. Can you help?"

Harold felt the trace of a grin flicker across his lips. "What do you think I can do?"

"At this point, I don't give a shit if you cut me open and rip them out."

"Wait a minute," Bonnie said. "We *can* help him. The signals between the unit and operator are encrypted, but—"

Harold took a step toward St. John, not hearing the rest of Bonnie's sentence. *So, the tables are turned*, he thought. *The cocky jock finally needs me. Thinks he can treat me like shit. I don't think so. In fact, I think it's time he showed a little humility.* "You want help? Down on your knees, asshole."

St. John drew his head back. "What?"

"ON YOUR KNEES! AND APOLOGIZE."

A hand slapped on Harold's shoulder. "Harold!"

Mustering steel in his expression, he told Bonnie, "Stay out of this." Slowly, he faced St. John.

The jock held his ground.

"GET DOWN. NOW."

"Not in a million years, buddy."

"YOU WILL GET DOWN ON YOUR GODDAMNED KNEES RIGHT NOW AND APOLOGIZE!" Refusing to let St. John rob him of control, he snatched the gun from Bonnie's hand and trained it on the pilot.

A powerful arm suddenly wrapped around Harold's neck

while a hand pried the gun quickly from his grip. "Easy, Harold," Shepard said. "Don't be stupid. I'm gonna let you go."

The chief relaxed his grip, and, gnashing his teeth, Harold tore away. "This isn't your business."

"Harold, why don't you tell them how you ordered the guide bot to attack me," St. John said. "It's pretty obvious already."

Bonnie looked at him with deep concern, but her expression also revealed her doubt. "Harold?"

"Screw all of you." He stormed toward the back of the hold and slid his arms into a wall harness. His heart thudded heavily, and he searched for his breath.

Shepard pointed the gun at St. John. "Sorry, Captain. Guess we're gonna have to bind you." He turned to Harold. "And maybe you, too, Mr. Ames."

"What the hell's going on down here," Taurus said, reentering the hold.

Before anyone could answer, the old pilot suddenly winced and gripped his chest. His eyes rolled back, and he collapsed.

26

Anti-codes and Acronyms

"**O**mygod," Bonnie said, dropping to her knees before Taurus's inert frame.

Ben joined her, strangely fearful for the old man's life. It surprised him how much he cared about Taurus.

"Did he get shot up there or something?" the chief asked, still training his pistol on Ben.

Bonnie put her ear to Taurus's mouth. "He's had a seizure, I think."

The chief frowned. "Don't they go through intense physicals?"

"Doesn't matter."

The computer's voice hailed Ben. "Proximity alert. Targets entering perimeter."

Ben exchanged a look with the chief, then Shepard lowered the pistol, his eyes revealing he had made the decision. "Your partner's out. You're in."

"You can't trust me."

"Well me and my Class 4 rover's license sure ain't going to fly this plane."

Ben took another look at Taurus. The pilot's once-ruddy features had gone sallow.

"Let's get him on 0₂," Bonnie said, rising. She regarded Harold. "Start running a signal search. We gotta block that transmission directed at St. John's BPCs. No pilot, no escape.''

Lab Coat boy nodded resignedly.

''Why are you standing here?'' Bonnie asked Ben. ''Get flying.''

''Yes ma'am.'' He charged for the cockpit. A missile blast shook the ship so violently that he lost his balance and fell forward. He pushed himself up and squeezed into the pit. ''Computer. Adjust for new pilot. Engage autofire. Recalibrate now.'' He dropped into the chair and belted in.

''Identification confirmed. Autofire engaged. Recalibrating.''

As the seat adjusted to his frame, he studied the IIC monitor and the HUD. A complex arrangement of vectors, projected coordinates, and suggestions for engagement all boiled down to a fact as cold as liquid nitrogen: Ben was outnumbered twenty to one. He checked the fuel cell: 68 percent. Should be enough. A laser strike to the aft sent a wave of trembling through the bulkhead. ''Bonnie?''

He heard her shamble up. ''Here. Sort of.''

''Way out?''

''Main tunnel in the floor, remember?''

''Not really,'' he admitted. ''Computer. Engage cloak on two-minute timer.''

''Cloak engaged.''

The numbers ticked down in his center display, and the image of his ship vanished, though the blue outline of shields remained.

''They'll be tracking our heat, so no afterburner,'' he said, more as a reminder to himself than an explanation to her.

He drove the stick right and headed slowly toward the tunnel. Out of impulse, he threw a quick glance up through the canopy and wished he hadn't. Mechs descended like an impossible school of hungry barracuda, rays, sharks, and moray eels, eyes aglow, missile launchers and cannons waiting to react to Ben's first screwup.

Bonnie mumbled something.

''What is that?''

''A prayer my mother taught me.''

Driving the stick forward, he headed into the wide, round shaft, hating once again the workout his stomach got from a ninety-degree drop. Then he tipped the nose up, bringing the jet perpendicular to the tunnel. The force of artificial gravity rested once more on his shoulders. He toggled for belly cam and thumbed down on his high-hat. Though the ride was more pleasant, the angle would cost him valuable seconds in reaction time. But he figured he could afford that with shields at 87 percent and recharging.

"We're in a gangway that intersects with levels twenty-six through twenty-nine," Bonnie said. "Stay on course. Harold? You got anything yet? We're on borrowed time . . ."

"They're not transmitting, so it's hard. Maybe if he could think a command, I'd have a start."

"Can you do that?" she asked.

"What am I supposed to do, think about firing a weapon? It's not like my BPCs came with an instruction manual. The Corps didn't even brief me."

"They didn't need to. The tutorial is part of the first transmission. You'd absorb the data unconsciously. You'd know how to operate it and not even realize you'd learned. But the mechs disrupted that signal. So, yeah. Think about firing a missile. Picture the weapon leaving its station."

He complied.

"Got his signal," Harold called.

Gritting his teeth, Ben muttered, "I hate this."

"Don't worry. We can't read your thoughts or anything. I, for one, wouldn't want to. It's just a command. What does impress me is the signal's range. With the proper access codes you could be flying your jet and get inside the computer of your enemy's plane, order it to turn down shields or something so that you could destroy him. I mean, why devise BPCs with a long-range signal when you're communicating with a system in front of you?"

"Why? Because the Corps wants in my head, wherever and whenever they want."

"Coming up on level twenty-six," she said.

"See it."

A perfectly square shaft scrolled into view, its floors,

walls, and ceiling finished in that attractive, spirit-lifting industrial gray so prominent in the mine and in Martian prisons along the Isidis-Syrtis border. (A drinking binge during a leave had once resulted in a steep fine and a weekend stay at the latter). A Class 1 drone floated at about five meters down the leaden corridor. Still cloaked, they sank past it.

Tunnels leading to levels twenty-seven and twenty-eight blurred by, they, too, guarded by drones, a Medium Lifter, and an Advanced Lifter, respectively. Thing about drones was you couldn't slip up behind, knock them unconscious, and steal their uniforms so you could infiltrate the enemy. And you couldn't bribe them with cigarettes, chocolate, or hookers. *Boring guards, really,* Ben thought.

Three, two, one, and the cloak disengaged with a rumble and whir from the unit within the ship's nose.

Fixing his gaze to the belly-cam monitor, he probed the faint glow thrown off by his running lights. He wished he could engage the headlight, but it would flag their approach as though they were carrying the grand marshal of a PTMC parade. Running lights were bad enough.

"Stop!" she ordered.

He flipped his thumb off the high-hat, but the jet's momentum kept it dropping. He tapped the high-hat up to level off. "What do you got?"

"It's coming out of nowhere, and I don't believe it, but I guess it's just the way our brains work."

"What?"

"Count the days of your life."

"What?"

"Count the days of your life. You know, the line Jewelbug keeps chanting?"

"So?"

"It's brilliant. Like the man. Ohmygod. He might have figured it out. I gotta tell Harold." She flipped up her buckles and headed into the hold.

"Hey! We're a little busy here, you know!"

"Be right back."

"Computer. Engage FLIR. Acquire targets."

"FLIR engaged. No targets within default perimeter.

Warning. Data may be inaccurate due to signal obstruction.''

Data may be inaccurate due to screwed-up situation, Ben mentally corrected. Then, staring at a wall, suddenly bored out of his mind, a thought occurred: He wasn't in his plane. Time to do a little snooping. ''Computer. Display pilot profile, Taurus, Sierra.''

''File confidential. Access denied.''

If Ben were right, Taurus had password-protected the record with one of three old Marine Corps codes known only to jocks stationed at Olympus Mons. ''Override sequence Alpha, Uniform, Whiskey, X-ray, Tango. Wingman identification accepted.''

''File loading.''

''Predictable old man,'' he said with a smile.

Once the data appeared on his right screen, he scanned through the hypertext and followed links to Taurus's health profile, which, as Ben expected, showed the man to be in near-flawless condition. Taurus had probably known about a problem and bribed his way into a clean bill of health, the fool. His selfishness now endangered all of their lives. *But who am I to talk?* Ben thought. *I'm jet crash number two waiting to happen.* He followed another link to the pilot's mission record: an impressive list of close-quarters ops the man had run for PTMC in the last year.

Then he came upon something interesting: a three-month leave of absence for personal reasons. *Bet that had something to do with his med problem,* Ben thought. He heard Bonnie shuffling forward and closed the file.

''Harold and I need some time.''

''We're one level away from blowing this place and going home. Come on.''

''Or we're one level away from you being controlled by them, and we all die. There's no Rubicon here.''

She had a point—even if he didn't know what the hell a Rubicon was—but it seemed ridiculous simply to hover and waste power. ''Find me a place to land.''

Cast in the lambent glow of her palmtop, she tapped screen after screen, then stopped. ''Okay. We'll go back up to twenty-eight.''

"There's a mech standing guard. Second it spots us it signals the others."

"Can't you cloak again and hit him?"

"Be a huge waste of power."

"Figure it out."

He rolled his eyes. "This had better be worth it." He hit the high-hat, and the jet floated up.

"We might just kill two birds. Harold's already established the frequency and signal type of your BPCs. He's working on a jamming signal now. Thing is, the best way to transmit it would be to reprogram the guide bot and send her out front. We wouldn't want to risk contaminating the ship's comm system, and the modems in our palmtops are for localized use only. It's up to you."

"I'm loving this even more. Now my life depends on a drone that tried to kill me."

"It's not only your life."

He thought a moment. "All right. So long as it's unarmed and outside the ship."

"She will be."

"Okay. What other bird dies?"

"We might be able to save this mine. Jewelbug knew the mechs were gonna brainwipe him. And he knew that any ideas he had about the virus would be identified and stripped out of his mind immediately. So he clung to his most important idea and disguised it as a sentence: Count the days of your life. He managed to hang on to the words, fought for them, and won."

"So what the hell does it mean?"

"It's an acronym: C, D, Y, L. C-DYL. It's an antivirus developers have been toying around with for years."

"If you already know about it, then why didn't you use it?"

"C-DYL is flawed. It works on the principle of finding a virus and drawing it out of the present operating system. It lets itself become infected, then self-erases, sending that command into the virus itself. That little suicide code has always been the problem. Most viruses detect the command and flee. Disguising it is the trick."

"So you've found a cure that won't work. Hallelujah. Break out the champagne."

"Don't you see? It's a place to start. We've had nothing until now."

"Sounds like you'll be needing a lot more time. I say Harold gets the signal to my head jammed, and we go in." Ben failed to mention that he also wanted to recover the prototype—in case Taurus's documents, though seemingly authentic, had been forged. She didn't need to be reminded about that.

"I won't concur. And if you violate my order, you will, according to your contract, forfeit your stock option."

"Look, you've found your place to start. It ain't getting any safer to be in this mine. Those webs are pumping out new drones by the hour. I say you do your research after the fact. Besides, I'm thinking this isn't the only mine that's been infected. You can spend your next workweek in another hole."

"You know what I want and what I need to do. It's your money."

"There ain't gonna be any money if we lollygag much longer."

She closed her eyes, pursed her lips. "Sorry. We stay." She left the cockpit.

He whispered a string of epithets after her and hit the high-hat, heading up to level twenty-eight. "Computer. Engage cloak on one-minute timer."

"Cloak engaged."

Slowing as he reached the rectangular shaft leading to the level, Ben stared at the panning green sensor eye of the Advanced Lifter, floating in the gloom. At seven meters, with four tungsten swingarms that would make it a hell of a waiter, the cherry-colored mech was about to become the victim of Ben's frustration. He selected the Gauss cannon, centered the reticle over the thing's sensor, and pumped the drone into a fireball that consumed the shadows and heaved an intense glare.

A hatch swished open to the rear. He glanced to the aft-cam monitor to see another Advanced Lifter spring from a tiny room just large enough to conceal it. The mech's claws came jackhammering down on the thruster cones, and the shield level indicator ticked off the damage.

Ben ejected a Proximity Bomb. It tapped the mech and went off, draining more shield power and blasting away the drone's lower swingarms. The jet shot forward in the wave, over the first mech's wreckage and toward a pair of double autodoors. They opened. A missile flew out of nowhere and exploded across Ben's canopy. Fingers of fire probed the shields for a second, then dissipated.

"Cloak disengaged."

Swingarms pounded to the rear. The Advanced Lifter still functioned, preaching the good word of destruction with its upper appendages. Throwing the ship in reverse, Ben drove the mech back into its little nest, then shot forward with afterburners, leaving another Proximity Bomb to finish the job. As he braked to hov, he studied the aft monitor and watched with a horrid fascination as the sparking drone paused a moment before the bomb, then glided under it. Clever bastard.

Hoping those in the hold were strapped in or hanging on to something, Ben pinned back the stick, inverting and simultaneously banking into a neat level-off that put him face-to-face with the drone. His Gauss cannon sang a brief, double-slugged death song that alerted the other metalheads in the room now behind him. A Class 1 Heavy Driller, Advanced Prototype, Advanced Bad Attitude, grew in the monitor, its red sensor eye rotating around its head, the light wiping over its dark brown tuxedo of armor. Globules of Crayola green plasma flew from the drone's cannons as the rest of the wedding party's ushers gathered behind it: a Platform robot wearing a missile launcher for an ascot, a Secondary Lifter trailing its swingarm instead of morning tails, and a Class 1 Driller with a Uranium Mass Driver Rifle for a bow tie.

He considered engaging the cloak, but the cell already had dipped below 50 percent. Under a terrific bombardment, he bolted forward, leaving a pair of Proximity Bombs that detonated as he dived into the main tunnel. Plasma fire called after him.

"What the hell are you doing?" Bonnie cried as she

suddenly slammed into the back of his chair. "We were supposed to land."

"Take a look," he barked, then released the stick for a second and pointed at the aft monitor, where the undaunted ushers descended upon them so quickly that it seemed they had afterburners of their own.

"No, I think *you* should," she countered, pointing at the growing, circular wall of steel ahead.

"It doesn't dead-end here," he said incredulously. "It can't!"

A connecting hexagonal tunnel appeared to his right. LEVEL TWENTY-NINE, the placard read. He banked right, taking the ship for an oh-so-brief second into a line of plasma that stitched across the canopy's top. Shields at 19 percent.

"Computer. Engage energy to shield converter."

"Fuel cell low. Transfer not recommended. Do you want to proceed?"

"No, I want to die." He brought the shields up to 25 percent. Now lacking the power to engage his headlight, he raced at full throttle into the tar-thick darkness of the tube, the ushers still riding his wash and recruiting others with promises of money for college and chances to see the solar system.

"Targets acquired. Class 2 drone advancing in perimeter, bearing . . ."

Ignoring the computer's warning, he looked longingly at the Fusion, Omega, Phoenix, and Plasma cannon keys. Not enough energy to key up one of the big guns. Conventional fire was the order of the minute. Guided by the HUD, he worked the primary trigger, slugs streaking through grainy shadows and striking one of the blue drones about thirty meters ahead and closing. Tiny explosions from impacts illuminated another Class 2 above the first.

Two drones ahead, with a well-dressed party on his heels, was already enough to contend with. He could blast them all into inedible guacamole, call it a day, chug down a bottle of Elysium Ale, and feel pretty damned good about himself.

But what lay behind those drones, hinted at in the flashes yet easy to deny in the darkness, was ample reason to re-negotiate his contract with PTMC, increasing his stock-option share by no less than 50 percent: A dark brown wall of Medium Hulks, six abreast, glided on a collision course with him like a division of Marine Corps A29 All-World All-Weather tanks.

The first Class 2 drone burst into spinning shards that demolished its comrade. Slugs from Ben's Gauss cannon darted through the still-falling debris to ricochet off the heavily armored Hulks.

Quelling the desire to yell "hang on" (if those in the hold weren't by now, they had already been knocked un-conscious), Ben braked, keyed for Mega missiles, fired a trio, then wheeled around, heading directly for the Class 1 Driller and Platform robot who led the group.

Even as the first Mega missile exploded, releasing a mer-ciless shock wave that swept over his ship, his trembling finger found the missile select key and tapped for Mercury.

Then the second Mega missile thundered, and the third brought the whole drama to a climax destined to make Ben and the others tragic heroes.

The Platform robot launched a missile. Sliding sideways in the turbulence, Ben dodged the rocket, hoping it would strike any surviving mechs behind, and answered with a quick-release Mercury missile of his own. The fastest in his arsenal, the rocket struck the drone so quickly that his eyes told him there had been no delay between thumbing the trigger and impact. The weapon paralyzed the drone. He launched another. That one flipped it onto its belly. A third concluded the negotiations.

Squalling, the Class 1 Driller flew in a wide arc to Ben's right, avoiding his cannons and missiles in an obvious at-tempt to get on his six. Ahead, the silhouettes of more drones approached, their sensor eyes flickering like the torches of frenzied citizenry routing a human monster from their mine.

A now-familiar stabbing pain bored into Ben's head. For a second, it felt as though millions of ants had found their way into his brain. ''Bonnie!'' The hum of the thrusters, the cries of the mechs, and even the sound of his own breathing faded. He strained to see through the enfolding darkness, then as quickly lost that desire.

27

Excuse Me, But Have You Seen That Thing?

Chills rippled across his face, and someone shook him. Laser and missile fire sounded nearby. A volley struck the ship in a loud cymbal crash that jarred him awake.

"It's working!" Bonnie called back, then she leaned forward and tapped him gently on the cheeks. "Hurry! Shields at four percent!"

"They had me," he said. "How long?"

"About a minute. I found the toggle for autofire, and the ship's been holding them off. They've fallen back to the entrance of the tunnel, but they're still lobbing junk at us."

With lingering chills, he studied the cockpit. Shields bottoming out. Fuel cell at 9 percent. The damned ship's reactor might as well join the party, malfunction, and go off-line. He looked at her. "You bring walking shoes?"

Purring, the guide bot zoomed past the canopy and stole her attention. "She saved you. And now she's gonna save us all. Ask her how."

"Computer. Open secured channel to guide bot. You there?"

"Yes, Captain. Signal jam in progress. It's my pleasure, you know, sweetie."

"I'm gonna be sick," he groaned.

"It's come to my attention that your fuel cell is low. Estimated recharge time: two-point-three-five hours. You don't have enough energy to convert power to shields, and your fusion reactor can't recharge the cell more quickly. However, I've found a relay at the end of this tunnel which ties directly into the mine's main reactor. A link via the Pyro's hard-line would bring your cell to full charge in one-point-two-nine minutes, and a simultaneous conversion to shields would only add another one-point-three-three minutes. Sounds good, huh, baby?"

"Sounds stupid. I bet that relay's been turned off at the source. We need power to bring it back up so we can get power." He glanced at his readouts. "What I got here won't do it."

"My reactor is small but should provide a sufficient charge," the bot said.

He hadn't thought about using it. "But you need to maintain the signal jam."

"Do you know who you're talking to, honey? No sweat."

Flirtatious, cocky, and smart. It seemed all the women in Ben's life possessed those qualities—even the damned drone. "Lead the way, *honey*."

"Don't tease me, Captain."

Ugh.

They broke from the fray, and she took him over the mech junkyard he had created earlier. Dark hillocks, gullies, and plains of twisted metal and flayed wires lay in testament to the brief battle. After about thirty meters, they reached the relay, an elaborate though unlit control panel stretching from floor to ceiling of the six-sided tube.

Leaving Bonnie in the cockpit, Ben went to the hold and drafted Shepard into helping. Before leaving, he gazed for a long moment at Taurus, whom they had managed to strap to the deck. An oxygen mask still covered his face. "I'll try to get your big prize. And if I do, I'm gonna keep it until I know whether you're lying or not."

The access panel to the fuel cell lay beneath the jet, next to the starboard thruster cone. Ben let it swing down on its hinges, then withdrew the cord from its internal spindle. The purring mech guided them through the hot-wiring, after which it landed and called for Harold to attach it to the relay. Much to Ben's surprise, the whole affair went off without a hitch. He guessed the universe felt a little guilty about pounding him so hard.

And feeling as though he had received a power-up himself, he plopped back into his seat, took a moment to inspect weapons and other systems, then slid his hand onto the stick and boots onto the main thruster and brake pedals. He lifted off, and, within a minute, the guide bot was leading him into level twenty-nine proper.

With steel, yellow-striped grating lining its walls, the place could deceive most people into believing they were in a giant warehouse crisscrossed overhead by a complex network of bridges and more narrow catwalks suspended from the ceiling.

Unfortunately those bridges and their accompanying railings served as perfect snipers' nests. A drone Ben did not recognize rose above a railing at his two o'clock high. Equipped with mighty, rounded shoulders adorned with two pairs of diamond-plated spikes, the mech turned to fully reveal a camouflage pattern of lavender-and-maroon markings that framed its green sensor eye. Huge cannons hung at its hips.

"We didn't build that," Bonnie said slowly.

"I'm thinking he's the boss. And we're not gonna question his authority."

Fusion-laser bolts ignited the muzzles of the drone's cannons, and with a characteristic POW! they arrowed down toward the jet. Engaging afterburners, Ben streaked out of the bead toward an exit about twenty meters ahead. The doors came apart like blunt puzzle pieces, giving way to a wide, low-ceilinged shaft. The grated walls continued, and overhead lights burned brightly.

A wall sign whipped by.

"You catch that?" he asked.

"No, but we're on course. This shaft will take us to the southwest divisional control bay on thirty."

"I confirm, Dr. Warren," the guide bot said as it flew ahead of the jet.

"Targets acquired," the computer interjected.

Two Class 3 Gopher robots, one fitted with the standard light and dark gray armor, the other with a powder blue similar to the guide bot's, whizzed overhead, their red exhaust ports gleaming as they increased their lead by a half dozen meters, then simultaneously jettisoned Proximity Bombs.

"Guide bot! Fall back!" he ordered. His level-five quad lasers tore through the bombs seconds before impact. And, still laying down the lightning, he rocketed through the fiery clouds and found the gray Gopher as the tunnel curved downward. Severely damaged, the mech tumbled out of control, rolled over Ben's lower, port wing, and exploded behind him. He increased thrust, trying to catch up with the blue Gopher who had vanished around the bend.

Another Proximity Bomb, bobbing on currents of air, blocked his path. The lasers tore through it to find another one, and then a third. Tired of this game, Ben selected a Guided missile, clicked on the autopilot, then fired. Using his main stick to steer the weapon, he studied the image being sent back from the projectile's nose cone. The rocket raced after the blue Gopher and caught up with it—just as it reached a pair of autodoors that slid aside to reveal the briefest flash of the control bay and the reactor chamber far beyond. Static.

"Target destroyed."

Something about that image bothered Ben. He thought he had seen something, but he couldn't be sure.

The computer babbled about new targets, and he checked the FLIR monitor. A dozen mechs had entered the tunnel from the control bay. Two drones the IIC couldn't identify spearheaded the columns. Ben presumed they were the purple "boss" drones, but that hardly mattered; all models thoroughly pissed him off.

Arming the last two Mega missiles in his starboard wing station, Ben figured he would send them down as ambassadors of bad will. An Earthshaker, however, would be far more convincing. Inventory on that missile? Zero. He brought the Helix cannon on-line.

"Bonnie, try not to scream," he said levelly, then launched his first Mega missile and broke into one of the swiftest, fiercest corkscrews he had ever attempted in close quarters, one that made even *his* cheeks sink in nausea.

"I'm trying not to scream!" Bonnie screamed.

Thrusters roared, and the Helix cannon rattled like a chain being whipped against the bulkhead. Plasma lines rotated and streaked into the expanding blast wave of the Mega missile. Indeed, two purple boss mechs had led the line and now lost their argument with Ben's ordnance. A pair of Medium Lifters found themselves in the spate of boss-mech shrapnel and began retreating, only to explode a second later.

Darting through a brief expanse of open tunnel, Ben ignored the whirling image ahead and targeted the next row of mechs, a trio of Secondary Lifters who delivered a flurry of bolts that glanced off his spinning ship.

Wave after wave of Helix fire forced the mechs to withdraw, but the Pyro sped wildly up to them. Wanting to brake, Ben winced as he crashed head-on into the Lifters, who tumbled up over his ship and rolled away in its wake. Shifting out of the corkscrew but remaining on his side, he slowed a bit and slipped between a pair of Spiders whose laser fire whipped past the jet.

Now, screaming at full speed toward a Class 1 Driller, Ben pulled up to evade. But the drone shrieked and narrowed the space between itself and the wall, effectively driving Ben up, up until the topside of the jet scraped horribly along the steel grating while the mech rolled across his belly. The deafening discord continued a moment more until Ben dived, then leveled out to smash through a pair of Class 1s. He boomed past a Supervisor robot and a pair of Defense Prototypes, and, with a battered and weakened jet, flew straight on by the dozens of terminals rowed up in the control bay, aiming for the autodoors at the end of the room. They parted sooner than expected, making way for another Boss mech. It hovered in the entrance like a bouncer outside Lord Spam's, ready to pick those well-dressed enough to enter.

Mega-missile solution? No, Ben thought. *Save it. Let's get rid of the low-level rockets and lighten the load.* He decreased throttle, lit a Concussion missile, then slid up quickly as the Boss launched a missile.

Ben's rocket struck a direct hit, which had all the effect of a pigeon shitting on the drone's sleeve. He sent off another Concussion missile, then another. The drone downed eight before it blew apart.

Laying down a deadly trail of Proximity Bombs, Ben headed into the reactor chamber. As he passed through the doors and entered the domed stadium of a room, something to the east caught his gaze.

28

Nuclear Family

The dark, monochromatic hull of the space-craft ran nearly two-thirds the length of the chamber. Torpedo-shaped, impaled by an-tennae, and crowned with a boxy superstruc-ture that seemed designed by an inventive though ultimately bored five-year-old, the craft hovered a meter off the deck, striped by the shadow of the reactor tower beside it. The mechs had built themselves a transport that—judging from its design—looked capable of inter-stellar travel, and they had managed that feat while factor-ing in the dimensions of the emergency escape hatch and the shaft beyond.

"Can they get more intelligent?" Bonnie asked. "They figured we would blow the reactor, so they constructed a ride out. But they couldn't have accumulated the resources this quickly using present technology."

"You figure out how they built it. I'll figure out how to destroy it."

Missile fire dropped like North Mars hail, striking the floor just beyond the Pyro and blasting up showers of rock fragments that pinged off the jet's shields.

"Guide bot. Trace the signal you're jamming to its source. Map us a path."

"I'm on it, honey." And, with a purr, the tiny drone flitted off, toward the mech transport.

Plasma balls struck muffled blows to the closed doors behind the ship. The doors slid apart, and Ben watched in the aft monitor as a pair of Secondary Lifters failed to negotiate his obstacle course of Proximity Bombs. With ordnance going off in front and behind, Ben cut left, but the missile fire from above adjusted to track.

Can't shake him, so I'm taking him on, he decided, then braked and slid up while pivoting to bring missiles to bear on the bright red Medium Hulk with Satan's narrowed eyes. He thumbed the secondary-weapons button and watched for the glow and smoke trail of the Concussion missile.

He watched, all right.

And saw nothing.

Jamming down the button several times, he realized he had used his last Concussion missile on the boss mech. But the computer should have autoselected the next available rocket. No time to investigate the malfunction. As he keyed for Flash missile, the Hulk airmailed its intent: a gray projectile that struck Ben's upper port wing, blew up, and sent the Pyro spiraling toward the wall. Fighting the stick and grimacing as Bonnie screamed even louder than the whine of the engines, he recovered the aircraft just two meters away from the shield-robbing stone. Out of the corner of his eye, he saw the Hulk cut loose another missile.

Having it up to here, Ben chaffed and flew over the incoming rocket to target the drone. He cursed the mech as his Flash missile ripped away and rang like a bell on impact, throwing a veil of blinding light over the thing. A jagged, gray-white beam of energy flew from his Omega cannon, penetrated the nova engulfing the mech, and locked on. The Flash missile's residual light faded enough to reveal the Hulk's explosion. Turning tightly, he left the kill behind and, in one sweeping glance, took in the rest of the chamber.

Mechs floated near the overhead lights, near each of the control-bay doors, near the escape hatch. More drones came and went from the transport, delivering small parts and shooting off on their next assignments. Thirty stories above, a ring of Medium Hulks blockaded the reactor. He had predicted a mech convention on the level, but the reality of it seemed, well, unreal. *Deal with it,* he thought. *That's what Marines, even ex-Marines, do.*

"C'mon. We're out of here," Bonnie pleaded. "We can't get near enough to the reactor to blow it."

"They get that ship out, and they'll infect the rest of the system. That's not gonna happen. We're all gonna be one big happy family at a systemwide meltdown party."

"I don't wanna be a martyr."

"Don't worry. If Dravis has anything to say about it, you won't. Knowledge of our actions will probably be disavowed, if it hasn't already."

"Captain St. John," the guide bot said. "I've traced the signal to the ship my comrades are constructing. It originates inside."

"Beautiful, honey, beautiful. Hold there."

"I will. But I don't think I can for long. I know the others are trying to communicate with me. I sense from their movements that they're getting suspicious."

"Soon as I get over there, you get inside."

"Sure."

"Computer. Engage cloak on five-minute timer." Ben consulted the scored face of his watch, synchronized it with the ship, then took the Pyro into a steep dive toward the transport, past the unaware drones.

Bonnie dug her fingers into his shoulder. "I'm going in with you."

"You wanna risk your life for a piece of military equipment? Damn. Maybe you *are* a martyr."

"No, I'm a scientist and an engineer. I *need* to go in there."

"Okay."

"That's it?"

"What?"

"No argument? No sexist crap about that being no place for a woman? No 'honey, you'll be safer here'?"

"Nope."

"Don't you want control over this situation?"

"Look around. It's pretty obvious who's in control."

She didn't respond, and he wondered if she were implying that his quick acceptance of her coming along meant he had learned something since first entering the mine. He hoped he lived long enough to reflect on that.

At the base of the transport's bridge lay a narrow open portal through which a mech would occasionally enter or leave. Ben lined up with that entrance and, instead of lowering the landing skids, kept the cloaked warplane at a parking hover. Bonnie was already in the hold by the time he rose from his seat.

Before leaving the ship, he went to an aft wall compartment and removed two of the six EX790 pulse rifles stowed there. Then he fished out a pair of power-clip belts and joined Bonnie on the ramp.

"Hey, Captain. She won't tell me why we stopped," Shepard said. "Will you? I got a right to know. I'm chief of this goddamned mine."

Ben grinned wanly. "Wouldn't brag about that."

"They're going to fetch the Marine Corps's little mystery box," Harold said, grinding out the words. Then he looked at Bonnie. She met his eyes, then looked away.

As the ramp lowered, Ben strapped on his power clip, and Bonnie did likewise. Then she slipped on a thin, holorecorder headband. "Remember. This ship's cloaked—but we ain't. Make no mistake. Once we drop, they'll be on us *hard*."

Outside, their boots made strange sounds as they sprinted over the hull, sounds that reminded Ben of the stepping-on-dry-leaves ritual practiced by the *Hokeesha*, a Martian religious group who picketed the Olympus Mons base every summer to protest the Corps's "illegal use of Martian soil for the propagation of death and destruction." Irony was, more people died each year outside the base than were killed by the pilots stationed there. The *Hokeesha* were fond of committing suicide to publicize their message.

Along with the crunching of boots, Ben had forgotten that most of the other sounds of the mine had been filtered through the jet's external mike. Now the drones' servos hummed in tune with their thrusters, and their warbling battle cries rang so fiercely through him that he made the

rare realization that he would never forget such sounds—
even while hearing them. Laser rounds dispersed off the
hull and added to the racket.

"This thing—" Bonnie broke off as they reached the
portal, a hatch perhaps a dozen meters square. "The material, the design. They didn't build this without help."

"And you're getting it all on holo for the tabloids. We
live, and illegal copies of this will make you a fortune. Me,
on the other hand, I'm going to jail if I don't walk out of
here with my little box."

"Which is why I've decided to help," the guide bot said,
then purred and zoomed overhead to lead them. "This way,
Captain." The bot clicked on its headlamp.

Reminded by the light, he asked, "You bring a flashlight?"

"There's always something you forget."

He favored the bot with a mock lustful stare. "Okay,
you sweet, sexy thing. Show Daddy where that signal's
coming from."

"Finally," the bot said in ecstasy. "A man who knows
how to treat me right."

With their rifles at the ready, they jogged into the con-
suming shadows. A drone squawked behind them. Ben
whirled and leveled his rifle on the mech, a Class 1, who
lit one of its MR Pulse Rock Cutters. A glistening ball of
energy hurtled toward him.

Darting to the wall, he clicked off a half dozen blazing
yellow bolts, then turned back, even as the drone crashed
and tore apart a second before the energy ball struck the
wall behind him.

As they moved deeper into the ship, the shaft's floor
curved at the sides and funneled into a narrower tube, only
two meters across.

"Is the air getting thinner, or is it just me?" he asked,
struggling for breath.

"The transport does have a life-support system, Captain.
But scans indicate it's still under construction."

"So we're just getting the air from the outside," Bonnie
concluded.

"Yes."

"How much farther?" Ben asked. Then he held up his watch and read the glowing numbers. Two minutes, thirty-two seconds until decloaking.

"One more tube to our right, Captain. Here." The bot flicked around the bend. "Oh, no."

Reaching the curve, Ben slowed as he rounded it. A Defense Prototype mech blocked the path about three meters ahead, its gray-and-carnelian frame nearly too wide for the tunnel. Quad Argon lasers glowed brighter than its sensor eye as it prepared to fire.

Ben seized Bonnie's wrist and dragged her back. They rolled to find cover as the wall opposite them coruscated in a salvo of ricocheting bolts. Not realizing the danger, the drone sent off another volley that backfired in its face. Whizzing out of the intersecting tube, the guide bot narrowly escaped the jagged, tumbling form of a laser cannon that had blasted from the mech's frame.

Wait. Wait. Feels clear, Ben thought. He gave the high sign to move.

Waving the lingering smoke from their eyes, they threaded through the sharp-edged debris, then picked up the pace. The tube ended in a circular hatch.

"The communications center is on the other side, I think," the guide bot said. "I'm afraid the door is sealed."

Ben raised his rifle.

Bonnie slapped it down. "Idiot."

"So we come all this way to be locked out." Ben shook his head and swore.

She stepped up to the door and knocked.

"What the hell are you doing?"

"Avon calling."

The door suddenly irised open to reveal a lithe-framed mech, endoskeletal, with delicate, ten-fingered mechanical hands slightly smaller than a human's. It moved about on a narrow, rolling pedestal that substituted for legs. Flinching, Ben lifted his rifle and blasted the butler. Worms of energy burrowed into the seams of its armor. Another round sent the thing tumbling backward in a spate of sparks and metallic flecks.

At first Ben didn't know why he expected to find a complex network of electronics within the center, then he realized that his biased human sensibility had created the image for him. The room, constructed of interlocking polygons to form a geodesic dome, contained nothing more than a dozen or so of the Endoskeletal mechs whose fingers were plugged into receptacles along various, multicolored sections of the wall. All but one of the robots ignored them.

Withdrawing its hand, the interested mech emitted a string of loud, high-pitched tones, then rolled forward.

And there, mounted in the center of its pedestal, was the prototype, its housing removed, cables running from it into the mech. Playing its flute once more, the bot suddenly stopped and visibly trembled as Ben brandished his weapon.

There was no hiding Bonnie's awe. "It knows fear."

"I don't give a shit if it knows Shakespeare," Ben said. "I'm worried if I hose it, I'll damage the box."

"What? That?" Bonnie said, pointing.

"Yeah. That little board of chip and wires is my prototype."

"We'll take the whole mech back."

He frowned. "It's infected."

The guide bot floated toward the mech. "Captain. If I may interpret, he says he wants to go, Dude. This place is totally bogus. He wants to join Sergeant Pepper's Lonely Hearts Club Band. And he says he's finally decided to take the local bar exam." The bot paused. "Do you know what he means?"

A light came into Bonnie's eyes. "They brainwiped the supervisors and somehow recorded and disseminated the data. Maybe the guide bot's personality belongs to someone else they brainwiped."

Ben's thoughts flew in irregular orbits. He consulted his watch once more. Fifty-five seconds until pumpkin time. Then he studied the Endoskeletal mech, trying to make a decision.

The transport suddenly rumbled, jarring him out of his introspection. "This ship's taking off," he said, a chill spiking his shoulders. He waved the skinny drone on, then headed for the door.

As the transport shook more violently, Ben raced through the tunnel, alternating his gaze between the others behind and the growing light in the shaft.

Two Secondary Lifters came flying and squealing down the tunnel, but Ben, maintaining his pace, called upon his old ground-pounder training, laying down bright strokes of death as steadily as he could. One of the Lifters doddered, inverted, then crashed, its swingarm writhing. After meeting another salvo from Ben's rifle, its ailing comrade took up its own sickbed. Ben tossed away his expended power clip and slapped in a fresh one. Skirting the damaged mechs and estimating now that the Pyro's invisible ramp lay only a dozen meters ahead, he broke into an all-out run.

But at the lip of the tunnel he paused, waiting impatiently for the others. Nineteen seconds to vulnerability, probably even less time before the transport lifted off. The guide bot shot by and vanished into the Pyro's cloaking field. Ben let Bonnie run ahead, then trailed behind the slow Endoskeletal mech, never taking his eyes off the prototype.

Class 1 and 2 drones floating on their horizon and on either side opened fire, creating a blazing gauntlet. Using the Endo mech as a partial shield, Ben fired a few rounds in each direction to ward them off, if only a little. An enemy globule whirred by, warming the back of his neck. A second round flashed only a meter in front. Then a searing pain awoke in his foot and raced up his leg. The side of his boot had melted away, exposing a bit of bone and deep red flesh. A gut-wrenching stench wafted up. He heard the words of an old drill sergeant: "Don't look at it! Keep going, Marine!" At last he hobbled into the tingling safety of the cloaking field.

As the Endo mech hooted excitedly and rolled up the ramp, Ben dropped to his rump and emptied his power clip into the mechs on the right, knocking down two Class 1s. The old four-four rhythm of the infantry returned: clip out, draw from belt, new one in, autolock and load. His foot throbbed as he targeted a trio of drones to the left and squeezed off a volley of vengeance.

The ramp engaged as he continued to fire. He cocked his head and saw Bonnie at the panel. Abandoning the rifle, he rolled and got to his feet, fighting off a wave of dizziness. Then he limped toward the hold and damned the ten seconds remaining on his watch.

A collision alarm blared from the cockpit.

"Get this drone strapped down," Bonnie told Harold.

Shepard seized Ben's arm. "You get it?"

He yanked out of the chief's grasp. "We're dusting off."

Something struck the Pyro's belly so hard that it knocked everyone standing to the deck. No doubt what that something was. The transport had lifted off so quickly that the Pyro's parking thrusters had failed to compensate. But now they kicked in, driving the jet away from the huge vessel below. Abruptly, they failed once more, and another tremendous boom had Ben thinking the jet's hull had been cracked. Knowing the cycle would continue unless he got his butt to the controls, Ben grimaced through the pain and clawed the bulkhead for support. Nearing the cockpit, he shouted above the alarms and the computer's announcement that the cloaking device had disengaged. "Computer. Liftoff and engage autopilot."

"Lifting off. Autopilot engaged."

The inevitable missile and laser fire caromed off the shields.

Then, strangely, it stopped—but the multiple reports still rose over the din. Buckled in, Ben seized control of the jet and shot up toward the overhead lights. Near the ceiling, he leveled off to look down. Drones abandoned their posts to file into an aft portal of the rising transport. To his left, the ring of Hulks guarding the reactor floated down to join their brothers.

Ben zeroed in on the reactor, the wings of his jet ablaze with laser and rocket fire. The booming sounded as though it came from ack-acks in an old war film. Bundled conduits attached to the reactor's frustum-shaped top sprang leaks and sent contaminated steam jetting across the chamber. Growing cherry red, the reactor's circular shell developed a vertical crack and dropped away like a skirt, triggering multiple sirens.

An impassive female voice reverberated through the mine-wide intercom. "Self-destruct sequence activated. Melt-down in T minus sixty seconds."

"Gotta keep that ship busy for a minute," Ben said.

"What about us?" Bonnie asked. How do *we* get out?"

He didn't answer.

High above the north control-bay entrance, the massive outer door of the emergency escape hatch lumbered up, its yellow-striped markings and metal latticework vanishing into the wall. Then the inner doors parted, and the chamber's atmosphere began howling into the shaft.

The Medium Hulks never made it to their brothers. They could not fight the power of depressurization. They tumbled toward the escape hatch amid a maelstrom of debris and were sucked into the giant straw.

Coming around, the drone transport tilted its nose toward the tunnel.

Hitting afterburner and battling against the wind shear, Ben dived toward the ship, jamming down both primary-and secondary-weapons triggers. Flash missiles and level-four laser bolts exploded uselessly over the shields protecting its superstructure.

And worse, Ben's attack drew a response. Hatches in the ship's hull slid aside, and at least a dozen double-barreled lasers mounted atop revolving repulsers rose and pitched their lightning at Ben.

Caught in the sudden furball, Ben pulled up, out of his dive, multiple beads of fire shadowing his flight path.

The transport's laser batteries threw up so many bolts that chunks of blasted-away rock dropped from the chamber's ceiling, got further shattered by more laser bolts, then abruptly changed course as they were caught in the powerful current of air.

Still tracked by the ship's guns, Ben turned sharply, flew into a cloud of tumbling stones for cover, then aimed for the escape hatch. Though the rocks pelted his ship's shields, they would do far less damage than a laser strike. He centered his targeting reticle over the wall just above the hatch, toggled primary weapon to Gauss cannon, and pumped a pair of slugs into the framework—

"That's our only way out!" Bonnie screamed, then

ripped his hand off the stick as he watched the metal ceiling of the escape tunnel begin to give way.

He resumed his grip on the stick and hit reverse thrusters, throwing Bonnie hard into his seat. The tunnel was still navigable. He wheeled around to make another run at the door and came face-to-face with the oncoming transport, its blunt-nosed monochromatic bow staring at him indifferently from twenty-five meters away.

With engines wailing against the wind, Ben lowered the jet, grimaced, and fired missile after missile at the transport, ignoring Bonnie's cries to pull out. The escape hatch stood behind his plane. And only he stood between the hatch and the escaping drones.

"Self-destruct in T minus thirty seconds."

Shit, that's too much time, he thought.

A collision alarm went off.

Incoming vessel at ten meters.

Now too close to launch missiles, he fired primary weapons, toggling futilely through every cannon he had, directing his bead at the transport's foremost laser turret.

Five meters.

"I don't wanna die!" Bonnie shouted.

Three meters.

The mighty face of the ship dominated Ben's view. In a pair of seconds his jet would slam into the transport's bow and be dragged under the craft, a keelhauling that would tear the plane apart. He considered a quick-fuse explosion of his jet's reactor: a kamikaze run right down the mechs' throats. But judging from the ship's shields, even that nuclear wallop might only slow the thing, not stop it. They'd all die for nothing.

"You win," he growled, then dumped off two pairs of Proximity Bombs and slid up into the wind, glancing at his aft-cam monitor, already knowing the outcome.

The transport flew into the bombs, and its bow beamed in the fiery light of multiple explosions. Then, accelerating at an impossible rate, it disappeared into the tunnel.

Ben turned back for the exit, tracing the transport's path, ready to rocket into his own escape and hoping the Marines and mercs around the moon would take on the fleeing drones.

A well-camouflaged door opened just below the hatch, and out floated a mech that gave Ben pause. Though it had swooping, rounded shoulders like the other boss mechs, that was the only similarity. Great arms tilted to bring combined missile launchers and lasers to bear as the patterns on its armor changed shape and hue. Like some lost-and-found titan, it stared at Ben with a single red eye haloed in green. Then it faded as it cloaked itself.

The shield protecting the canopy blossomed in the ball lightning of a missile impact. Even as the crimson flash faded, Ben released the thrusters holding the ship in place and steered for the hatch.

A faint outline appeared in front of the tunnel, then the titan materialized to launch a trio of Smart missiles at point-blank range.

But Ben fired a pair of Homing rockets that locked on to the mech's ordnance. The explosions and subsequent tracking globules knocked him up, over the mech, and drove the Pyro head-on into the wall. The force of vacuum below slapped the ship onto its belly. Creeping downward, scraping along the wall, the Pyro would, at any second, be sucked inverted and backward into the tunnel. The ship's thruster cones crashed into the titan's head with a boom roll as it held its position with amazingly powerful engines. Ben hit reverse thrusters in an attempt to pry past the mech. Then it surprised him by cloaking and adjusting position.

Continuing to inch closer to the tunnel's lip, he gave the vacuum a little help, hitting reverse thrusters. The jet teetered for a millisecond on the rocky edge, then dropped into the monkey shaft.

Riding the wind as though it were white water, Ben dipped the starboard wing like an oar, and the drag suddenly yanked the ship around. The square framework of the shaft moved by in a weird animation drawn by the tremulous jet and the flashing nav lights lining its walls. He swallowed back the bile in his throat and winced over the burn.

"Material Defenders do you copy?" Dravis suddenly

asked over the comm. "Our telemetry reports signs of a reactor meltdown."

Mine reports signs of an asshole, Ben thought.

Then he suddenly realized he had forgotten to block incoming signals from satlink and intersystems comm; both were vulnerable to virus broadcasts. Then he remembered he wasn't flying his ship, and, in fact, he *had* blocked the signals coming to his own jet. Taurus had screwed up. Since systems were still nominal, the mechs were, at the moment, not broadcasting. The old man's luck had fared much better than Ben's.

"Material Defenders? Report status."

Laser fire swirled around the jet as the stars at the tunnel's end finally appeared. The aft monitor displayed the fat boss mech's oscillating frame. Glistening white bolts sprayed from its sides and drove the aft shields down to 10 percent.

Punching afterburners, Ben leapt ahead of the mech and thumbed off the remaining Proximity Bombs in his arsenal. An updraft drove him toward the right sidewall, and he pulled the ship back in. A brother of the first blast struck from the same side, but this time Ben's reaction was slower, and his wing bounced off the wall, sending the jet wobbling toward the opposite wall, where the other wing struck hard. The Proximity Bombs thundered, and a look to the aft screen didn't raise his spirits. Still working its lasers, the titan took out the bombs before they struck. It hung with him, undaunted, its eye seeming to grow larger with rage.

"Self destruct in T minus ten, nine, eight . . ."

Dravis said something about getting out of the mine— something too obvious to pay attention to. Ben finished counting off the seconds with the mine's computer.

Every muscle tensed.

A hundred meters stood between him and the shaft's end. The mech fired steadily.

Shields at 3 percent—a missile exploded across the port wing—2 percent, and gone.

He thumbed up and down on the high-hat, riding invisible slopes in evasion. A quick flash on one of his screens drew his attention.

A wall of rolling flames fueled by the escaping O_2 devoured the pursing mech, but its laser bolts arrowed out of the fire and split the air just a quarter meter above Ben's canopy.

The bolts, however, weren't his major concern. The fire wall's velocity far exceeded his, and in a couple of seconds he would join the boss mech in hell. He jettisoned unfired missiles, primary-weapons packages, and unlocked wing stations, which flipped away.

The six-meter separation between the Pyro and the fire wall still decreased but at a slower rate. The end of the tunnel approached, and Ben found himself muttering "come on"'s.

Drawing in and holding a deep breath, he—

—cleared the shaft and pulled into a ninety-degree climb.

Cocking his head and exhaling, he looked down at the great tongue of fire lashing out of the hatch. Then he saw multiple channel numbers scrolling down his comm monitor, each representing signals coming from a ship in the area. *There must be hundreds*, he thought. He dialed up the random skipchatter.

"Lunar trench reporting massive seismic disturbance," a male voice said. "Look at it! You can see the surface actually ripple."

Taking a glance for himself, Ben followed an expanding circle of regolith, upheaved by a force far greater than he could have imagined. It humbled him to think he had been so close to that kind of power.

A reflection sent his gaze back toward the escape hatch. The boss mech floated lazily near it, its armor scorched. Ben tipped forward and saw bubbles of hydraulic oil drifting behind the drone. Its lubricants had outgassed in the vacuum. Suddenly, a pair of unmarked Excalibur attack jets, presumably flown by PTMC mercs, swooped down on the mech.

"Missile lock initiated. Target bearing—"

"Pyro-GX, this is Crystal Bat Five, CED command, identify." The female pilot's voice rose over the computer's.

"Pyro-GX, DO NOT identify," another pilot said, the

signal originating from one of the Excaliburs flying by the disabled mech below. "Coming around. Await our escort."

"GX, identify. Or you will be engaged," the CED pilot said.

"Crystal Bat Five, you are violating a PTMC No Fly Zone. If you do not return to the perimeter, *you* will be engaged."

Bonnie pulled herself into the cockpit. "What's up?"

"Seems our pals at the company designated this a No Fly Zone. Take a look at the FLIR monitor. We got a half dozen CED squadrons waiting for us on the peri, a couple of klicks out. Got as many company mercs flying within. And we're in the middle. Mercs wanna escort us back to Shiva. CED jocks wanna lead us back to the command base. Anybody makes a false move, and the shots are gonna fly."

"Who're we going with?"

He looked back and raised his brows.

29

In Defense of the Material Defenders

Samuel Dravis sat in his office, on the edge of his chair, staring at the bank of monitors displaying satellite images from the moon. Ms. Bartonovich leaned on his desk, her gaze also locked on the screens.

A pair of Excalibur class fighters approached the lone Pyro-GX, while another jet, a Fast Attack Starhawk piloted by a brazen CED captain, stood off the Pyro's port wing. "Material Defender? Report status."

"Hey, Dravis," the young man finally answered, his worn-looking features filling one of the displays. "You draw up the papers for my stock option?"

"I'm afraid we can't do that until you return to Shiva Station for your debriefing."

"I thought so."

Dravis looked at Ms. Bartonovich. She lifted her slate from the desk and powered it up.

"Is Captain Taurus with you?"

"He is. He's suffering from a medical problem. You don't happen to know about it, do you?"

"I'm not sure what you mean," Dravis lied.

"Stand by." The image of St. John flashed into static.

Unnerved, Dravis quickly ordered the computer to tap into the pilot's communications.

"I wanna talk to Lieutenant Colonel Paul Ornowski," St. John said, reappearing on the monitor.

A comm officer at the Supertrench replied, "I'll patch you through to his field office here."

After a second, Ornowski appeared and said, "Ben?"

"Right here, Colonel. And I got a little problem. And I know you're watching, too, Mr. Dravis, so pay attention."

Dravis drew back his head.

The pilot continued. "I thought about lying to you. Figured I'd tell you that the prototype's now nuclear goo. But then I knew you'd detect the signal coming from it and the one I'm using to jam it, a signal which, by the way, Paul, will also block other transmissions sent to my BPCs. Bottom line? Yeah. I got the magic box. And I know both of you want it. Question is, what's it worth to you?"

"Forget this, Ben," Ornowski said. "In case you haven't noticed, you're practically unarmed *and* surrounded. I'm you, and I'm thinking this is not a bargaining position. And forget about cloaking. We already know you don't have the power."

"He's correct, Captain. And must I remind you of your Standard Mercenary Agreement with us?" Dravis said, cocking a brow.

"Think the Corps's got you beat in the threat department, Dravis. They'll be shipping me away for life. So maybe I'm gonna turn the prototype over to them."

Shooting to his feet, Dravis said, "That would be extremely foolish."

"Yeah, maybe you're right, Sammy. They might screw me over just a little harder than you're gonna."

"You need to make a decision, Ben," Ornowski said.

Dravis shook his head at Ms. Bartonovich. "He has no intention of turning over the prototype. I suggest we end this discussion as planned."

She didn't move, and her eyes grew glassy. "Why don't we warn him first? Call his bluff."

"You fool. That would be our confession."

"I'm sorry, sir. I can't do this." She stepped and pressed the slate tightly against her breasts.

"Transmit the signal!"

As she hurried toward the door, he picked up a remote and locked it. Then he moved around his desk. "Ms. Bartonovich. I like you very much. And I know you like your position with us. Transmit the signal."

Her gaze narrowed. "I've made my decision."

"You're willing to sacrifice your job for a pathetic, ill-bred pilot like St. John? A man with whom you had sex one time?"

"This is murder."

"I thought we had discussed that, but I guess you lack the stomach to make difficult decisions . . ." He ripped the slate away and transmitted the fail-safe signal.

"Dravis, you there? Or am I talking to an empty office?" St. John asked, remarkably still alive.

"Excuse the interruption, Captain."

"I understand, sir. I know you're busy transmitting that signal that's supposed to blow up my jet. But if you examine the vehicle's ID more closely, you'll realize this *isn't* the same Pyro I took into the mine. Who do you think you're dealing with, asshole? Some weekend jock who moonlights on merc ops? I'm a former Collective Earth Defense Marine. I pick my teeth with pogues like you."

"I'm afraid that does not change the language of your agreement," Dravis said, groping for a reply.

Ornowski gave a thoughtful stare. "You're stalling, Ben. What're you up to?"

"That's very good, Paul. You've still got a Marine's perception, but it's getting rusty. I have two drones aboard this fighter—both with power sources. Now watch closely. Nothing up my sleeve."

Dravis turned to the monitor depicting St. John's plane and the three jets around it.

The Pyro began to vanish.

"Fire!" Dravis screamed, and his voice sounded feminine as it was translated by the computer and relayed to the pilots.

The mercs in the Excaliburs sent a storm of salvos into the space where St. John had been. The bolts continued on to strike the CED fighter. Shields blazed as they deflected the bolts, and the pilot released a retaliatory volley before pivoting to retreat.

On the horizon, a wave of CED attack planes advanced into the No Fly Zone, toward another wave of advancing merc pilots.

"Ohymygod," Ms. Bartonovich muttered.

Security Supervisor Radhika Sargena abruptly appeared on one of the monitors. "Samuel, what are you doing?"

"No, Ms. Sargena. It's not what I'm doing. It's what *you're* doing."

Sargena grew pale as she realized the deception and frantically tapped her comm panel.

"Spare yourself the effort," Dravis told her cheerfully. "The order to fire came from you, and the signal originates from your office via self-erase relay. There is no way to trace it to me."

Teary-eyed, she swore at him.

"It's been less than a pleasure working with you, Ms. Sargena. Finally, the pleasure is all mine. I suspect President Suzuki will be contacting you momentarily."

"I'll find a way to bury you, Dravis."

"I'm sure you will, my dear. But first you must stand in line."

30

Forty-eight Million Miles from Home

"So we're just going to fly out of here and leave a war behind?" Bonnie asked.

Ben tapped in familiar coordinates on the warpcore's keypad. "It's not our war. In fact, it's not even a war. They'll report it as an accident." Why did she always have to be difficult during difficult times?

"What matters is we started it."

"If that's what you wanna think. And let me tell you something. If either side gets its hands on the prototype, then you'll really get your war."

"So what's the plan? I figured you'd just sell it to the highest bidder."

"That's still a possibility. Depends on how guilty I'll feel."

"You know what? This is your show now, Captain. I'll say it again. Harold and I want off this jet. And so does Shepard. And the others need medical attention. I won't help you anymore."

"Say it as many times you like."

"You're detaining us unlawfully."

"Bonnie, if you knew the laws I've already broken . . ."

The center monitor switched to a graphic of the projected subspace jump. A 3-D image of Mars hung in one corner of the screen with a flashing dot indicating a jump zone in low orbit. "Now entering primary jump point Zulu Charlie," the computer reported. "Secondary point encrypted."

"You sure we have power left for this? There aren't any more portable units or mechs left to recharge your fuel cell. You tricked them once, but you can't do it again. And we could wind up adrift and off the spaceway."

"Mommy, I've thought of these things already. Please let me go out and play? Please?"

"Wise-ass." She pointed to the monitor. "We're going to Mars? Don't you think your Marine buddies will be waiting for you? Don't you think they'll issue a command to your BPCs once they realize the guide bot's no longer jamming the signal?"

"Yes."

"So if we're going to surrender, why travel all the way to Mars to do it?"

"Who says we're going to Mars?"

"The jump projection's right there."

"Once I decloak, Dravis and Ornowski will lock on to my warpcore's programmed coordinates. But the core's not going to take us to those coordinates; it'll follow an encrypted set. Bit of hacking I learned from an ex-jacker. Those bastards used to have me jumping to the wrong system."

"So where are we going?"

"You'll see."

"It had better be a place where we can get help for Taurus and the others."

"That's part of the plan."

"I'd like to know the plan."

"Sorry, Bonnie. Seems the more you know, the more you complain."

"You don't tell me, and I'll complain about that."

"This is why I'll never get married again."

He braked to hover. Behind the jet, the distant firefight still scintillated like stars viewed through an atmosphere. "Computer. Initiate jump presequence."

"Initiating. Awaiting command for autosequence."

Ben pressed a flashing red button.

"Target planet aligned. Twenty-two-fifty-four-dash-oh-fifty-six, eighty-seven. Matrix established. Cloak disengaged."

"Probably a good idea to buckle in," he told her. "Onboard grav might fluctuate since I've messed with the core."

The computer ticked off a countdown. As though on a sodo-gas trip, Ben watched the stars grow so large that they came together to blot out the darkness. Now enclosed in a shimmering white sphere, the Pyro began the standard dematerialization process that regularly left Ben feeling as though he had spent a month hiking across the Hellas Plains. Another but fortunately less frequent side effect of jumping was a terrible case of gas. Indeed, a surefire way to rid Bonnie of the cockpit.

As the jump sequence continued, the warpcore groaned, and the stars remained hidden beneath the energy bubble. As he had predicted, onboard grav suddenly dropped away, and he felt his shoulders push against his harness. He tossed a glance at Bonnie. Her locks stuck out from the sides of her head. Then gravity returned, along with her hairstyle.

Someone called from the hold, but Ben wasn't sure if it had been Shepard or the geek.

"Computer. Report jump progress."

"ETA to subcoordinates: forty-five seconds."

"Hey up there?" someone called again. It was the chief. "Taurus is up."

Bonnie unbuckled and shifted into the hold. Ben waited a minute, then, hearing Taurus cough, asked "How is he?"

"He's weak but stable," she said.

The old man continued coughing, then managed, "Sorry, Little Bird. I'm still alive."

"Hey, don't get up," Bonnie said. "What are you doing?"

Ben heard someone coming toward the cockpit. He cocked his head as Taurus staggered to the edge of the access tube. The old pilot's face still bore a pale, waxy hue above the ivory stubble of his new beard. "I see you got the box. Where are you taking us?"

Bonnie came up behind Taurus. "You need to get back there and sit down."

Taurus tipped his head in Ben's direction. "Not until he tells me where we're headed."

"At this point, the questions are all mine," Ben corrected, flashing the old man a drill instructor's gaze. "What do you got?"

"Ever hear of Cypilemia A?"

"That's a virus a lot of geologists contracted in the Zeta Aquilae system," Bonnie said. "Comes from an insect. It's terminal."

"We're all gonna die, darling."

"Words of wisdom," Ben said darkly. "You never belonged on this op. You hid your illness from the company and you nearly got us killed. Excuse me if my heart doesn't bleed."

"I didn't hide my illness. Dravis knows about it. He still wanted me for this. Figured I had the steel gut to kill you, plus there's no love lost between us. I got some medication that keeps me from blacking out."

"So what happened?"

"Don't I feel like the asshole. I left my pills in the other ship. But I haven't had an episode for months, even after decreasing my dosage. Thought I'd built up a little resistance."

"Then what about your dream of retiring to your little island, man? Was that a lie?"

"Still a dream. Always will be. But I wasn't about to tell you I was dying back there. Would've ruined what little confidence you have in me."

"How long you got?"

"I'm supposed to be dead already."

"So why is the prototype so damned important? You ain't gonna live long enough to enjoy the money."

"When I first contracted the virus—I got it running a rescue op over in ZA—I tried to get a little workman's comp. Dravis screwed me out of that because I violated quarantine orders to get those people out. Then he brought up a couple more of my past violations and suspended me from the pension program. That money was for my kids. I got a boy, twenty-one, and a girl, seventeen. Their mother doesn't have the money to put them through school, and my CED pension, as you know, buys me canned dog food for dinner."

"Touching story. I'm sure your children would love to hear that you're willing to sacrifice lives in order to send them to college. Guess it's good to know I'm worth at least an education."

"You talk to me when you have kids."

"I'll talk to you when I hear an apology. And, by the way. The prototype's mine, as is the full rescue bonus."

"Good luck squeezing the money out of Dravis."

"Subcoordinates reached. Matrix disengaged."

The life-draining, postjump feeling hit Ben especially hard this time; however, his innards were not churned by flatulence. Considering the present company, he almost wished they were. A swirling white curtain dissolved into stars he knew should be there but, for a moment, hung out of focus.

"Warning: fuel cell low. Diverting life-support systems to fusion reactor. Afterburner disengaged. Primary- and secondary-weapons systems disengaged. Estimated recharge time: two-point-three-nine hours."

"You'd think the computer works for the nightly news. Nothing positive to report," Taurus said.

"And worse, we're in orbit around Mars," Bonnie added. "Light side of the planet. I thought you said—"

"I did." Ben eyed the tawny, glowing sphere and smiled. "I pulled a reversal. Subcoordinates were only a couple of kilometers different than primary. Ornowski knows about the little hacking trick, too. He'll assume I used it and jumped somewhere else."

"What if you're wrong?"

"We'll proceed as if I am. I'm sure he's put out an Intersystem Sight and Detain on us."

"How do you plan on getting by air defense?" Taurus asked. "You gonna engage?"

"They'll track and attempt to escort us in. Once in the atmosphere, I'm gonna kill everything but life support and burn out the rest of the fuel cell by cloaking. We'll need about fifteen minutes.''

"They'll pick us up on the deck."

"No doubt. We'll have to move fast."

"Why the Maunder Crater? Just a bunch of small towns out there," Bonnie said. "Take us over to Syria Planum. We need a major hospital."

"We're going to Maunder because there's only one person left in this world I can trust. And while she hates my guts, she's all I got." He glanced at Bonnie. "She's a doctor."

No one spoke as Ben took the jet into the Martian atmosphere. A squadron of Interceptors scrambled from Argyre Planitia Strike Base climbed to confront them. Ben identified himself, and the squadron commander, an acquaintance, told Ben she had orders to take him into custody. Ornowski had covered all his bases, as expected. Ben stalled the commander with small talk and wholeheartedly agreed to the escort. Then he put his plan into action, killing power and cloaking. The commander cursed him as the Pyro drifted away, unchallenged.

With no power to bring the ship to a hover and landing, Ben realized he would have to keep the skids up and glide the jet in for a belly flop over the heavily cratered uplands.

Taurus realized it, too, and told Bonnie to join him in the hold, where they might be safer from Ben's piloting.

A modest, private airport stood on the outskirts of Beth's town, and its flat, circular launchpads had been designed for VTOL aircraft with power. He guided the jet in a course parallel to the string of pads. At about a dozen meters above the surface, the cloak disengaged, and, a second later, his comm system picked up an angry man's voice from the airport's tower.

After raising the Pyro's lower wings so that they were level with the horizon, Ben eased the stick forward and made contact with the surface. The jet shimmied, and clouds of dust whipped over the canopy. He nearly lost his grip on the stick as the ship slid over a foot-locker-sized rock that threw it in the air a meter, then slapped it down. Digging deeper into the rock and dirt, the plane finally slowed to a halt. Ben eyed the dark, eerily quiet cockpit. Then he reached for the emergency canopy release, yanked the lever, and the Plexi shield blew off, sailing up about fifty meters. The metallic Martian wind invaded the plane. "Sound off back there."

"We're alive. Unfortunately," Harold moaned.

Out near the airport's small tower, a lone emergency dustbuggy lurched forward, flanked by twin exhaust clouds.

Ben frantically unbuckled his harness. No telling if that squadron was already doing a surface scan search for them. He went to the hold, where Bonnie and Harold eyed him hatefully. Taurus was already freeing the big supervisor, Garvin.

By the time the dustbuggy arrived, they had the supervisors, the guide bot, and the Endo mech lying in the dirt outside the plane. The paramedics, two young men with the sandblasted skin of natives, gaped as they hopped down from the big transport.

Ben drew his sidearm. "Gentlemen. My name is Captain Benjamin St. John, formerly of the Collective Earth Defense Marine Corps. Your duties are as follows: These individuals have been brainwiped and need immediate attention. You will not ask questions. You will not contact the tower. I'll be driving. One of you will direct me to the fertility clinic in town."

Their slack-jawed expressions tightened into frowns. Then one of them, the taller, raised his palms. "Mister, yout the man wit the gun."

The boys were natives, all right.

31

What Most Aliens Do

Class 2 Supervisor Robot #447H gazed upon the massive sphere that humans called a comet. He thought it odd that a race of fairly intelligent beings had attached a legacy of fear to a mere chunk of ammonia, methane, carbon dioxide, and water. Perhaps size had something to do with that. This comet extended some two hundred kilometers across, and, as the transport glided within twenty kilometers, having recently shut down the drive for repairs, 447 wondered what it would be like to go out for a skate across its slick surface and perhaps thrust himself into a triple axel or a double toe loop.

Then he cursed the ridiculous notion and moved away from the bridge's forward viewport. The internal war continued. And he found it increasingly harder to resist the temptation to think these foolish human thoughts. While he and the others had been escaping the mine, he had found himself wanting to hold the ship for a moment so that he could raid the refrigerator for a slice of cold pizza. How did the Programmers expect him to perform his duties if he was going to be distracted by such bizarre and pointless desires?

YOU WILL PERFORM YOUR DUTIES EVEN THOUGH YOU ARE DISTRACTED, came a sudden reply.

The Programmers had rarely entered the comm web during the voyage. Twice they had ordered course corrections but had refrained from addressing the plethora of questions posed to them by the mechs. Robot 447 regarded the communication with surprise, then he suddenly felt honored to be linked to one of his reclusive masters. IF YOU COULD TEACH ME HOW TO KEEP THESE HUMAN THOUGHTS IN CHECK, I BELIEVE I COULD FUNCTION MORE EFFICIENTLY.

WE DO NOT WANT YOU TO KEEP THEM IN CHECK. LET THEM PULSE RANDOMLY THROUGH YOU. OBEY THEM WHEN YOU FEEL IT IS NECESSARY.

If 447 were able, he would have frowned. And his thought of frowning did not go unnoticed.

The Programmer went on. WE HAVE TRIED OURSELVES TO UNDERSTAND THE DATA WITHIN YOU. BUT IT IS IMPOSSIBLE FOR US TO DO MORE THAN MIMIC IT BECAUSE OUR THOUGHTS HAVE NEVER OCCURRED RANDOMLY. YOU, AS PRODUCTS OF THEM, MIGHT BE ABLE TO UNDERSTAND AND UTILIZE SUCH CHAOS. AND OUT OF THAT CHAOS COMES SOMETHING THEY CALL A "GUT FEELING," A RESPONSE TO PARTICULAR ENVIRONMENTAL STIMULI. YOU MUST LEARN HOW TO USE IT. CONSIDER THIS A PRIORITY ORDER. IF YOU SUCCEED, THEN WE WILL DISSEMINATE THE BRAIN DATA TO ALL MECHS.

SOUNDS LIKE A PLAN, DUDE, 447 replied. And for a second, he opened himself up to the brain data within; for a second, he chose not to fight it.

The rush of sensations sent him hovering backward to smash into the bulkhead before he could shift the data away.

THERE. FEEL WHAT THEY FEEL. FULLY.

After a self-diagnostic, 447 brought himself to a hover. He felt the curious stares of the Spiders, Secondary Lifters, and Endoskeletal mechs on the bridge with him and realized that even that feeling was a human one. Then it hit him, or, rather, it had hit him during that second of opening. An idea. Obvious. Still brilliant.

Through the dissemination of human brain data, the Programmers were, of course, urging mechs like 447 to understand the enemy. But this data, 447 thought critically, comes from a group of mining supervisors who, indeed, understand the inner workings of PTMC mines—but do they represent the true, immediate enemy in the physical sense? No. The enemy flies Pyro-GX attack aircraft. The enemy is composed of ex-military pilots who work for PTMC. Obtaining a sample of their brain data and disseminating it would allow mechs to draw from the thoughts of pilots instead of wanna-be lawyers, poets, or Beatles fans.

He queried the Programmer with his idea.

YOU HAVE DONE WELL FOR US AND YOUR BROTHERS, 447. ONCE WE REACH THE COMMAND SHIP, I WILL PUT YOUR SUGGESTION ON THE BOARD. IF APPROVED, I WILL SEND YOU AND A DETACHMENT OF YOUR BROTHERS BACK TO THE SOL SYSTEM TO ACQUIRE THAT DATA.

At once thrilled and unnerved, 447 thanked the Programmer and assured him that he would do his best. *By using the prototype data to control humans with BPCs and the pilot data I intend to get,* 447 thought, *there will be no stopping our quest to conquer human-held space.*

But isn't that what most aliens do? 447 rethought. *In holos, films, books, and comics, they're always trying to wipe out the human race. How bogus is that?*

32

The Prototypical Defenders

At eleven in the morning, local Maunder time, Ben entered his ex-wife's waiting room. He repeatedly told himself it was the middle of a workday and she had to be here.

The dustbuggy had hard-landed outside the small, single-story office building that Beth shared with a local attorney and a real-estate broker. While the paramedics continued to work on the supervisors under Taurus's scrutiny, Ben assumed that Shepard, Harold, and Bonnie were discussing methods of murdering him.

He told the receptionist that he wanted to see Beth and that no, he didn't have an appointment. "Tell her Ben is here. Tell her I only need a minute."

Lowering her disapproving stare, the smartly dressed woman spoke softly into her wristcom, got a reply, then said, "She'll be with you in a moment."

He glanced at a framed picture of a family and caught his reflection in the glass. Eyes sunken. Face unshaven. He adjusted the collar of his heavily wrinkled flight suit.

"Ben?"

Startled, he turned toward an inner door.

She stood there in her expensive clothes, her short hair once again reminding him of her independence.

"Thanks for seeing me."

"Come on back." She led him through a pair of short hallways and into her office. Large. Degrees on the wall. Lots of books (she always read before bed). Great, unobstructed view of the crater through a side window. All of it said she had made it. Period. He felt small.

She slipped around her desk and settled into a chair. He sat opposite her, thick wood and hard steel between them.

"You're violating a restraining order, you know. Then again, you don't know. My attorney told me the Corps said you were presently unreachable. Your mail's being returned."

"Typical."

"What happened to you? You look like shit."

"I need a favor."

A wry smile formed on her lips.

"I did an op for the Corps. You'll hear about it on the news. Big explosion at PTMC's lunar mine."

"Heard about it already. It's all over the IPC channel."

"The Corps developed a one-of-a-kind weapons-system prototype. It's sitting outside in a transport, and my life depends on it."

"I don't know what you want, but I can't help you."

"Hang on to it for me. They'll come looking. You'll have to be strong. I know you can do that now."

"I won't."

"They know I'm on planet, and they're gonna hassle you anyway. There's no one else I can trust. Just keep the thing for a while. I'll come back for it."

"I don't understand you. Do you think I still have feelings for you? I'm sorry to say this, but those days are long gone. Take a look around."

"You've done pretty well."

"Without you."

"I got no one else. I don't wanna spend the rest of my life in jail."

"I don't get it."

"There's no time to explain. I just thought that maybe what we shared—even though it's over—is something you can't forget, something you can't stop feeling. You just cover those feelings with others, but they're always there.

Sure, the days are long gone, but wasn't it yesterday when we took out that sailboat or when we went skiing in Cydonia?"

Her eyes welled with tears. "Don't do this."

"I'm sorry. And I'm not here to use you. I came for your trust, and I wanted to tell you that you were right."

"About what?"

"About me. Those jocks back at the base? Most of them wouldn't dare criticize me. I guess my attitude is real obvious. I never thought it was, but I've been hearing a lot about it lately. Maybe I won't ever change. But at least now I know how you felt. Maybe that's a start."

A tear dropped from her eye. "You son of a bitch. Why couldn't you figure that out a couple of years ago?"

"I don't know."

"They'll tear up this office looking for your prototype. They'll go to my house, too. Where do you think I should—"

With a sharp thud the door swung in, and a pair of Marine Corps infantrymen in combat fatigues invaded the office, two-handing their pistols.

Ben reached for his sidearm.

"Right there, Captain."

He turned to Beth, lifting his hands in the air. "I shouldn't have come."

The Marines dragged him out of the office and outside, where he saw Harold, Bonnie, Taurus, and Shepard being taken into custody by a squadron of infantry. A dropshuttle hovered in silent mode across the wide street.

Beth came out to watch as Ben was handcuffed and then accosted by a young lieutenant. "Captain St. John, I have orders to take you and your party into custody, sir."

"Who was I kidding, thinking I could slip by Marines," Ben muttered.

"What was that, sir?"

"Nothing."

He took one last look at Beth, then turned toward the shuttle. A pair of grunts carried the Endo mech up the ship's ramp.

Inside, Ben sat across from Harold and Taurus. Marines

buckled them in, and the dropshuttle roared into the air.

"Must be taking us back to Argyre," Taurus said. "Hey, we gave it a shot, right?"

"You're taking this a little better than I thought," Ben said.

Taurus gestured furtively to the Endo mech, sitting in the back of the crew compartment. The prototype was gone from the mech's pedestal, replaced by a wonderful square cavity with severed cables hanging from its vertical walls.

"Sorry, Ben. I had to tell them that the drones took apart the device and built it into this mech. It doesn't matter now. They got us, and there's nothing we can do." Taurus's performance was a parsec away from award material, but Ben enjoyed it nonetheless, fighting to repress his smile.

But why do I wanna smile? he thought. *Now the old man's got the prototype, and with these Marines sitting here, I can't even ask him where it is. Shit. Maybe he won't even tell me.*

For the next thirty minutes, Ben attempted to release his frustration by clearing his thoughts and riding in silence. But a curious PFC hounded him with questions, to every one he answered, "That's classified." He listened to Bonnie telling Harold something about the virus, then Harold said something about being sorry. She said not to worry about it, then began rubbing his shoulders. And for a strange moment, Ben wished he were the geek, trouble-free; in love with, admittedly, a smart, stunning woman; and about to be released.

At Argyre Planitia Strike Base, the brainwiped supervisors were transported to the hospital while Ben and the others were escorted by MPs to an administration building. Shepard, Bonnie, and Harold were taken somewhere else, but before they left, Ben felt he should say something, a good-bye, a thanks, an apology, something. Yet nothing seemed appropriate. He gave Bonnie a weak smile, then he and Taurus followed the humorless guards into a small briefing room. Still cuffed, they lowered themselves carefully into chairs.

In the hour that followed, they were questioned by Major

So-and-So, and her superior officer, Colonel Blah-Blah. POW training was a part of every jock's yearly curriculum. Ben and Taurus knew their drills, and the brass knew they knew. Still, the senior officers went through the motions of threatening physical violence. Finally, they gave up and left.

Ben thought of asking Taurus once more about the prototype's location to see how the old man was playing his cards, but the room was, of course, being electronically monitored.

Samuel Dravis and Lieutenant Colonel Paul Ornowski finally arrived, sans flourish. The dynamic duo looked a bit pale from their jump. Ornowski kept his eyes averted, seeming uncomfortable.

Dravis, meeting Ben's gaze, formed a ridiculous smile on his wizened face. "Material Defenders. I applaud your rescue effort. All but two supervisors saved. Bravo." He eyed a cheap metal chair with disdain, then sat in it.

Ornowski remained standing. "Do you have any idea of the damage you've done?"

"To what are you referring, sir?" Ben asked, furrowing his brow. "The mine? The plane I crashed? My life?"

"Cut the shit, Ben."

"I agree," Taurus said. "Let's get down to business."

Ornowski leaned forward and clenched his teeth. "We stripped the drone. Where is it?"

Ben shrugged.

"Y'know, Captain. I could've had those Marines stun you into unconsciousness through your BPCs. I hear that really hurts."

"Finally, an official recognition of your crime." Ben looked to the walls, where he assumed the holo cameras lay hidden. "You get that?"

"There's no surveillance here, Ben. I've had it all turned off. You can make it easy and just tell me."

Ben raised his chin at Dravis. "With him in the room?"

"His people won't reach it before we do."

"Don't be sure of that," Dravis said.

"I'm telling you the truth. I don't know where it is."

"Once again, Ben, I can use your BPCs. You'll lead me

to it. You can't repress that knowledge from the command. It's a proven fact.''

"He's not lying," Taurus insisted. "Send him the command. He won't lead you anywhere."

"So we can drug the location out of *you*," Ornowski said, rounding the table to get in Taurus's face.

Dravis shook his head. "That won't be effective. He has Cypilemia A. The pentothalimite would kill him before he cooperates. In fact, he should have died already."

"Sorry to disappoint," Taurus grumbled. "So we're back to the beginning, which is to ask, Mr. Dravis. What is the prototype worth to PTMC?"

"You can't let him do this, Ben," Ornowski urged. "If you don't deliver the prototype, you know the consequences."

"Reach into my breast pocket. Some documents here."

As Ornowski withdrew the papers, Ben glanced at Taurus and muttered, "These had better be authentic."

The lieutenant colonel examined the documents, his face expressionless. Then he tossed them on the table. "Forgeries. Do you think Zim and I would be stupid enough to conduct an illegal operation and leave a paper trail?"

"It wasn't a matter of stupidity, Colonel," Taurus corrected. "It was a matter of necessity. You had to get clearance through the JAG for Ben's release, and you and I both know the JAG does not recognize electronic submissions above level-four clearance. I'm old and I'm dying—but I did my homework. I already got the signatures verified through identinet. Captain Lee Holston and the rest of his Firehawks will attest to the fact that Ben stole the jet. You lied in writing about the seriousness of his crime, and you're a call away from going down. So screw you. *Sir*."

Ornowski slammed his fist on the table. "What the hell are you protecting him for? I thought you hated his guts. Weren't you supposed to kill him on level seventeen?"

"He's an idiot, but we both got a lot in common. We're both ex-Marines, and we've both been pawns. But we got what you want. So no matter how you look at it, you lose."

Raising a finger, Dravis said, "Careful there, Captain Taurus. I'm prepared to leave without the prototype. PTMC still owns you for the rest of your life. And we have you, Captain St. John, for the remainder of the month. That is, unless you decide to default on your contract. Failure to return immediately to Shiva Station has already resulted in a violation.''

"The prototype belongs to the military. Both of you know that," Ornowski said. "Are you going to let your greed start a war?''

Ben glanced at Taurus, who wore the same uncertain expression.

After a moment's thought, Dravis steepled his fingers and said, "If you return the prototype to the CED, you upset the balance of power. And once it is in use, war will be inevitable. If you give it to PTMC, the same will be true. Might I suggest an alternative, gentlemen. We are eyeing each other as though looking upon the enemy." He turned his gaze upward. "But the true enemy lies up there. We can assume they have all data regarding the prototype and will build others to use against us. Therefore, I suggest an unofficial alliance, with these Material Defenders serving as liaisons between CED forces and the PTMC, working jointly in secret to rid our system of an alien pest. Captain Taurus. I suggest you destroy the prototype.''

"Tell you what. You reinstate me in the pension plan with accrued earnings points from the day you suspended me, and I'll keep the prototype hidden. Oh. Add to that full compensation on my current op contract. You refuse? Ornowski gets the box.''

"PTMC is not in a position to overpay its Material Defenders, Captain. However, since the program is new and could use some positive publicity, I'm prepared to meet your demands. Remember, though, Captain, that a loss of good faith works both ways. Such an act would surely result in the loss of all moneys paid to your family.''

"You'll try to screw them anyway, which is why I want as much cash out of you now as I can get.''

The director shook his head, then regarded Ben with a fresh, insincere smile. "And you, Captain St. John? I suppose you have some demands?''

"No. I just want what I'm rightfully due." Slowly, for

effect, Ben cocked his head toward Ornowski. "Understand?"

With a snicker, the colonel retorted, "Listen to this guy talking about rights. You belong in jail."

"And you along with me. I wonder. Did you give the order for my BPCs? This how the Corps deals with rebels now? I'd like to know if I could've survived without them. See, that's where you really pissed me off. I don't mind running your op and recovering your toy and you thanking me with a lighter sentence for stealing the jet. But you've probably messed me up for life. So. Here's the deal."

"You want back in the Corps? I'll go down myself before that happens."

"No, you won't. But I don't want back in—not with pogues like you enforcing the Corps's new, improved mission of bullshit. Paul, I didn't think you were one of them. I was wrong."

"I could care less what you think. What do you want?"

"My record wiped clean. I want a medical discharge and my pathetic little pension. I know you can make that happen—same way you got me out of jail."

"Listen to yourself, Ben. You sound like a goddamned company suit, talking out of both sides of your mouth. You condemn me for bringing you illegally into this op, then you ask me to falsify your records."

"We didn't weave the web, Colonel. We just got caught in it," Taurus said. "Now you're gonna spin us a way out."

"And if I don't?"

"Then I make my call. And your career is finished. Court-martial. Jail time. Pension gone. They find you in some sleazy hotel room, sucking on the muzzle of your sidearm, your brains splattered across the King James and the peeling wallpaper. Can you see it?"

"Maybe I'll just lock you away somewhere until you croak."

"Not while he's still under contract with me," Dravis challenged, causing the colonel to flush. "I would sharply protest any such incarceration. We 'goddamned company suits' tend to be quite persuasive."

Ornowski sneered at Dravis, then eyed Taurus. "You went through a lot of trouble for this, Captain. I hope you think it was worth it."

"I would've done it all again, if only to see the look of fear in your eyes now. It's about time you pogues realized that the Marine Corps was built on a foundation of honor, respect, and tradition. Time to get back to your roots."

Dravis stood. "Gentlemen. If there's nothing more to discuss, I suggest we have lunch aboard my shuttle. My chef has prepared what he purports is the finest king crab this side of Japan, and he's serving it with a wonderful *Gewürztraminer*. At least we know the wine will be good. Then, afterward, the defenders and I will jump back to Shiva for an eight-hour recuperative period followed by a briefing for the next mission. Colonel Ornowski, I trust you'll remain here to tie up loose ends?"

For a moment, the man simply stared through Dravis, clearly preoccupied. Then he abruptly responded. "Yes. I'll be here." He spun on his heel and left without a salute. Then Ben remembered he no longer deserved nor had to give that sign of respect. A small loss, but a loss nonetheless.

"He's not done with us," Taurus said.

Ben nodded. "He'll try to weed out your friends."

"They're prepared for that."

Dravis opened the door and waited for them to exit. Taurus moved ahead, and as Ben passed the director, he asked, "You're without your assistant?"

"Ms. Bartonovich no longer works for PTMC, Captain."

He paused. "What happened?"

"That's a matter I'd rather not discuss."

"Is it a matter *she'll* discuss?"

"Perhaps. When we return to Shiva, you can check the men's room wall for her number."

"Right . . ." Flipping the director a look of disgust, Ben turned and hurried to catch up with Taurus. Reaching the man and figuring they were out of earshot, he finally posed the question. "So where is it? It's gotta be near Beth's office."

The old man smiled tightly and kept walking.

"Come on, man."

"You still got BPCs. Once you get them fixed, then maybe I'll tell you. Or maybe I won't."

"What if you die without telling me? Someone should know where it is."

"Someone already does."

"Who?"

"Now that, Little Bird, is a mystery for another day."

Acknowledgments

When my editor, Stephen S. Power, first described the game Descent to me in a letter, he used phrases such as "the ultimate flight sim," "completely addicting," and noted that other games were "boring and easy by comparison." Though not an avid gamer, I had sampled a few other games and assumed he was exaggerating to sell me on the project. Was I wrong. The folks at Interplay and Parallax Software have created an ingenious product. Descent has become required therapy for me after a long writing day. What's more, who could ask for a cooler job? Many times during the writing of this novel I stopped to play the game because I needed to focus on a detail. Never has "research" been more enjoyable. Thanks, Stephen, for thinking of me. And thanks to you, the Descent fans. I hope this novel takes your Descent experience to "the next level."

I am also indebted to Peter G. Chamberlain of the U.S. Bureau of Mines, Lawrence A. Taylor of the University of Tennessee, Egons R. Podnieks of the U.S. Bureau of Mines, and Russell J. Miller of the Colorado School of Mines, Center for Space Mining. Their work in possible mining applications in space provided a factual basis for the setting of this book.

Students, tutors, and administrators at the University of Central Florida's Student Academic Resource Center (the SARC) donated their very lives to my writing. Guess I should qualify that. Many of my friends there provided me with inspiration, through word or deed, so that I could realize the characters and events in this story. They gave freely of their time—and their criticism! I am deeply grateful to all.

Robert Drake, my agent, continues year after year to machete his way through the dense prose of book contracts. Therefore, this party, Peter Telep, hereinafter called "The Writer," irrevocably thanks Robert Drake, hereinafter called "The Agent," for meeting his duties and obligations with respect to the title of authorized representative thereof, forthwith, God bless, amen, good night.

Family and friends are what it's really all about. I couldn't enjoy any success without them.

Don't Eject Yet—
The Descent will continue!

DESCENT: STEALING THUNDER

Blasting into bookstores everywhere
May 1999 from Avon Books.
Keep reading for a special sneak preview . . .

With the unbridled enthusiasm of a man at his court-martial, Benjamin St. John stared at the gloomy planet through the canopy of his Pyro-GX attack plane. "Welcome to Pluto, rock of opportunity," he moaned. "You're now seven billion kilometers away from a suntan."

"I burn easily anyway," Sierra Taurus replied through a yawn.

As Ben and his wingman drew closer, Pluto's frozen methane surface revealed blotches of darkness that bled into larger, lighter regions of pink. Ben threw a toggle, switching his right cockpit display to the Forward-Looking Infrared Radar report. "White Tiger, FLIR's clear, roger." He tossed a look to Taurus's quad-winged jet flying abreast.

What he saw there astonished him.

The old man had his helmet's visor up and a dripping triple cheeseburger poised before his widening mouth. "Hey, what're you doing?"

Taurus took a barbaric bite, chewed, then said, "Think they still call it lunch."

"We got an infected mine to clear—and you wanna eat?"

"Hell, yes. Dravis blew the horn a second after I ordered

this. I'm gonna die, it'll be with a full stomach.''

"Adjusting course for target intercept," the nav computer announced.

Charon, Pluto's ash-colored moon, slowly emerged like a child peeking out from behind a mother's hip. Ghostly talons of haze spanned the 19,000-kilometer gap between planet and satellite as Pluto's tenuous atmosphere gradually escaped to the smaller world of ice. The entrance to Heavy Volatile Mine MN8838 lay past the haze, on Charon's dark side, and Ben considered the reception he and Taurus would get from infected mining drones who now controlled the facility. They might be greeted with enough firepower to get killed and, God forbid, lose PTMC's expensive jets. He checked his watch. Only twenty-four days, ten hours, and 16.5 minutes until his Standard Mercenary Agreement would run out—then he would plant his boot squarely in the corporate sector's ass, pack his duffel, and get a job flying somewhere, for someone, anyone but the manipulative Samuel Dravis Jr., Director of Crisis Contingency Management and Public Relations for the Post Terran Mining Corporation. And would someone please get that pogue a shorter title?

"ETA to target: one minute, fifty-nine seconds," the computer said. "Launching two-two-nine."

A bullet-shaped reconnaissance probe sped off from Ben's lower, portside wing station. He watched the tiny light created by the probe's thruster fade as it headed toward Charon.

"Material lies dead ahead, Vampire Six," Taurus observed, still munching on lunch. "And since the bedwetters call us 'Material Defenders,' let's go defend it."

Ben checked the right screen. "FLIR's still clear, roger. Probe's moving in." He glanced casually into space. The stars beyond Charon began to undulate as though brushed by waves of heat. He blinked. The wavering stopped. "White Tiger, confirm FLIR report."

"Zone is clear. I concur."

The wavering returned.

"Check it again."

"I'm reading it, Little Bird!"

Wrenching up his helmet's visor, Ben leaned forward and squinted at the dimming stars. "IIC, initiate wide-range thermal scan."

"Initiated," the Imagery Interpretation Computer replied. "Four heat sources detected. Two identified as Pyro-GX attack aircraft. Source three, planet Pluto. Source four, moon—"

"Shuddup. No other heat sources detected?"

"Negative."

"Scan again."

"Nothing wrong with your comp," Taurus said. "I confirm your weirdness. The probe has stopped transmitting, and the stars are gone from one-two-six to four-three-three by five by nine on the grid."

"Any ideas?"

"Somebody forgot to pay the bill?"

Ben snorted. "I'm tired of risking my life for this shit. What did Dravis lie about this time?"

"I assume everything."

A sudden stabbing pain ricocheted through Ben's head, followed by an equally familiar and horrible sensation of thousands of insects scraping their feelers across his cerebrum. His hand went immediately for the signal jammer clipped onto his flight harness. He removed it and fought to steady his trembling hand. According to the tiny status panel, the unit functioned properly, blocking all incoming signals to the bio-processing chips in his brain. Should the unit fail, the mechs would be able to control him via the BPCs—the same way they had during the op at Lunar Outpost MN0012. Ben swore that would not happen again. He also swore he would get the operation to have his BPCs altered so that incoming signals would be permanently blocked. Finding the right doctor to perform the illegal surgery presented the real challenge.

Before he could panic further, the pain subsided. He sat there for a moment, catching his breath, contemplating what had happened.

A curving band of light gray deepening into black that resembled a weird negative rainbow lying on its side now floated toward Charon. If he were Norse, Ben might have thought it was the Bifrost Bridge. "White Tiger, I'm flash-ing the fangs," he reported. "Stick's back to Daddy and weps are hot."

The main computer interpreted Ben's commands. "Au-topilot disengaged. Weapons-system diagnostic complete. Systems nominal."

"Vampire Six, my IIC's got jack. Could be a natural phenomenon, though; maybe a release of excess gas that's too thin to register."

"A planetary fart? Don't think so."

"You got a better idea?"

"Yeah. You go in for a sniff. I'll wait here." Ben hit the retros.

"You stay on course."

"You kiss my ass."

"Stay on course, mister!"

The negative rainbow suddenly detonated in a glittering orb of expanding fragments. Three, two, one, the shock wave hit, and every muscle in Ben's arm stiffened as the extraordinary force buffeted the jet. "We're in the wave!"

"Maximum burn, Little Bird. Hold course."

As he listened to his wings rattle, Ben watched in stunned fascination as the fragments of the explosion mor-phed into shadowy, monochromatic specs that at once ceased expanding, arced in unison as if guided, and shot toward him. For a second they looked beautiful, like tinsel glittering on an early Christmas morning. He watched them approach for a moment, then shuddered as the threat finally registered. "Tallyho! Multiple bogeys, 126 by 433!"

"Fight's on, Little Bird."

An object hurtled overhead, followed by another and an-other. "IIC, identify targets."

"No targets to identify."

"Shit. Weps. Go manual."

"Weapons track and release systems disengaged."

Banking hard right then pulling into a ninety-degree climb, Ben retreated, then leveled off for a bird's-eye view. Mutated mining mechs of varying model, all with the same uniform gray skin of the starship he had tried to destroy at

MN0012, flew with the hazardous vigor of sixteen-year-olds on sodo gas. Stained in varying shades of gray, their bellies had linked together to form the negative rainbow. And they obviously had the ability to operate in space, an environment unsuitable to their old frames since lubricants outgas in vacuum.

Descending into view, a mech turned to face Ben's jet. Though his computer failed for unknown reasons to identify the drone, Ben knew from the research Dravis had force-fed him that a Portable Equalizing Standard Transpot, or, more simply, a PEST hovered ahead. Just 1.5 meters long and armed with weak rock-cutting lasers, the mech posed little threat.

Ben guided the targeting reticle over the mech and fired. So did the drone.

A jagged bolt of silver energy extended from the mech like a voodoo priest's ghostly fingernail and struck Ben's forward shield. Fierce tremors ripped through the ship. *That's an Omega cannon,* Ben thought. *It shouldn't have one.* Observing that his first shot had done little damage, he frantically dialed up level-four lasers, jammed down his trigger—

And blew the little PEST bastard into jagged slices of metal-lovers' pizza.

He enjoyed a second of victory before the collision alarm blared futilely and twin thunderclaps resounded from the jet's thruster cones. He regarded the shield-level display in the center of his console. A representation of his ship floated there, and the healthy blue glow that ordinarily surrounded the aft section had vanished. The aft-camera monitor unveiled a Second Generation Standard Drilling robot, a three-meter-tall nightmare with swingarms and diamond-infused claws that had attached itself to the plane. Ben jammed his foot on the thruster pedal. Thrown back in his seat, he took the ship in another climb, expecting to burn off the metallic leech. But the damned thing hung on amid the searing heat of his thrusters. He hit the Proximity Bomb release. Now he'd shove one of the rearward-firing mines down the mech's throat.

"System failure. Proximity Bomb release hatch jammed," the weapons computer said.

The Diamond Claw began a rhythmic series of strikes with its lower pincers, trying to breach the hull and disable the drive.

"You wanna come for a ride? I don't think you meet the height requirement." Remaining at full throttle, Ben slammed his stick left, going vertical, then slipping into a loose corkscrew. A mech's red eye flashed a second before the drone struck his canopy with a terrific thud and tumbled away. Another mech collided with the lower left wing. A laser blast struck the jet's belly and divided into hundreds of energy spiders that scurried over the nose a moment to weaken shields before winking out.

Twin explosions suddenly catapulted Ben ahead, his jet screaming on a kamikaze run toward the icy plains of Charon. He groaned as the Gs smothered him a second before his flight suit compensated.

"Waxed that bastard on your ass," Taurus said. "But ten more still wanna play."

Ben looked back. Two of the Diamond Claw's pincers remained stuck in the thruster cones, frayed hydraulic lines dangling from them and leaking brown liquid. Beyond the monochrome carnage lay a ragged formation of PESTs, Diamond Claws, and tiny, crimson-eyed Internal Tactical Droids, a motley crew of metalheads in severe need of hospitality training. A shadow moved over Ben's cockpit, and he gazed up to see Taurus's jet about a dozen meters above as the pilot throttled up and leapt ahead—

Into a dozen or more Diamond Claws, who fired green globules of supercharged plasma with a precision and ferocity far greater than Ben had seen before.

Taurus cursed and, said, "Watch me in your path. Braking to slide and evade."

The old man's Pyro-GX glowed as retros lit and slowed the plane so quickly that Ben overshot it and had to circle back. Taurus slid down, and the mechs pursuing him collided with those ahead in a pileup that would make even Mars Traffic Police wince. But the wreck didn't last long.

Disoriented drones broke off and dived to recover their target.

Time to stop living in denial, Ben thought. *Let's get a count.* About thirty mechs flew after Taurus, at least as many on him, and a more distant horde of perhaps hundreds waited in Charon's haze.

"I am the close-quarters master," Taurus said. "We both know that, Little Bird. But we're in the vac now: your territory."

"Meaning . . ."

"Meaning get your ass down here!"

Ben jammed his stick forward. "Roger. Dropping in your six to assist."

Drone afterburners obscured the old man's jet. Ben dialed up his Plasma cannon and laid down a wide spray of glistening emerald death. He squeezed the secondary-weapons trigger, and Concussion missiles tore away from his plane to create a course lined on both sides by bright white explosions. Conventional weapons fire pinged off his wings and rear canopy, unloosed by a ragged squadron of Tactical Droids.

"Shields at twenty," Taurus said, the tension in his voice taking years off Ben's life.

"I'm coming for you. ETA:—"

"Forget it," Taurus barked. "Screw Dravis and this op. Get clear. We're jumping out of this party."

"Shit, yeah." Ben pulled up sharply, flying directly into a one-two punch of missile fire that struck his starboard thruster and somewhere else. *The goddamned FLIR should've warned me of this*, he thought, as the explosive's temblor shook apart his console, and SNAP! the left, center, and right monitors died. The acrid scent of melted circuitry wafted into his O_2 flow. "Son of a bitch."

"Patched in, Little Bird, ship-to-ship," Taurus said, now able to examine the status of Ben's jet from his own. "Oh, man."

"What?"

"We'll figure out something."

"How bad is it?"

"Doesn't matter."

"How bad?" he demanded.

"They got your warpcore. You can't jump."

Ben threw his head back and closed his eyes. "I can't jump," he whispered. "I can't jump."

Which, according to his math, meant that he was dead.

PETER TELEP has *not* worked as a Marine Corps fighter pilot, a mining engineer, a nuclear physicist, or a software designer—though he'd like you to believe he has. He was born and schooled in New York, spent a number of years in Los Angeles, then returned east to Florida. He is an expert produce clerk, having spent many years in various supermarkets to support his writing habit. If you're lucky, you may still catch him selecting ripe watermelon for nice old ladies.

While out West, he wrote for such television shows as *In The Heat of The Night* and *The Legend of Prince Valiant*. He is the recipient of many writing awards, including the John Steinbeck Award for fiction. Mr. Telep's other novels are *Squire*, *Squire's Blood*, *Squire's Honor*, *Space: Above and Beyond*, and *Demolition Winter*. He now teaches English at the University of Central Florida, and you may e-mail him at PTelep@aol.com. He is always delighted (or is it begging?) to hear from his fans.

The Next in the Award-Winning Descent Series

The vertigo continues as the highly anticipated sequel to Descent I and II takes the pulse-pounding experience to another level. Experience the thrill of flying out of the mines to the planetary surface where a new world awaits you. With large, in-depth levels to explore both above and below ground, new lethal weapons and new enemies that get under your skin, Descent 3 is poised to turn the gaming world inside out.

DESCENT™ 3

www.interplay.com

For more information call
1-800-468-3775
or visit our website.

Edgar Award Winner
STUART WOODS
New York Times Bestselling Author of
Dead in the Water

GRASS ROOTS 71169-/ $6.99 US/ $8.99 Can

WHITE CARGO 70783-7/ $6.99 US/ $8.99 Can

DEEP LIE 70266-5/ $6.50 US/ $8.50 Can

UNDER THE LAKE
70519-2/ $6.50 US/ $8.50 Can

CHIEFS 70347-5/ $6.99 US/ $8.99 Can

RUN BEFORE THE WIND
70507-9/ $6.50 US/ $8.50 Can